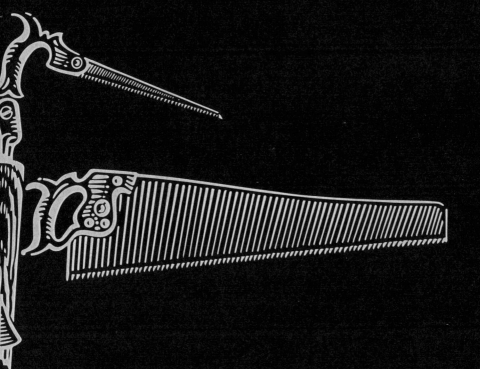

THE DIRECTION
OF MURDER

ALSO BY JOHN NIGHTINGALE

The Appearance of Murder
The Sky Blue Parcel

THE
DIRECTION
OF MURDER

JOHN NIGHTINGALE

SPIDER MONKEY BOOKS

LONDON

**SPIDER MONKEY
BOOKS**

First published in Great Britain in 2020
by Spider Monkey Books
82 Wroughton Road
London SW11 6BG
spidermonkeybooks.com

ISBN: 978-0-9933788-4-3

Also available as an ebook
Mobi ISBN: 978-0-9933788-5-0
Epub ISBN: 978-0-9933788-6-7

A catalogue record for this book is available
from the British Library.

Typeset by Chandler Book Design

Printed and bound in the UK by
TJ Books, Padstow, Cornwall

For Molly and Flossie

PART ONE

SATURDAY – SUNDAY

1

OVERTURE

I'M NOT A CRIME writer who likes to get close to anything
illegal. I don't ride around in police cars, have forensic
pathologists for neighbours, or attend court proceedings. My
fact-finding is done online or from books. My plots hark back
to the Golden Age of detective fiction and are laced with sherry,
fruitcake and sudden death. They feature locked-room mysteries
and impossible crimes and have a neatness not normally found
in life. One thing they do possess, however, is certainty. My
detective, Tom Travis, always solves the case and returns order
to a troubled world. When they have read the last page, my
ideal reader turns off the bedside light, savours Tom's deductive
powers and drops into a contented and deep sleep.

As it turned out, events at Langham Hall had none of the
elegance of my Tom Travis stories, despite the fact that one
of the reasons I was there was precisely to advise on Golden
Age crime conventions. But that was only one of the reasons I
was there. Another was because my agent convinced me that I
should be. Was that where the nightmare started? Was it that
lunch in an Italian restaurant six weeks ago?

'Kenneth Preston,' Debbie, the literary agent in question, had said in tones that savoured every syllable of his name. '*No one* says *no* to *Kenneth Preston*. And he wants your help.'

I remembered a momentary feeling of power. Perhaps I *could* say *no*. Perhaps I *should* say *no*. I had mixed feelings about the *enfant terrible* of British stage and screen. Like everyone else, I had heard the rumours that he had turned down both a knighthood and a peerage. When the question arose in interviews he would simply deploy a disdainful smile that suggested he had little concern for personal advancement. For himself, he cared so little about such matters that he would neither confirm nor deny that he had been approached. Maybe I had seen too many clips of the great man on the internet, but I had a lingering sense that if he had been offered something approaching his own estimation of his worth – a dukedom perhaps – he might have been inclined to accept.

Kenneth was in his mid fifties, a lean, wiry man who dressed in dark jeans, a black t-shirt and casual leather jacket. His thinning hair was cropped short. Incised on one cheek was a scar that he declined to explain and which, with his high cheekbones and thin lips, gave him a sinister appearance that meant he was in demand in Hollywood to play megalomaniac villains with British accents.

'Are you sure it's a good move?' I said to Debbie. 'I mean, I've never written a screenplay. A play, yes, but not a screenplay, and the play wasn't that good. It was for an amateur group. They weren't that good either.'

'You're too modest, David, I've told you before.'

I wasn't aware that she had, certainly not with any great emphasis, and certainly not before the movie deal.

Until that had happened our chief topic of conversation had been my inability to deliver Tom Travis books on time and the disappointment this must cause my fans. But six months ago, unbelievably, everything had changed and Debbie had sold the screen rights to *Murder Unseen* for a million dollars.

It seemed that an American star with a desire to play a British role had been looking for a heroic part with a darker side. *Murder Unseen* (no more than a 20,000 word treatment) fitted the bill. Add in two film studios eager to retain the star's services and a couple of chief executives who didn't believe in coming second and Debbie had orchestrated a bidding war. It was, my wife Kate had said, proof of the maxim that, in life, one needs to take *the smooth with the rough*.

In the space of a week (and a few noughts on a cheque) I had become Debbie's premier client for whom nothing was too much trouble; and for whom she was always available; and would, in another new departure, take out to lunch. The other crime writers on her books ceased to be mentioned, even as comparative sticks and carrots.

'So where precisely are we?' I said, as I wondered whether anyone ever turned Kenneth down and which of Aldo's specialities of the day I should choose, 'I'm not sure I'm entirely up to speed.'

As far as I knew, the original American star was in rehab for substance addiction having discovered that the shadows in his own life outweighed any he might find in my detective.

'It is a bit complicated,' Debbie said. 'But Kenneth Preston is still on board. More than that, Fire Ring International is now in overall control. Most of their money comes from Asia.'

'Fire Ring?' I said. 'Are they interested in crime films?'

3

'They might want more action and fewer words than you're used to, but yes. They're keen on Kenneth and the prestige he will bring.'

'That's good.'

'It's better than good,' Debbie said. 'This could be the best outcome. Fire Ring has more resources to devote to the project. They'll be able to do full justice to the material. Once the deal is announced it should do wonders for the sale of your existing books.'

I smiled wanly. I had a number of difficulties with *Murder Unseen*. Firstly, I hadn't sent the manuscript to Debbie. Worse still, I hadn't written it. Then, to compound matters, I hadn't said that I hadn't and finally, when the offer came in, I kept silent and accepted it. The whole matter had become particularly difficult because I had also been involved in some suspicious deaths six months before that had echoes of *Murder Unseen*. Although I hadn't been arrested, the policeman in charge of the investigation, DCI Bob Addinson, had become convinced I hadn't been telling him the whole truth. Even when events had been concluded to the satisfaction of the average, fair-minded citizen, part of him, or perhaps most of him, remained certain that I had cheated Justice and had been involved in some bizarre criminal enterprise that he had failed to get to the bottom of.[1]

Gradually, my fear of exposure had faded and I managed to convince myself that even if the precise details of *Murder Unseen* had been written by another hand, the fabric of the series had been dictated by my own efforts. Given, also, that I was unlikely ever to see Bob Addinson again, the problem only troubled me once a day, rather than once an hour. There was, however, another difficulty. *Murder Unseen* was a prequel

---

1 See *The Appearance of Murder* for a full account of David's involvement.

to the other books in the Tom Travis series. That would have been fair enough except that Tom had been given (and therefore must also have in the later books) what, even if euphemised, can only be described as *murderous* (there's no other way of putting it) tendencies. More than having murderous tendencies, he had committed a murder.

I'd taken such care with Tom. The private means he needed to be fully independent had been democratically acquired through a lottery win. His girlfriend, the mysterious Claire Moriarty, a Detective-Sergeant in the Met (old Wiltshire family, nouveau poor, jet-black hair, eyes you could fall into, alluring, intelligent, slim, above average height) made only the most fleeting of appearances so as not to distract either from the plot or the fantasies of my female readers. Tom's dedication to investigating esoteric areas of knowledge had been positively Sherlockian. It had all been going so well, if not for Debbie's expectations of a book a year. But then, faced with a wall of money, I had stayed silent and abandoned him and his moral welfare.

My wife Kate had come to the conclusion that my diffidence on the whole matter was most likely explained by my suffering from an acute attack of imposter syndrome. Her view was that I had been lucky, but that was all. The other matter that I found surprising was that nobody had questioned whether I thought compromising my hero's moral character, in the way that I had, was worth it.

'Kenneth's prestige means that Fire Ring will get a great cast,' Debbie said.

'Like who?'

'I've heard it's likely to be Matthew Tabard, Emma Hale and Rufus Stone.'

'Is it?' I was fairly sure who Matthew and Emma were, but Rufus?

'There's always a queue to work with someone like Kenneth.'

'Is there?'

'Of course there is.'

'I didn't think he normally did crime films.'

'He doesn't. But he wants to do Tom Travis. You should be delighted.'

I remember nodding. One of Kenneth's directorial advantages was his ability to extract the last ounce of passion from his actors and actresses. His relentless demands for heart-rending integrity had led to multiple BAFTAs and Oscars for his emotionally drained leading men and women, and acceptance speeches in which his charges were reduced to speechlessness when expressing the depth of their gratitude to him for taking them to the hidden and tortuous places in their souls they had previously been unaware of.

'I'm not sure I get it,' I said. 'What precisely is it that Kenneth wants me for? I've always said I'm happy for them to make what they want out of *Murder Unseen* and Tom Travis. I mean, you did say when they bought the rights that I would have to be prepared to give up control of the film version of Tom and how he was developed. Maybe I should just stand aside.'

'You're being far too modest about the material and your abilities,' Debbie said, leaning back in her chair. '*Murder Unseen* was a masterstroke, a defining moment in your career. I was exultant when I looked at it. I could see why you were compelled to send it without any explanation. You wanted the work to speak for itself. I always knew you were capable of finding Tom's true essence.'

'Weren't you surprised?' I said.

'Not at all. You could have written reams but you realised that the most effective way of communicating was simply to give me the work in outline. Masterly.' Debbie gave a silvery laugh. 'And of course it was about Tom, so it couldn't have come from anyone else, although it was a different Tom from the one I was expecting. But once I had started reading it, I understood completely.'

I nodded again. There wasn't much else I could do. When I had heard the Hollywood star was off to rehab I had checked the contract to ensure I would be paid, whatever happened, and spent a happy couple of days planning Tom's rehabilitation to the straight and narrow. Then Debbie had phoned to reassure me everything was still on and to express admiration for my impressive *sang-froid* under such trying circumstances.

'But,' I continued, 'this workshop Kenneth wants to run. What precisely is it for?'

'Helping to make everything fall into place,' Debbie said expansively. 'Kenneth likes to prepare longer with his actors than most directors. It's his theatrical background. He says he can only find the perspectives he wants in the rehearsal space, whether it's film or theatre. He needs his actors and actresses to inhabit the roles they are given. In the light of the reaction he can spark from them, he develops the script. That's where you come in. You should be flattered. He personally asked for you.'

'Did he?'

'Yes.'

'So tell me again about where this is taking place?'

'Langham Hall in Suffolk. It's near the sea, not far from Southwold. Fire Ring has rented it for a couple of weeks.

In addition to the rehearsal studio there's a swimming pool and gym, and the food is meant to be very good, so there will be plenty for you to do even if you're not screenwriting all the time. It's no more than a three-hour drive from where you are in London. Think about it. You'll be a central cog in the development of the searing love triangle you've created. It will burn up the screen if Kenneth can get it right. That's why he needs a screenwriter – and who better than you?'

'I'm not a screenwriter.'

'He admires your dialogue. He's read all the Tom Travis books.'

'Did he tell you that?'

'Nick told me. The producer lined up for the film – Nick Wallace. He's an attractive man, got a lot about him. I don't think he's married but he should be. He's been part of Kenneth's team for the last couple of years. Used to be a soldier. He told me that Kenneth was insistent you were there.'

'So you didn't get this from Preston first hand?' I said ignoring Debbie's obvious infatuation with Kenneth's right hand man.

'Didn't need to. Nick and Kenneth are hand in glove. In fact, the offer is better coming from him. If Nick is involved you can be sure it's all been properly agreed.'

'So how much is it?'

'They'll pay £30,000 a week and guarantee two weeks work. 60k minimum. I might be able to squeeze them for a bit more. And it's not just the two weeks you need to think about. If this all goes well they'll need you when the film is actually made.'

'Will they?'

Debbie nodded vigorously.

'And this is still going to happen in the first two weeks in December?'

'Absolutely. They'll want you full time of course. Is that a problem?'

'Kate said she could manage.'

Debbie beamed. 'So, you can sign up now?'

'You did say that Kenneth Preston admired my dialogue?'

'Yes.'

'And we don't think he's just doing it for the money do we? I've heard he does commercial work so that he can get the wherewithal to make his film about Graham Greene.'

'Nick told me he's genuinely interested in you, Tom Travis, and the crime form. Besides, Fire Ring intend to put up the money to make the Greene film, if *Murder Unseen* is a success.'

Debbie fixed me with her unwavering gaze that indicated I should give in. It was impressive. I wondered if she ever blinked.

'I'll do it then.'

'Good decision.'

I had a moment of euphoria that focused on the boys' joyful upturned faces as they clutched their new laptops. Kate was in the background smiling contentedly, free of the burden of being the family's primary breadwinner. Then I returned to earth. Debbie was taking something out of her handbag.

'I had a contract drawn up earlier,' she said. 'Why don't you sign it now? Then you can celebrate with some profiteroles – they're particularly delicious here and they're Tom Travis' favourite dessert, aren't they?'

I ignored the offer of pudding and suggested that I might take the contract away to look at the detail but Debbie said that it was pretty standard and she had already been through it. She produced a pen when I said I had lost mine. I signed.

'You shouldn't underestimate what you bring to the project,' she continued as I gave the pen back to her.

I imagined Debbie was referring to my minor celebrity status in the minds of readers of the *Daily Mail*. I had featured in headlines that had exaggerated my authorial fame to better cast doubt on my character. Even the more serious newspapers had featured salacious headlines along the lines of "Crime Writer Found With Body" with the clear implication that the whole matter had not been a chance occurrence.

On the way out of the restaurant I remembered the question I had been meaning to ask.

'Kenneth Preston,' I said, 'didn't he marry somebody famous?'

'He married Miriam Stanhope if that's what you mean. Twenty years ago.'

'He was twice her age wasn't he?'

'At least.'

'And wasn't there something recent?'

'Miriam Preston was back in the papers earlier this year. Her father and brother were killed in an accident. A light plane they were in crashed flying back from Normandy. Her mother had died of cancer years before. All of the family wealth suddenly descended on Miriam. She's a very rich woman.'

And a beautiful one as well, I recalled, if the pictures of the wedding twenty years before were to be believed. Miriam had been a radiant eighteen-year-old in love with the world and her own good fortune. Kenneth had been engaged in discussions to direct a modern stage version of

Beauty and the Beast. The headlines in the newspapers had made the inevitable connection.

'You never know,' Debbie said, putting the pen back in her handbag, 'She might come with him.'

She did of course. And if she hadn't, events would have been different. For one thing, the murders wouldn't have happened.

2

BACKGROUND MUSIC

LANGHAM HALL WAS AT the end of a long avenue of lime trees leading from a gatehouse manned by a couple of security men. It appeared out of the gloomy afternoon sky as a silhouette of towers and chimneystacks.

Just before the house a metal pole blocked the road. A burly man dressed in the same blue uniform as his comrades at the gatehouse asked my name. Then he subjected the car to a check on its underside with an illuminated mirror on a pole, gave a grunt of what seemed to be satisfaction, raised the barrier and waved me in the direction of a low wooden building to the side of the drive.

I parked the car by the side of the building he had indicated. It looked as though it had once been a barn. Inside, in an interior that was part office and part gift shop, a shapely, good-looking woman, who looked as though she was in her early thirties, was glancing alternately at her mobile and a clipboard. Her hair was expensively curled and unnaturally blond. She looked me up and down.

'David Knight?'

'Yes.'

'Welcome to Langham Hall. I'm Molly Whyard. Please let me know if there is anything I can do for you. We try to do everything we can to ensure all our guests have the best possible stay. You're in the main house. You can park in the courtyard over the drawbridge. Here are your keys. And you'll need to put this in the front of your car.'

She handed me a laminated card marked P6. To emphasise her directions she tapped a framed photograph on the counter in front of her. It was an aerial view of Langham Hall and its grounds. The Elizabethan manor, in the shape of an E with the central stroke missing, was surrounded by a moat that also enclosed an area of lawn and trees.

'The security people here seem very efficient,' I said.

'They're all ex-army,' Molly Whyard said by way of explanation. 'The chap in charge of them, Jack Catesby, served with Kenneth's producer, Nick Wallace, in Iraq. In fact a lot of them were there. They're very good at following orders, which is an advantage I suppose. They have a lot of celebrities to look after here.'

I must have raised an eyebrow.

'The stars of the film,' she added by way of explanation. 'Emma and Matthew, and that Rufus Stone.'

I waited for her to add Kenneth Preston, or his wife, or the producer, Nick Wallace, or me. But she was silent.

'Sounds as though they'll keep us safe,' I said. 'Where do I go when I get to the hall?'

'If you go to the main entrance somebody will be there to greet you. There's an introductory dinner tomorrow at nine and food in the dining room from seven tonight.'

'Fine,' I said. 'Thank you.'

I drove across something that looked like a drawbridge and parked the car. The ground rooms of the building were ablaze with light. Through the mullioned windows I could see that a Christmas tree, bedecked with tinsel and lights, was providing a festive welcome. As I was getting my suitcase out of the car, a figure that looked familiar emerged from the main doorway, walked over to a sports car and retrieved something from it.

I found myself in step with the figure as we moved to the entrance hallway. On one side was a heavy oak table with a scattering of papers and a young woman, who looked as though she had just left school, sitting behind it. She got up as we came in.

My companion stopped abruptly so that we almost bumped into each other.

'I'm not sure we've met,' he said.

'David Knight.'

'David Knight? Good to meet you.' He stretched out his hand. 'Tom Travis. At your service.'

I've never been sure about the "*at your service*" introduction I use in the books, although here it seemed to hold up reasonably well. It was the first time I had heard it in person rather than in the interior recesses of my imagination. I nearly hadn't included it in the first book of the series because Kate said that it made Tom appear old-fashioned. Her observation had troubled me for a week but then I had concluded that harking back to the golden days of crime fiction was no bad thing. Serial killers and gore are not for Tom. Exotic and inventive methods of murder are.

I managed to take the hand outstretched toward me and was treated to a decisive grip that Tom would have approved of. I found myself at a loss as to how to respond. The person issuing the greeting I recognised as the actor, Rufus Stone. He certainly looked like Tom Travis. Indeed he probably looked more like Tom Travis than Tom Travis did. In the books I've only included the briefest of details about Tom's appearance. I've always thought it best to leave something to the reader's imagination. Here there was nothing that jarred. Perhaps I could use the detail before me to give a fuller description of Tom in the next book. He would be perfectly happy wearing chunky silver cufflinks.

His mobile rang.

'I'm so sorry,' he said in an embarrassed manner as he moved away, 'I need to take this.'

Debbie had told me that Rufus Stone was a method actor who liked to immerse himself in his roles. I hadn't previously noted her gift for understatement. She had also said that part of the purpose of the Langham weekend was to enable Kenneth Preston to decide which of his two male leads would be best suited to playing the role of my detective. That pass seemed to have been made. The man I needed to convince that Tom's murderous nature had been over-emphasised in *Murder Unseen* was Rufus Stone.

The young woman behind the oak table had got to her feet. She was slim and willowy and had reddish-brown hair cascading over her shoulders. She was wearing a black and white striped top underneath a black jacket. Tom would have deduced two things: she didn't dye her hair and she had been a prefect at her school.

'David Knight. Helping with the script.'

My companion summoned up a smile.

'Florence Hammond, BBC.'

'So how does the BBC fit into this?'

'I'm trying to find out, to be honest. I think we get limited showings about a year after the film is released but apart from that, I'm not clear. To be frank, I only joined the BBC and got this job on Thursday. I'm a graduate trainee.'

'So what do you do?'

'I'm just trying to work that out. At moment I'm running errands for the producer, Nick Wallace, and filling in forms for the BBC personnel. The work is fine. He's fine. I get to see what's going on and he's great to work for. Never panics and thrives on a crisis.'

'He's worked with Kenneth Preston before hasn't he?'

'He certainly worked on Kenneth's last film. They're a bit chalk and cheese. Kenneth likes to improvise, Nick likes to plan.'

I pointed towards my erstwhile companion who had his mobile clutched to his ear.

'And that's Rufus Stone?'

'Yes.'

'It's just that he introduced himself as Tom Travis.'

'That's Rufus for you,' she said brightly. 'Nick Wallace gave me a tip. If you want to really engage with him, address him as Tom. He likes to immerse himself totally in the role when he's awake. If you catch him first thing you might still be able to have a straightforward conversation with him, but not this late in the day. He'll have been pure Tom Travis for the last ten hours. Nick says it's better to go along with it. And if he can't have a meaningful conversation with you, he can't have a meaningful conversation with anyone, can he? You know Tom Travis' world inside out.'

'I suppose I do,' I said, doubtfully. 'But what about Rufus' family? If he stays in whatever role he happens to be playing at the time, they must find it difficult surely?'

16

'That's just the point. He doesn't have any family. Nick Wallace told me he was taken into care when he was six months old. His mother died of a drug overdose and he doesn't know who his father is. There were a succession of foster parents and local authority homes. Despite all that he managed to complete a first class university degree and get into acting. He's very bright. I can't say I blame him for wanting to be the character he's playing. There was an article about him in *The Sunday Times* colour magazine a couple of weeks ago. Did you see it? At least he's playing somebody able-bodied in *Murder Unseen*. In one of his previous roles he was pushed around in a wheelchair for six months. Lost a lot of muscle tone that he had to work hard to replace. When he's deeply immersed in a role, he really thinks he is the person.'

'I suppose he must.'

I looked round. Rufus, or Tom, was nodding his head as though the call was about to end.

'So what room am I in?'

'Heisenberg. All the main rooms are named after physicists, except for the Chinese Suite. Look, here's a floor plan and a key. The rooms will be open anyway. Your luggage will be perfectly safe here if you want to leave it while you explore. He's coming back over so now's your chance. Remember it's Tom.'

Her last words were no more than a whisper.

'David,' Rufus said, 'I've got a bottle of Sancerre in the library which I was just about to sample when I remembered I left my mobile in the car. Then I had to deal with this wretched phone call. But, if you've got a few minutes, why don't you join me?'

'I'd be delighted,' I paused for a second, 'Tom.'

In a corner of the library two deep leather armchairs were set round a small table on which an open bottle of wine, a bowl of nuts, a napkin, and a glass were occupying a silver tray.

'You'll need a glass.'

He returned twenty seconds later with glass and a napkin. I sank into the armchair as he passed me a drink.

'Have you heard anything from Claire?' he said.

It was a couple of seconds before I worked out he was referring to Claire Moriarty. As far as I could remember I hadn't decided when she would reappear.

'Special duties,' I said in a low and confidential tone. 'I'm not sure how much I can tell you. She's keeping a low profile, a very low profile, away from family and even the closest of her friends. It's undercover work of the greatest importance to the state. It's very hard for her. Any communication might blow her cover. I'm afraid I can't tell you more at the moment except that she's operating mostly in the Home Counties. I shouldn't really have told you that – please keep it to yourself.'

He nodded sagely.

'I knew there must be some reason why I hadn't heard from her.'

'It must be difficult,' I said. 'For both of you. I know Claire isn't happy about it.'

'Is she not?'

The archaic sentence construction was plausible enough but there was a vulnerable tone to his voice that was far from Tom's normal calm. But then I had intended that Claire should be linked to him by one of those strings of fate that tie two people together. They were destined to be lovers, circling stars that would never break free. Their magical cord could stretch or tangle, but never break. At least that had been the plan. It had occurred to me once that perhaps Claire should be implicated in some shady dealings, perhaps even murder, to protect her family. Tom would be torn between his natural inclinations to pursue truth and justice and his feelings for her.

'She regrets you've had so little time together,' I found myself saying in a confidential whisper.

'Then... why?'

'Family honour. She promised her father, the General, before he died. It's something she has to see through whether she is happy about it or not.'

'I'm being selfish.'

'Hardly.'

'I don't know,' he said. 'This thing about Rob. It's been worrying me. It gives the game away doesn't it? I'm not worthy of her. When we met I had suppressed the memory but it's welling up. It makes a mockery of everything I told her. I'm not who I said I was.'

He took a deep draught of the Sancerre and looked into the middle distance as though seeking somebody to rid him of the universe he was in. He'd obviously read all of the *Murder Unseen* treatment in which a young Tom Travis decides to rid himself of a long-standing friend and rival in love – the Rob he had referred to.

'I don't recognise myself. It all seems like a bad dream. Sometimes I wake up and forget it has happened for a few moments and then it all comes flooding back.'

'You shouldn't be too hard on yourself. I'm pretty certain Rob would have died whatever anyone had done.'

'It needn't have been with my help.'

'It's marginal.'

'Maybe. But when I met Claire I'd obviously suppressed the memory of what had happened. I'm going to have to tell her when we next meet.'

'She'll understand.'

'Will she?'

'Definitely.'

'I wish I could share your optimism.'

'Think of your past cases. Think of the good you've done. Paul and Sylvia Henderson wouldn't have reconciled if you hadn't deduced that it was the wrong snake in their shed. And nobody else would have thought of looking for the crossbow bolt that had been fired through the door handle that had been removed in the same case. Pure genius. The police would never have been able to work that out in a thousand years. There must be half a dozen people, maybe more, who would have suffered the gravest miscarriages of justice without your intervention. There's a lot in the scales on your side. Besides, I'm not sure you've got this Rob story quite right.'

Ten minutes of weakening Tom's conviction that he was primarily responsible for the death of Rob Crane, together with a subtle blackening of Rob's character and a focus on his passive-aggressive nature, seemed to cheer him. A few examples of the other triumphs of deduction in his cases and the addition of a glass or two of Sancerre restored his confidence in himself. It was a re-born Tom Travis who left half an hour later contemplating a lifetime with Claire.

My case was still in the entrance hall where I had left it. Somewhere close there was the sound of voices but the oak table was unmanned. I looked at the floor plan Florence Hammond had provided. It seemed straightforward enough and probably would have been if I hadn't been mentally exhausted by the efforts I had put in to convince Rufus that Tom was really blameless in what had happened. It was also the case that I mistook north for west, a mistake exacerbated by the Sancerre and the fact that I hadn't eaten anything since breakfast. I stumbled in and out of a number of rooms before I found Heisenberg.

Looking around I was pleasantly surprised. It was on a larger scale than most of the other rooms I had come across in my search. Indeed it wasn't so much a room as a suite. I decided I needed an infusion of caffeine to clear my head. The milk I needed was in a mini fridge that was also stocked, encouragingly, with a bottle of Krug.

There was an inexplicably bright light outside the window that was dazzling. It seemed that some sort of mini Spielberg spaceship had just landed on the lawn. I decided to turn off the light in the room to see if that made what was going on on the other side of the window any clearer, but didn't manage to come to any great conclusion as to what the light was. I took off my jacket. I needed a shower to freshen up.

I was just going to turn the room light back on when I heard a sound behind me. I must have been silhouetted against the dazzle outside.

'You've found it then,' a woman's voice said invitingly. 'I thought you said we couldn't meet until tomorrow. Why don't you come here?'

3

BODY DOUBLE

IT WASN'T AN INVITATION I had any prospect of refusing. A slim pair of arms entwined themselves around my waist and then under my shirt, which had become unbuttoned at the front. I would have said something but I was transfixed by an intoxicating aroma from the person behind me and a disturbing mental image of a man who wasn't me scenting the fragrance from her hair and daring himself to breathe in more deeply.

Then there was the sense of touch. There's something about being touched by someone you don't know that is quite different from the touch of someone you do. But that really didn't get to the heart of the matter. I was experiencing being touched by someone else who thought I was someone else. It was unusually rewarding. I wondered who she thought I was.

There was a slight tensing of the fingers that were stroking my skin and then a gradual, but only very gradual, disengagement. The arms slid away from holding me, the heady balm in the air faded slightly, and the main light of the room was switched on.

'And you are?' There was no alarm in her voice, more a languid curiosity. I turned round.

Emma Hale was a beautiful woman. She would have been a beautiful woman in Troy before the horse appeared, or pretty much anywhere else at any time. For the average British male she was a telling mixture of the girl next door and some exotic international beauty. She emanated a languorous physical ease. She was wearing a close fitting robe and looked as though she might have been preparing for bed. Whoever she had taken me for was clearly an individual of good fortune. I wondered if he knew it. There had been both a familiarity and newness to her touch.

'David Knight, I'm doing the screenplay.'

'Emma Hale.'

She didn't add what she was doing but she didn't have to.

'Could I ask you a question?' she continued.

'That is a question.'

'So it is,' she said carelessly. 'But what I really want to know is – why are you in my room?'

'Your room?' I said in surprise.

I must have sounded genuine for she offered her hand and led me to the door of the room and outside into the corridor. She pointed upwards to the top of the doorframe. Carved into the wood was Newton.

'This isn't Heisenberg then?'

'No. I imagine Heisenberg has *Heisenberg* carved on the doorframe.'

'I'm so sorry,' I said. 'I must have missed it. I was looking for names besides the doors. I wondered why I wasn't finding any. It never occurred to me to look above them.'

'That's mildly plausible. I suppose you have a bad sense of direction?'

'Atrocious. Worse than bad. Hopeless. I normally go in the opposite direction to the right one.'

'Really? And you're doing the screenplay?'

'Helping with it.'

'And it wasn't just a ruse to get into my room?'

'I'm afraid not.'

'How disappointing.'

She seemed momentarily deflated.

'So have you met the boys?' she said after a moment.

'Only Rufus Stone. I gather he's playing Tom Travis. He seems to be getting into the role.'

'He would be. He's like Daniel Day-Lewis when it comes to method acting, but worse. He's certainly better cast as a detective. You wouldn't want him playing Rob, would you? I mean Rob's depressed and a potential suicide risk. Rufus would take that into the blacker shadows. What is Tom Travis' attitude towards women by the way? If I'm going to go to bed with him, I'd like to know.'

'He likes women and they like him. They find him attractive. Otherwise, he's upright and honourable. He's in love with a policewoman but she's disappeared on special operations so he's at something of a loss.'

'That sounds reasonably promising. To be frank, I'd much prefer to be in bed with Matthew Tabard but I think there's only one intimate scene with his character. We're coupling on a Persian rug where I'm coaxing the life force back into him. Could be fun.'

'I'm sure it could,' I said. I couldn't remember the detail but then I hadn't written it in the first place.

'Care to join me?'

I was still partly dazzled by the spaceship lights outside and hadn't seen that she had picked up the bottle of Krug and was now fishing out a couple of glasses from a wooden cabinet.

'Why don't you open that?'

'So,' I continued, after I had absorbed the fact that in Langham one was never more than five feet away from alcohol, 'why did you take the part?'

'Of Jan Pearson? Harry asked me. He's calling the shots on the project. The champagne will be from him. He's always very attentive.'

'Harry?'

'Harry Leung. Sir Harry these days. He's a bigwig in Fire Ring. Does a lot of fixing with the Chinese for the film market there. I couldn't let him down.'

She was edging toward me in a slightly provocative manner.

'That light outside,' I said, moving backwards. 'Do you know what it is?'

'The moth man.'

'The moth man?'

'Yes. He's doing a survey.'

'Are there moths in December?'

'Apparently so.'

'And won't it keep you awake?'

'Oh no. They said they would turn it off in an hour or so. Not that it would bother me. I don't really like the dark, at least not the pitch-black version you get in the country. But I suppose this way if we both look out the window we can see the stars. There's only you and me on this wing at the moment. The room between us is reserved for the policeman that's meant to be protecting Harry, but he's not expected for a day or two. Though if he did turn up I'd tell him we're more at risk from intruders inside the building. I'm not sure what's to be done. Some of them are passably attractive.'

She was standing close to me. There was that heady scent again. I put down my glass. It was half full and the bubbles were fizzing.

'I think I should find my room. It should be along the corridor. I need to shower before supper.'

'If you can't find your room, or the shower doesn't work, do come back. And remember to take your jacket with you. You can't walk around the house half naked.'

In the next moment she had disappeared into a different part of the suite. I put my jacket on and picked up my case. Heisenberg was the next room but one as she had suggested. It hadn't got the lavish proportions of Newton. Indeed, for a moment I thought it might not have its own bathroom until I noticed a narrow corridor in the wall at the end of the room. Looking down it I could see the middle of an unusually large bath. I put my case on a Victorian four-poster bed and sat down. Scattered round the room were odd bits of furniture that seemed to have been arranged at random. A guide to the room praised the wallpaper above everything else. The decor was apparently French, dating from the 1820s. The mini bar had an assortment of soft drinks, a selection of snacks and a bottle of champagne of more dubious parentage than the Krug in Newton.

Twenty minutes later I was feeling renewed. The bath, which could have accommodated at least two adults, had a shower at one end, which, once it had creaked into life, delivered an invigorating stream of hot water.

I dressed and headed back towards the entrance hall.

Florence Hammond was talking to a burly man dressed in the same blue uniform as the men at the gatehouse.

'Have you met?' Florence Hammond said, turning to me. 'This is Jack Catesby. He heads up security for Nick. They were in the army together. But there's somebody in the library eager to meet you. I said I thought you'd be around and here you are.'

'And it's...?'

'Didn't I say? Harry Leung.'

I might have said something more but Catesby was measuring me with an intense look that would have made sense if he had been a sergeant major appraising a new recruit.

4

UNDEREXPOSURE

THE OCCUPANT OF THE library was a man wearing an open necked white shirt and light blue cashmere pullover beneath a jacket that shimmered expensively in flecks of yellow and brown. In his top pocket there was an embroidered blue handkerchief that only years of opulence could have given him the confidence to adopt. His skin was a light golden brown and his shoulder length grey hair framed features that were a mixture of Chinese and western.

'Harry Leung,' he said, in tones that suggested he had been educated at a number of private schools. Then he proffered his hand. 'Fire Ring International. You must be David Knight?'

'Yes.'

'My dear chap, I'm so pleased to see you. But haven't we met before? Were you at Cannes?'

'No.'

He looked me carefully up and down.

'Wimbledon?'

'No.'

'Ascot?'

'No.'

'New York?'

'No.'

'You're trying to tease me, I'm sure. There's somewhere I know you from. It'll come to me eventually. And our director, Kenneth, is eager to get your ideas, positively slavering in anticipation the last time I saw him. Do you know Kenneth and Miriam?'

'I'm afraid not.'

He looked surprised. 'Too busy writing I imagine.' I wasn't clear whether he considered his remark a criticism or a compliment. 'But it's a treat in store,' he added. 'They're both terribly interesting. I thought they might be drifting apart at one point but they've just renewed their wedding vows. It was something Kenneth arranged. I'm not sure I would have expected such a charming gesture from him but there we are. Why don't you have a cocktail? I've ordered mine but I'm sure they can make it two.'

'Great,' I said. 'Perhaps we could have some nuts with them.'

Harry Leung gave me a slightly odd look.

'What a good idea!'

He disappeared through the door at the far end of the room. Debbie had been at pains to emphasise that, apart from being a socialite, a billionaire, a playboy, a wit, and one of the best-connected men in London, Harry Leung was also a major player in the film business and import/export markets. The UK Government regarded him as a key fixer for deals involving the Asian market, particularly anything that got anywhere near Beijing. He was also a player in Fire Ring International which probably explained why he was at Langham rather than his more usual haunts – his house in Belgravia; his villa on the Riviera; his apartment in Hong Kong; his condo on the Upper East Side; or the suite available to him in any luxury hotel in the world.

'Tell me,' he said when he reappeared with a remarkably large bowl of assorted mixed nuts, 'would you say Suffolk was dangerous?'

'Not particularly,' I said. 'Is there anything specific you had in mind?'

'I'm told I might be the subject of a terrorist threat. There's a Tibetan community in Beccles, isn't there? That might be it, although we've only optioned the hotel in Lhasa. Anyway, your government is insisting on providing me with a senior police liaison officer while I'm here, although he's not likely to be here for a day or two – the cuts I imagine. But I hardly think it's a *Black Special*, or whatever they're called. To be frank, I'm not sure there is any real threat at all. They probably want to keep tabs on me in the mistaken impression I'm someone important. But there we are. Tell me, have you done much screenwriting?'

'No.'

I couldn't tell whether Leung was surprised by my answer or not. He adopted the inscrutable face of a poker player.

'It's your experience of crime writing that matters I imagine,' he said reassuringly. 'That's what Kenneth wants to explore. When it comes to the film proper, we can get a team on it. The important thing at the moment is to keep Kenneth happy. Nick told me he was very keen to get you to work on the film.'

'I'm very flattered. But hasn't he got some other major project in mind?'

'Oh that,' Leung said airily. 'You mean the Graham Greene film. He's been trying to put together the finance for that for ages. He intends to set it when they're making *The Third Man*.

He even talked about making it in black and white at one stage. It's the casting he should be worried about. I'm not at all sure who he has in mind for the Orson Welles part.'

'Harry Lime?'

'That's the one. Shades of Greene in the name of course.' An expansive smile crossed Harry's face. 'Kenneth will have some fun with that. And he's thinking about having Kim Philby in the film. He and Greene remained close friends even after Philby was unmasked and fled to Moscow. He seems to want to start it from the point at the end of the film when Alida Valli, playing the mistress, walks past Joseph Cotton, who's playing the character who writes Zane Grey westerns. In the film she doesn't look at him and the leaves descend from this avenue of trees that looks as ruined as the rest of Vienna. But in the version Kenneth is planning, she goes back to him and puts her hand through his arm, as she did in Greene's original novel. So it looks more like the start of something rather than the end. The Philby angle might be interesting. It's not everybody who has been awarded both the Order of the British Empire and the Order of Lenin. I imagine he can't have held them both simultaneously, or perhaps one of them was a secret award. I imagine the Palace would cancel the OBE pretty quickly if they found out. It's rich material and it could be Kenneth's masterpiece. He's absolutely obsessed with it. I've told him we might be interested in backing him if *Murder Unseen* is a success. Though we'll need to avoid the problems that happened in *The Third Man*. Orson Welles wouldn't film in the sewers. He said that where he came from, sandwiches were always wrapped in cellophane and he wasn't risking his health. They had to use all sorts of doubles and even rebuild a version of the Vienna sewers in a London studio. At least we might avoid that, especially if Nick Wallace produces it. I imagine you've met him?'

'Not yet,' I said, 'although we did speak on the phone.'

'Next best thing. I'm sure he'll want to see you as soon as he arrives. He's definitely the man to go to if you've got any problems. Kenneth trusts him implicitly.'

'As a matter of fact I've been talking to Rufus Stone. He seems very keen to play the Tom Travis part but he's not sure that accentuating Tom's murderous tendencies is the right way forward.'

'Discuss that with Nick,' Leung said after a moment. 'Rufus could be right. We need to keep it simple if we're going to sell into the Far East.'

Emma Hale shimmered into the room.

'Harry,' she said, 'there you are!'

Florence Hammond was behind her. For a moment, as Emma curved herself seductively around Leung like an oversexed limpet, I saw an expression of distaste slide across Florence's features. A moment later, when I looked again, the expression had disappeared so completely that I thought it might be the product of my imagination.

'Kenneth Preston wants to see you,' Florence said, turning to me. 'He's in the studio. I can take you to him.'

The sound of Kenneth's name forced me back into the present and what I might do to convince him that Tom might best be returned to a traditional detective role. I wondered if the most effective argument might be to pick up on Rufus Stone's concerns. I've always found that the best way to get someone to take account of the pressing concerns you have is to present them as somebody else's ideas.

5

PRINCIPALS

'THE OWNERS HAVE MADE all sorts of improvements to the house in the last few years,' Florence Hammond said with an expansive gesture. 'The studio is where the bake house and laundry used to be. They've knocked through three floors to create the space and put in a balcony area so you can look down on what is going on. The best way of getting there is back through the entrance hall. Kenneth is always on a tight schedule so, if you could follow me…'

As we left the library I could see that Emma Hale was still coiled around Leung in a sinuous embrace. If my son Iain was to be believed, her true love, according to the usual tabloid sources, was now her future co-star in *Murder Unseen*, Matthew Tabard.

'This way,' Florence said.

'So,' I said, as I followed her across the entrance hall, 'the owners of this place. Where are they?'

'William and Helen Graves? They're off buying antique furniture in France. They want to create a "French" room here. Lafayette stayed here for a night in the 1820s, which is all the excuse they need. Nick Wallace tipped them off about a sale in Deauville. They didn't think they would be able to go but Nick insisted and they've decided to turn it into a bit of a holiday. Molly Whyard told me they're always looking for period pieces for the house. William Graves made a lot of money in rock music promotion and decided to retire in his late thirties. Helen made a couple of records but her career fizzled out. So they decided on a new project – buying this house and restoring it. It started off as an Elizabethan manor house and the exterior hasn't changed very much, but internally it's been knocked about a bit and the Graves' are still changing things. They want it to be self-financing. You can rent it for weddings and conferences, join the exotic dog show, although I imagine you need a dog, do the Jane Austen garden walk, or the Halloween "Fright Night", or any number of things. There should be a pile of leaflets in your room telling you what's coming up. The theatre has only just been finished. Molly Whyard told me the builders only left a week ago. Anyway, here we are. I'll leave you to Kenneth.'

Here was a massive pair of wooden doors at the end of a corridor leading off from the entrance hall. A thin strip of light was visible at the bottom. Behind me Florence's footsteps retreated down the corridor. I pushed against the right-hand door, which swung open to reveal a large, shadowy space that was more a small theatre than anything else. Illumination came from spotlights on an overhead gantry. As far as I could see the space was as high as it was long. As Florence had said, two or three floors of the original building must have been knocked through to create it. There were flagstones on the floor and the walls were black painted wood that seemed to absorb the light rather than reflect it. At one end was the balcony that she had mentioned that looked to me more like a modern minstrels' gallery. It had a steep set of steps leading up to it. In the space below there was a scattering of seats facing a performance area. There was also the slightly bitter aroma of 'new', the sort you get from fresh paint in a room where there hasn't been time for any dust to return.

Suddenly a new pool of light revealed the shadow of a bird. It was angular and oddly terrifying, like some ancient pterodactyl in the nightmares of early man. I moved forward and looked up. The bird was directly above me, looking down. A taut trail of rope attached to its body led up to a pulley mechanism fastened to the ceiling.

It had saws for wings, their serrated teeth pointing backwards, handles fixed at right angles to the bird's body. It looked as though it was planning to glide endlessly in its search for prey. Its neck was the handle of a scythe and its body the blade of the scythe, encased in two oval shaped pieces of wood that tapered to a tail. The head of the bird was a more delicate saw with a pointed beak. It was hung from a ring of metal that had been bolted on to its wooden body.

The bird was descending slowly toward me, a process that stopped when it was about six or seven feet off the ground. I reached up to touch the bird's beak. In the cone of bright light round the bird's head I could see there was a pinprick of bright red blood that slowly got bigger.

'So, what do you think?' a voice above me said, 'could you use this to kill someone?'

Kenneth Preston was at the edge of the minstrels' gallery looking down. The scar on his cheek had caught the light, so that for a moment it looked newly formed. I licked my finger.

'Come up. You need to see it from above. I'll put more lights on.'

As I walked up the stairs, light fittings on the walls lit up the corners of the room. The bird was suspended from a rope that stretched up to a pulley on a gantry, suspended from the ceiling. The rope from the pulley was coiled round an iron hook embedded in the wall.

'So, what do you think?' Kenneth Preston said again as I got to the top of the stairs. 'Would it put the fear of God into you?'

He was wearing the black leather jacket, black t-shirt and jeans that he had been wearing in the television interviews I had seen. He probably had wardrobes full of the same garments in the house in Chelsea he and Miriam used as their main base. I wondered whether he could have been the man Emma Hale had been waiting for.

'It's going to drop down is it?'

'There will be a camera on the floor looking straight up. Her eyes terrified as the blade of the beak descends.'

'Her eyes?'

'He's not going to stop at one corpse is he? Murdering Rob Crane is just a taster for him. The murdering detective, great character.'

Kenneth said the words with relish. I gathered he was taken with the concept of *the murdering detective*.

'It's quite an exotic form of murder, isn't it?' I said, injecting as much doubt as I could muster into my voice.

'That doesn't matter. When it comes to film, if you can see it, you can believe it. I can make it work. It will be terrifying. Have you talked to Nick about death? He's the expert on mortality. He's killed people and he's seen people killed in Afghanistan. I envy him. It's a line he's had to step over. I wonder whether there's any way back once you've done it? It could become a habit.'

36

There was a relish in Kenneth's tone that was unsettling. His film version of *Murder Unseen* would be littered with murders, each one more extravagant and gory than the one before, and all committed by Tom Travis. The film would be two hours of celluloid mayhem charting Tom's descent into the lower depths.

'It must vary from person to person,' I said, 'Tom's crime, if one can call it that, is hardly a serious one. I'm not sure he's crossed any sort of line.'

'Of course he has, that's what makes him interesting. But let's get back to the bird. Could it kill someone?'

'I don't see why not. Exotic murder methods are a traditional focus of the classic detective story. Although that may not work with a character that is morally ambiguous.'

'Give me both,' Kenneth said in a way that suggested he had stopped listening. 'And hold this.'

He was uncoiling the rope from the wall. Then he handed it to me. The weight of the bird was more than I had anticipated and for a moment it threatened to plummet to the ground.

'Can you lower it to the ground when I'm down there?'

Kenneth was walking down the mezzanine steps to the flagstone floor below. He looked up.

'Slowly as you can.'

I let the rope slip through my fingers, at Kenneth's direction, until the beak of the bird was no more than a foot or two above the flagstones. Kenneth had produced some chalk from his pocket and was marking the point where the bird's beak would impact with an X.

'It should fall pretty straight. Although why anyone should be lying on the ground is another question.'

'Work something out for me,' Kenneth said. 'That's what you're being paid for. Remember you don't have to explain too much in film if the shot works. And this one will.'

'I...' I said.

'And give me a list of any other exotic methods of murder you can think of,' Kenneth added, before I had time to work out what I was trying to say. 'The more you can come up with, the better.'

'Fine,' I said. 'I...'

'We'll discuss it tomorrow. It'll give you time to get your thoughts in order.'

I was saved from having to say anything else by another presence in the room.

'Are you boys having fun?'

A figure was moving towards Kenneth. She was dressed in a black jumper and black leggings. She had probably left her black leather jacket in the entrance hall. Miriam Preston must now be about two-thirds of her husband's age rather than less than half. Marriage, to outward appearance, seemed to have made them the same person.

'David is helping me work out how we can kill someone with this, preferably a woman.'

'You really shouldn't be giving him ideas,' Miriam said in a teasing tone looking at me. 'You never know where they might lead.'

'But you can help us Miriam,' her husband said. 'If you could just lie on the ground underneath the bird's beak.'

'What on earth for?'

'We need a beautiful corpse.'

'Really Kenneth, you'll be the death of me.'

'Not today. Look, it's simple.'

Kenneth positioned himself on the floor, his chest a few inches below the bird's beak. Miriam managed to lift the rope a little. The bird rose and fell an inch.

'Your turn.'

Kenneth scrambled to his feet and was replaced by Miriam. As corpses go she was more than acceptable. She gave a moan of distress and threw out her right arm in a pose of abandoned death. Despite the theatricality of the gesture, she managed to induce a shiver down my spine. Debbie had told me she had been about to go to RADA when she met Kenneth.

He was drawing a chalk line round her body. There was a ripple of applause from the mezzanine floor. I looked up. Harry Leung was clapping approvingly. At his side another man joined in.

'Why don't you all come down?' Kenneth said.

'So why would anyone agree to lie on the ground with a murderous bird above them?' Miriam said, removing a speck of dust from her leggings.

'Ask David,' Kenneth said. 'That's what he's here for.'

'It's a good question,' I said.

'And have you got a good answer?'

Miriam's tone was playful. Beyond her I could see Kenneth was looking enquiringly at me, as was Leung and whoever our new companion was, a wiry, good-looking man in a green Barbour jacket, cord trousers and wellingtons. If William Graves, the owner, was away in Paris, this was most likely to be the producer, Nick Wallace. There was an expectant hush. I realised they were waiting for me to speak.

'The person doesn't know the bird is above them,' I said. 'They've been asked to lie down. Maybe they're blindfolded. The position they need to be in has been worked out in advance. They are led to the spot and a surprise is promised. A second or two later it arrives. The murderer removes the blindfold and the whole thing is made to look like an accident.'

'That's not a bad beginning,' Kenneth said, 'but you need to colour it in.'

'Seems a little elaborate for me,' Miriam said.

'So how would you get rid of someone?'

'Nothing complicated. Poison. A poison that is untraceable. What would you recommend?'

'I'm not too good on untraceable poisons,' I said. 'They're not really allowed in crime novels for obvious reasons. But if you could find something that was readily available, that any number of people might have access to, that might do the trick.'

'So,' Miriam said, 'what is readily available? What would a sleuth use if he was tempted for once to turn to murder?'

'You're going to have to wait, darling,' Kenneth said, 'the first thing David is doing is compiling a list of exotic murder methods for me.'

'I'm sure adding a few simple and readily obtainable poisons won't be too much additional trouble, David, will it? Tom Travis seems to know about them.'

The words were said with the reasonableness of a confident Lady Macbeth. From the confidence of her tone it seemed that Miriam had read the *Murder Unseen* material as well.

I didn't know whether to be heartened or dismayed. Debbie had given me the impression that I would be lucky if the Prestons (I now looked on them as a unit) or any of the actors would have had the time or inclination to look at the *Murder Unseen* material in any detail. But they obviously had. Matters weren't a blank slate on which I could colour in Tom's road to redemption. While there was still some hope that Rufus might be coaxed down a new road, Kenneth Preston would be more difficult to turn round.

The man in the green Barbour jacket and wellington boots had turned to me.

'Nick Wallace,' he said, extending his hand and giving me an appraising glance that was weighing me up as an ally or an enemy. If Kenneth was to be swayed on the direction that Tom Travis' murderous tendencies needed to be channelled, Nick Wallace needed to be on side. 'You must be David Knight. Pleased to meet you.'

I nodded in reply and returned the handshake. Tom Travis, who is used to making deductions about people from any source, would have judged it a pleasing mixture of the resourceful and trusting, not too hard and not too soft. He ushered me into a corner as Leung took a call on his mobile and Miriam Preston went back to her role as a beautiful corpse.

'That's promising,' Nick Wallace said.

'What is?'

'Kenneth's reaction to your suggestion.'

'I didn't think he seemed too enthusiastic.'

'Believe you me, most people get a lot worse than that. Kenneth likes to be abrasive. The fact that he wants you to do more work on what you were saying is a good sign, a very good sign. I'm not surprised. He, both of them actually, seem very interested in classical crime fiction.'

Behind us, Miriam Preston was looking enquiringly at Nick and muttering about being hungry.

'There's rather a good restaurant in the local village we could try. But we need to go now if we want to get a table. You could come along too David,' Nick Wallace said.

'That's kind,' I said, 'but I think I'll give it a miss. I need to do some thinking.'

I did. If I was going to convince Kenneth that Tom Travis was better at solving murders rather than committing them, I needed as many allies as I could get. I had a feeling that Nick Wallace could be one of them.

6

FOREGROUND

THERE WAS A NEWCOMER in the entrance hall as the two limousines that Nick Wallace had miraculously managed to conjure up, sped away into the night. It was Kenneth's other leading man, Matthew Tabard. As I got closer it was apparent that the film critic who had described him as "the most handsome actor of his generation" hadn't been far off the mark. He had blue eyes and an honesty of feature that suggested that you could buy a second-hand car from him with total certainty, preferably a vintage model, most probably an expensive one. This was allied to upper class English good looks, a delicate bone structure, and a frame of auburn hair around his face.

'David Knight,' I said. 'I'm here to help with the screen-writing.'

I might have been speaking Chinese for all the recognition the words produced.

'I write the Tom Travis series,' I said, hoping for some sort of affirmative nod that indicated we were both inhabiting the same region of space-time.

He looked as baffled as ever.

'Have you read much crime fiction?'

'Sherlock Holmes,' he said after a moment. 'At school,' he added after a period of further reflection. 'Actually it was read to us. Our history master always used to read us something in the last period on a Friday afternoon.'

'No better place to start,' I said cheerfully. 'So did you continue with the genre?

'I bought a Patricia Highsmith novel once. I think it was a crime novel. My girlfriend recommended it as holiday reading but my case got lost at Rome airport. The book was in it. I hadn't even opened it. It was about somebody called Ripley I think. Not sure I've read anything much since.'

I wasn't sure he had read anything at all since, but I let the matter pass. I had been hoping for something that I could use as a hook to persuade him that playing a murder victim wasn't necessarily his best career option. It might have been a plan with little hope of success but it wasn't any sort of plan given Matthew's complete absence of interest in crime fiction.

'If you'll excuse me,' Matthew Tabard said. 'We can talk later.'

'Of course,' I said. 'Nice to have met you.'

I remembered there had been some complaint that Matthew Tabard in any film role he played was essentially... Matthew Tabard. But then that might have been an accusation aimed at the greats like Cary Grant, or Hugh Grant. Tonight he hardly seemed to be Matthew Tabard. Quite how he was going to interact with Kenneth's desire to push his actors to their psychological limits was an interesting question.

I needed to take stock of what had happened in the few hours since I arrived and what it meant for any overall strategy I might employ in the next few days. That was best done with a friend. Where was Jerry? Where was the man I could explore possibilities with? Where was my friend, confidant, consultant (with a three week gap to his next job), master of any gadget known to mankind, and sounding board? Debbie had been certain that she could find something for him, given that they had been so anxious to land me and given, as she had put it, Jerry's obvious qualities. The basis of her otherwise inexplicable faith in him seemed to be the miraculous repair of one of the upmarket office chairs that she had been told would take weeks (not minutes) and several hundred pounds to fix. At the time I had nodded at her idea. Now, I embraced it wholeheartedly. I needed Jerry's consultancy confidence that anything could be solved. If he couldn't be employed as a consultant at least, I had suggested to her, he could be employed as my chauffeur.

So why had I heard nothing? Debbie had promised to let me know when something had been fixed up but she had been unusually silent. Could it be Faith, Jerry's wife, and the newly born twins? I still didn't understand how they hadn't known, until the twins were born, that they were of opposite sexes, rather than two girls. Or why that needed to involve so many changes in colour schemes. Or why Faith's aversion to the smell of newly applied paint meant that she felt obliged to take the twins to stay with her sister in Edinburgh. Was this what had delayed him?

With his family doubled in size, the upcoming redecorating bill, and a gap until his next job, his priority should be earning as much money as he could. He didn't need to be supervising paint finishes. He needed to be here.

Not that I could talk to him about everything that had happened. He might have shared in the events of six months ago but he didn't know the full story and he certainly didn't know that I hadn't written *Murder Unseen*. Perhaps I should have confided in somebody completely but I hadn't. At least Jerry knew there were some matters that I wasn't prepared to share with him. It was the same with the policeman who had been involved in the events as well – Bob Addinson. But the chances were that I would never see him again or have to face that quizzical glance, or his annoying use of the word *sir*. The other good thing about Jerry was that if I simply said I had changed my mind about Tom, he would click into his consultant mode and feel obliged to offer up solutions.

I chatted idly with Molly Whyard for a few minutes. She hadn't liked Kenneth's last film, or indeed any of his films that she could remember. Indeed, she seemed to have a blind spot when it came to his films although, surprisingly, she seemed to have seen almost all of them. She didn't seem to have a particularly high opinion of Kenneth's wife either.

She was more enthusiastic about Langham's other visitors. She had found Matthew Tabard enchanting, if a little shy. She thought Rufus Stone intense, Harry Leung amusing, and Nick Wallace handsome and unflappable, and, after I had pressed her on the point, influential. I mentioned Florence and Emma but she seemed to have no particular views on them, or at least no view she was prepared to share, although she did say that Matthew and Emma should make a nice couple. Following the directions she gave me I eventually found the dining room where I had a slightly disjointed meal that matched my mood and failure to come up with any killer arguments that would convince either Kenneth or Nick that Tom's murderous tendencies should be played down.

When I got back to my room I found I had left my mobile on the bedside table. I rang Kate.

'David? Did you get my messages? How's it going?'

'I mislaid my phone,' I said. 'I'll catch up with them later. I'm just finding my feet. I've met Matthew Tabard, Rufus Stone and Emma Hale. At least the boys will be impressed. I wanted to say goodnight to them if they're still up.'

'Did you say Matthew Tabard was there, Dad?'

Iain was on one of the extensions.

'He certainly is,' I said. 'Actually, to be frank, he was looking a bit out of sorts.'

'That's because he's broken up with Abbey Frost.'

'I thought he was with Emma Hale.'

'He is *now*.'

'So who is this Abbey Frost? I've never heard of her.'

'Of course you have. She's the tennis player with long legs that got to the quarterfinals in the mixed doubles at Wimbledon. You watched the match.'

'Did I?'

'You thought she was rather attractive,' Kate added. 'Particularly her forehand.'

'I vaguely remember.'

'C'mon Dad, concentrate. Anyway, that's the explanation.'

'What is?'

'She found him with someone else and gave him the boot. She hasn't won a match since. He's bound to be regretting it.'

'Perhaps,' I said. Matthew Tabard could be experiencing a strong sense of guilt. That might explain his rather weary response to anything I had said. It was valuable intelligence although I was becoming concerned about my eldest son's comprehensive knowledge of tabloid gossip. He might even be looking at *Mail Online*. If he was, he was bound to have found the less than flattering references to *crime writer David Knight caught in one of his own mysteries.*

'David?' Kate was saying, 'are you still there?'

'Yes.'

'Did you say Emma Hale, Dad?' Iain asked.

'Yes.'

'I was thinking,' Iain said, 'there's a charity football match coming up at school. She could kick off.'

'That's not a bad idea,' Kate said. 'Kicking off. Iain is team captain next term. Getting Emma Hale involved would be great.'

'You could ask her, Dad.'

There was a new level of fervour in my son's voice.

'I'll do my best.'

'Great Dad. I've got to go. Oliver has fallen asleep and I need to wake him to tell him what's happened.'

'Tell him in the morning,' Kate said.

'Do you think that's best?' Iain sounded doubtful.

'Your mother is right.'

'OK then. Night Dad.'

'Goodnight Iain,' I said. There was the sound of the receiver being replaced.

'There was something else Iain was going to mention,' Kate said. 'Apparently, the Prestons renewed their wedding vows a couple of days ago at a church in Kensington. It was an A-list celebrity attendance according to him. I haven't seen him so impressed for a long time. Are they both there?'

'Yes. But I'm not sure renewing their vows is still the top thing on their mind. When I was introduced to Kenneth he was obsessing about using a bird sculpture as a murder weapon. Miriam seemed more interested in what poisons were available locally.'

'They sound interested in crime at least. But I can hear noises upstairs. I think I'd better go and make sure Iain doesn't wake Oliver.'

'Goodnight then,' I said.

'Goodnight, darling. Thanks for phoning.'

I looked at my watch and plugged a capsule into the coffee machine. There was notepaper next to the leaflets advertising Langham's forthcoming attractions. I might not be able to think of reasons that would convince Kenneth to turn Tom back from the gates of darkness, but if he wanted a list of the unusual in the homicide stakes, I was the man to provide it. I paced round the room for what seemed a long time and then started writing -

Methods of Murder

a. the disappearing weapon – bludgeoned to death with frozen leg of lamb (also, when cooked, provides the investigating officers with a meal), the ice bullet;

b. weapon in full view but not seen – the detachable newel post on the stairs, the new oven door, the rowing oar as stair rail;

c. murder as accident – car, cliff edge, tube train platforms, bomb on plane (but collateral consequences);

d. murder as temptation – the poisoned Petrus '89, takeaway food to the wrong address, the 1807 College sherry, profiteroles, medjool dates, lemon meringue pie , (what flavour best disguises poison?);

e. unusual murder – the bells (Wimsey) – dehydration in the locked room that doubles as a furnace, or gassed/frozen;

f. unseen murder – local GPs;

g. crushed by a giant cheese;

h. the poisonous goldfish;

i. murder with memory loss;

j. the wrong assumption – e.g. the arrow which isn't fired but used as a dagger.

I looked at the list. I yawned. A little time later there was the sound of the returning limousines. I yawned again and climbed into bed. The last thing I remember was the sound of a clock chiming midnight.

7

ESTABLISHING SHOT

WHEN I WOKE THE next morning, I stretched an exploratory arm across the bed but all I found was a cold sheet. It took me a few more moments to deduce that I wasn't in London; the bed I was sleeping in wasn't my own; and Kate wasn't with me.

I opened my eyes, got out of bed and pulled the curtains back. The chalky light of dawn was making a feeble attempt to break through a blanket of fog that had reduced everything to a pointillist grey haze. I drew a face in the condensation that had settled on the window and stepped back. The face looked gloomy, mouth downturned.

Half an hour later I was feeling better. The antique looking shower in the bathroom had delivered as bracing a shower as it had the night before and the coffee machine had delivered a more than acceptable espresso. In the entrance hall Molly Whyard was back behind the oak table.

'Good morning, Mr Knight. They're serving breakfast in the dining room from now until ten if you're hungry.'

'I think I'll go for a walk and work up an appetite,' I said. 'I need to clear my brain. Is anyone else up?'

'Not that I've seen.'

'Not Matthew Tabard or Emma Hale then?'

'She's very attractive of course but I hope he isn't on the rebound. He's such a nice man.'

'It was that tennis player he was involved with wasn't it? What was her name? Abbey Frost?'

'That was it. You are well informed Mr Knight. But that comes of writing detective novels, I suppose.'

Outside, a number of cars were parked next to mine. A new gleaming black Bentley almost totally hid a Fiat 500 painted in creamy pastels. Next to them was an antique Jowett Jupiter sports car, in immaculate condition. The paintwork of the car, a racing green, was gleaming brightly under the application of what must be a regular coating of polish. It was the car that Rufus had gone back to the evening before.

I walked across the drawbridge. The moat that surrounded the house and its accompanying area of garden was a good six metres wide. On both sides the banks dropped steeply into water that was deep and uninviting. I decided to walk around the main building. Debbie always says that one needs to get a sense of what any place is about, to help descriptive passages write themselves.

There was a bridge across the moat to the side of the house where there was a collection of lower lying buildings that must have originally been kitchens or stables. The bridge had three brick arches and, halfway across, a sort of gatehouse with a solid wooden door.

There was also a figure looming out of the mist that looked familiar.

'Jerry?' I said.

'Oh hello David,' he said, stifling a yawn.

'You got here then?'

'Last night.'

'I didn't see you.'

'That's because I didn't get here until midnight, and if you get here once the drawbridge is up, there's no way you can get into the house proper. The entrance across the footbridge is locked. The security people told me when I arrived.'

'So what did you do?' I said. There was something different about Jerry's appearance from the last time I had seen him but I couldn't work out what it was.

'They found me a bed in the buildings round the corner from the barrier. It used to be the stables but now it's a restaurant and a gym with some bedrooms attached.' He gestured vaguely in the direction of a collection of buildings indistinct in the haze. 'To be fair, they gave me a bacon sandwich and a cup of tea as well. The security people bunk down there. It's a bit like a barracks but it was comfortable enough. Anyway, that was last night. Tonight I've got a room in the main house. It's pretty impressive isn't it?'

'What is?'

'This place,' Jerry said, expansively holding his arms wide. 'It could be the perfect setting.'

'For what?'

'For plotting your next murder mystery. Bit of a cliché I know but look around you. Isolated country house – check. No way in when the drawbridge is up – check. Eccentric owners – check. Assembled group of the celebrity great and the good – check. It must be the ideal setting for Tom Travis mustn't it? If you take some notes while you're here, the plot will write itself.'

'It will, will it?'

'Absolutely,' Jerry beamed.

'So,' I said, unwilling to contest Jerry's long-held assumption that plots for crime novels could spring fully formed from a location, a headline in a newspaper, or a chance remark in a pub. 'To turn to practical matters. What car have we got?'

'What do you mean?' Jerry said.

'You're my chauffeur, aren't you? I mean we're not going anywhere, are we? But that rather makes the point doesn't it? *Better to have a chauffeur if you don't really need one.* Although I suppose you could nip down to the village for anything I might want.'

'Chauffeur?' Jerry said. 'You think I'm here as your chauffeur?'

'Aren't you?'

'No.'

'So why are you here?'

'I'm the assistant screenwriter.'

'You don't know anything about screenwriting.'

'Who edits your novels?'

'You look at them when they're nearly finished, before they go off to Debbie and Angie. Kate looks at them and so does Debbie and...'

'And you'll want a nodder,' Jerry insisted before I could finish.

'A nodder? Why would I want a nodder?'

'It will look much better.'

'Will it?'

'Undoubtedly. More than that, you will look much better.'

'Will I? Why?'

'Because I'll be agreeing with you.'

'How?'

'Because I'll be nodding.'

Jerry started moving his head up and down as though he was part of some affirmative action programme.

'It won't just be nodding,' he continued. 'There are inflexions of the facial muscles that can be used.'

'Like what?'

'An insouciant smile might be just the thing at an appropriate moment. A careless acknowledgement that you're the top dog when it comes to matters concerning Tom Travis could come in useful.'

'And so that's all you're going to be doing? An insouciant smile and nodding at the appropriate moment?'

'That's just for starters.'

'It doesn't sound an enormous amount even for starters. What else can you do?'

'General advice on crime, general advice on anything come to that. I'm pretty clued up.'

'Give me an example.'

'The family that used to own Langham were Catholics. That means the house probably has a priest's hole. It's the sort of thing that could be useful for the film.'

'Fair enough,' I said as I noticed I had involuntarily started nodding, 'although there is one other thing.' I had finally worked out what was different about Jerry's appearance.

'What's that?'

'Those glasses. Are they new?'

'Oh these?'

'Yes, those.'

'Neat, aren't they?'

The glasses had a chunky black frame of the sort made fashionable by Clark Kent when he was not being Superman.

'They're reasonable enough,' I said, 'if that is the sort of retro look that you want. But I didn't know you had problems with your eyesight.'

'I don't. Faith found them. They block out all sorts of harmful rays. The only drawback is that you need to keep them on all day if you want them to be fully effective. I must say they seem to work. My eyes don't feel nearly as tired as they used to. Anyway, we should press on.'

'We're on a walk are we?'

'You should see it more as a reconnaissance. This place could be gold dust. You need to get to know it.'

'Do I?'

'Of course you do. Frankly David, your descriptive stuff in the Tom Travis series isn't necessarily the clearest, or the best. If you're going to use this setting in your new book, you need to absorb it so that it's second nature to you.'

I would have argued further but Jerry had already set off. As I trailed reluctantly behind him I found the back of the house was less formal than the front, with a series of yew hedges that had been playfully clipped into the shape of chess pieces. A pawn at the end was ragged and careworn, the victim of a storm. I shivered, not because the house was promising as a Tom Travis murder venue, but because the breeze had suddenly picked up and was beginning to chase the mist away. One moment the house was turning into a hazy outline and the next it was in full view.

'So,' Jerry said expansively, 'you look as though you've got something on your mind. I'm here to help. Why don't you tell me?'

'It's Tom Travis,' I said. 'It's these murderous tendencies he's developing.'

'I thought that was the point.'

'I'm having second thoughts. I'm not sure it's a road he should travel down.'

Jerry looked nonplussed. Never mind the promise of nodding or an insouciant grin; he looked as though he was about to shrug his shoulders.

'I regret it,' I said firmly.

'What?'

'Allowing it to happen. Allowing him to become a quasi-murderer. Frankly, I would be much happier if he could revert back to a traditional detective.'

'I can understand that,' Jerry said, nodding.

'Can you?'

'Bearing in mind what you have been through, it's clear enough.'

'What do you mean *what I have been though*?'

'That stuff in the *Daily Mail*. It virtually implied you were a murderer. That's bound to leave a bit of a shadow.'

'That's nothing to do with it. I'm worried about Tom.'

'He's fiction.'

'He's still my creation. I don't want him to have murderous tendencies.'

'They're not so much tendencies as actualities, aren't they? I mean, nobody else murders Rob in *Murder Unseen*, do they? You should know. You wrote it.'

'That's as maybe. But I've reconsidered. I'm not sure I want Tom to be a murderer, whatever the provocation.'

'It was sexual jealousy, wasn't it?'

'Whatever it was, I'm still going to try and turn it round. I think Rufus Stone, who is playing Tom, is as uneasy as I am.'

'He's bound to be isn't he? He'd have to face up to his own nature if you go through *Murder Unseen* as written. I imagine the Jowett Jupiter is his?'

'I thought you said you hadn't been up to the house?'

'The security people were discussing it. It is his, isn't it?'

'Yes,' I said reluctantly.

'There you are then,' Jerry said. 'He just happens to drive the same car as Tom Travis does. I imagine it's a green one. Give him murderous tendencies as well and you have no idea where you'll end up. Still, if you think you can bring him round…'

'Kenneth Preston may be a problem as well. Even if I can convince Rufus that Tom isn't a murderer, I think Kenneth is determined to plough on into the depths. Debbie and Harry Leung told me he's planning to make a film about Graham Greene's dark side. Maybe this is just a dry run for him.'

'You could be right,' Jerry said with an unhelpful certainty to his words. 'Graham Greene. There's a man for you!'

'Is he?

'Of course he is. He wrote two versions of his own diary. Allied to that, he drank to excess, flirted with suicide, investigated whipping establishments, chased prostitutes, and volunteered to spy against his own country. Tom's not going to develop that fast, but he must be promising material for some sort of dry run of such a character. Kenneth probably sees him as a springboard for the excesses to come.'

'That's hardly reassuring.'

'It's the truth. There's no point in me nodding if nobody believes a word you're saying.'

'In that case there's not much point in having…' I started saying, but stopped. There was a new figure emerging from the billows of mist. Nick Wallace, in the hazy light of morning, was a wiry man dressed in slacks, boots, and a chunky green jumper with leather patches around the shoulders. He looked as though he had just dropped in from an army helicopter and seemed none the worse for wear from the previous evening's gastro pub adventure.

'David, we didn't have time to introduce ourselves properly yesterday. So let me just say I'm so glad you're here. And this is?'

'Jerry Davis,' Jerry said.

'And you are?'

'The assistant screenwriter,' Jerry added quickly.

I nodded reluctantly.

'Good to meet you.'

'Debbie Hunter said you would be bringing some expert help.'

'Yes,' I said. 'Jerry is very much my go-to man on any problem.'

'Great,' Nick Wallace said enthusiastically. 'As I said in our phone call, Kenneth is very keen to get you – both of you – involved in the work he's planning with his principals. He wants to make sure his stars have got the necessary chemistry between them and understand what classical crime is all about. You were talking to Rufus weren't you? How was he?'

'I haven't met enough method actors to know, but he did seem a little intense.'

'That's Rufus. He put on a stone and a half in his last role.'

'I think I missed it.'

'It was a romantic comedy about a pizza chef in New York. It's done very well at the box office. Luckily, filming only took six weeks. He's got most of the weight off. So that shouldn't be a problem. Tom Travis has a good diet, doesn't he?'

'Pretty much. Drinks a bit too much Sancerre but not enough to impair his deductive abilities. And he eats lots of fish.'

'Any weaknesses? Doughnuts? Chocolate? Dates?'

'Profiteroles are pretty much his only vice.'

'Good.' Nick said. 'We can cope with that. Besides, I think you said in one of your books that Tom has something of a lean look. That could be helpful.'

'But I was wondering,' I said.

'What?'

'His method acting,' I said. 'Could that be a problem if Tom is portrayed as a murderer...'

I had half-expected Nick Wallace to dismiss my concerns out of hand but instead he seemed to be taking what I said seriously. Out of the corner of my eye I could also see that Jerry was engaged in some judicious nodding.

'I certainly think it's something we need to keep an eye on,' Nick said after a few seconds reflection. 'I'm sure Rufus ultimately does know he's playing a role but he takes his identification with character much further than any other actor I've ever come across. We need to manage the situation. I think Kenneth said you and he had an initial discussion yesterday. Have you discussed it with him?'

'I didn't really have an opportunity. He just asked me to think about exotic methods of murder. Ice daggers and that sort of stuff. I've started to make a list.'

'That's good. Those might be murders that Kenneth envisages Tom Travis investigating. And do bear in mind that a lot of these projects never get made, even when they get to this stage. You may be disappointed but the thing to remember is that you get paid, whatever happens. In fact, a lot of screenwriters make a very good living from projects that are never made. But come to me the moment you've got any concerns. Rufus could be a problem.'

'Well,' Jerry said as Nick Wallace disappeared into the mist. 'You've got an ally there. A problem shared is a problem halved. His job is to hold everything together and make sure everyone is happy. He seems to know what he's talking about as well. I'm sure he'll help keep matters under control.'

Jerry seemed to be adding a faint, almost imperceptible, nodding motion to his words. It was eerily effective. For a moment I thought of confessing that my real problem wasn't so much that I was concerned that Tom had been allowed to develop murderous tendencies, so much as the fact that it wasn't me who had invented those tendencies in the first place. I almost said something but Jerry had become indistinct in a billow of mist and the moment passed.

8

BACKSTORY

'I'D BETTER FIND MY room.' Jerry said. 'Then we should meet up. You'll look more imposing if you've got an entourage.'

'Just a moment,' I said. 'There's something you could do for me. Miriam Preston said she was interested in poisons, the more untraceable the better. If you could do a bit of research on what might be available locally, that could be helpful. It might create leverage with her.'

'Suffolk poisons,' Jerry intoned, 'available locally.'

'Precisely,' I said. 'Make it as Agatha Christie as you can. Give it a traditional feel.'

'Consider it done,' Jerry said.

'She might want to talk about it later today.'

'When I say consider it done,' Jerry said grandly, 'I mean just that. It is done. I could do it now if she asks. I imagine there will be wolf's bane, or some other variant of aconitum here, for example. There used to be a Suffolk tradition of creating a death garden on these sorts of estates. You never know, there might be one here. I thought it was a topic that might come up and I had time on my hands so I thought it was an opportunity to do some research.'

'Excellent,' I said. 'That's really helpful.'

It seemed that Jerry was turning himself into a master of facts as well as gadgets. It was a surprise, but a pleasant one.

'Anyway, I need to find my room,' Jerry said. 'I'll see you later.'

There was a cough behind me. I turned. Molly Whyard was at the desk. She looked nervous.

'There's something I meant to ask you, Mr Knight.'

'Which is?'

'It's this,' she said. It was a hardback copy of *A Grave Mistake*. 'I wonder if you could sign it.'

'I'd be delighted to,' I said. 'Can I dedicate it to you?'

'Oh, it's not for me!' she said in an alarmed tone. 'It's for my sister Julie. She's the Don Travis fan. She reads lots of crime fiction.'

'Tom,' I said. 'Tom Travis.'

'What did I say? Of course it's Tom. That's what I meant to say.'

'No problem,' I said. 'Normal spelling for Julie? A small dedication? My name and the date? Would that do?'

'That's perfect. She'll be very pleased.'

'There you are then,' I said as I signed the book. 'But you might be able to help me on something. Do you know if there are any secret rooms or anything like that at Langham? The family who used to own it were Catholics weren't they? They might have had a priest's hole?'

'Julie would know. I'll ask her. She's interested in that sort of thing. She helps with the library here. She wants to be an archivist.'

'Ideal,' I said. 'Any detail welcome. I always like to know everything about any house I'm staying in.'

'And thanks so much for this,' Molly said, flourishing the copy of *A Grave Mistake* in her hand. 'Julie will be very pleased. Would you like some coffee and biscuits? I can easily order some.'

'That would be good,' I said. 'I'm not sure I want a proper breakfast. Could you send them in there?'

I pointed towards the library. Once I had walked into the room I found myself drawn towards the fiction section by an invisible hand. Gratifyingly, under K, there were hardback copies of all the Tom Travis novels with the exception of *A Grave Mistake*. Perhaps I had just signed the library copy for Julie Whyard. Telling myself that the matter was of no purpose, I picked up *The Sunday Times*, installed myself in a green leather armchair with a high back and side panels, and started filling in the general knowledge crossword. I found a reasonably sharp pencil in my jacket pocket that must belong to one of the boys. One across, the Tarzan of the 30s, was obviously "Weissmuller" and I spent a happy twenty minutes filling in clues with the only interruption being the arrival of coffee and some tempting dark chocolate ginger biscuits with a hint of orange.

I was just coming to the conclusion that I must have got one of the clues for the crossword wrong when there was a sound behind me.

'So, you're here,' Jerry said. 'I've been looking for you,' he added in an accusatory manner that suggested, at the very least, that I was guilty of a serious moral fault, or that he had noticed there was only one biscuit left.

'Well you've found me,' I said. 'I've remembered something I meant to ask you. On this poison stuff, make sure you cover ones that can be disguised in food and drink. Miriam may be a way into Kenneth. We need to over-deliver. But I need to leave that to you. Tom Travis isn't in to that sort of thing.'

'You said he was an expert on poisons in *Death of a Socialite.*'

'Did I?'

'Right at the beginning.'

'I might have done, I suppose. I think I made him an expert on all sorts of things. But I never followed up with anything concrete on poisons. Are you sure I said that?'

'I'll show you the passage if you like,' Jerry said.

'No, no, I believe you. In fact, I was going to poison Jennifer Tyler, wasn't I? But then I found I couldn't go through with it.'

'She was shot by the gamekeeper, wasn't she?'

'Accidentally. Nobody would have wanted to murder her. And it was an instantaneous death that she would have no knowledge of. I liked her.'

'Anyway,' Jerry said, 'consider it done. You can leave poisons and Miriam Preston to me. I'll tell her that I advise you on technical details.'

'Great. You might be able to help me with the crossword as well. 10 across. I thought it was "fog horn" but 10 down must be "Charles Manson" and it doesn't fit.'

Jerry picked up the newspaper. 'It would if you made it "car horn". And 10 down is "bodkin". There's that Cyril Hare novel, *With a Bare Bodkin*, isn't there? Unusual murder weapon. And 22 across is "assegai". I think I saw one in the dining room on the wall, come to think of it. Could be useful.'

I filled in the clues and put the paper carelessly to one side before Jerry could come up with any further answers.

'So?' I said. 'You came in here with something in mind. What is it you wanted to tell me?'

'Oh nothing much,' Jerry said in a self-deprecating tone that suggested he might have accidentally stumbled across the secret of nuclear fusion. I bit my lip and waited.

'I've just seen Matthew Tabard and Emma Hale,' he said after a dramatic pause. 'They were talking together. They didn't see me because they were engrossed in each other.'

'Is that it?'

'It looked pretty intimate. Besides, Matthew Tabard is meant to be quite the lad isn't he?'

'I imagine things tend to look that way with Emma.'

There must have been a note of the dismissive in my voice because I found myself offering up details of my encounter with Emma in her bedroom. At first, Jerry seemed unwilling to accept my account as being part of anything other than my own wish fulfilment. Then, after I had convinced him that what I had said was an accurate picture of what had happened, and he found out that Emma's room had been called "Newton", he spent a happy couple of minutes discussing equal and opposite attraction and the laws of motion, which he seemed to find amusing. He seemed uninterested in the identity of whoever it was that Emma had actually been expecting, but perhaps I hadn't emphasised that as much as her tactile attraction. Anyway, it seemed to me, if Jerry's description of what he had seen was anywhere near accurate, that it was confirmation of the tabloid theory that Emma and Matthew were now an item.

'It looked like an intimate embrace from where I was,' he continued ruefully. 'I could have taken a snap on my phone. It would be worth a fortune.'

'But you didn't.'

'No. One has certain standards. But it's something you could put in your next book. *Crime passionnel*. It's an obvious motivation.'

'It's in *Murder Unseen*.'

'I suppose it is,' Jerry said. 'Yes, good point. You're on the case already. I should have registered that. But there's something in the air here. There must be if Emma Hale fancies you.'

I had a feeling that at the back of Jerry's brain there was more accumulated badinage lurking on theories of equal and opposite attraction. Luckily, before it could emerge, there was a ping on my phone.

'It's a message from Nick Wallace,' I said. 'Kenneth wants an initial discussion with Emma, Rufus and Matthew, starting at eleven, to explore the dimensions of their roles. But we're not needed, neither is Nick, although Kenneth might want a word with me later in the afternoon.'

'Shame,' Jerry said. 'It would be interesting to see how Matthew and Emma relate to each other.'

'If I'm meant to be seeing Kenneth this afternoon, it might be helpful for you to be available as well. Are you going to the dinner tonight?'

'Everyone is.' Jerry said. You're sitting next to Kenneth on the seating plan Molly Whyard showed me. There are pre-dinner drinks at seven.'

'We need to do some thinking then.'

'Do we?' Jerry didn't look convinced.

'Of course we do. Poisons that Miriam Preston can hide in food and drink.'

'I'm prepared for that. I don't want to over-train.'

'You could think of the questions that she might ask you.'

'Perhaps,' Jerry said doubtfully. 'But I want to be spontaneous. Ask me some questions now.'

'I don't want to think about poison at the moment,' I said. 'I need to concentrate on the methods of murder Kenneth asked me about and what we're going to do about Tom.'

'He's a fictional character, you can do what you like.'

'Not in the film version, I don't have any control there. If they pay you a million dollars, they expect to be able to do what they like.'

'So it was a million dollars was it?' Jerry's eyes gleamed. 'That's what the papers said but I didn't know if it was true.'

'Debbie leaked it. It was remarkably good for sales. But it was one of those lucky accidents. Two sets of people wanted something at the same time. I don't suppose it will happen again.'

'There's no need to look quite so agonised.'

'You're probably right,' I said. For second time I felt like confiding there was also an authorship problem with the material, but I managed to keep silent.

'If you're not prepared to ask me about poisons, I need to do some thinking instead,' Jerry said. 'I'll take another stroll in the grounds.'

'See you later,' I said.

No sooner had he left than Molly Whyard appeared and went bustling down to the far end of the library. After five minutes she came back with a box file in her hands. She opened it to reveal a series of architectural drawings and floor plans.

'Julie told me about them. She said thank you for the book by the way. There's never been a priest's hole at Langham but we might have had one installed in the last few months.

It's the work Mr Graves had carried out last month. He was very secretive about what they were doing. Julie told me what I should be looking for. This is the one.'

She was pointing to a plan of the ground floor at Langham.

'That's where she thinks it is.'

'Where what is?'

'The priest's hole you were talking about. Julie thinks it's something William Graves got put in. They're quite the jokers, he and his wife. Nick Wallace was pleased they were away in France. I'm not sure he was looking forward to the pranks that William might play. Anyway, that's neither here nor there, but if you still want to find a secret room that's where it's likely to be.'

She tapped the plan indicating an area of the corridor leading to the theatre in which the bird was displayed. 'Julie says you can see the wall is bending out when it should be bending in. That doesn't make any sort of sense unless there's something else there. It's the sort of thing they might not have got planning permission for if they'd been totally open about it.'

9

BIT PART

I'M NOT PARTICULARLY GOOD at understanding plans but, once the inconsistency had been pointed out, I didn't doubt that Molly Whyard was likely to be right and the wall bulging in the wrong direction might indeed indicate that a secret room had been built. I made my own sketch of the plan and put the box file back in the gap on the shelf that Molly had withdrawn it from. I breathed a sigh of satisfaction. Events at Langham had taken an upturn. One: the film of *Murder Unseen* might never be made. Two: Jerry seemed to be an expert on poisons. Three: a secret room, if there was one, was a staple of classic crime fiction. I walked into the entrance hall and gave a thumbs up sign to Molly Whyard's friendly wave as Jerry appeared.

'You seem happy,' he said. He gestured towards the main door. 'It's beginning to turn cold out there. It wouldn't surprise me if it was a bad winter.'

'There will be time to talk about the weather later,' I said. 'In the meantime, I could do with your help. I think I may have found the secret room here.'

'There you go,' Jerry said. 'The benefits of historical research.'

'It's not a priest's hole,' I said. 'It's a modern secret room. This could be just what I need. Molly's sister, Julie, thinks that William and Helen Graves have just built their own version. If it's true, it could open up new ways of dealing with Kenneth. We could convince him that he should look to the house for inspiration. If we can find a secret room here he's more likely to make a traditional crime film. He's already obsessed with turning that bird into a murder weapon. If we can throw in a secret room, we'll be in business. Anything that reeks of a traditional crime puzzle must be good for turning Tom Travis back to being a traditional detective. And Molly and her sister are saying William and Helen Graves are likely to have built it.'

Jerry was nodding. 'They seem to have every interest in making themselves part of the traditions of the house, perhaps they want to create more artefacts…'

'Just a minute,' I said. 'Traditions of the house? Artefacts? How do we know that?'

'Because of the portraits of themselves in Elizabethan costume they've put in the library illustrating the fate that awaits *Virtue and Vice in the Garden of Earthly Delights*. It's quite well done. You probably wouldn't notice that it wasn't one of the historical family portraits that adorn the walls unless you looked closely. One of the tapestries looks rather new as well. You should check it out.'

I should have looked more closely. Tom Travis would have done.

'That's a detail at this stage,' I said, authoritatively. 'Let's go and see if we can find this room. It could be a crucial lever in winning Kenneth over.'

'Give me five minutes,' Jerry said. 'There's some equipment I might need. I'll see you there.'

By the time he joined me in the corridor leading to the studio, I had almost convinced myself that there was nothing to be found. My preliminary tapping on the panelling hadn't produced anything but the firm echo of a solid wall.

'It should be about here but I don't think it is,' I said.

'It seems pretty solid,' Jerry said, 'but let me see.'

He was getting a contraption out of a canvas bag. It had a couple of chrome tubes attached to rubber hoses, which ended in more chrome and some sort of probe. The top chrome pipes were curved at right angles and had small bits of plastic on each end. Jerry inserted one into each ear.

'That's an odd sort of stethoscope, isn't it?' I said.

'That's because it's a mechanic's stethoscope, not a medical one. It was in my room in a glass case but that wasn't difficult to get open. This is quite old but it's still a functioning bit of kit. I can see why they wanted to preserve it. We used them a lot when I was studying engineering.'

'What for?'

'Listening to internal sounds made by machines. I used to be a whizz at detecting worn ball bearings.'

'And why is that going to be useful here?'

'Detecting if there is a gap behind the wall. If there's some sort of secret room here, there's bound to be a space behind the panelling and this is the best way of detecting it. If you listen, there's a particular sort of echo effect you get. Here, you could try it for yourself.'

'No thanks,' I said. 'I'll trust your expertise.'

'There you are then,' Jerry said, a couple of minutes later, 'it's behind here as the Whyard sisters suggested.

I'm impressed. Have you ever thought of having a female pair of detectives?'

'No,' I said. 'But even if the room is here, are we any further forward? How do we get in to it?'

'That shouldn't be difficult,' Jerry said, reaching up above his head. 'Yes, look here. There's a lever. Not too difficult to find if you know something is here, but not something you would notice otherwise. And hey presto!'

A section of panelling rolled back smoothly to reveal a small passageway leading to a robust wooden door that wouldn't have looked out of place as the entrance to a dungeon managed by the Inquisition, particularly one on a Hollywood film set. The door was secured by a large metal bar.

'There you are,' Jerry said.

'Does it draw back?'

'Let me see.'

Jerry pulled on a knob on the bolt. It slid smoothly out of a housing recessed into the wall. 'That's interesting,' he said, 'it's...'

'Let's get in there first,' I said. I pushed the door and it swung open. An overhead light flicked on as I entered. I was in a small round room painted a hazy white that made its walls seem insubstantial. The ceiling was a shallow dome. The only furnishings were a small, round, wrought iron table and two metal chairs in a friendly green that looked as though they had just been bought. On the chairs were cushions. On the table was a bat that was obviously a child's toy. Its wings emitted a rustling sound when I picked it up.

On the inside of the door, as on the outside, there was a large bolt. One could be locked in or locked out, or both. I bent down. It might be possible to slip a sheet of paper under the door to the outside world, but nothing more. I tapped round the walls. They were solid despite their misty appearance. The floor was composed of flagstones cemented in concrete. I tapped them with the toe of my foot and then exerted more pressure with my heel. None of them moved. I slid the bolt forward and back. It moved easily. The door was the best part of three inches thick and made of solid oak. On the ground some electric wires protruded from the bottom of the wall. Otherwise, the chalky white walls were unblemished, apart from a small hairline crack on one side of the doorframe that suggested that the room had been constructed recently and was still in the process of drying out.

'Health and safety,' Jerry said to himself. 'I wonder?'

I sat down at the table. There was the same aroma of the new as there had been in the theatre. The rooms had been completed at the same time and William Graves had hidden the installation of the secret room under the cloak of the bigger project. Jerry was looking at the wires protruding from the wall.

'So?' I said. 'What are they for?'

'I'm not exactly sure but I think it's the wiring for an escape button. You'll need one if you've got a room like this. Think about it. You can be bolted in from the outside and there is nothing you can do about it. Hence this. I wonder what it's all for.'

'"Fright Night",' I said.

'Pardon?'

'New thrills for "Langham's Fright Night". There'll be a brochure in your room. This is one of the thrills. Locked in a secret room. It's obvious.'

'It could be a locked room in a murder mystery. Do they do a "Crime Night"?'

'They're not advertising one, as far as I'm aware. No, it's "Fright Night". But that doesn't matter. Kenneth Preston is going to be interested. But keep it to yourself. I need to use it at the right moment. Would anybody know we had been in here?'

'Not unless they had a fingerprint kit with them. Are you going to tell the Whyard sisters their hunch was right?'

'I think I'll say we think they are on to something but we haven't found anything concrete as yet.'

'A secret room in the bag,' Jerry said softly as he slid the panelling back in place. 'Things are on the up!'

It was a phrase I remembered later. It hadn't been entirely accurate, in fact it hadn't been accurate at all. It would have been more accurate if he had said *things are on the down*.

10

SOFT FOCUS

'SO HOW MUCH IS she worth?' I said idly as we waited for coffee at the end of lunch.

'Who?'

'Miriam Preston.'

'Miriam Preston, how much is she worth?'

'You don't have to tell the whole world Jerry, just me.'

'Sorry, asking the question helps me remember the answer. About £100 million.'

'That much?'

'Probably a bit more. Most of her wealth is in the company. There's property as well. Why do you ask?'

'No reason,' I said.

'There's always a reason for a question, even if it's a subconscious one. You're thinking about a new book aren't you? Langham would be the perfect setting. We've just discovered a secret room; Kenneth is obsessed with using a mechanical bird as a murder weapon; his wife wants to murder everyone with poison; the drawbridge goes up every night so nobody can get in; Rufus Stone seems to think he is

Tom Travis; Matthew Tabard has a new love in his life; Harry Leung is a mysterious Oriental; Emma a *femme fatale*. What more do you want?'

'Motive would be helpful.'

'Apart from Miriam Preston's money, do you mean? If money isn't good enough for you, what about Emma? You could have any number of men fighting for her favours. In fact, you could include yourself in that.'

'That's ridiculous.'

'I don't mean you-you, but a fictional you.'

'I suppose, fictionally, any environment with Emma Hale is bound to have men falling over themselves.'

'Precisely,' Jerry said. 'It's in the air. Can't you feel it? Emma used to be Leung's mistress. That's another plot point. He might not take a new liaison well and seek revenge on the man concerned. He could contract the killing out to some burly henchman. What are those criminal gangs in Hong Kong called? Maybe he could employ one of them as a bodyguard?'

'Leung's mistress?' I said.

'Didn't you know? It's not exactly a secret. She can't have been much more than eighteen when it started, or twenty-one when it finished. Probably saw him as a father figure. Anyway, there are no hard feelings on either side.'

'They still seem to be pretty close.'

'They are.'

'So when did all this happen?'

'They broke up a couple of years ago. She had a dalliance with a film director that didn't last very long. He didn't treat her very well. Not sure he's made another film. Leung is a powerful man in the movie business. And she and Harry are still the best of friends. She's always at that annual party on his yacht in the Med. But if you want to use it in a Tom Travis book, you could make it more of an open wound. If Matthew Tabard meets an untimely end here, we'll know it could work.'

'It's not just Matthew,' I said.

'What isn't?'

'I didn't give you all the details of my encounter with Emma. She was wearing a bathrobe and I had partly undressed because I was thinking of taking a shower to freshen up.'

'You were?' Jerry said.

'Yes. I thought her room was my room for some reason. I may have been a bit befuddled. I'd been drinking with Tom, I mean Rufus, and I hadn't eaten since breakfast. I should have realised my mistake when I found the bottle of Krug in the mini fridge, but I didn't. It was all perfectly innocent.'

'You mistook her room for yours?' Jerry didn't sound convinced.

'Easily done. And she opened the champagne, not me.'

'If you say so. Have you told Kate about this?'

'No.'

'Well I wouldn't. Not in any detail anyway. Or, if you do, just stick to one excuse. Mistook the room, or the drinking. I wouldn't use them both. It sounds unconvincing if you pile on the excuses. And don't mention the Krug, it sounds as though you've got something to hide.'

'The point I wanted to make is that she was expecting someone,' I said. 'That's why we ended up in a sort of embrace. It wouldn't have happened otherwise.'

'An embrace?'

'She put her arms around me before she realised I wasn't the man she was expecting.'

'And how long did she take to realise that?'

'I don't know. A few seconds. When her fingers started stroking my stomach she seemed to tense a bit, then she relaxed again. But she knew it wasn't a stomach she was familiar with.'

'Your stomach?' Jerry said.

'I was silhouetted against the light outside.'

'Were you?'

'Yes.'

'So it could have been Matthew Tabard she was expecting? He's your sort of build. That means it couldn't have been someone like Jack Catesby or any of his security colleagues. They're too muscular.'

'Rounded certainly.'

'Too rounded then, for her to think it was one of them. Who does that leave? Obviously you're excluded so that leaves me, Matthew, Rufus Stone, Nick Wallace, even Kenneth Preston. And there are a couple of guys who work in the kitchens who would also qualify. If the light was as dazzling as you say, it could be any of them. And it couldn't have been me because I hadn't arrived.'

'Not Leung?'

'Hardly. He's shorter than the rest of you, and stockier. And it wouldn't make much sense would it?'

'I suppose not. But the rest of us aren't exactly all the same height are we?'

'Near enough in a darkened room. Anyway, the point is that she's having a fling, or whatever, with someone here, probably Matthew Tabard. And from what you're saying you don't even have to make anything much up for a character based on you do you? Or what happened? Bathrobes and Krug are a good start.'

'It was all perfectly innocent.'

'It may very well have been but it wouldn't look that way to any outside observer would it? You just happen to be in a bedroom with the UK's most attractive woman and start drinking champagne with her and we're all expected to believe it's totally innocent. I mean I know you but even I'm finding it hard...'

I was summoning up a protest when chance, in the person of Florence Hammond, intervened.

'Kenneth wants to see you,' she said. 'Nick asked me to track you down.'

'You as in us?' I said, signalling towards Jerry.

'No, you, as in you. Kenneth is over in the gym in the new buildings. He'd like you to join him.'

'Fine,' I said, 'I'll get over there straightaway.'

I nodded curtly towards Jerry, and left.

Outside, the mellow light gave Langham Hall more of the appearance of a dreamy country house hotel than Jerry's suggested setting as a hotbed of sexual intrigue. I walked across the drawbridge. The gym buildings were behind the reception area where Molly Whyard had greeted me the day before. As I entered, there was the sound of rhythmic exercise from the next room.

Kenneth Preston, dressed in a grey sweatshirt and shorts, was alternately raising and lowering a weight on the apparatus behind him. He had unusually well-developed biceps for a man of his age, and a small tattoo of a scorpion on his right arm. He didn't stop his exercise pattern as I approached, or as we subsequently spoke, so our exchange was punctuated by the swish of weights sliding up and down well-oiled poles. There was also an instructor present; a man dressed in a singlet and white gym trousers. He nodded from time to time in harmony with the rising and falling weights, but was otherwise immobile.

'Murder,' Kenneth intoned on an upswing, 'tell me what you have.'

I must have been there for half an hour while Kenneth's rhythmic exercises continued to a tempo that never varied. He systematically evaluated the list of exotic methods of murder I had prepared, mostly returning to the bird of prey in the studio. Midway through our conversation he turned to another piece of apparatus that involved him lifting weights on his shoulders, rather like Atlas bearing the burden of the world. As we talked, sweat advanced down from the top of the grey sweatshirt so that by the end, with the bird firmly established as his preferred method of death, there must have been an advance of damp fabric of at least six inches.

I said it seemed to me that Rufus had clearly decided that the role of Tom Travis was destined for him. Kenneth made a non-committal grunt in response that might have meant anything. He was similarly opaque about his thoughts concerning Emma and Matthew. Gradually it became clear that, as far as he was concerned, the conversation had reached its end. As I left he switched to a rowing machine.

Outside a slim figure was lighting a long, filter-tipped cigarette in the gathering gloom. There was a glow of flame that revealed fine cheekbones. It was Miriam Preston. As I watched, she took deep pulls on the cigarette and then exhaled the smoke with gusto. It looked as much a regular exercise as her husband's. The little clouds of smoke were a sudden swirl of white. I moved away but a twig snapped under my foot. She turned round.

'Oh, it's you,' she said.

I walked towards her. There was an eddy of something exotic and enticing mixed with the smoke. She was wearing a close-fitting black jumper under a short, fashionable, black coat.

'Do you?' she said proffering the packet of cigarettes.

'I don't,' I said. 'Used to, but never inhaled. I always found the first cigarette much better than the second in any case. Maybe if you could buy cigarettes singly I wouldn't have given up.'

She proffered the packet again.

'If you're not addicted, why deny yourself the pleasure? It'll only be one, won't it?'

'Does Kenneth smoke?'

She shook her head. 'In some things he's risk averse. He got me to cut down but I can't give up entirely. So I limit myself to a packet a week. To be fair to him, he hasn't mentioned that I should give up for a couple of months. But then I'm discreet.'

I stretched out my hand for a cigarette.

'I imagine you'll need a light for that.'

She reached inside her coat. The flare of flame illuminated her cheekbones and then her eyes as I bent forward.

'Are you married?'

I nodded.

'With children?'

'Two sons.'

'And is your wife at home?'

'She's a lawyer.'

'Handy,' she said, 'if you ever get into trouble.'

'I suppose it would be,' I said, 'if that were to happen.'

'I've got to pick up something at the office,' she said, 'if you want to keep me company.'

We strolled back to the buildings where I had checked in the day before. I had the strange feeling that I might have failed some sort of test, or perhaps passed one. I ground my cigarette beneath my heel and followed Miriam inside.

'It's in the safe,' a woman I hadn't seen before was saying to Miriam. 'I'll get it for you.'

I must have raised an inquiring eyebrow.

'It's a present for Kenneth.'

The woman was coming back to the counter. She had a cardboard box under her arm.

'I'm afraid I'll have to ask you to sign for it,' she said.

'Of course,' Miriam said. She took the pen held out to her. 'Well, I suppose I ought to hide this.' she said to me. 'Kenneth doesn't know anything about it. Maybe he shouldn't. Maybe I should give it to someone else. Although that might be difficult.'

'You've bought it for him now,' I said. 'I'm sure he'll be delighted, whatever it is.'

'He'd better be. It was rather expensive. But can I tempt you to a last cigarette outside?'

'It might be habit-forming.'

'Not for you, apparently. But I'd forgotten, you don't like the second cigarette do you?'

'Not in normal circumstances, but I'll make an exception.'

There was a flash of flame as she lit one cigarette and then another, holding them both in her hand. It reminded me of a scene in a black and white Hollywood film that I remembered watching one night when Kate and the boys had gone to bed. The flame had emerged from a chunky petrol lighter that qualified as a museum piece. It was gold in the sudden light. She handed a cigarette to me and took a deep breath that pulled the smoke down into her lungs. A look of contentment crossed her face.

'There's nothing quite like it,' she said. 'Particularly if you have to do it secretly.'

'I wouldn't know,' I said, 'I never breathe in.'

'Probably not worth changing your habits now,' she said. She didn't sound as though she entirely meant it.

11

FLASHBACK

AN HOUR LATER THE image of Miriam Preston and the golden glow from the petrol lighter's flash of flame was still in my mind. Perhaps Jerry was right and there was something seductive in the Langham Hall air; a heady blend of Emma's sinuous greetings and Miriam's swirl of cigarette smoke. It had made it seem as though Miriam and I had some sort of history together, but, if we had, I was totally unaware of the fact. It was probably nothing more than the fact that she shared Emma's flirtatious nature. I found myself wondering if Julie Whyard was as attractive looking as her sister.

In the entrance hall Molly Whyard was removing books from their cardboard packaging. Some Dürrenmatt crime novels were stacked on top of a book on sleep disorders. Next to them was a hardback copy of *The Practical Poisoner*, which I thought had been banned. I was about to ask whom the books were for when Jerry appeared.

'You're looking happy,' he said. 'Did you try out the secret room idea on Kenneth?'

'I wasn't sure it was the right moment so I decided to hold it in reserve.'

'Fair enough,' Jerry said after a moment. 'In fact, that could be a good tactic. So are you thinking about the possibilities this place offers for the next Tom Travis?'

'You could be right about sexual intrigue as a motive. I'll think about it.'

'I've just remembered you've got a book on the go, haven't you?' Jerry said. 'I mean apart from *Murder Unseen?* What was it called? You know the one I mean – the book about the art collector, Crispin Cruickshank, and his nephews and nieces?'

'*Murder is Equal.* The clue is in the title.'

'I'm not sure that's much of a clue,' Jerry said. 'Besides, I'm not sure your readers pay that much attention to titles.'

'Well they should. As far as I'm concerned, every bit of the book is relevant, whether it's the title, illustrations, or anything else.'

'If you say so,' Jerry said, unconvinced.

'I am the crime writer here,' I said. I almost believed it.

'So let me give you a test. How would you account for this in Tom Travis terms? I've just been talking to Miriam Preston.'

'And?'

'She was talking about cyanide. She wanted to know how it works. I told her that it interferes with the red blood cells' abilities to extract oxygen from the air. The victim literally suffocates to death as he breathes in oxygen he cannot use.'

'He?'

'I think she had a man in mind. Anyway, she was also interested in how long it took. I told her the effects are pretty instantaneous when it's swallowed. It causes immediate unconsciousness, convulsions, and death within fifteen minutes. Then she asked me how detectable it was.'

'And?'

'You get a bitter almond odour at an autopsy but not many people can recognise it.'

'So, if you're a murderer, you need a Home Office pathologist with a poor sense of smell?'

'Pretty much. But don't you think it's a bit suspicious? Being interested in that level of detail.'

'So who is she thinking of murdering?'

'Most murders are committed by people who know each other. Kenneth must be the prime candidate.'

'They renewed their marriage vows the other day. An immediate poisoning doesn't seem the obvious follow-up.'

'You could be right,' Jerry said reluctantly. 'Molly Whyard told me a photographer from *OK!* turned up and took some photographs of them looking lovingly into each other's eyes in the Chinese suite this morning. Curious really. I would have thought it was you Miriam Preston was interested in.'

'Why on earth do you think that?'

'I saw her outside with you an hour ago. It was obvious. I could tell.'

'We were just exchanging a few words.'

'She lit you a cigarette. It wasn't that so much, as the way she did it. Actually, now I recall, she didn't just light you one cigarette, but two. And you followed her into reception and came out with that parcel. What was in it by the way?'

'A present for Kenneth. Presumably something to do with this wedding vows celebration the photographer was covering. But what it was I don't know, although I gathered it was something expensive. Miriam was asked to sign for it.'

'And the cigarette?'

'I had a sudden craving, I don't know why. It was just a momentary thing.'

Jerry looked unconvinced.

'Not for her.'

'Meaning what?'

'She didn't go back into the house immediately. She stopped in those trees. She put the parcel down on the ground. After a moment she lit herself another cigarette. She was blowing smoke rings into the air in a languid, yearning fashion, or that's what it looked like. She wanted to capture the moment.'

'Probably decided to light up while she could. Kenneth doesn't smoke.'

'Neither do you.'

'That was hardly smoking. Besides, it's not so much that Kenneth doesn't smoke, it's the fact that he disapproves of the fact she does. Not that I smoke normally. It has always been diminishing returns with me. I've never liked the second cigarette as much as the first.'

'It didn't seem to bother you today.'

'That was different. I was being polite.'

'Is that what you call it?'

'It's the truth.'

'So you're not falling in love with her?' Jerry said provocatively.

'Of course not.'

'If you say so.'

'If you must know I suppose I felt sympathetically inclined towards her. I had just spent half an hour watching Kenneth lift weights. That wasn't a great deal of fun. He didn't speak much.'

'That could be good.'

'How precisely?'

'His subconscious mind was probably mulling over all those murder possibilities you gave him. Let him sleep on it and you might have a different Kenneth Preston tomorrow morning.'

'Murder possibilities?' a voice said.

Nick Wallace was behind us.

'Kenneth asked me to think up a few possibilities for exotic forms of murder.' I said.

'Did he indeed?' Nick Wallace said. 'Did he interrupt you much?'

'Not really.'

'That's good. If he's not talking, he's more likely to be concentrating on what is being said. I was thinking about what you were saying about not letting your detective stray too much into darker areas. It's a perfectly good point, particularly if there is any chance of making it a series. A flaw in character isn't necessarily a bad thing, even in a detective. It could be a springboard. Let me know how things progress. We can talk about it later. Just at the moment there's something I need to sort out with reception.'

'Which is?' Jerry said.

'The original police superintendent assigned to liaise with Harry Leung can't come. His daughter has been taken ill. It's a shame because he served a secondment in Hong Kong and it looked like the perfect fit. Harry likes to have someone he can impress with his knowledge of local customs. Anyway, I need to make sure his replacement has the right passes to get through security. It wouldn't look good if he didn't.'

'It would prove your security worked,' Jerry said.

Nick Wallace smiled. 'You could be right. I'll make sure he's rigorously checked before they let him through.'

He bustled away to speak to Molly Whyard.

'Nice guy,' Jerry said. 'If I'm any judge, you're getting through to him about Tom.'

He tapped the side of his nose in an irritating, know it all, sort of way. It was a gesture I had played with in the first Tom Travis book but decided it was too tiresome to continue with. I wondered for a moment where he had been standing when he had been spying on Miriam Preston and myself. Come to that, why had he been outside in the first place?

'I wonder who they'll have lined up?' Jerry continued idly.

'I don't mind,' I said, 'as long as it's not Bob Addinson.'

'That's hardly likely to happen is it?'

'I suppose not. But I meant to ask Molly Whyard something and Nick seems to have finished his business.'

I crossed over to the reception table and pointed to the pile of books she had unpacked.

'Those books?' I said. 'Are they all for Rufus Stone?'

'Checking up on what your detective is reading are you?' Molly Whyard said brightly. 'Actually no, they're not. There's only the two for him. Those,' she pointed towards the pile of Dürrenmatt paperbacks, 'are for this policeman coming tomorrow. He phoned me ten minutes ago to check who was here and see if his books had arrived. It's remarkable how quickly you can order things these days isn't it? I think he said he ordered them five minutes after he knew he was coming here.'

'He'll be in the room next to me won't he?'

'That's the plan. He should be near Sir Harry but we're running out of space in that part of the building. We could have moved people around but Nick Wallace said that would cause too much upheaval, so he's next to you.'

'So it's a policeman who is interested in crime fiction?' I said. Addinson had been interested in crime fiction.

'They're certainly for him,' Molly Whyard said. 'But they're a bit slim aren't they? Julie always likes a thicker novel than that, like the ones you write, something she can get her teeth into. And I'm not sure about these covers.'

I picked up the top book, *The Pledge*. The publishers had made the books look old and slightly tattered. On the top one they had added a picture of a man walking into the distance in snow. When I looked more closely I saw that he was leaving too many footprints. Either that or his movements were basically sideways rather than forward. Perhaps he was following someone, or perhaps whoever had designed the cover had used elements from two photographs rather than one.

'I think they're mostly crime reprints from around the world. Most of these were published in the 50s as far as I remember. That's why they've gone for these distressed covers. And you're right. They are quite short – more a novella than a novel. But then they're not quite traditional crime novels either, more a critique of crime fiction.'

Molly Whyard raised enquiring eyes.

'Dürrenmatt took the view that there was a major problem with crime fiction. It's the way the detective goes about his work, like he was solving some form of mathematical puzzle. It just needs the odd clue to fall into place and the murder is always solved and, of course, crime fiction is always trying to raise the bar on that by having crimes committed in locked rooms or in impossible circumstances. There is always the feeling that if the detective is clever enough, he or she is bound to solve the mystery. In real life things don't work out like that and chance comes into it as well. There's a novel he wrote where the inspector can't put a particular case behind him. A young girl has been brutally murdered and a local simpleton is pressured into confessing he has committed the crime. The inspector is convinced that he hasn't and works out that it must be someone else. He also knows where that person is likely to be at a certain time, and lays a trap. But the real perpetrator has been knocked down in a road accident and never turns up so the trap stays un-sprung and the brilliant inspector begins to doubt himself and goes mad.'

'That's interesting,' Molly Whyard said. 'But I'm not sure I really understand. You should talk to Julie. She reads lots of crime.'

I looked up. I wasn't sure I really got it either. The words I had just uttered had seemed to fit together well enough but they had been delivered from some pre-packaged part of my brain that was linked to a blog that I had started on my author website. This had been in response to Debbie's view that the person most responsible for author publicity was the author himself, although she had said that the tone of my pieces was academic. That was before she had secured the million-dollar deal.

'Does he have a name, this policeman who the books are for?' Jerry said to Molly Whyard. 'I did a bit of training with the police last year. I might have met him.'

'He's Superintendent something. I've got his name some-where here.'

'At least it's not our friend,' Jerry said to me in an aside, 'wrong rank.'

'Yes, here it is,' Molly Whyard said, 'Superintendent Bob Addinson.'

I felt a buzz in my brain as though it was malfunctioning in some way. Surely I had misheard? But in the next moment I realised that I hadn't. My nemesis would be at Langham on the following day. Luckily the telephone on the table rang and Molly Whyard answered it, so she didn't notice the effect that her words had caused.

'Well,' Jerry said as we walked away, 'that's a bit of a turn-up isn't it? I can't say I could have predicted that in a million years. I suppose there are only so many senior policemen in England so it's not totally unexpected. Or perhaps it is. But I suppose you could look on the bright side. You could use it in one of your novels and then tell anyone who questions the improbability of a plot that's based on coincidence that it happened in real life.'

'That's hardly a comfort,' I said.

It wasn't. I had thought that the major problem that I faced at Langham was doing everything I could to ensure that Tom Travis wouldn't develop into a full-blooded murderer. Now I also had a police superintendent who was convinced that I had got away with murder to contend with.

12

PRODUCTION VALUES

'IT COULD BE ANOTHER Bob Addinson,' Jerry said for the second time. 'He was a DCI last time we came across him.'

'And the chances of there being two senior policemen with the same name are what? No, don't answer that, I don't want to know. It's the same man. He's been promoted.'

'I can't see why he would be. It was hardly a shining performance in the case we were involved in was it? And he was involved in that car accident with Blenkiron.'

'I'm not sure that promotion works like that. He's probably been rewarded for taking the strain, or maybe they've got a quota for policemen who have worked their way up the ranks. It can't be anyone else. It's him.'

'Then it's just one of those things that happen. We should ignore it and concentrate on things we can change – like Kenneth's view of Tom Travis. Here we are.'

Langham's ancestral hall had a large, round table bedecked with a white tablecloth, gleaming silver and a generous selection of wine glasses. On the seating plan I was, as forecast, sitting next to Kenneth Preston. Moving round the table to his left were places for Florence Hammond, Nick Wallace, Matthew Tabard, Jerry, Miriam Preston, Harry Leung, Emma Hale and Rufus Stone.

In the corner of the room Harry Leung was holding court. He was wearing his own version of smart casual, an immaculate blue-black mandarin outfit that would have looked equally at home at a state banquet. Florence, Nick and Emma were gathered round in an affirming circle. The most serious sartorial competition to Leung was Emma who shimmered in a strapless silver full-length dress that glittered in the light and which would have been suitable for an Oscar acceptance speech. To one side, Rufus Stone was in an immaculate tailored jacket of the sort favoured by Tom Travis.

'So,' Jerry said from behind me. 'What are you thinking?'

'Nothing much, just an idle thought. I was wondering. Whyard. It sounds unusual. Is it a Suffolk name?'

'Common Suffolk names,' Jerry intoned. 'Is it one of them?'

'I've just said that, haven't I?'

'I thought you wanted an answer. Phrasing the question again helps me concentrate. As you ask – it is.'

'What is?'

'A name more common in Suffolk than the rest of the country.'

'How do you know that?'

'I did some research before I got here, including members of staff,' Jerry said in a slightly offended tone. 'The only problem I had in London was finding the air filters that Faith had specified. They're unusually high spec but I've got contacts in the business. It didn't take me more than twenty minutes. I had a lot of spare time.'

Matthew Tabard came into the room, and looked warily from side to side.

'I'm surprised he's here at all,' Jerry hissed.

'Why?'

'There's stuff all over social media.'

'What stuff?'

'I thought you were up on that, or maybe that's Iain. Anyway Matthew was apparently on the job when he fell asleep.'

'What?'

'Too many liaisons had exhausted him.'

'Are you sure that's what happened?'

'Well, some of the stories were pretty euphemistic, but that was the gist.'

'Really?'

'Really.'

'Matthew, so pleased you're here,' Nick Wallace was saying in front of us. 'I'm sure you know Emma, but have you met Florence Hammond?'

'I wonder what he means by *know*?' Jerry hissed. 'Do you think it's biblical?'

'What are you talking about? She's not even looking at him.'

'Precisely,' Jerry whispered. 'Enough said.'

'And do you know our writers?' Nick Wallace turned toward us. 'David Knight and Jerry...'

'Davis,' Jerry said.

A minute later Kenneth and Miriam Preston arrived in matching black outfits that gave them the appearance of cat burglars. Kenneth was only an inch or two taller than his wife and any advantage he might have had in muscular development was offset by the fact that Miriam was wearing a black leather jacket with shoulder pads. They might have been brother and sister rather than husband and wife. They snaked through the group as though bound together by an invisible string and then separated to sit opposite each other at the round table. I was reminded of Bergman and Bogart in *Casablanca* when they are both dressed in stripes and we know symbolically that they are the same person and share the same values. Then I shook my head.

'So,' Kenneth said, as I sat down next to him. 'I've been looking at your website about the lure of the Golden Age of crime – all those murders in country houses and intrigue in every corner of the guilty vicarage. Do you think setting crimes in domestic circumstances is more disturbing than having murderers out there in the wild city streets? *Village noir*? I was intrigued. It's not based on experience is it? How do you know they will work? Nick and I were discussing the murder in *Killing Spree* when Tom works out how the jack has been used to lift the oil drum in the garage. It sounded plausible but I wondered how you checked, or if you checked? If it's going to work on film it must be able to work in reality.'

'I make some things up,' I said. 'But I try to ensure that everything that happens is possible, however an improbable model it may seem.'

'That's good,' Kenneth said, and for a moment I saw the professional man behind the mask of the spontaneous artist he appeared to be. Everything about him seemed more calculated than it had been before.

'In real life as much as your books, I imagine,' he added with an edge to his voice.

I tried to remember what the *Daily Mail* had actually said about me. There hadn't been any direct accusation, simply a series of insinuations that left the reader to jump to their own conclusions in the matters that had engulfed Stephen and Francesca Angell. Those conclusions would suggest that I was, or might be, far from innocent. It had been skilfully done and nothing that had been printed, according to Kate and Faith, would give me a case for defamation that I could win. Debbie, my agent, had been more relaxed, muttering about all publicity being, in the end, good for sales, and that people never remember the detail, particularly in this case as the detail was so indistinct. I looked back at Kenneth. He was beaming encouragingly as though the prospect that I might once have been involved in something shady was a distinct advantage. He had nodded as he spoke, an invitation to a shared confidence that I had no intention of taking up.

'So you can work something out for the bird?'

'It certainly has possibilities as a murder weapon,' I said. 'The beak is sharp enough if it was descending at speed. But as we were saying there are other exotic forms of extinction.'

'I've been thinking about them,' he said with a distinct relish. 'But you'll need to choose what you're eating. Mine is a steak and kidney pie but that's something Miriam arranged for me. It was what I ate at the first meal we had together.'

I wondered if Kenneth had his own wine to serve as well. I needed to look out for a waiter with his hand over the label. I would have said something more but Kenneth, suddenly losing interest in exotic weapons of personal destruction, had started talking to Florence. I felt a momentary sense of regret. I had a feeling that I'd failed some test in not being more forthcoming about the *Mail's* innuendos. Perhaps if

I had indicated there might be some substance in the story I might have hung on to Kenneth's attention a few minutes longer and he wouldn't now be talking so animatedly to the young woman beside him. I looked round the table. Jerry was having an animated conversation with Miriam Preston, while Matthew Tabard was contemplating the ceiling. Harry Leung and Emma had managed to sit closer together than dining chairs would normally allow, Nick Wallace was issuing instructions to one of the waiters and Rufus was assessing whether any clues might be present.

I took a deep breath and tried again to assemble the best case for restoring Tom's reputation. Surely Kenneth's interest in the mechanics of exotic murder must offer the possibility of a conversation? A remark that Kenneth had made when we first met had convinced me that he had read my blog piece on the ubiquity of the locked room murder mystery in cultures that had a history of crime fiction. Something could surely have been made of that but I had the feeling that the best way forward with Kenneth was to offer him something personal, some story that I didn't want repeated. But the moment had passed. Kenneth was occupied with Florence Hammond.

Under the onslaught of food and wine, the company gradually mellowed in mood, and the anxious chatter of voices that had once been nervous and shrill, gradually subsided into a more relaxed hum. By the time I was eyeing up my sea bass and Kenneth was poised to tuck into his steak and kidney pie, everyone, even Matthew Tabard, was beginning to relax.

That was the moment when everything went deep black, a power failure that left the room in complete darkness.

A moment later a cry of pain rent the silence that had fallen across the room.

I don't know how long the darkness lasted. Then, almost simultaneously, a burst of flame lit up Miriam Preston's face and the powerful beam of a torch swept across the room like a searchlight.

The beam from the torch successively illuminated the faces of Matthew Tabard, Nick Wallace, Florence Hammond and Kenneth Preston. The first three were registering various states of surprise but Kenneth Preston was clutching the side of his face trying to staunch a flow of blood. At the other end of the table Miriam Preston looked unnerved, the golden flare of light revealing her strained features.

More light was springing up around the table. I reached for my own phone but there was only an empty space in my jacket pocket. I remembered that my mobile was recharging in my room.

Nick Wallace was asking in a calm voice for whoever had the powerful torch to shine it on Kenneth Preston's face. At least I knew who the owner of the torch was – Jerry. His emphasis in life might have switched from universal gadgets to universal knowledge but he hadn't abandoned his ability to have the right kit always to hand. No torch function on a phone for him, but a real light.

Nick Wallace had moved round the table and was dabbing at the blood that was trickling from the right side of Kenneth Preston's mouth, uttering a calming mantra.

'It's okay; it's just a cut. Nothing serious.'

In the coalescing pools of light I could see blood on the tablecloth next to me. Next to it something glistened. I reached out to whatever it was and succeeded in getting Kenneth's blood on my fingers. I was aware that a shadowy Miriam Preston was moving from the other end of the table towards her husband. Then the lights came back on.

I looked around. Leung had a comforting arm around Emma Hale. Rufus Stone was scanning the room in a forensic manner and Matthew Tabard looked anxious. Nick Wallace had his mobile to his ear and a concerned look on his face. A few seconds later he put the mobile down and tapped a wine glass with a spoon as though calling a dining club to order.

'If I could have your attention,' he said. 'I've just been talking to the security people. They think some additional lights they were installing may have overloaded the mains. Everything is now working properly and we should get on with the dinner. But there does seem to have been an accident. Kenneth, are you all right?'

'I will be once I can get my blood to clot,' Kenneth said, dabbing his mouth. 'I've cut my lip. It's something to do with this steak and kidney pie. There's glass in it.'

'Glass? Glass?' Nick Wallace said. 'Are you sure? You could have done yourself a serious injury.'

'I have, ' Kenneth Preston said. 'This is blood you know.'

'Of course it is,' Nick Wallace said soothingly. 'We need to get you a plaster and some antiseptic.'

Five minutes later Kenneth Preston had calmed himself and was apologising for over-reacting. He was patting Miriam's arm that was curled around him. 'Let's not spoil the party. It's an accident. Can someone rustle something else up?'

'I'll sort it out,' Nick Wallace said.

'And if someone could pour me another glass of wine...'

Kenneth put down his napkin. It was covered in spots of blood. It left the room a few seconds later along with the offending pie. Miriam kissed him and returned to her seat at the other side of the table. A new section of tablecloth was rustled up magically from the kitchens to cover the stains. Leung reluctantly released his reassuring grip on Emma Hale. I left the room to wash the blood off my hands and when I returned it was difficult to remember that anything untoward had happened.

Surprisingly, the incident seemed to improve Kenneth's spirits. Nick Wallace provided a small plaster for Kenneth's cut lip that covered the wound without impeding, in any way, Kenneth's power to talk, which had become supercharged. The mood of the company changed from the subdued to the elation of a group has come through some sort of test. Even Matthew Tabard seemed less wary than he had been.

Over dessert I found myself talking to Rufus Stone.

'So what do you make of what happened to Kenneth?' I said. 'Do you think somebody tampered with his steak and kidney pie?'

'Somebody could have done,' he said carelessly. 'But it's fairly obvious what's happened isn't it?'

'Is it?'

'I would have thought so. There are three possibilities.'

'Three?' I said surprised.

Rufus paused to reflect. 'That's true. You could be right. I see what you mean. Four then. If you think tampering is a possibility. I suppose it could be.'

He didn't sound convinced but wouldn't add anything more. An hour later, after the consumption of a great deal more wine at Kenneth's insistence, the party started to break up. Matthew Tabard slipped away first, closely followed by Florence Hammond. Then Kenneth and Miriam left leaving

Rufus Stone examining the table where Kenneth had been sitting. Nick Wallace was talking to Harry Leung who was still somehow connected to Emma Hale.

'So,' Jerry said, 'I saw you talking to Rufus. Does he know what happened?'

'He may do but he's not telling, other than he thinks there are four possibilities.'

'Four? Surely it's an accident or it's not?'

'Tom's mind doesn't work like that. He likes to keep all the options in play in the early stages of an investigation in case he's missed something, or the murderer is actively misleading him.'

'I thought that's because you didn't want to give your readers too much information that would spoil the twists at the end.'

'I suppose that might have something to do with it. Anyway, whatever the reason, Rufus is tight-lipped.'

'So what do you think happened?'

'I don't know,' I said.

I didn't. I only knew the failing of the lights and Kenneth cutting his lip would give Bob Addinson something to investigate. If he thought something untoward had happened, I knew who his chief suspect would be – me.

PART TWO

MONDAY — TUESDAY

13

CONTRAST

ADDINSON ARRIVED SHORTLY AFTER dawn the next morning (in a chauffeur driven police car, Molly Whyard told me later). I hadn't slept well. My dreams had consisted of an endless series of meetings in which Addinson had quizzed me about steak and kidney pies, and unexplained deaths, in the Home Counties. Even a bracing shower and a supportive phone call with Kate did little to lift my mood.

I went to the library and wandered over to the fiction section. All four of the Tom Travis books were back on the shelves glowering at me. The missing book had been *A Grave Mistake*, the same book in which I had written a dedication to Julie Whyard. I told myself that whether she had purchased her own copy of the book was neither here nor there. What I needed to remember was that she was a fan. Or perhaps she wasn't. Perhaps she and her sister always got visiting authors to sign books to increase their value or perhaps they had a little sideline in book dealing. Some people say that *A Grave Mistake* is the best of the Tom Travis novels. It does have, after all, my definitive version of a locked-room mystery in it.

That was why I had been pleased that Julie Whyard had chosen it.

Somebody had straightened up the row of books when they had put *A Grave Mistake* back. It was with nervous fingers that I took the book from the shelf and opened it. The title page was free from any inscription. I gave an audible sigh of relief and spent a happy couple of minutes reading a paragraph here and a Tom Travis aphorism there. Then I put the book back, ensuring that it was lined up with the other books, as it had been, all the spines a precise two inches from the edge of the shelf.

I let out a further contented sigh but I was aware that something was wrong. There was somebody else in the room. There had been somebody else in the room all the time I had been concentrating on *A Grave Mistake*. I turned round. Addinson was observing me in his usual condescending manner.

'Mr Knight. Good morning.'

'Superintendent.'

'I see you're consulting a book, sir? I imagine crime writers are always searching for new ideas.'

'Not always.' I said. 'In this instance I simply wanted to check that one of my novels was here, *A Grave Mistake*. And there it is. Job done.'

'Your own book, sir? How interesting. I couldn't help noticing you were looking at some passages in it in detail.'

'I like to read the odd page. It reminds me of the composition process.'

'And inspiration for future novels I imagine, sir?'

I didn't like the way Addinson was sprinkling *sirs* into the conversation.

'I...' I said, but stopped. Saying that I had entered the library simply to check whether the copy of *A Grave Mistake* had been signed or not would only provoke a host of further questions that would paint me in a neurotic and unflattering light. I needed a different explanation. Luckily one came to mind, ready dusted and polished.

'It's a little difficult to explain. There's a passage about a locked room. I just couldn't remember what I had written. I was thinking of going back to a similar theme in my current novel. I just didn't want to go over the same ground twice.'

'Very commendable, sir. I'm sure your audience wouldn't appreciate a re-hash of an old idea, however skilfully it was done. But isn't that Mr Davis I see? Perhaps the three of us could have a word together. I'm sure you're both very busy and a conversation now would make best use of all our time. Perhaps we could sit in that corner?'

'So, Mr Knight,' Addinson continued, when Jerry had been summoned and we had settled into three chairs, 'I hear you're working on the screenplay of a Tom Travis film. But I'm not sure I quite understood your role, Mr Davis? What is it?'

'I'm assisting Mr Knight,' Jerry said.

'Indeed, sir. In what way?'

Addinson made the arrangement sound conspiratorial.

'With the screenplay,' I said.

'I didn't know you were a writing partnership?'

'We're not as such, but Jerry advises me on the technical aspects of my novels. Besides, he's very familiar with all aspects of Tom Travis. But before we go on I must congratulate you on your promotion.'

'That's very kind, sir. Thank you. But the truth of the matter is that my promotion was more accidental than deserved. You remember Mr Blenkiron and the crash. He may have been blinded, as he claimed, by the blue flashing lights but, as it turned out, the key point was that the collision occurred on a private road.'

'Are you saying he got off? He was half cut.'

'He has strong links with the new American administration.'

'And?'

'*Realpolitik* prevailed.'

'That's outrageous.'

'Very possibly, sir, but there may be an opportunity to catch up with him if he ever returns to British soil. Sometimes Justice needs more than one opportunity if it is to be effective. Lord Dunsany's stories capture the longer view of retribution rather well. I'm sure you have come across them sir, given your interest in such matters. In this instance it was not entirely an ill wind. Thanks to Mr Blenkiron's vengeful tendencies, the Americans insisted I was moved. The only available immediate posting, as it turned out, was liaison with the Diplomatic Service. But it was a promotion. So here I am. And here you are. And we need to understand each other.'

'So how do we do that?' Jerry said.

'The first thing to say is that my job here is to act as a contact point between HMG and Sir Harry Leung. Sir Harry is a key conduit for maintaining our influence in the East. We also believe there is a credible threat established against his person. Events like those that occurred yesterday evening are not welcome. Nick Wallace has briefed me on them. I'm prepared to think the occurrence was an accident.'

'So why do you think that?' Jerry asked with an unwelcome trace of belligerence in his voice.

'There would need to have been a degree of co-ordination that seems difficult to achieve if anyone was intending to do Kenneth Preston harm. Causing the lights to fail at precisely the right moment would be tricky.'

'I don't see why,' Jerry said. 'There are a number of gadgets that could do that.'

It wasn't a helpful intervention.

'Are there indeed?' Addinson said with a hard edge to his voice. 'So if you could control the lights remotely, somebody sitting next to Mr Preston could *spike* his meal. Somebody like Mr Knight, perhaps?'

'I didn't say that,' Jerry said. 'It was obviously an accident.'

'You're not suggesting we were in any way involved in what happened yesterday, are you?' I said before Jerry could say anything else.

'Only you know whether you are or not,' Addinson said. 'As I was saying, there is a threat to national security. In those circumstances I must emphasise that no pranks will be tolerated.'

'*Pranks*?' Jerry said.

'You know perfectly well what I mean, sir.'

'Do I?'

'Yes.'

I could see that Jerry was inclined to argue further. Luckily I managed to dissuade him with a slight shake of my head.

'I shall be keeping a close eye on both of you. I thought you should be aware of the fact.'

'We haven't done anything,' Jerry said.

'Indeed you haven't, sir, if you say so. I just want your assurance that you won't think of doing anything in the future.'

'You can certainly have my assurance, Superintendent.'

Addinson was looking at Jerry.

'And that of Mr Davis,' I added.

'That's very good of you both. That's all I wanted to hear.'

Addinson rose and walked out of the library.

'He's got a nerve,' Jerry said. 'Why on earth would he think we would be involved in anything like that?' He looked thoughtful. 'Actually I suppose you could argue there was a bit of logic to it.'

'How?'

'The lights going out. There's that scene in *Terminal Man.*'

'What scene?'

'The one in the station waiting room when the lights fail.'

'That's hardly comparable. Nobody ended up dead yesterday.'

'That's different, certainly, but otherwise it's pretty much identical.'

'Just a minute,' I said. 'In *Terminal Man* the wrong man gets killed. It's ironic. That's not what happened here. Only Kenneth was having the steak and kidney pie. If somebody put some glass in it they would know where it was going.'

'That's as maybe,' Jerry continued, 'but that wasn't what Addinson was talking about. What about the body we moved six months ago?'

'He never found the body.'

'That's the point isn't it? There must be a lot of professional pride involved. One moment you are about to uncover a body and the next it isn't there. Then there was the body you were found with.'

'That was all explained.'

'I'm not sure it was. To judge by that stuff in the *Daily Mail,* you were the prime suspect.'

'They apologised.'

'Most people didn't notice they had. Page thirty-seven, wasn't it? And in small print! Look, if I'm going to help you properly, I need to know the full story of what happened.'

'Too complicated. Besides, it's easier if you don't know.'

Jerry didn't look convinced. 'The problem is,' he continued in a more reasonable tone, 'if anything happens, we're going to be the first two in line. If somebody steals a cheese straw from the canteen, Addinson is going to come looking for us.'

'Nothing is going to happen.'

'It better not,' Jerry said. 'But in the meantime we need to make sure we don't put a foot wrong. Did you see the sketch in that notebook he was flourishing? It was a seating plan. That's why he knew you were sitting next to Kenneth when he cut his lip. Whatever he says, he doesn't think it was an accident. Anyway, I've got to phone Faith. The twins should be having their mid-morning nap by now. There's a window of opportunity. I'll see you later.'

I sighed. I hadn't even noticed that Addinson had a notebook. In search of distraction I looked round for the crossword I had half-completed but it was nowhere to be seen. I wondered where Rufus Stone was. I needed to talk to him. Unless I was mistaken he seemed to have some idea of what had actually happened to Kenneth.

Eventually I settled back into one of the high backed chairs the library had in abundance and swivelled it round to ensure that I could see anyone who entered the room. I took a sheet of Langham Hall headed writing paper from a letter tray and a pen from my pocket. Make a list, Kate always advises; of the things you want answers to if your mind isn't clear. Or maybe it wasn't Kate but Tom Travis. Or maybe it was both. Anyway, it was sound advice…

1. *Who had Emma Hale been waiting for when I had blundered into Newton?*

2. *What is the best way of influencing Kenneth Preston?*

3. *Why had Leung been convinced we had met before?*

4. *Was the steak and kidney pie incident an accident?*

5. *Why was Miriam Preston so interested in poison?*

6. *Could I get Tom Travis' career back on the straight and narrow?*

7. *Did I have any chance of signing up Emma Hale for a charity football match?*

8. *Why is Matthew Tabard in a mood?*

9. *Is Rufus Stone certifiably insane?*

10. *Why did I have a sense that events were about to get out of control?*

I looked at the list. *Out of control* didn't really sum up my feelings. It was more that I had an impending sense of doom. Suddenly the advice to make a list, wherever it had come from, didn't seem so helpful. I crumpled the paper into a ball and threw it in the direction of the fire. Instead of being consumed in the flames it bounced back onto the carpet. I'm not superstitious but it seemed to be some sort of sign, so I smoothed out the paper, folded it into four, and put it in my jacket pocket.

14

CAMERA ANGLE

THE LIBRARY DOOR OPENED behind me. I turned round. Harry Leung was in the doorway dressed in slacks and an immaculately cut blazer. His shoes also gleamed with polish.

I turned back to the shelves. I felt the need to straighten the row of Tom Travis books even though they didn't need straightening. It was a habit I had picked up at school when I hadn't been allowed to sing because I was *out of tune*. It passed the time. Luckily, most of my fellows assumed I was involved in some elaborate ruse to avoid being included in the singing practice and I enjoyed an entirely unfounded reputation as a silent rebel that increased my popular standing. I almost embarked on an explanation but it wasn't a story I wanted repeated in the luxury hotels of the world.

'I was trying to find a copy of *Terminal Man*,' I said instead, picking a Tom Travis at random. 'Luckily there is one here.'

Harry Leung nodded in a manner that suggested he was hardly listening to what I was saying.

'It's work I'm doing for Kenneth,' I continued. 'You know he's obsessed with the mechanical bird in the studio. He just wants to make sure it can kill. There's something in *Terminal Man* that I thought might be helpful but I can't quite remember what it was. Looking at the book will help refresh my memory.'

'You're fortunate to have copies here,' Leung said. 'I can't find a copy of my book on modern etiquette. Nick Wallace assured me he had seen one here but he may have been mistaken.' He looked distractedly around him. 'It's quite a small format book – you could put it in a hunting jacket pocket, although whether one should ever take it on an actual hunt is quite another matter. I was told it was most likely in the reference section but I can't find it there and apparently there's no formal checking of books in and out so anyone can take anything they like. William and Helen Graves are somewhat libertarian in their approach to such matters.'

'If it's not on the shelves, someone must have borrowed it. That means it's a book in demand.'

Leung's face brightened.

'You're right.'

'Or Julie Whyard might know something. She seems to be the closest thing to a librarian here. Her sister Molly could get a message to her.'

'Is that the blonde woman in the entrance hall?'

'That's her.'

'I'm not sure it's entirely appropriate to be asking after one's own book.'

'She's very discreet. You could say that Nick Wallace had asked you if they have a copy here.'

'That's not a bad plan. But there's something I need to ask you,' Leung said. 'It's Superintendent Addinson. I met him in the entrance hall. We had hardly been talking for more than a minute before he assured me that any threat from the Tibetan community in Beccles was exaggerated. I think he was being serious but I thought they were sending someone who had served in Hong Kong.'

'I understand the daughter of the original officer has been taken seriously ill so they sent Addinson instead.'

'He didn't make that clear,' Leung said. 'But you know the man don't you?'

'We had some dealings six months ago. There were one or two sensational reports in the press that were never properly withdrawn but that's all. I prefer not to talk about it.'

'Of course,' Leung said, with a reluctant ring to his voice. Clearly the rules of modern etiquette didn't permit the discussion of subjects that participants might find sensitive.

'He's also something of a crime fiction fan, isn't he?' Leung continued. 'Including your own work, or so he says. He seems very knowledgeable about it. I gather he's studied all your books in detail. He also tells me you're something of a crime fiction critic in your own right.'

'Nothing of any great substance.' I said dismissively. 'A few articles on my website.'

'That's not the Superintendent's view. He tells me that you're at the cutting edge. I'm sure you're underestimating your own importance. Kenneth also told me he was interested in that aspect of your work.'

'It's nothing at all. Nothing more than amateur scribbling.'

Leung seemed undeterred by the denial.

'Miriam Preston was telling me that your associate, Mr Davis, is also an expert on crime. She said he was briefing her on poisons that are locally available. She seemed particularly taken with aconite from monkshood or wolf's-bane.

You could grow that here, a blue flowered variety would add contrast to the garden. It still kills the odd unwary gardener apparently. Although I suspect she would probably favour polonium poisoning. She was impressed that a gram of vaporised polonium could kill a million and a half people in a couple of months.'

'Polonium is hardly likely to be available in Suffolk. If she wants something practical, the answer is probably in the garden here, as Jerry says.'

'Polonium might look better on the big screen.'

I might have argued the point or pointed to Miriam's interest in cyanide but Leung's mobile was ringing, a subdued regal fanfare.

'No, I can talk to the Prince, if he's there. No, no, it's very convenient, couldn't be a better moment...'

Sign language, to judge from Leung's fluency in it, was still part of modern manners and we parted on cordial, if silent, terms as I tiptoed out of the room. In the entrance hall I bumped into Jerry.

'So,' I said, 'what's up?'

Before he had time to answer there was the dull thud of something falling and a scream of terror from somewhere nearby. Even muffled, the howl of fear was recognisable as a man's voice, and more than that, as belonging to a man we knew, a man more used to directing fear rather than confronting it. The voice belonged to Kenneth Preston.

'That was the studio,' I said. 'We need to find out what's going on.'

When we got to the studio we found Kenneth Preston examining a gash in his black leather jacket. By his side, on the floor of the studio, the mechanical bird was sprawled on the flagstones. Around it a long coil of rope that had once attached it to the ceiling was scattered over the floor.

'What's happened?' I said. 'Are you alright?'

'Bloody thing!' Kenneth said. He gestured in the direction of the grounded bird. 'It must have worked itself free. This jacket is ruined.' He was pointing at a gash a couple of inches long in the leather. 'Do you know who gave this to me? Of course you don't!'

There were other people crowding into the studio.

'Kenneth! What's happened? I thought someone was being murdered. Are you all right?'

It was Nick Wallace, slightly breathless, with Harry Leung behind him.

'There's been an accident with the bird,' I said, 'but nothing too serious by the looks of it. I don't think there are any actual injuries.'

'I shouldn't have to be here working out scenarios for myself,' Kenneth said. 'That's what you're paid to do.' He was pointing at me. 'Congratulations on not coming up with anything convincing yet! This has been bloody terrifying!'

'I think you're suffering from a bit of shock,' I said, in as soothing a voice as I could muster.

'Yes,' Jerry said. 'Why don't you sit down? Relax while we work out how this happened.'

'It's bleeding obvious isn't it?' Kenneth said, pushing away Jerry's consoling arm. 'Something went wrong with the pulley up there. This thing is heavier than you think. When the script writer in chief here comes up with some ideas, I won't need to do this.'

I gathered the notion of personal responsibility wasn't one on which Kenneth placed much reliance at moments of stress. I was tempted to say something but I was aware of a faint scraping sound on the mezzanine floor above us. I looked upwards but there was no one to be seen.

Nick Wallace had produced a hip flask.

'You need a drop of this Kenneth.'

Kenneth looked as though he was about to argue further, but then took the flask with an element of ill grace.

'My tailor can fix your coat,' Leung said. 'You'll never be able to tell it's been damaged.'

'If you'll excuse me,' I said. 'I need to check what's going on up there.'

I ran up the stairs. Rufus Stone was bent down on the far side of the mezzanine level examining the wooden floorboards under the hook in the wall on which the bird had been tethered. He had a magnifying glass in his hand that he put away in his jacket pocket as he saw me approaching.

'I always carry one,' he said, in response to my enquiring glance.

He was right. He did.

'What are you doing up here?'

'I heard the commotion and came in to see what was going on. I looked over and saw Kenneth on the ground. What I heard was more a cry of alarm rather than pain, albeit a little theatrical in manner. He was more shaken than injured, so I thought my time was best spent on working out how it happened.'

'He could have been killed.'

'I think not.'

He seemed firm in his view. I supposed it was long odds against any accident with the pterodactyl being fatal.

'So,' I said, in a more relaxed tone, as I wondered whether to call him Rufus or Tom, 'any other deductions?'

'You can see for yourself can't you? Look at the rope and the marks on the floor – not an accident, possibly a warning.'

There was a growing hubbub from below. Miriam Preston had a consoling arm round her husband. Jerry was standing to one side. In a far corner Leung was talking animatedly to Nick Wallace. Jack Catesby, the head of security, had also appeared and was hovering behind them.

Rufus was walking down the stairs. As he went up to Kenneth, who was now on his feet, he casually fingered Kenneth's damaged jacket in his hand and then left.

The next person to enter the studio was Bob Addinson. He looked round the space, his gaze lingering a little too long on Jerry and myself. Then he announced he needed to ask everyone about the incident. Starting with Kenneth, he asked brief questions of the company and recorded their replies in shorthand in a notebook. As far as I could see, he was keeping Jerry and myself until last.

'So,' Addinson said, when everyone else had left, 'I imagine you know nothing about this?'

I shook my head. Jerry was shaking his head too, a little too much in time for my liking.

'Who was the first person here?' Addinson said.

'That's a little difficult to answer,' I said. 'On this level it was Jerry and myself, then Nick Wallace and Harry Leung who arrived together. But Rufus Stone was on the balcony area. I heard a movement so I went up the stairs and I found him looking at something on the floor.'

'And what was he looking at?'

'I'm not sure I know. Marks perhaps.'

'Marks?'

'As I said, I don't know. There was something that attracted his interest on the floor below where the bird had been tethered. Then he went to the ground floor of the theatre, looked at the damage done to Kenneth's jacket and left, just before you arrived.'

'The detective at work,' Addinson said dismissively. 'And where were you and Mr Davis when the alarm was first raised?'

'In the entrance hall.'

'Can anyone vouch for that?'

'I don't think anyone was at the table. But I'd just come out of the library where I had been talking to Harry Leung. I'm sure he'll corroborate that if you ask him. I found Mr Davis in the reception area. Then we heard Mr Preston's cry of alarm.'

Addinson put his notebook down.

'No further questions?' I said.

'Not at the moment.'

'You ought to have a word with Rufus Stone,' I said.

'I'm sure I'll have a word with everyone, sir.'

'Mmmmh,' Jerry said when Addinson had left the studio.

'What does that mean?'

'He thinks you're up to something.'

'Why would he think that?'

'These so-called accidents that Kenneth has been involved in. Addinson obviously suspects you of tampering with his steak and kidney pie. You were sitting next to him after all.'

'Us,' I said.

'What does that mean?'

'I could only have tampered with his pie if I knew the lights were about to go out. You told him how easy that would be to arrange remotely. He knows I'm not capable of arranging that. If he suspects me of doing anything, he suspects that you're my accomplice.'

'So that is how you are going to play things is it? *Oh I don't understand how those lights could have gone out. Really, I don't have a clue. So I must have had an accomplice in anything I was planning.*'

'You know I'm not good at anything technical.'

'I know that's what you say. The reality might be very different. What you need to bear in mind is that whenever Addinson looks at you he's reminded of the difference between factual and legal guilt.'

'What do you mean by that?'

'He knows you're factually guilty but legally he can't prove it. The weight of evidence isn't right.'

'I don't think that's what he thinks. I think he thinks I can't tell the difference between fact and fiction when it comes to crime.'

'That's hardly any better.'

'It's not a problem if there's no crime here is it?

'I think Rufus thinks there has been a crime.'

'Rufus is bound to think he's involved in some murder mystery in which everything that happens is significant. But nobody has died. That's what you need to remember.'

'Kenneth looked rattled,' Jerry said decisively.

'Rufus didn't think he was in any danger.'

'You didn't make Tom Travis infallible did you?'

Quite what Jerry meant by this remark I was never to know because Florence Hammond was hovering behind us, looking worried.

'Can you help?' she said. 'Nick wants the bird back where it was. He thinks it's bad for morale to have it on the floor like this. If you two can help me I think we can pull it up to where it was.'

Five minutes later the bird was happily poised thirty feet above my head. Jerry and Florence were talking about how best the rope could be secured to the wall. I couldn't see how it could have come free in the first place. But then I couldn't see how glass could have got into Kenneth's steak and kidney pie either.

15

AUDITION

I STILL HADN'T COME up with anything like a satisfactory explanation when, a few hours later, Jerry and I found ourselves involved in Kenneth's acting workshop. We had started in the room of childhood, where we were each encouraged to remember the first sadness we had encountered and the darkness it had thrown over the rest of our lives.

'Now we're beginning to know ourselves,' Kenneth said, after Jerry had completed his denunciation of his primary school, 'I want to talk about each of the roles before us. Creating a character on screen is a collaborative process between the director, the actor, and the writer. Some people consider the director is the *auteur* when it comes to the finished work, but my view is that we need everyone's perspective. The primary reason we are all here is that the creator of Tom Travis had a new and deeper insight into his character.' Kenneth gave a brief bow in my direction. 'David, why don't you tell us how you discovered his flaw?'

'That's an interesting question,' I said.

'And what's the answer?' Kenneth said.

'It was something that came to me.'

It was truthful enough. It had come to me, or rather I had been handed it by Angie, Debbie's assistant, when I had gone to the office to say that whoever had written *Murder Unseen,* it certainly hadn't been me. I had, however, failed to set the record straight.

'Fully formed like all the best inspiration?' Kenneth said encouragingly. 'Tell us more.'

'I,' I said. 'I...'

'I'm sorry everyone,' another voice said, 'can we all take five? There's something I need to discuss with Kenneth.'

It was Nick Wallace. He and Kenneth walked to one end of the studio while Matthew, Emma and Rufus split into a group of their own.

'That's unfortunate,' Jerry whispered beside me. 'I've always wanted to know why you wanted to give Tom a darker side. But what did you think about what happened to Emma? Who would have thought that she had been through such bleak times?'

Emma had recounted that her parents had been killed in the 9/11 attacks when she was little more than a baby. Her mother's brother, a career diplomat, and his moneyed wife, had brought her up. They were a well-heeled cosmopolitan couple that mostly spent their time travelling the world. It was, she had said, an idyllic childhood to the outside observer. For once Kenneth had listened without interrupting.

'She must feel vulnerable,' Jerry added. 'That might explain her attitude to men in general.'

'Meaning what?'

'Meaning that she's always looking for a protector.'

'I think there was a little more going on than that.'

'Meaning what?'

'Meaning that she didn't put her arms round your waist. She put her arms around mine. I could tell there was something substantial in her feelings. I appreciate they weren't directed at me but even so, there was something going on. Perhaps she's found the love of her life. Something was happening anyway. Whoever it was she was pleased to see him.'

'If you say so…' Jerry said, unconvinced. 'But that wouldn't rule out the love of her life being older and more in command would it?'

Jerry's question went unanswered as Kenneth and Nick were coming down the mezzanine steps.

'Sorry,' Nick said. 'We're going to have to pull this. Kenneth has some calls he needs to make on the Graham Greene project that can't wait.'

Whatever urgent business Kenneth had to attend to on his favoured project had been completed two hours later because Florence phoned my room and said that Kenneth would like to see me in the Chinese Suite. I had just about managed to prepare a hotchpotch of reasons why I had made Tom Travis a murderer in *Murder Unseen* and a more solid set of reasons why any self-respecting film director might favour a more traditional detective.

As I walked I wondered about the exact nature of the relationship between Kenneth and Nick. Kenneth hadn't hesitated in agreeing to Nick's request to interrupt the workshop. Five minutes later he had agreed that it should be postponed to the following day. Nick obviously had a great deal of influence over him. Perhaps I should concentrate my efforts to redeem Tom Travis on Nick.

The door of the suite was open when I arrived and there was the sound of voices coming from the end of the corridor. Nick Wallace was talking intently to Kenneth on one side of a round table covered in a white cloth that probably served as a breakfast table. They both looked up as I entered, like conspirators in a Shakespeare play.

'David,' Nick said, smiling, 'perfect timing. Kenneth told me he had something to discuss with you that couldn't wait. I'll get back to housekeeping and leave you and Kenneth to get on with the creative work.'

'If there's something you need to finish discussing, I'm very happy to park myself somewhere for a few minutes.'

'No, no, we're done.'

'So,' Kenneth said as Nick left the room, 'I hear you're an expert on locked-room mysteries. Tell me anything and everything about them. The locked room is a never-ending source of inspiration for crime writers, I'm told.'

It was a phrase I had used on my author website. Kenneth had obviously done his research. I wondered how much of my material he had read. Apart from a number of reflections on locked rooms, I had also posted a piece on "impossible crime".

'The basic point,' I said, 'is that a locked-room mystery is a detective story in which a murder is committed under circumstances where it seems impossible for the murderer to commit the crime. The most common form is the locked room, normally bolted on the inside with no other form of exit, in which the victim is found dead.'

I nearly added that Langham Hall probably had its own version but checked myself. I needed to keep something in reserve.

'There are any number of variations, like the body found on a rocky outcrop on a wet beach where there are no tracks in the sand. Then there is the house surrounded by snow, where the murderer has left, but there are no footprints. In fact you could say Langham Hall is a version of the same thing. If somebody was murdered here after the drawbridge was raised, the murder must have been committed by somebody on the premises.'

'Stick to the room,' Kenneth said. 'Make it one entrance, locked from the inside. The victim is a woman. She's young, beautiful; her clothes are ruffled, disarrayed. Her dead eyes look up at the camera from a once alluring face, high cheekbones, and sensual lips. She's sitting in a chair away from the door. The gun is in her hand. A shot is heard. Tom Travis breaks the locked door down and finds her. There's a policeman following behind him. So what happened?'

'The shot heard isn't the shot that kills her. Tom enters the room first and shoots her dead in the chair with a gun fitted with a silencer. Before the policeman enters the room he puts a different gun of the same make in her hand. He can do everything he needs to in a couple of seconds. He's bending over her when the policeman enters the room. He screams at the policeman to get a doctor while he sees what he can do. When the policeman has gone Tom unscrews the silencer from the gun, wipes his own prints off the butt and presses the gun into her hand. He puts the other gun and the silencer into his pocket. When the policeman returns he insists that nothing is touched. When the gun is tested it turns out that it is the one that fired the fatal bullet and that only her fingerprints are on it. She might have been drugged beforehand so that he can get close to her and shoot her but nobody is going to test for any such substance given the cause of death is so obvious.'

'Reasonable enough,' Kenneth said encouragingly, 'it could work on film at least.' He seemed to have recovered from the incident with the bird. Perhaps the news on Graham Greene had been good.

'You need to remember,' I added quickly, 'if we're talking about Golden Age crime, murders don't have much to do with practicality, either in the way they're executed or in the way that a solution is arrived at. It's almost part of the convention. People are always firing crossbow bolts through three sets of open windows or hovering above isolated outcrops of rock and landing by a helicopter.'

'Let's keep it simple,' Kenneth said. 'I don't want to use a gun. I want to use that bird. Think of it hurtling down toward her and the look of fear in her eyes. Maybe we could get something reflected in her pupils, opening wider as the bird descends. Work me up something on that. We can talk later.'

Kenneth's mobile was ringing. I gathered Kenneth's interest in classical crime had ended for the time being and that the meeting was at an end. He made a perfunctory gesture of farewell as I walked out of the room and into the corridor.

'David?' a voice said.

There was the scent of something intangible and exotic in the air. It spoke of the warm summer scents of the South of France rather than a cold Suffolk winter. Miriam Preston was standing in the doorway of what could only be the bedroom. Her hair was attractively disarranged as though she might just have woken from some sleep or daydream. She was wearing black jeans and a dark green top. Her feet were bare.

'Have you been seeing Kenneth?'

'Yes. We're done for the time being – locked rooms, impossible crimes, all dealt with. And he wants me to do some more thinking about the bird.'

'How fascinating. But don't give him anything too original or you'll find it isn't your idea but his. It's the way he works. If he's got a question he can't answer he makes it someone else's responsibility. So if there isn't an answer, it's not down to him. He's not really one for taking responsibility unless everything is a success. He should have gone into politics. But never mind about that. There's something you can do for me if you come in here.'

Here was the bedroom of the Chinese Suite, which featured a four-poster bed that was adorned with silk drapes on which embroidered kingfishers darted between green spiked leaves. Miriam Preston had picked up something that she cradled in a silk scarf. It might have been a baby by the care she took, but it wasn't. She put the object down on a side table by the bed.

'What do you think?'

Nestling in the scarf was a bottle of whisky, a Glengowrie 1965.

'Hold it up to the light,' she said. 'Look at its colour.'

'It's magnificent,' I said. 'The man who gets this will be lucky.'

'It's a shame it's far too old for you,' she said. 'Ten years at least I would say.'

'That's a good guess.'

I had a feeling it wasn't a guess. She might not have Jerry's omnivorous control of facts but she had done her research on me. David Knight, crime author, would locate me and avoided confusion with David Knight, the amateur squash champion from the Isle of Man; or David Knight, actor; or that nine-year-old comedian from *Britain's Got Talent*.

'Are you going to give it back, or do you want to keep it?'

Her tone was playful and the dark green top she was wearing was loose-fitting, something that she probably wore in bed. I looked down at the bottle I was cradling in my hands.

'Sorry,' I said. 'It's just interesting to hold something that has been around for all these years. Kenneth is a very lucky man.'

'He has his good points. The renewal of our vows was unexpected. I need to give him credit for that. He put a lot of effort into the arrangements. But I've been married to him long enough to know he'll want something in return. If 1965 wasn't so obviously the wrong year, I might tease him by giving it to you.'

It might have been a trick of the light but her eyes had become luminous.

'Put it down on the side there if you would,' she pointed towards a small lacquered table. 'I'll give it to Kenneth when we go to bed.'

She was close to me and ran the tips of her fingers lightly over my right cheekbone.

'Do you base Tom Travis on yourself?' she said.

16

TIGHT ON

I HAD THE IMAGE of Miriam Preston in the Chinese Suite in my head as I went to bed. I had been slipping in and out of wakefulness and it was with a sense of weariness that I opened my eyes. Sleep had been playing a game, threatening at one moment to sweep over me like a healing balm and then, in the next, to withdraw the offer. I looked around me. The room was various shades of black. I remembered I had also been thinking about Matthew Tabard.

According to online media he had incurred the displeasure of the tennis player, Abbey Frost, not only by his unfaithfulness to her, but also because of the attendant circumstances. In the midst of what should have been a rapturous moment with a new, unnamed, partner, he had apparently fallen asleep from sexual exhaustion. This had left his reputation floating in the space between admiration for his sexual appetite and doubts about his capacity for delivery.

I took a deep breath and tried to reconcile the stories online with the reality of the man who was at Langham. I wondered whether Iain would understand the full extent of the innuendo that had been employed in descriptions of Matthew's supposed actions. Then I thought I could detect the scent that I had recognised in Miriam Preston's bedroom as also being present in my own room. I breathed more deeply but whatever it was, or had been, seemed suddenly distant and then non-existant.

I closed my eyes. There was something else to remember. I had been on the brink of sleep but something distinct had woken me. It had been a door being opened and closed, a sound in the middle distance, not the door of the next room, but the one after that. The sound hadn't come from Addinson's room but Emma Hales'. I fumbled for the switch on the bedside lamp. A cone of light sprang into life but most of the room was in deep shadow. The moth man's light, the light that had dazzled Emma Hale in her encounter with me, was no longer shining. I walked over to the window and looked out. What before had been a brightly lit area of path and lawn outside Emma Hale's room was now an impenetrable blackness.

I put on the dark blue silk dressing gown I had acquired the week before I met Kate that I only used when she was not with me. I also put on the white complimentary slippers that had come with the room. It would be much easier for me to describe Tom's feelings if he were to venture out in the middle of the night in a country house, if I had had that experience myself. Then I walked to the door and opened it. It creaked loudly. I looked out.

The lights in the corridor brightened magically. For a moment I was at a loss to understand why but then I remembered that Molly Whyard had told me that Helen Graves was a Green councillor for the local district and had included a whole series of state-of-the-art energy saving measures when Langham had been refurbished. This must be one of them. As I watched, the overhead lights dimmed again. They were movement sensitive.

I eased the door shut behind me and stepped forward. I moved past Addinson's room. For a brief moment I had the feeling that the door to his room would open and that he would be staring at me with that expression on his face that suggested that whatever I said he would not believe me. But nothing happened and the door remained closed. I told myself he was fast asleep. The door of Newton, Emma Hales' room, was also firmly closed but a sliver of light at the bottom of the door indicated that at least some of the lights inside were turned on. The opening door must have been Emma's. I padded on, my slippers emitting a faint scuffing sound on the wooden floor.

In an alcove at the end of the corridor, where the ornate carved stairs led either upwards to the next floor of the house or downwards to the rooms below, a naked woman lay voluptuously on her front amid crumpled bedclothes. The Italian ballerina before me was captured in eternal youth and white marble. According to the guide to the house in my room, she had caught the third Baronet's eye while dancing at the King's Theatre in the Haymarket and had lasted long enough in his affections not only to be commemorated in this life size statue but also in a painting by a student of Gainsborough. The smooth stone was curiously lifelike, the stretching figure satiated with lovemaking.

I had a sudden craving for a cigarette that I couldn't explain. I stood immobile behind the sculpture for a few seconds, my hand pressed against her cold naked shoulder. Somewhere in the house there was another sound. Footsteps, light and strangely regular, were approaching from below. I moved into the shadows behind the sinuous back that curved seductively in front of me. The footsteps stopped. I held my breath. Then they started again, slower and more deliberate than before. I dropped down behind the crumpled sheets of marble.

Emma Hale, dressed in a figure-hugging tracksuit, walked past my hiding place. For a moment I thought she might be sleep-walking – her gaze was fixed and her eyes glassy. She seemed lost in her thoughts. It was only when she got to the door of Newton that she paused and looked both ways along the passageway. Then she opened the door and closed it behind her. I took a deep breath. She hadn't seen me.

I thought back. It must be at least half an hour since she had left her bedroom. In that time she would have been able to reach any corner of Langham. Had she been going to meet someone and, if so, who could it be? Was it the same person she had been expecting when I blundered into Newton when I first arrived? Why was she looking so pale when she returned? Had Matthew Tabard rebuffed her? I got to my feet and edged back towards Heisenberg. Hiding behind the sinuous arms of an Eighteenth Century mistress wasn't necessarily the best way of working out the love life of the present. The lights in the ceiling increased in brightness and the house creaked in the night. At the doorway I permitted myself the same glance over my shoulder that Emma had made. There was no one to be seen.

Inside, I sat on the bed. I was wide awake. After a moment or two I switched off the bedside light and made my way across to the windows on the east side and opened one. I looked out. There was no light visible from Newton's windows or any light showing from Addinson's room next door. Emma Hale seemed to have wasted no time in returning to bed. I closed the window with exaggerated care. Jerry's suggestion about using Langham as the setting for the next Tom Travis novel floated back into my mind. There's a moment in any Tom Travis novel when you need to ensure that you've assembled all the characters for the reader. If I could only find a plot, I could start a novel now. Everybody had been assembled at Langham. The drawbridge was up and we were all effectively locked in for the night. Perfect in fictional terms.

Did I have a plot? There were the incidents that Kenneth Preston had been involved in. He must have upset more people than most, surely? And Miriam was a very rich woman. There were likely to be reasons to get rid of both of them. Then there was Leung, a man with powerful connections and an ex-mistress, Emma Hale, who was normally not averse to dabbling with men's affections.

Added to that, Florence Hammond seemed in a permanent state of nervousness and what was anyone to make of the rumours surrounding Matthew Tabard? And what were Nick Wallace and Kenneth up to? Or Miriam, for that matter? Who was precisely allied to who? Addinson clearly thought Jerry and I were in cahoots. What had Jerry been saying? That he was convinced of my guilt from six months ago and was looking to even matters up for Justice? How was he going to do that?

I lay back down on the bed and tried to dismiss the thoughts from my mind. I had more pressing matters to deal with, like salvaging Tom Travis from the murderous career that Kenneth Preston and Rufus Stone had mapped out for him, rather than the plot of the next book or these sort of unhelpful speculations.

Gradually I must have fallen back into sleep. I remember a clock striking one and then nothing very much after that. I must have been very close to wakefulness again because I remembered the dream I had been having. Emma Hale had lit me a cigarette and seemed ready to confide in me, although why she was reclining on a chaise longue barely dressed was another question. It was her features that I remembered. It wasn't that her nose had been put out of joint, but more that she had been betrayed. That was why she was wearing a fixed stare as she moved back along the passageway to her room. Gradually all the speculations died away and sleep finally decided to engulf me. The last thing I remembered was the look of despair on Emma Hale's face on her return to Newton. Whatever had happened on her night-time jaunt, had seriously upset her.

17

VERTIGO EFFECT

MOLLY WHYARD WAS BEHIND the table in the entrance hall the next morning.

'You're up early, Mr Knight. I hope you slept well.'

'Tolerably well I suppose,' I said, 'but I'm surprised to see you. Weren't you on duty last night?'

'Oh, I didn't go home. There are staff rooms in the main building here we use if we stay over. I was on early duty this morning so it didn't seem worth the effort. The bedrooms on the top floor are too small for guests but good enough if you just want to sleep.'

The telephone on the table was ringing.

'No, I'm sorry to hear that... have you tried his mobile number? Yes, I appreciate that... I'm so sorry... yes, I'll pass the message on as soon as I can.'

She put the phone down.

'Is there a problem?' I said.

'That was another call for Mr Preston. There was one about five minutes ago. They were both from America. They've been trying to get him on his mobile but he isn't responding.

Americans are so impatient, aren't they? I should have asked them whether the mobile was actually ringing. That could be the answer. Coverage here can be patchy. I said I'd pass the messages on but I didn't want to wake him up unless it really is urgent. Langham is meant to be a retreat for guests. It's one of our rules. I'm not sure I know what to do for the best.'

'Apparently he only needs five hours sleep,' I said, 'so more than likely he's up and about. The calls could be about this Graham Greene film he's so keen on. Nick Wallace interrupted the workshop yesterday because something had happened on that front. Sounds as though it could be urgent. If you write the numbers down I'll slip round to see if he is about. I need to talk about methods of murder.'

'Well, that would be a relief,' Molly Whyard said. 'We're not meant to leave the table here once the drawbridge is down. Jack Catesby gave me a lecture about it. These are the names and numbers. Can you read my writing?'

The men – they were both men – who wanted to speak to Kenneth were called Brent and Karl and represented, respectively, Netflix and a company called Crushed Suede Productions, whose precise purpose was less clear. I had a momentary sense that matters might once again be heading in my direction. If Kenneth was obsessed with Graham Greene he might have less time to develop Tom's flaws.

I knocked discreetly at the door to the Chinese Suite but there was no answer. I knocked again, this time more loudly. Again there was no response. I turned the handle. The door opened.

'Kenneth? Miriam?' I said as I walked in.

The door to the bedroom was open.

'Kenneth? Miriam?'

I looked inside. The room was deserted. There was a hint of the perfume she had been wearing the day before when she had run her fingers across my cheek and shown me the bottle of Glengowrie.

I looked at the four-poster bed. The kingfishers still inhabited a heaven of green spiked leaves and the duvet on the bed was disarrayed. There was something different about the room. The bottle of Glengowrie that I had put down on the dressing table was no longer there although, gratifyingly, there was a copy of *Terminal Man*. What had Miriam Preston said about the whisky? That she would give it to Kenneth when they went to bed that night? Last night. Perhaps she had.

I don't know what it was that made me do what I did next – I couldn't find a satisfactory explanation for Addinson later when he questioned me about it. Perhaps it was no more than writer's curiosity. Anyway, for whatever reason, it was too good an opportunity to miss. I opened the wardrobe to reveal a phalanx of black leather jackets, each of which could have belonged to Kenneth or Miriam. Only at either end of the rail was clothing gender-specific. At one end there was a red dress that would have clung to Miriam and at the other a dinner jacket that Kenneth could wear to denounce establishment values.

In the en-suite bathroom an expensive pot of day cream that pronounced itself "anti-wrinkle" probably belonged to Kenneth. There were no lines around Miriam's eyes that I could remember. A series of mysterious blue and red glass bottles with glass stoppers were most likely Miriam's. They might have been old-fashioned poison bottles. Calvin Klein's *Escape* was certainly hers. Who was the owner of the white pills in a transparent plastic case was more problematic.

The room where I had my discussions with Kenneth the day before was also deserted. The drawer in the desk by the window was locked but it was a matter of a few seconds to work out the hiding place of the key. Kenneth made notes. Looking at what he had written could get me ahead of the game. The drawer was empty. I looked round to see whether there were any other obvious depositories for notebooks but found none. I walked back along the internal corridor and closed the door.

'You were a long time. Did you find Mr Preston?' Molly Whyard said when I got back to the entrance hall.

'Nobody in,' I said. 'The door to the suite was open and I waited around for a bit thinking they might come back, but no luck. Maybe they've gone outside for a walk to get up an appetite for breakfast? It's a pleasant enough morning.'

'They can't have done. I was here when the drawbridge went down. There's no way they could get out without me seeing them.'

'Has there been anybody about at all?'

'No, but it's only a few minutes past eight. If they're not in their room they must be somewhere. Maybe they've gone to the dining hall for an early breakfast. It's open from seven. They could have gone there.'

'That's probably it,' I said. 'I'll check it out.'

Kenneth and Miriam weren't in the dining room. The only occupants were a couple of bored looking young men in white tunics who said they had just come on duty.

I drank a cup of black coffee and tried to work out where they could be. The answer, when I thought about it, was blindingly obvious. Kenneth was obsessed with the bird of prey in the studio and its murderous possibilities. Miriam had helped Kenneth develop his ideas before by playing the bird's victim. They had come up with a new idea on how the bird could be used as a murder weapon and were trying the method out. Maybe they had even pinched the idea from *Terminal Man* and that was why a copy was in their room.

The door to the studio wasn't locked and pushed open easily. I was half-expecting to hear the sound of voices but the room was dark and there was a faint aroma of Miriam's ethereal perfume mingling with the acerbic scent of the new wood. But this time the smell was real. I had come to the right place. I switched on the lights.

For a moment I had difficulty in understanding what I saw. The bird had crashed to the floor but that wasn't the problem. There was a body lying close to it. It was on its side facing away from me, a broken heap that had once been a living being. I moved forward. The bird was in front of it, crash-landed but whole. On the underside of its wooden body there was a matted mass of something brownish that turned out to be a mixture of hair, skin and dried blood. It had inflicted a catastrophic blow on the person lying before me. That person was Miriam Preston. Around her was the mixed scent of her ethereal perfume and her blood.

I inched forward. Miriam Preston's face was serene, her features relaxed. The messages from her brain that catastrophe had struck hadn't time to reach the muscles of her face and change their look of vitality and contentment.

I had a mental picture of Miriam lighting me a cigarette, her illuminated face favouring me with a look that suggested we were involved in some gigantic conspiracy together. On this planet, here and now, that would never come to fruition. What had it meant – the tremor of the lips and the all-knowing eyes? As I looked at the beautiful features before me, unknowing of their own death, I was struck by an overwhelming sense of waste.

Not that the sense of desolation was final and all encompassing. Instead, the sense of loss that had gathered first in the pit of my stomach spiralled into a profound sense of unease. Suddenly I seemed ghostly, as though I was looking down on myself from a great height. I thought of the copy of *Terminal Man* that I had seen in the bedroom in the Chinese Suite. Jerry and I had been discussing mass, velocity and motion, or Jerry had been saying that was what we might want to take into account, given Kenneth's desires for new murder methods. It was the method, he had said, that we had used in *Terminal Man*. What had been a theoretical discussion, that I had scarcely understood, had turned into a live demonstration before me. The difficulties that Jerry had enumerated had been overcome – what he had been proposing theoretically was clearly eminently practicable.

There was a sound from the mezzanine floor. I looked up. Addinson was looking down. His eyes flicked between me and Miriam Preston's body.

'If you could just stand away, sir.'

'It's Miriam Preston, Superintendent. She's dead.'

'As I said, sir, please stand to one side. I'm sure you appreciate the importance of not disturbing anything. Just take a step back.'

'I was trying to find the Prestons,' I said. 'I've just been to the Chinese Suite. The door was open so I went in. I thought they might be having an early breakfast but there was no one there. Molly Whyard will tell you. There were people that wanted to talk to Kenneth, from America, I've got the names and numbers here.'

'Just hold onto them sir. They could be important. I'm coming down.'

The sound of his footsteps was like the sound of slowly approaching fate. I tried to get my thoughts into order. Miriam had been hit in the back of the head by the bird. That was just the sort of killing scenario her husband had been urging us to develop. The bird might not have skewered its victim as Kenneth had wanted, but it had been converted into a killing machine. Addinson would see the connections with *Terminal Man*. He had probably already worked them out. He had come down the steps and looked me up and down. I didn't feel entirely well.

'A bad business,' I said. 'A terrible accident.'

'Indeed, sir,' Addinson said. 'But what makes you think it was an accident?'

18

PULL BACK

'SO WHERE IS KENNETH?' Jerry said.

It was two hours since Addinson had found me bent over Miriam Preston's corpse. In that time no trace had been found of Kenneth Preston despite an extensive search organised by Addinson and Nick Wallace. Then a police forensics team had arrived swathed in all-enveloping blue protective clothing. The doors to the studio and the Chinese Suite had been sealed with tape: *POLICE LINE – DO NOT CROSS*.

'I have no idea,' I said.

'Still,' Jerry said. 'Kenneth missing is good news.'

'Is it?'

'Of course it is.'

'How do you make that out?'

'Look at it this way. If they think what has happened to Miriam is in the slightest bit dodgy, you're the prime suspect. You discovered the body.'

'Somebody has to discover the body.'

'That may be the case. But a lot of the time it's the person found with the body that is most likely to be the murderer.

The point is that they don't discover the body. They are found with it before they can escape.'

'In that case, maybe it was Addinson,' I said. 'He seemed to be there the moment I was. It was one hell of a shock. I wouldn't necessarily have noticed anything else that was going on – Addinson slipping out of the way for example. And then slipping back in.'

'Why on earth would Addinson murder Miriam Preston?'

'He's determined to frame me so that justice will prevail in the longer term. He may not have been able to get me for a previous crime, but he can for this one.'

'You don't really believe that do you? You're saying he would murder a perfectly innocent woman just so that he could bring you to justice?'

'It was your suggestion.'

Jerry rolled his eyes.

'That's was just a speculative idea,' he said firmly. 'What you've just said is crazy.'

'If you think that's crazy, what motive do you think I could possibly have for murdering Miriam Preston?'

'Better than any Addinson has for murdering her,' Jerry said in his most reasonable voice. 'It could be a sudden infatuation or something far more long-standing. You could be after her money. Sex or wealth – either of those would be plausible. Or you could have murdered Miriam to stop Kate learning about your affair. You have been seen with her in what even the most neutral onlooker would describe as, well, intimate circumstances. But then by your own admission, much the same thing happened with Emma Hale and, come to that, I've seen Molly Whyard looking at you in an appraising manner.'

'Molly Whyard? She's not exactly my type.'

'She's an attractive woman. She would certainly be a notch on any man's belt.'

'Notch on my belt! What on earth are you talking about? I'm not that sort of man.'

'She doesn't know that.'

'Look, Miriam Preston is dead in the studio and all you can do is speculate that I killed her for some sexual motive.'

'It's what other people will be doing. It's human nature. Although,' Jerry paused significantly, 'Kenneth is nowhere to be found. He must be the obvious suspect. Think about it. The husband of a wife who has met her death in mysterious circumstances has disappeared. How suspicious is that? What do real murderers do? They flee the scene of the crime. It's obvious what has happened. Kenneth has murdered Miriam and then he's scarpered. You'd be surprised how many husbands and wives or partners murder each other, let alone when one of them is worth a hundred million quid.'

'Would I?'

'Yes.'

'So how many do?'

'Murder their partners in the UK as a percentage of all murders?'

'If you want to put it like that – yes – what's the answer?'

Jerry was looking up at the heavens.

'A little over twenty-five per cent as far as I remember,' he said, after a moment. 'So he'd be the person Addinson would look to first, whether he's disappeared or not. And he's *fled* the scene. That's not something Addinson can ignore. You're in the clear.'

'Until he turns up.'

'Even if he turns up, he'll have a lot of explaining to do. What happened last night in the first place? They were together in the Chinese Suite. Now Miriam is dead in the studio and Kenneth has disappeared.'

'That's what I don't understand.' I said. 'How could he?'

'How could he what?'

'Disappear, or flee the scene, or whatever he has done. Molly Whyard was adamant that nobody left this morning after the drawbridge was down. She was manning the reception area. Nobody could have left without her seeing them.'

'Then he must have got out some other way. I don't know. Could he have used that other bridge? Or a boat? But that's not our problem. He must have found a way because he's not here.'

'I...' I said, but then I stopped. 'Did you wake up or hear anything during the night?' I continued, after a moment.

Jerry looked at me suspiciously.

'No,' he said firmly.

I tried to think back to what had happened since I had found the body. Harry Leung had appeared, dressed in an expensive grey suit with a flamboyant red handkerchief tucked into the breast pocket. It wasn't the way a murderer would dress was it? Florence Hammond and Emma Hale looked as though they had been crying which meant that somebody must have told them what had happened. If anything, Florence had weathered the situation the better of the two. But Emma had been wandering the building the night before.

Then there was Matthew Tabard. He had seemed as disengaged as ever. But then he had been at the centre of a tabloid storm for days, in which his only guarantee was that most people would put the worst interpretation on the events that had occurred. He could surely be ruled out of anything to do with Miriam's death, couldn't he?

'You need to keep your facial expressions under control,' Jerry said.

'What?'

'I can see you thinking. You're not quite talking but you nearly are. You don't want Addinson to think your mind is in turmoil do you? Shocked by Miriam's death yes, but nothing else.'

'You weren't there. You're not in a position to judge how I feel.'

'I didn't say I was. I was just saying that you need to be as calm as possible when Addinson questions you.'

'He'll be questioning everybody else as well.'

'Of course he will. I didn't say he wouldn't. He'll certainly be questioning me. I just said the calmer you are the better it will be. You're the one he found standing over Miriam's body.'

'Somebody had to find the body. I just happened to be the first person there.'

I thought for a moment that Jerry was going to start going through the significance of me being found with the body for a second time but instead he said 'And then there's Rufus Stone.'

'Meaning?'

'Have you seen him this morning? He looks positively energised.'

'Of course he does. There's been a suspicious death. He's a detective. That's what he thrives on – murder.'

'He may do if he thinks he's Tom Travis. He can't really think he is, can he?'

Before I had time to respond I saw that Addinson was in front of us. 'Mr Knight, Mr Davis,' he said. 'I've just been speaking to Molly Whyard. I understand the two of you have been looking for a secret room that William Graves and his wife might have installed here. Is there anything you can tell me about that?'

'It exists and we know where it is,' Jerry said.

'We've just found it,' I added. 'It was something we were holding in reserve to tell Kenneth. It was all part of the unusual murder weapons and classical crime stuff that he was interested in.'

'So you didn't tell him that it existed?'

'No. As I said, we were biding our time.'

'And you didn't think to mention it to me?'

'I was shocked by Miriam's death. I didn't think.'

Addinson seemed to be weighing up my explanation.

'Anyway, perhaps we could check it out now,' he said, after an uneasy silence. He beckoned towards a young and exceptionally tall policeman. 'You can come with us Richards. Why don't you lead on, sir?'

'It's about here,' I said, walking down the passageway to the studio. 'What do you think Jerry?'

'Back six inches. I'll show you.'

Jerry slid back the panelling like a professional. In the light the door looked slightly less a Hollywood prop than it had. The outside bolt was in its housing in the door but not drawn across.

'There's another bolt on the inside,' I said, 'it's basically the same as this one.'

'So you can be locked in or locked out.'

'Exactly.'

Addinson pushed against the door. It didn't budge.

'Sergeant!'

The door was subjected to additional force by Addinson's colleague. It remained shut.

'So does this mean the door is bolted on the inside?'

'Looks like it,' Jerry said.

'So there's somebody inside?'

'It couldn't have been closed otherwise,' Jerry said. 'Do you see those wires protruding through the wall that haven't been connected to anything yet? They're the wiring for a fail-safe device. You couldn't have a public attraction where people could lock themselves in, have a heart attack, and nobody could get to them. Health and Safety wouldn't allow it and you'd have no chance of getting insurance. You'd need to be able to open from either side in an emergency. They're some more wires there as well if you look. My guess is that they're all part of the same system.'

'So,' Addinson said, 'the way things are at the moment, if you're outside and wanting to get in there's no way you can, if the inside bolt is in place.'

'Or vice-versa.'

'I see,' Addinson said, turning to the tall policeman. 'Richards can you get an axe or something similar?'

'That door is a three inches thick,' Jerry said. 'You'd be better off with a battering ram. Besides, there's another way.'

'Which is?'

'The door has an internal magnet that can be used to draw the bolt back remotely. If those wires can be connected up you should be able to make it work from this side. Give me ten minutes and I'll see what I can do.'

'Ten minutes?'

'About that.'

'What do you need?'

'Nothing.'

Jerry produced a screwdriver and a wire stripper from a pocket in his jacket. He ignored Addinson's look of surprise.

'Let's see what you can do then,' Addinson said.

Ten minutes, or perhaps more like a quarter of an hour later (Jerry maintains ten minutes and I always opt for longer) Jerry gave a grunt of satisfaction and pronounced himself finished.

'If everyone could stand back,' he said. 'We don't want anything to jam. Here goes.'

There was a whirring sound of something moving on the far side of the door.

Jerry took a step back. 'That's my bit done,' he said. He was putting the screwdriver and the other tools he had been using back into a canvas pouch that he had also miraculously produced. Addinson looked at the tall policeman.

'Sergeant,' he said.

The policeman eased the door open and looked inside the room.

'You'd better see this, sir.'

Addinson was looking at Jerry and myself. For a moment he seemed unwilling to tear himself away from the forensic glare he was subjecting us to. Then he walked into the room.

I edged forward to look round the door. A figure was slumped in one of the green metal chairs. On the green metal table was a bottle of whisky and a glass. The bottle was the Glengowrie 1965. The glass was a tumbler with a heavy base. The figure at the table was Kenneth Preston. He was dead.

19

PLATO'S ALLEGORY

'HE WAS A BIT high-handed wasn't he?' Jerry said. 'I mean, asking us to leave like that. If I hadn't wired up the fail-safe device they'd still be outside the room with that policeman trying to bash down the door with an axe. In fact, they probably wouldn't have realised that was what the wiring was for in the first place.'

'It was standard procedure. The last thing a policeman would want to do would be to contaminate a crime scene. He was polite enough.'

'More curt than polite. Anyway, I don't know if it was a crime scene. What on earth could have happened?'

'I don't know. His wife dies in mysterious circumstances and he dies in a room which he just happens to lock from the inside.'

'It sounds like one of your plots.'

'Does it?'

'Absolutely.'

'You were convinced that Kenneth had murdered Miriam a couple of hours ago.'

'When I thought Kenneth was the murderer, I didn't know he was dead. But you can see how the whole thing could have happened can't you? They have been swapping ideas about how to use the bird as a murder weapon haven't they? You told me they were fooling about with it on Saturday before I arrived. You said that Kenneth was obsessed with using the bird in the film. They've got a new idea so they go back to the studio to try it out but it goes wrong. Kenneth releases the bird and Miriam is in the way. She's dead instantly. Kenneth hasn't had time to shout a warning. It's a freak accident. He's horrified. It's his obsession with the bird that has killed his wife. He wants to be alone. Mind you, that doesn't explain why he has the bottle of whisky with him. It was a bottle of whisky on the table wasn't it? Maybe that's all wrong.'

'No,' I said, 'the whisky was a present from Miriam to mark the renewal of their marriage vows. She was planning to give it to him. So it looks as though she did it last night. They take it with them to celebrate the new method of death they have thought of. But then something goes wrong and Miriam is killed.'

'So,' Jerry continued enthusiastically, 'he goes to the secret room to lock himself away from a world he can no longer bear. He decides to drown his sorrows. He opens the bottle. He drinks and everything is suddenly too much for him and he has a heart attack.'

'These incidents with the glass in the steak and kidney pie and the falling bird are just accidents are they?'

'You shouldn't be too influenced by Rufus and his theories. He isn't Tom Travis.'

'You could be right,' I said. 'But we need to take stock. I mean, the secret room isn't quite as secret as we thought, is it?

Kenneth knew about it. The Whyard sisters suspected it existed. William and Helen Graves planned it, so they know about it as well.'

'So do the builders who put it in. All sorts of people must have known about it.'

'Are you sure Kenneth closed the door from the inside before he died? Perhaps somebody could have joined up the wires?'

'Absolutely not,' Jerry said. 'The wires were in pristine condition before I connected them. Kenneth shut the door. Nobody else could have done.'

'That's not good,' I said.

'Why isn't that good?'

'You need to think about it from Addinson's perspective. The only people he is aware of that know about the secret room are you and me. Of course the owners and the builders must know as well, but they can't have been involved in last night's events. Who are going to be the first two names on Addinson's list of suspects if he suspects foul play?'

'The fact that he thinks you're a pathological liar isn't going to help us much either,' Jerry added with a hint of malice.

'I don't think he thinks I'm a liar. He just thinks that I don't always tell the truth.'

'It's not white lies we're talking about David,' Jerry said forcefully, 'it's your habit of not being straightforward with him in areas which policemen hold dear. Moving dead bodies in particular. It may have been a few months ago, but it will be imprinted on Addinson's memory as if it were yesterday.'

'Fine, fine,' I said, 'let's not discuss that now. We can work this out for ourselves. Let's suppose the worst and they were murdered. Kenneth and Miriam were alive when the drawbridge went up last night so, if anyone was involved in their deaths, it was one of the people who were in the main house here last night. It should be easy enough to make a list.'

'OK,' Jerry said reluctantly, 'let's make a list.'

'So there's the cast – Matthew Tabard, Rufus Stone and Emma Hale. Those three are all accomplished actors so they'd probably find it easy to act a part. That could be significant.'

'Let's keep it as simple as we can for the time being,' Jerry said. 'There are another three who aren't actors – Harry Leung, Nick Wallace and Florence Hammond. And there were the staff who stayed over. Jack Catesby and Molly Whyard. Count in you and me and what do you have? Ten suspects.'

'You're missing someone.'

'Who?'

'Addinson. If you're the murderer, what better way to cover your tracks than to be in charge of the investigation?'

'So you think he's going to turn accidents into murder so that he can pin responsibility on us?' Jerry didn't sound convinced. 'You think he would frame us for something we didn't do because he can't get us for something we did? It's not going to happen.'

'People are always being framed.'

'Not in real life. You've written too much crime fiction. You just need to admit that to yourself and move on. We need to find the positives in the situation.'

'Which are?' I said, to fill the silence that followed.

'At least we can eliminate each other,' Jerry said after a moment. There was an element of doubt in his voice that I didn't find reassuring.

'I certainly don't have a motive for killing Kenneth,' I said.

'Are you sure?' Jerry said.

'What do you mean by that?'

'You didn't want Tom to be branded as a murderer, if you remember. You just wanted the whole project to collapse so you get back to Tom investigating straightforward cases. What better way of ensuring that than by murdering the director?'

'That's absurdly far-fetched. I wouldn't even put that in a Tom Travis plot.'

'Maybe Kenneth found out you were having a secret affair with Miriam? He was going to tell Kate about the two of you and you were desperate to stop him.'

'That's ludicrous, Jerry.'

'I don't think so. Look at the way they were both murdered. You're an expert on locked-room mysteries and impossible crimes. At least that's what your website claims. Kenneth was in the equivalent of a locked room, and not just a locked room, a room locked on the inside that couldn't be opened from the outside. That's a classic locked-room mystery isn't it?'

'Except that you opened it.'

'Only in a way that couldn't have been used before because of the state of the wires.'

'Addinson won't believe that.'

'He will once he's consulted his experts. That's not our chief worry. Think about the bird.'

'What about the bird?'

'All this stabbing stuff you were going on to Kenneth about was fair enough, but the bird was used as a bludgeon. That was the next murder method you had lined up for Kenneth, wasn't it?'

'I never spelt it out to him in detail. I didn't have time.'

'You didn't have to. He could have worked it out for himself. There's the pulley murder in the train station in *Terminal Man*.'

And the Prestons had had a copy of the book in their bedroom. I thought back. As I had been writing the book Jerry had devised something that he assured me would work in practice. It had involved a heavy wooden object flying through the air on the end of a rope. To be frank, I still didn't understand how it was meant to work. But nobody had written in to query it as they had to the material I had included without consulting Jerry, such as the improbable burst of bullets from the automatic in *Killing Spree*, or the unusual dissolving pearls in *Death of a Socialite*.

'That's not the same,' I said firmly.

'Not in the specific detail maybe but the *modus operandi* is pretty much identical. If Kenneth has read all the Tom Travis books, as you claim, I'm surprised he didn't come up with it himself.'

'It's hardly obvious.'

'It is, if you know anything about engineering or mechanics. Did you look up at the roof in the studio? The rope connected to the bird was also connected to a pulley, wasn't it? There's no other way you could generate the force required to cause the injury you described. It's the method in *Terminal Man*, no question.'

'I can't see it.'

'That's not going to save you from Addinson's suspicions.'

'It could have been an accident,' I said.

'Which is probably the best defence you've got,' Jerry said, 'if you can stick to it. All you need to do is to ignore any suggestions about locked rooms and forget that Miriam's death is also pretty much an impossible crime, which just happens to be another area you are an expert on. Why would she just stand there while somebody lined her up to be bludgeoned to death by the pterodactyl? She'd have to be mightily distracted not to notice what was happening.'

'She was more interested in poison. That was what she was talking to you about. She just went along with Kenneth's interest in the bird.'

'You shunted her in my direction.'

'You're here as the assistant screenwriter. You're an expert on poisons, or so you claim. Of course I steered her in your direction.'

'Tom Travis is an expert on poisons.'

'Tom Travis is an expert on a lot of things I don't know much about. You told me the pulley murder in *Terminal Man* would work. If I get the particular details right then people are likely to believe that Tom is the polymath that I describe. It's just a technique. I do a bit of research on the detail and people think I've mastered the complete subject but, of course, I only need to be an expert in a small area. I don't need to have the breadth of knowledge that a true expert would have, and anyway I can rely on people like you. To be frank, I've been impressed by the mugging up you've done. I didn't know you had a photographic memory.'

'Did I say I had a photographic memory?'

'Yes.'

'That was a bit of an exaggeration.'

'I wouldn't have said it was given what I've seen over the last few days. It's been impressive. Anyway, whatever type of memory you have, it's a lot better than mine.'

Jerry nodded in a half-hearted manner that was pretty much the equivalent of shaking his head.

'But I'm not the man in the driving seat,' he said. 'You're the man who has got this million dollar deal. Some of it may be down to Debbie but you're the main man as far as Addinson is concerned. Miriam was murdered by a method you outlined in *Terminal Man*; Kenneth was murdered in an impossible locked-room mystery, an area in which you are generally acknowledged to be an expert.'

'That may be the case, but there's no evidence against me.'

'Are you sure about that?'

'Of course I'm sure.'

'You were sitting next to Kenneth when he cut his lip.'

'Chance.'

'And I did see you smoking with Miriam.'

'And you were advising her on poisons. But that's neither here nor there. What matters to policemen is the weight of the evidence. There's nothing of substance that incriminates me.'

'If you say so,' Jerry said in a voice that suggested he was not entirely convinced.

He was right. I wasn't convinced either. The evidence was mounting up against me. More than that, it was mounting up against us. Not just small bits, but lots of it, all pointing in the same direction. I looked sideways at Jerry. He had been the man, after all, who had got the door to the secret room open. He was certainly knowledgeable about fail-safe devices. And that opened up all sorts of other possibilities. Who was to say that he couldn't have found another way of opening that door? Maybe Kenneth hadn't known about the existence of the secret room but had had his heart attack, or whatever had killed him, somewhere else at Langham? If there was another way to trigger the fail-safe mechanism, all bets were off. And the person most likely to know how to do that was Jerry. So Kenneth might have met his death anywhere in Langham and then been transferred to the secret room by someone else. And it was that someone else I was looking at now.

I shook my head. I told myself that suspecting Jerry was as ludicrous as Addinson suspecting me. This wasn't some sort of game with a murderer moving pieces across a criminal chessboard. This was real life. Kenneth and Miriam Preston were both dead. Miriam's eyes would never sparkle again and Kenneth would never direct his Graham Greene film.

Jerry announced that he needed fresh air to clear his head and suggested a walk around the grounds. I declined to join him. I needed to work out who I could trust.

20

SHUTTER SPEED

AN HOUR LATER I found myself in the library staring at the collection of Tom Travis books. I needed to know whether the copy of *Terminal Man* that had been in Miriam and Kenneth's bedroom had been taken from the shelves here. The answer was no. The next question I needed to ask myself was whether I was prepared to believe that what was happening was some sort of plot weaving together the fictional world of Tom Travis and corpses in the all too real present? It might have been if the two people who had expressed so much interest in methods of murder in classical crime fiction, the couple who had their own copy of the book, Kenneth and Miriam Preston, hadn't both been dead.

'Have you got a moment David? There's something I need to ask you.'

Rufus Stone was sitting by the fire. I hadn't noticed him.

'I've just found out that Bob Addinson has been appointed the Senior Investigating Officer,' he continued. 'Actually I've heard he pretty much appointed himself. The thing is that it's always been Dick Fosbury that has dealt with my cases up till now. I was hoping it might be him again, although I suppose Suffolk is a bit off his normal beat. I've had a friendly word with Addinson to offer my services but he isn't at all keen to share information in the way that Dick is prepared to. It seems I'm a suspect first and a potential resource a distant second. You've had dealings with him before, haven't you? I thought you might have worked out the best way of doing business with him. I need to get him to trust me if we're going to get this straightened out. Any thoughts on how it might be done?'

I looked him up and down. He seemed perfectly sincere in what he said but he couldn't really believe deep down he was Tom Travis, could he? Perhaps Jerry was right and Rufus had been unhinged by recent events. Was there some sort of medical condition in which people actually believed they had become someone else?

I wondered how he would react if I told him that Dick Fosbury wasn't a real person. Fosbury was a fictional Met. Detective Inspector whose main purpose in the novels was to feed forensic evidence to Tom that he would not otherwise have access to. Crime fiction abounds with such unlikely relationships between police inspectors and amateur detectives. I had thought of rounding out Dick a bit by making him divorced, or hard drinking, but steady and efficient was all he needed to be.

'There is something else,' Rufus said, as I struggled to find anything to say about how to handle Addinson. 'There's a rumour that you found Kenneth Preston's body.'

'Not just me,' I said, 'there were four of us. It was in a secret room that's been built here,' I said. 'You know the passage leading to the studio...'

I don't know why I let the words spill out of me. Perhaps I had more faith in amateur detectives than the police. At least he listened intently. But when I had finished speaking he didn't come up with any great conclusion, although he seemed to be weighing up the options.

'Kenneth's death doesn't make a great deal of sense unless, well, I suppose that could be it, or maybe not...' was his most detailed pronouncement.

It wasn't the definitive diagnosis I was hoping for but I was prevented from pushing him to any conclusion when he declared he had to go.

'So what was all that about?' Jerry said from behind me, once Rufus had left. 'You seem to have frightened our detective away. What were you talking about? I only got the end of the conversation.'

'I'm not entirely sure I know. He asked me about finding Kenneth's body. I thought it best to tell him. Then he burbled on about things either making sense or not which was logical but not illuminating. I was hoping to press him on what he thought when he decided to leave. I'm not sure quite what to make of it.'

'Bear in mind he could be the murderer,' Jerry said bleakly. 'I wouldn't get too close to him. Being hand in glove with someone who appears to think he's your detective will simply feed Addinson's fantasies, particularly as your last significant act with Tom was to give him murderous tendencies. But he must have said something else, surely?'

'He was worried he wasn't getting the same access to forensic intelligence from Addinson that he's used to. If you remember, Tom has a friendly police contact in Dick Fosbury.'

'Oh him,' Jerry said dismissively. 'He's hardly here or there is he? I don't know why you didn't make him a bit more interesting. You could have given him a drug habit for starters.

Then he would have been much more rounded and vulnerable. In fact he could have been an extra suspect in Tom's cases if his habit was bad enough and he needed to keep it hidden. Any number of murderers could have blackmailed him.'

'That's hardly for here and now Jerry. The reason I was talking to Rufus was that I thought he might be able to provide some insight into the key questions we're facing.'

'Which are?'

'Who was Emma Hale expecting when I went into her room and who was she going to see on the night of Kenneth and Miriam's deaths? Then...'

'Just a minute,' Jerry said. 'I agree it would be good to have an answer as to what is motivating Emma or what we should believe of the tabloid rumours that Matthew Tabard is experiencing, but that's not what we need to know, is it? What we need to know is what we don't know. I mean, for all we know, the key to this whole matter might be that Molly Whyard had had a fling with Matthew Tabard or something like that. The point is that it is all to be uncovered.'

I might have added that the other question I wanted answered was how Jerry had become so knowledgeable. His display of learning on any topic raised was beginning to get to me. I could accept his engineering expertise and his fruitful relationship with gadgets of all kinds, but he must have had a lot of time on his hands to become an expert on poisons and the etymology of Suffolk surnames.

'There was one thing that Rufus asked,' I said. 'Miriam Preston told him you gave her a briefing on world poisons and where to find them.'

'Only because you asked me to.'

'Did I? I don't know anything about poisons.'

'There's a poisoning in *Killing Spree*. You must know something about them. Tom Travis is a bit of an authority on them isn't he?'

'He may be, but I'm not.'

'You should be. You're misleading the public by posing as an expert.'

I was about to argue the point when a young policeman came into the room and cheerfully requested Jerry's finger-prints. For a moment I thought he was going to refuse to give them but, after a moment's reflection, he announced that he was more than happy to be the first to clear his name.

I looked round the library. An open fire blazed cheerfully in the fireplace in front of me. Out of the corner of my eye I could see that Florence Hammond was searching for something on the shelves at the far end of the room. I walked across to her.

'You're not looking for a Tom Travis book are you?' I said.

'Oh no,' she said. 'It's Sir Harry's book on modern etiquette. He mentioned it to me last night and I promised I would look for it. I thought it might have been put back in the shelves out of order, but I can't see it.'

'Then I should give up,' I said. 'Let me order us some coffee. If you'd care to join me we could sit by the fire.'

'I enjoyed the Tom Travis book I read,' she said nervously before sitting down.

'I'm glad to hear it,' I said. I saw that she was giving me an appraising look, the sort of look that one gives someone who discovers dead bodies.

'Kenneth's and Miriam's deaths,' I said. 'A bad business.'

'Oh yes,' she said, 'very sad. Nick is terribly cut up about it. He must have worked on lots of films with Kenneth but this was going to be their first crime film together.'

'Kenneth seemed very keen on classical crime,' I said.

'So Nick said. But it wasn't just Kenneth. Miriam was interested as well, and so was Nick. It was a new departure for all of them. They were pleased to have you and Mr Davis here to guide them on all those exotic methods of killing. Nick told me that Mr Davis thought there had been a poison garden here.'

'A poison garden?'

'They were quite common according to Mr Davis. There was one here in Jacobean times. William Graves and his wife are thinking of re-creating it. Miriam said Mr Davis knows all about them. The one here wasn't very big but it did have dozens of toxic plants.'

'Really?' I said.

'Yes,' Florence Hammond said with growing enthusiasm. 'Mr Davis thought it was probably over in the far bit of the garden where the wall has been partly demolished.'

I was scarcely listening. I found I couldn't get the image of Kenneth slumped across the table in the secret room out of my head. Florence was talking again but my mind was filled with a picture of a body next to a bottle of Glengowrie. Then it all began to make sense. It wasn't a heart attack that had killed Kenneth Preston. It was poison. The poison had been in the whisky. That was why they were fingerprinting Jerry. But they wouldn't find Jerry's fingerprints on the bottle – they would find mine.

21

OVERCRANKING

'I CAN'T LEAVE?' I said. 'Why?'

'It's not just you,' Nick Wallace said soothingly. 'It's everyone who was here last night. It's an edict of the Superintendent. It shouldn't be too bad. Everybody is contracted to be here in any event and I'm sure it won't be more than a few days. And if you want to leave Langham for a meal or something there's nothing to stop you. Simply tell Addinson or any of the policemen here that you're leaving the grounds.'

'So is there anything to do on *Murder Unseen*?'

'Harry Leung told me that Kenneth wasn't the only director they had in mind, so I think we need to wait and see what happens. I'd expect some movement in the next couple of days when the shock of what's happened dies down. But that's not the main thing I had to tell you. Addinson wants to see you. He's set up an incident room.'

'Has he?'

'Yes.'

'So when does he want to see me?'

'Now would be good.'

The incident room turned out to be the estate manager's office. Addinson had installed himself behind an old wooden desk with a red leather top. He waved me towards a seat in front of the desk, an upright wooden chair. There was a newspaper in front of him that he pushed in my direction. Do you recognise this?'

'It's a crossword.'

'And you were trying to complete it?'

'I'm sorry, I don't quite see the relevance.'

'Crosswords can give interesting insights – particularly the clues you've completed. The way that people fill them in can provide a snapshot of their concerns. The clues that relate to the issues at the top of their mind are likely to be those that you complete first.'

'If you say so.'

'And the other helpful thing is that it's been completed in pencil. As the pencil has got blunter the strokes you've used have got thicker. So, helpfully enough, you've pretty much provided an order in which the clues were completed, even if you yourself can't remember. As far as I can see you've started with Mr Weissmuller.'

'He's one across. Everybody does one across if they can, don't they?'

'Tarzan is a representative of male authority. A beguiling figure if you believe in physical force as a way of solving your problems. He provides a starting point for action.'

'If you say so.'

'Towards the end of the clues you've completed you seem to have ended up with a Mr Manson. A repellent individual in real life, as I'm sure you agree. As far as I remember he believed the apocalypse was coming and that somehow justified his actions, murderous as they were. But you seem to have your own doubts about him; the "a" on Manson is almost rubbed through. Perhaps your subconscious was rebelling against your conscious mind.'

'It's a far more prosaic than that. There was a difficulty with another clue I'd filled in. I thought it was "fog horn" but it turned out to be "car horn". I had to pencil over one letter with another.'

'So you were in two minds, sir?'

'Not at all. I made a mistake and I corrected it.'

'And the last two words you added, where the pencil lines are at their thickest because the pencil is getting blunt, are "bodkin" and "assegai". They're both weapons aren't they? So you realised that the alarm you were considering wasn't a fog horn but a car horn, put in Charles Manson's name, and then added two stabbing weapons. Might that not suggest you had decided on a course of action and were visualising the weapons you could use?'

'That's fanciful in the extreme,' I said. 'And that bird didn't stab Miriam Preston. It bludgeoned her to death. You can't have it both ways. Besides, I was just adding answers that Jerry had provided.'

'Mr Davis?' Addinson said. 'I hadn't realised he was present.'

'He wasn't. At least, he wasn't until the later answers were being filled in. He suggested the *assegai* and *bodkin* answers. I just wrote them down.'

'So I should also be questioning Mr Davis about this?'

'You shouldn't be questioning anybody. The whole thing is absurd.'

Addinson contemplated the ceiling before he spoke again.

'You may be right. I can't see any jury convicting you on the basis of the way in which you've compiled a general knowledge crossword. Besides, I'm sure any defence counsel would make a great deal of the fact that you are a crime writer and weapons of murder are always somewhere close to the top of your mind. No, I can't see that anything would stand up in court. But it does build up the picture.'

'Of what?'

'Of your thought processes and behaviour patterns. I like to think of them as the thread between imagination and reality. It's useful background.'

'Is it?'

'I think so.'

'There's another thing you could help me on. I understand that you and Mr Davis might have handled the mechanical bird in the studio.'

'Florence Hammond asked us to put it back up after the accident with Kenneth Preston. Nick Wallace didn't want it on the ground. And I was experimenting with Kenneth and Miriam Preston earlier.'

'Experimenting? In what way?'

'Kenneth wanted to use it as a murder weapon in *Murder Unseen*. He asked me to work out how it could stab someone.'

'Quite, sir, but of course in the end, as you've just pointed out, it was used as a flying bludgeon, not dissimilar to an incident in one of your books.'

Addinson was subjecting me to a teasing smile, as though we were participants in some complicated game in which the rules were uncertain.

'I don't deny it,' I said, in the most reasonable tone I could muster. 'But as you will be aware, there are a number of murder methods described in my books. In fact, there are at least two in each. So you would expect me to have described at least eight murder methods in the four books and, of course, there were more in *Killing Spree*. So it's probably not a surprise that there are some similarities between the murders I devise and events in real life. I'm sorry that Miriam Preston has been killed, I really am. But are you suggesting she was murdered?'

'I'm not suggesting anything one way or the other. But let's move on to Kenneth and the secret room. You say that you had already been in the room before the internal bolt had been drawn across. So one would expect to find traces of your DNA and fingerprints.'

'And fibres from clothing. It's Lockard's exchange principle.'

'*The perpetrator of a crime will bring something into the crime scene and leave with something from it, and that both can be used as forensic evidence,*' Addinson intoned.

'Precisely.'

'Except that of course both you and Mr Davis have been in the secret room and handled the bird, so that any fingerprints, say, of yours that might be found in either location would have a ready explanation of how they came to be there.'

'And?'

'I'm told you also have rather a poor sense of direction.'

'I'm sorry, I don't see the relevance…'

'Miss Hale told me that you blundered into her room the first night you were here.'

'I mistook her room for Heisenberg. It's easily done.'

'Is it, sir?'

'Absolutely. Have you seen the room map they give you? It's difficult to understand, or at least it was for me. I mistook which was north.'

'So you went into a number of rooms that were not Heisenberg?'

'I must have done.'

'So can you tell me which rooms you haven't been in?'

'None of the rooms on the third floor,' I said. 'And I'm sure there must be others but I'm not sure I could be entirely accurate about which they were. It was a new house, it was gloomy, I've not got a good visual memory.'

'Indeed, sir.' Addinson looked as though he had some difficulty in judging whether he should believe me.

'Having difficulty in recalling precisely where you have been in new surroundings is hardly a crime.'

'Indeed not, but you do see the difficult position this puts me in don't you? As a crime writer I'm sure you will understand.'

'Understand what?'

'In many cases, forensics are the bedrock of any investigation. They help to tease out the truth. Of course it's more a plot for one of your novels but supposing the perpetrator of a crime decided to put counter-measures in place? Supposing he decides to leave a fine spray of fingerprints, DNA and clothing fragments over any area in which a crime might be committed?'

'Such a strategy would be too open to chance events, surely? Suppose Emma Hale had locked her door.'

'Emma Hale? I think you've got me wrong, sir. What I was saying was simply speculative, not linked to what has happened at Langham. Background.'

Addinson managed to keep a straight face and for a moment I wanted to believe him.

'If we're talking about background,' I said, 'I'd like to ask you a question.'

'If you wish to.' Addinson seemed unduly relaxed for a policeman with two dead bodies on his hands.

'Molly Whyard was unpacking some novels by Friedrich Dürrenmatt. She said they were for you.'

'Indeed they are. I had hoped they would provide some diverting reading for my time here. But that plan has been rather shattered by events.' Addinson made an expansive gesture that seemed to dismiss the deaths of Kenneth and his wife as hideous distractions from something more interesting. 'Did you have any particular reason for asking?'

'Nothing in particular, I just wondered why you might be interested...'

'To tell you the truth, I was alerted to Mr Dürrenmatt's work by one of your own pieces in your *Musings on Crime* series. I must say I have found those essays of enormous interest. You should really think of putting them out in book form and not just as electronic pieces. Personally I print them out and put them in a folder. Old-fashioned I suppose, but I do like to have a physical copy of anything like that. It gives it due substance...'

Addinson's voice had transformed itself into that of an academic giving a lecture, rather that a policeman with two suspicious deaths to deal with.

'...I was particularly taken with his novel *The Pledge* which I am looking forward to reading again...'

In which the killer's accidental death prevents the zealous detective Matthäi from even proving that such a person exists, precipitating his own mental disintegration.

'...of course, as you pointed out, *The Pledge* is also subtitled *Requiem for the Detective Novel*, and I was pleased to see that it had been included in the paperback version I was sent. Some editions don't include it anymore...'

Dürrenmatt had been a critic of the neat solution of murders in detective fiction. In his view the detective is not disentangling some mathematical puzzle and chance had much more of a role to play.

'...the more traditional a detective is, the more rational and dogged in their pursuit of truth, the less able they are to cope with the real messiness and randomness of life...'

Tom Travis had never been asked to cope with anything other than the most complex problems. Perhaps he wouldn't be able to cope with anything more haphazard. But why was Addinson talking like he was addressing a seminar on crime fiction?

'There is one thing I should tell you,' I said abruptly, 'before we go any further. There will be fingerprints and fibres and DNA and all that sort of stuff, traces of me if you like, not only in the places you mentioned but in a number of other locations.'

'Really? Where for example?'

'The bathroom and bedroom in the Chinese Suite. I was in there yesterday morning. I'd been speaking to Molly Whyard and she said she had a string of messages for Kenneth but she couldn't get hold of him. I said I would go and investigate and when I got there the door was open so I went in.'

'And?'

'The bedroom door was open. The bathroom door was open as well.'

'Was the light on?'

'No, no, I don't think so. I think I may have switched it on. I was interested in what I would find.'

'And why was that, sir?'

'It's a writing thing. I found I couldn't help myself. I mean, for the most part you have to make things up but

176

sometimes you just want to describe what's there. It's a tendency I try to curb but I'm not always too successful in doing so. I have this unfortunate habit of, what shall we say, rootling through things.'

'Rootling through things?'

'Yes. I'm afraid so. I picked up a number of things. I can't remember them all. But there was definitely a pot of face cream, a phial of perfume that looked expensive and some white pills in a plastic container.'

'Like these?'

Addinson was producing something from a drawer in the desk. The pills and their container were now in an evidence bag.

'That looks like them.'

'I see.' Addinson paused for a moment and then reluctantly put the pills back in the desk drawer. I had the feeling that I had ruined the big moment he had been leading up to.

'So,' he said. 'What else do you need to tell me?'

'I can't think of anything,' I said.

It didn't sound convincing.

22

ABOVE THE LINE

'YOU'RE LOOKING THOUGHTFUL,' Jerry said.

'I've just been talking to Addinson.'

'So what's going on? None of us are allowed to leave.'

'I get the feeling that if he thinks that there is something going on, I'm his prime suspect. We fenced around the subject without coming to any conclusion. Then we talked about crime fiction.'

'I'm surprised he had the time. But it makes sense in a way.'

'Why?'

'Addinson thinks you're some sort of criminal prankster, doesn't he? And he is a fan of the Tom Travis novels.'

'I've got lots of fans. There's a woman in Eastbourne who always writes to me the week following publication. She's very appreciative.'

'She may be but think about it. What are you known for? What did that review say? "*For the lover of ingenious plots and good-natured old fashioned murder.*" And what have we got here? An impossible murder and a locked-room mystery. You're bound to be in the frame.'

'It may have passed your notice,' I said, 'that murderers in Tom Travis books tend to have motive as well as opportunity and expertise.'

'I've been thinking about that,' Jerry said, 'and, as I said, if anyone had motivation, it was you. To the outside world you and Miriam were getting close. You kill Kenneth out of jealousy and Miriam because you don't want Kate to learn of the affair that has been going on. The renewal of wedding vows that Kenneth organised was a desperate attempt to win back Miriam's affections. He suspected that Miriam had taken a lover. Not that one could blame her if she had done so, given his own reputation for dalliance. Nick Wallace told me all about his inclinations. So there's your motive, or at least the start of one. Added to that there are echoes of your books wherever one looks. Addinson isn't going to miss them.'

'He hasn't. Maybe he was just trying to humour me by talking about crime fiction, but the whole thing is ludicrous. It hasn't been confirmed that anybody has been murdered yet but I seem to be facing thirty years in jail.'

'You could enter a plea of diminished responsibility,' Jerry said. 'You could say you were trying out a plot idea that went wrong. Addinson might go for it.'

'You're being absurd,' I said.

'I don't know about that.'

Quite where the conversation would have gone after that I was never to know because yet another police constable I had not seen before said that the Superintendent was eager to ask me some further questions.

'Delighted,' I lied. 'The sooner all this is sorted out the better.'

Addinson was still seated behind the desk, but this time a police constable was lurking in the shadows behind him. It looked as though he was there to create a sense of intimidation. It was effective enough. There was a sheet of notepaper in a clear plastic folder covered in writing in a neat but small hand. Addinson pointed to them.

'This purports to be a confession Kenneth Preston made,' he said.

'What?'

Addinson repeated the sentence. I hadn't misheard.

'But you think it's a forgery?'

'Why do you say that?'

'You said, "purport".'

'Did I? Oh yes, I did. A good deduction sir, although I suspect most people would pick up on the word *confession* first.'

'Nobody says *purport* and doesn't expect to be taken up on it. So what is all this about?'

Addinson eased back in his chair and looked at me.

'This confession is a forgery. How do I know? The handwriting? No. In fact, as far as my experts can determine the matter, Kenneth could certainly have written this.'

'So what is this a confession to?' I said.

'Didn't I say? No, no, you're right. I didn't say and, of course, there's no reason why you should know.' Addinson paused, his voice full of irony. 'It's Kenneth's confession to murdering his wife. And, as I was saying, as far as the handwriting analysis goes it's a genuine document. But he didn't write it. There are no fingerprints on the paper for example. Why would that be? Why is there no visible link between Kenneth writing the paper and the piece of paper itself? If you want to write a remorse-ridden confession, why go out of your way to ensure there's no way of physically tracing it back to you? Again, that makes no sense at all. But luckily there's another way into the problem. Kenneth was always making notes – about a scene in a film, snippets for his autobiography, instructions to his actors, his interest in classical crime, the financing of his Graham Greene film, anything and everything. Many of them are lengthy. The analysts are looking at them in more detail as we speak but they've come to an initial conclusion about this confession. The language isn't right. This note sounds superficially like Kenneth but it uses words he never used elsewhere in his writings and the words he was prone to use don't appear as regularly as they should. No one changes their style like that, whatever pressures they are under.'

Addinson leaned back to let his words sink in. I didn't know what was coming next but it didn't seem to be something I would welcome.

'So,' Addinson said in a confidential tone. 'Brilliant, really quite brilliant. How did you do it?'

'Do what?'

'Imitate Kenneth's handwriting so perfectly. In fact, as I said, if we didn't know that Kenneth hadn't written the note, the experts would have concluded, beyond reasonable doubt, that he had.'

'If that's what the handwriting people say, maybe he did. And if he was writing in gloves, so be it. It may not be normal but it's not impossible. It's perfectly straightforward for him to do that. Much easier for him than it would be for me.'

'So you admit you could have done it?'

'If Kenneth didn't do it, anyone with the proper skills could. But this whole thing is absurd. You don't have a shred of evidence for your suppositions. Your handwriting people tell you Kenneth Preston is the most likely author of his own note. He could have worn gloves. There's nothing to suggest it was anybody other than him.'

'Oh but there is,' Addinson said. 'As I said, it doesn't match up with his normal use of language. We're talking about stylometry. Wincenty Lutoslawski 1890. His *Principes de Stylometrie* was the foundation of a whole new branch of science. It has taken us more than a hundred years, but it's becoming an essential part of our diagnostic kit. And, of course, the march of technology and the computing power that has become available over the last ten years makes it a more effective technique these days. I'm sure you will have come across it in your researches. Tom Travis always likes to keep up with developments, doesn't he?'

'I'm sorry,' I said, 'I really don't know what you are talking about.'

'If you say so, sir,' Addinson didn't sound convinced. 'But indulge me for a moment. Stylometry is an area where my forensic colleagues are only beginning to develop the necessary depth of expertise that will convince a court of law. There is one advantage to that, however. Investigation methods are much more effective when those who commit crime have no prior knowledge of them. Those who plan to flout the law, by committing murder for example, can counter most of our techniques. They might decide, for example, to provide themselves with a series of actions that would account for any *forensic* traces that might be found.'

Addinson looked me up and down.

'I've explained. I haven't got a good sense of direction. I couldn't find my room when I arrived, and the room I thought was mine turned out not to be. To be frank, I also drank too much on an empty stomach. And I've told you I went into the bathroom in the Chinese Suite. Perhaps I shouldn't have done, but I did. Perhaps I shouldn't have handled Kenneth's bottle of Glengowrie either, but I did.'

'You handled the bottle of Glengowrie?'

'Miriam Preston showed it to me. It was a present for Kenneth.'

'So you picked it up?'

'Yes.'

Addinson nodded.

'I'll bear that in mind, sir, but as I was saying, it's more difficult for any criminal to take countermeasures against techniques he has no knowledge of. Which gets us back to stylometry. It's a technique for determining who might be the author of a particular text. Did Shakespeare write all his plays or are many of them collaborations with Marlowe and Fletcher? As a technique it used to be based around the use of particular words that appear only, for example, in works that Marlowe is known to have written. But the science has moved on since then and we're now able to look at the structure of language individual writers use. Of course it helps if there are substantial bodies of known text to compare. And when it comes to you and Kenneth Preston, that is very much the case. I'm sure you will be aware of his seminal work, *On Directing*, and his other writings. It's a rich pool to dip into.'

'Is it?'

'Very much so. It turns out there are all sorts of anomalies in the confession document. Your use of adverbs for instance.'

'*My* use?'

'I'm so sorry sir. I meant to say *the* use of adverbs. But the point is that the word patterns in this note,' Addinson tapped the sheet in the plastic folder for emphasis, 'aren't like the word patterns in the Tom Travis novels.'

'There you are then.'

'The note has more of a feel of the immediate and day-to-day, certainly not the polish of your fiction. But there the good news ends. There are strong similarities with your other writing style, the one you employ on your blog. In fact, it seems the style is pretty much identical.'

'Between the confession and my blog?'

'Exactly. There may be no structural connection between this note and your Tom Travis writings. But with the blog there's a match.'

'Is there?'

'Yes.'

'But that doesn't make sense does it? Why would Kenneth write in a style he never uses, wearing rubber gloves so there are no fingerprints on the paper?'

'There's an obvious explanation. He didn't write it. Somebody else did. You, Mr Knight.'

'That's absurd. Anyway, what's happened to Kenneth? He's dead in a locked room in which he has bolted the door from the inside. How do you explain that?'

'I was hoping you would help me there. You are an expert on locked-room mysteries, although I imagine you would say you have the appearance of an expert but, when it comes to the practicalities, you look to Mr Davis. And I freely admit he is an impressive resource. He was, after all, able to get us into the locked room without difficulty.'

'Look,' I said, 'is there any evidence that foul play is involved in Kenneth's death? I mean, couldn't what happened to Miriam simply be some sort of terrible accident? Kenneth retreats to the secret room, tries to shut out the world, and has a cardiac arrest or something. Isn't that what happened?'

'Hardly, sir. We'll get the full autopsy report in a few hours, but it seems that Kenneth Preston was poisoned.'

23

REDLIGHT

'POISONED?'

'Cyanide. It interferes with the red blood cells' abilities to extract oxygen from the air. Kenneth Preston suffocated to death as he breathed in oxygen in the air he couldn't use. But you probably know that, or Mr Davis does.'

'Jerry?'

'My understanding is that he advised Miriam Preston on how long the poison took to work. And the answer he provided was that once it had been swallowed, the effects were pretty instantaneous. Unconsciousness and death within fifteen minutes.'

'So how do you know all this?'

'A bitter almond odour can be detected with this form of poisoning. The Home Office pathologist I called in luckily has an acute sense of smell.'

'No, I don't mean that. I mean how do you know Jerry, Mr Davis, told Miriam Preston that?'

'Miriam Preston also kept a diary. It seems to have been something of a family habit, particularly in recent months.

She certainly wanted to capture her thoughts on her and her husband's renewal of their wedding vows. But she also covered a number of other events, including her conversations with Mr Davis about poison. And she seems to have also developed a keen interest in you. There are a number of paragraphs concerning aspects of your life – your charm, your wife and children, and your writing. They're all covered at some length. She seems rather in awe of you. And she seems to have been struck by the thought that the marriage that she and her husband were renewing, hadn't really delivered. For many couples, the last positive action they take together is deciding to get married. They think that's what will solve any difficulty between them. But the marriage simply forces them to face up to reality. Maybe the renewal of wedding vows that Kenneth has organised doesn't pull them together but forces them apart. Miriam Preston is still a young woman. She became an heiress when her father and her brother were killed in the plane accident. Her brother left no family. She finally has the family money she had never expected and is free to do anything she likes. Sir Harry also tells me Kenneth Preston has got something of a reputation when it comes to young women. But let's not make this too one-sided. Kenneth reveals in his diary that he thought Miriam might be finding, what shall we say, companionship, elsewhere? But I imagine you know nothing about that, sir?'

'So you suspect that I might be this companion?'

'There have been a number of sightings of you and Miriam Preston together, apparently enjoying an intimate conversation. But perhaps that's because the fact she had already strayed had given her a taste for a different life? But then perhaps you knew each other before you got here?

Who knows? But this is all conjecture. So we need to return to hard facts. There is something you could explain to me. Kenneth Preston was poisoned by cyanide. The cyanide was in a bottle of Glengowrie 1965. There were two sets of fingerprints on the bottle – Kenneth Preston's and yours.'

'I told you. That's easily explained. I admit I handled the bottle.'

'So let's just run through that again.'

Addinson drew himself up an inch or two and the police constable behind him leant forward expectantly, as though equipped with a ticket for the front row of the stalls. I looked at the ceiling.

'You picked up the bottle with her from the outside reception point on Sunday at 3.38. One of the people from the local village they employ here – Sarah Farquhar – was manning the office in the reception area. The Glengowrie was in a cardboard box that Miriam Preston signed for. For the delivery of valuable items it's office procedure to keep a record of delivery and pick up times. Sarah Farquhar noted down the time it was picked up – 3.38 – but the clock in the reception office is a couple of minutes fast hence the more accurate time is 3.36.'

He flipped the notebook shut.

'She might have misread the clock,' I said. 'It's digital as far as I remember. It's easy to transpose figures, particularly a six and an eight. It could have been 3.36 which would make the time the parcel was picked up 3.34.'

'She recorded the time contemporaneously.'

'That doesn't stop her making a mistake.'

'If this was some sort of fictional murder mystery,' Addinson said pointedly, 'the timing could be important. And open to all sorts of manipulation by the cunning writer. The broken alarm clock lying on the ground but with the murderer changing the timing of the hands once the clock has been smashed. I'm sure your friend Mr Davis could manipulate a digital clock as well. But you don't contest the facts Mr Knight, do you? You'd been talking to Mr Preston in the gym in the new buildings. You'd come out from the gym and accepted a cigarette from Mrs Preston, although I believe you claim to be a non-smoker.'

'I don't normally,' I said wondering quite how Addinson knew so much about what had happened.

'The point at issue,' Addinson continued, 'is not the precise timing that Miriam Preston picked up the bottle of Glengowrie, which was intended as a present for her husband, but that she did, and that the bottle then, or at some subsequent moment, was laced with cyanide, and that the only other fingerprints on the bottle, besides those of Mr Preston, were yours. But you were about to explain how your fingerprints came to be on the bottle. You said Miriam Preston showed you it. When was that?'

I had a mental picture of Kenneth Preston in the secret room slumped over the green table with the bottle of Glengowrie on it and a tumbler to hand. Why had he bolted the door from the inside? Why had he poured himself a whisky? Why had he drunk it?

'I'm sorry, what was the question?'

'When did Miriam Preston show you the bottle? When were your fingerprints deposited on the bottle itself? It was heavily packaged when I'm told you both picked it up from the estate office.'

'Monday evening. '

'And how did that come about?'

'I had been talking to Kenneth in the Prestons' suite.'

'What about, sir?

I hesitated.

'Locked-room mysteries.' I said. For a split second I had thought of making something up but I couldn't think of anything plausible. Besides, for all I knew, Kenneth might have told Nick Wallace what he wanted to talk to me about, or recorded the fact in a diary.

'On which you are an expert,' Addinson said.

'There's an exegesis in one of the Tom Travis books.'

'Indeed there is, sir. And a very interesting exposition, if I may say so. So you were talking to Kenneth about locked-room mysteries. How did Miriam Preston get into the picture?'

'I bumped into her as I was leaving. Kenneth had asked me to put together some more ideas.'

'On what?'

'The bird of prey in the studio. How it might be used as a murder weapon.'

'So you bumped into Miriam Preston as you were leaving?'

'She was coming out of the bedroom. I don't think she had been awake for too long. She asked me whether I had been seeing Kenneth and I said that he had given me a few hours to come up with some new ideas. She was reassuring about the demands Kenneth makes on people. She said if he had a problem he couldn't deal with he made it someone else's responsibility.'

Addinson noted something down in a notebook on the table in front of him.

'So what happened next?'

'She asked me into the bedroom to look at a present she had for Kenneth – the Glengowrie. She told me to hold it up to the light and look at the colour. She might have been nervous he wouldn't like it.'

'That's unlikely isn't it? My understanding is that Kenneth Preston was very fond of a drink.'

'I think she was nervous that he wouldn't think it value for money, or frivolous.'

'Really? Anyway, for whatever reason, she handed the bottle to you, did she?'

'She was cradling it in a silk scarf. I picked it out of that. She must have been using the scarf for something. She might have been polishing it.'

'So that would explain why her fingerprints are not on the bottle?'

'I imagine so.'

'And you didn't hand the bottle back to her?'

'I put it back in the silk scarf she was holding.'

'So what did you say to each other?'

'I said it was a good present and that Kenneth was a lucky man.'

'Nothing more?'

'Not that I remember.'

'And this all took place in the bedroom while Kenneth Preston was in the room at the end of the suite?'

'The door was closed. He was doing his business calls. Apparently he had half a dozen to make. He lets a few build up and then deals with them in the evening before he eats. It's a daily routine that he has.'

'So there wasn't any danger of you being interrupted?'

'Miriam didn't seem to think so.'

'And you didn't think it might be embarrassing if Kenneth Preston had found the two of you together?'

'I was curious to see why she wanted me to go into the room.'

'Would you describe your relationship as flirtatious?'

'It was nothing serious. As a writer I spend a lot of my life in front of a computer screen imagining characters interacting. It was an opportunity to be part of such a scene. I thought Miriam Preston would be a good basis for a character in one of the Tom Travis books. I don't deny she was an attractive woman but there was no more to it than that. I did accept a cigarette when she offered me one outside but we talked about my wife and sons. Anyway, who told you about our meeting?'

'Mr Davis.'

'Jerry?'

'Yes. But there is one other matter I meant to ask you about. I wonder if you remember this?'

Addinson slid a photograph across the table. In it David Knight and a similarly cheerful Harry Leung beamed cheerfully at the camera. The surroundings looked familiar. They were. It was the College. I was one of the alumni they had managed to round up who was not a Nobel Prize winner or Lord Chief Justice. Leung would have been there as an expert on the film industry. If I had connected Leung with the College I would have remembered.

'Sir Harry told me when you came across each other at Langham that he was convinced that you had met before, but you denied it.'

'I remember now,' I said as Addinson looked unbelievingly on. 'I think the second Tom Travis was about to be published. The first one had been a minor success and I'd been invited back to the College for a careers conference. There was a celebratory banquet in hall and my agent thought it would generate a few sales. I can't think why I didn't remember, it's amazing what one can forget, although Leung couldn't remember the circumstances in which we had met either, could he?'

'At least he could remember you had met.'

'But not when and where.'

'So, let me get this straight. You have a bad sense of direction which means that you blunder into a number of rooms you can't remember and leave fingerprints, fibres from your clothing, and DNA traces round them all? Miriam Preston asked you to hold the bottle of Glengowrie which explains why your fingerprints are on it? You decided on a whim to go into the Prestons' bathroom and handle their belongings? Kenneth Preston's suicide note is written in a style you use on your blogs, and you can now remember that you have met Harry Leung?'

It didn't sound terribly good put like that. If he suspected anyone of murdering either Kenneth or Miriam Preston, or both of them, it was me. And if he was doubtful about motivation he could always consult Jerry for reassurance. Add to that the fact that Kenneth had been found in a locked-room situation, a crime fiction area in which Addinson regarded me as an authority; fingerprints on a whisky bottle that contained poison; methods of murder that had strong resemblances to those in the Tom Travis books; stylometry; and my general habit of leaving traces of myself everywhere. All in all the evidence against me was reaching saturation point.

In addition, he had read far too much crime fiction for a policeman. He was perfectly capable of creating his own fantastic motives for my actions. He had probably convinced himself that I was engaged in some bizarre game with Justice.

Somehow I would contrive a plethora of evidence against myself but none of it would be sufficient to convict me.

Addinson was tapping the table in front of him with a pen. The police constable behind him was looking expectant. Addinson was speaking again, a blur of words that I had difficulty in following.

'Is that it? I said.

'Not quite,' Addinson said. 'There is one other thing. Miriam Preston's fingerprints. How is it that they come to be in your room? Not to mention traces of her DNA.'

'In Heisenberg?'

'Yes.'

'But they can't be.'

Addinson was saying something else but I was hardly listening.

'...have to say anything. But it may harm your defence if you do not mention when questioned... anything you do say...'

I could see the police constable moving forward. Addinson was looking at me with something like triumph caressing his features.

'...arresting you on suspicion of the murders of Kenneth and Miriam Preston... Cuff him, Constable!'

24

SUBPLOT

THE HANDCUFFS WERE CUTTING into my wrists, leaving patches of inflamed red skin. A strong hand was propelling me to my feet. Most of my body was imploding as though there was a small black hole near my heart sucking my vital organs into it.

'Just wait in here.'

The room had no windows. Addinson probably had a specialist team of carpenters on tap, in addition to his stylometry experts. Police resources in the universe I normally inhabited were scarce or not available. Here it seemed temporary cells could be constructed in minutes. A long fluorescent light bulb suspended overhead struggled into life, emitting a faint burring sound. The room met every definition of sparsely furnished. It had a rudimentary table and a wooden bench. I sat on the bench and closed my eyes.

I was trying to find some way of massaging my left wrist – physical pain is always a good antidote to mental introspection – when the door opened and another figure was pushed inside; Jerry. There was something strange about him.

He wasn't moving properly. Then I recognized what it was. He was handcuffed as well. He was pushed down onto the bench next to me by the policeman who had been standing behind Addinson. For a moment we looked at each other and then at the policeman, who left.

'What the hell is going on?' Jerry said.

'I wish I knew.'

'I've just been arrested as an accessory to murder.'

'Kenneth and Miriam Preston?'

'Has anybody else died?' Jerry said witheringly.

'It's not my fault you've been arrested.'

'Isn't it? Everything you do fuels Addinson's suspicions. I'm not sure how Faith is going to take this. I don't think any of her family have ever been arrested.'

'Kate's cousin was.'

'What?'

'Kate's cousin. He was arrested for burning down the school pavilion. Claimed it was a political action. He's something in the City now, a loss adjuster I think.'

'You seem to think this is some sort of game,' Jerry said. 'I can't think what Faith is going to say.'

'You haven't exactly been dampening down Addinson's wider suspicions have you? Why did you tell him about that cigarette Miriam gave me?'

'He asked me. What was I meant to say? There could have been someone else who saw you, and saw me seeing you. There probably was. He could have got the story from multiple sources.'

'He told me you'd told him.'

'Of course he would. Can't you see he's trying to drive a wedge between us?'

'Well, he seems to have succeeded. What was all that stuff you were going on about? Wiring and secret rooms? It was virtually an essay in guilt acceptance. Did you really have to appear so knowledgeable about panic buttons and health and safety regulations?'

'They were lucky I was there. There are not many mechanical engineers around the place with my expertise. Besides, I've done some consultancy on those sorts of systems. I'm pretty much an expert witness if it comes to a court case, although they won't be able to call me if it's my trial. But it's clear what happened. Kenneth Preston drew the bolt across from the inside. There's no question about it. Then he poured himself a glass of whisky. Then he drank it. Then he died. There's no possible alternative sequence of events. Nobody killed Kenneth Preston but himself.'

'Except we've just demonstrated we could have done it!'

'No we haven't. We've just demonstrated how it could be done if the wires had been connected up. But they weren't. It couldn't have been done that way because the wires hadn't been twisted together to form a circuit. Those wires had never been twisted. That would be obvious to anyone who bothered to give them a cursory inspection.'

'And the lights that failed when Kenneth had the encounter with the steak and kidney pie?'

'Anybody could have done that. It's simple. All you need is...'

'No, don't tell me,' I said. 'I'm never going to remember. Besides...'

'Besides what?' Jerry said.

'Besides, all this speculation is hopeless. The fact is that I'm innocent and so are you, that's what we should concentrate on.'

I raised my finger to my lips.

Jerry looked baffled but lapsed, with some reluctance, into silence. Five minutes later Addinson came into the room with a police constable tagging along behind him. He looked us up and down and seemed to come to a decision.

'Gentlemen, I owe you an apology. I'm afraid I got the wording of the caution wrong when arresting you – in both instances. I must offer you my sincere apologies. The consequences are that neither of the arrests is legal. In some ways you could look on it as a lucky chance. Perhaps I was a little hasty in proceeding with the arrests in the first place.'

Addinson favoured us with a beatific grin that seemed to suggest that wrongful arrest was one of the necessary hazards of a policeman's life.

'So I haven't been arrested?' Jerry said.

'No, sir. In fact I'd be obliged if you would regard the whole matter as never having happened.'

'Fine by me,' Jerry said benevolently. 'A good result.'

'That's excellent. And I would be grateful if you could take the same view Mr Knight. It would avoid embarrassment all round. It could be a mutually beneficial outcome. These sorts of matters always get misreported in the papers in my experience. If we're not careful they'll run a story not simply that you've been arrested, but that you've actually been charged with murder!'

Addinson emitted a throaty chuckle that suggested such outcomes were one of the unavoidable vagaries of the world.

'If you could remove these handcuffs I might agree with you. These things really are very uncomfortable.'

'I'm sorry to hear that sir. I must confess I've never tried them myself. Something I need to rectify. One should always try to see matters from both sides. It's important to understand the physical, as well as the psychological effect, handcuffing might have on criminals.'

'Or people like myself.'

'Or indeed people like yourself, if you want to put it that way. And why wouldn't you?' Addinson emitted another benevolent chuckle and turned to the policeman hovering behind him. 'Perhaps we could free this gentleman?'

Ten seconds later I was pointedly flexing my hands while the tall policeman was unlocking Jerry.

'Is there anything else I can do for you, Superintendent?' Jerry said as he started idly massaging his wrists.

'I don't think so, sir,' Addinson said cheerfully. 'I think we all know where we are for the moment.'

'Then we're free to go?' Jerry said.

Addinson nodded.

'So,' Jerry hissed as we walked down the corridor, 'What was that all about?'

'Not here. Let's go outside.'

'So?' Jerry said again as we crossed the drawbridge.

'Give me a moment or two. Yes, I think that's it.'

'What is?'

Addinson did make a mistake when he arrested us. But that was intentional. I was distracted when he was reading out my rights so I'm not certain what he got wrong, if indeed he got anything wrong. He's made arrests hundreds of times. There is no way he could have messed up the process – not with both of us – unless it was intentional in some way.'

'I don't get it.'

'Don't you see? You and I get arrested and thrown into a room that looks pretty much like a cell. The whole thing is done with a touch of the brutal. We were in their power. It was meant to break us down.'

'They certainly weren't that friendly when they arrested me.'

'There you are then. The shock of the whole thing is meant to unnerve us. The room was bugged. They could hear everything we said.'

'That can't be legal, can it? I mean, any evidence obtained that way would be inadmissible in a court of law, wouldn't it?'

'That wasn't the point. They thought the stress of the whole occasion would make us turn on each other and give them an insight into who had murdered Kenneth and Miriam.'

'Where they suspect you,' Jerry said.

'They don't suspect *me*,' I said. 'They suspect *us*. They think we're working together, although they haven't managed to fathom out how yet. More than that they're bound to think you're the technical expert for anything we do. That was what that was about.'

'To create pressure and hope one of us let something incriminating slip out?'

'Exactly.'

'So we've seen them off.'

'We certainly have.'

'Although,' I said a moment later, 'maybe I played that wrong. I mean, I suddenly realised the room was most likely bugged and I wanted him to know that I had. That's why I thought it was best for us to be silent. But it could be a mistake. They could have a camera in the room. Addinson doesn't exactly seem short of resources. They could have been observing us and what they might think they saw was me recovering my *sangfroid*.'

'What?'

'Composure, equilibrium, aplomb, poise – whatever you like. The point is he was hoping the shock of the arrest would lead us to be unguarded in our comments – perhaps it would have been better if we had gone on talking.'

'Why?'

'It would have been more authentic. Tom Travis always maintains that the truth is most convincing. If we'd behaved naturally we might have convinced Addinson that we hadn't got any involvement in Kenneth and Miriam's deaths. As it is, he probably thinks we knew we were being listened to all along and adjusted what we said accordingly.'

'So what about this relative of yours who was an arsonist? Why would that go down well? Anyway, how long did he get?'

'Richard? I don't think he got anything in the end. It was a conditional discharge, or something like that. He didn't go to prison. Both his parents were lawyers, which helped, but the key thing was that he owned up when his school was threatened with a group detention which impressed his headmaster who was a character witness at his trial.'

Jerry looked less than convinced.

'Anyway, I didn't mention arson, I said he burnt down the school pavilion.'

'The precise words hardly matter, do they? You're most likely right. Addinson thinks you've twigged what he was up to. The whole experience reveals to him just how resourceful you are. It would have been the perfect opportunity to break down under the pressure and behave like innocent people do when they have suffered the shock and indignity of arrest. That's why they put the handcuffs on so roughly. We should have been broken men letting slip the truth. Instead of that, the only thing you've revealed is that you have an unpunished arsonist in your family. Addinson is probably looking up the case now. In fact –'

'Just a minute,' I said. 'Let me think. Perhaps matters aren't so bad after all. Was what you said about not being able to draw back the inside bolt in the secret room unchallengeable?'

'Of course it was. If they get any sort of expert in they'll corroborate what I've said.'

'There you are then.'

'I don't see how that helps.'

'Of course it does. If that's true and if what you say about how easy it would be to fuse the lights in Kenneth's steak and kidney pie episode is true as well, anything of substance we said is true. Addinson can independently verify that.'

'What about Miriam Preston and the cigarette?'

'Did you say we were flirting?'

'I can't remember exactly what I said.' Jerry looked furtively around him.

'There was nothing in it,' I said firmly.

Jerry looked unconvinced.

'Maybe it was unfortunate. But we need to stay positive – although we're not out of the woods, we're not further into them either are we?'

'Does Tom Travis say that?'

'No. Do you think he should?'

'Not really.'

'Fair enough,' I said, 'but we need to take stock.'

'We could ask an expert,' Jerry said.

'Sorry?'

'Rufus Stone, he's the shadowy figure over there.'

'I'm not sure he's entirely in touch with reality,' I said.

Whether he was in touch with reality or not, the approaching figure seemed preoccupied.

'I was looking for Florence Hammond and Matthew Tabard,' he said. 'Have you seen them? I imagine they'll be together.'

'Sorry, no, we've just been speaking to the Superintendent.'

'Have you?' Rufus said. 'Do you think he understands what's going on? I'm not so sure he does myself. There are factors that he is ignoring.'

With a curt nod Rufus strode on into the night.

'We need to find out what he knows,' Jerry said as he disappeared into the blackness.

'Why?'

'He thinks Addinson is on the wrong track. We know he is. We need to know what he thinks and why, because we know he's more likely to be right than Addinson, who we know for a fact is wrong. We can see the direction in which this is heading.'

'Can we?' I said, but Jerry had been swallowed up by the darkness and didn't reply.

PART THREE

WEDNESDAY – THURSDAY

25

PRE-CODE

THE REST OF TUESDAY passed inconsequentially enough. Kate phoned just as Jerry and I were entering the dining room and I spent ten minutes confirming that both Kenneth and Miriam Preston were dead and concocting a series of fluffy white lies and evasions on what had happened. My own role in events was seriously downplayed. I justified my actions by telling myself that there was no point in worrying my wife unnecessarily. When I finally got to the table I found that Jerry had poured me a large glass of red wine. After that, and another glass or two, everything became indistinct and faintly comforting. It was only when I was climbing into bed that it occurred to me that Jerry had not spelt out the direction in which we were heading.

The next morning was cold and damp with the sky full of threatening clouds and a breeze intent on turning itself into a malevolent wind. Inside Langham everyone talked in whispers. Only Leung seemed to retain much of his previous vitality. We bumped into each other in the library. Leung looked round to check that we were alone. Then he seized my hand.

'My dear fellow,' he said, 'I'm so sorry it has taken me so much time to remember when we met. I was sure I recognised you but I didn't connect you with the College. I can't think why. You must be the only crime writer the College has produced in five hundred years. You should have stood out among all those professors and doctors with their Nobel Prizes and strange initials after their names and of course you do, and you did, now that I remember. But I wanted to know how you are coping with what has been going on here? I've heard that Superintendent Addinson has been giving you a hard time over...' Leung seemed to be searching for the perfect words. There probably wasn't an etiquette guide that advised the hostess or the eager reader what to do in the event of multiple corpses being discovered in their country home. '...the events here that have so shocked us all,' he finished. Then he added, with renewed vigour, 'but you know Addinson don't you? And he's an enthusiast for your work.'

'He does seem to be a Tom Travis fan.'

'But that's not what I wanted to discuss with you. To be frank, I'm not sure that Bob Addinson is the right man to be in charge of a high profile case like this. I was wondering what your view was. I could have a word with Anthea.'

Was the Home Secretary "one of us"? Had she been at the College? Surely it hadn't been co-educational in time?

'Do you know her husband, Crispin?' Leung was looking enquiringly at me.

'Crispin?'

'That must have been before your time; of course it must!' Leung said with a fervour that suggested he might have committed a serious social gaffe. 'The thing I wanted to ask you is,' he continued, 'whether you're happy with what he is doing? I mean, I understand he's had a number of interviews with you.'

'I was there when the bodies were discovered, so he would want to talk to me. But if it came to anything serious... I mean if he were to arrest me or Mr Davis...'

'I'm sure there's no question of that,' Leung said quickly.

'Let's hope not.'

I gathered by the speed of his response that he hadn't heard about Addinson's apparent blunder, which meant that the *Daily Mail* hadn't heard about it either, which meant that Iain wouldn't pick anything up from his online browsing, which meant that what I had told Kate remained solid.

'It's good of you to take everything that has happened so reasonably,' Leung continued, 'of course, I personally vouched for your character once I remembered where we had met. One can't have this sort of thing going on. Remember, if this is a sticky wicket you can always come to me. We need to make sure it doesn't get unplayable.'

We passed a few moments in mutually supportive chatter – instant networking – in which Leung assured me there were enormous possibilities for crime fiction and film, suitably handled, in urban China; and revealed that the College was likely to have another Nobel prize winner for science (something to do with the existence of dark matter that he was uncertain about). After more general protestations of help and my mention of his monograph on Robert van Gulik, we parted on the best of terms.

In the entrance hall Molly Whyard was behind the large oak table looking at her watch.

'I wonder if you've got a moment,' I said. 'There's something I need to ask you.'

She looked over her shoulder. 'I'm just coming off duty. Jenny from the village is taking over. She's just putting her coat away. If you order us some coffee we could sit down over there.'

She pointed to a table and a couple of comfortable chairs in an alcove at the end of the entrance hall. I took a deep breath. Now it came to it, what precisely did I want to ask her about the planning drawings? The anomalies they had noticed or whether they had discussed the plans with Kenneth Preston? Perhaps I should get straight to the point.

Molly Whyard sat down in the armchair opposite.

'So what's this about?' she said.

'Kenneth Preston,' I said. But then I stopped. Perhaps a direct question about what Kenneth had known about the secret room wasn't a subtle approach.

'Oh him,' Molly Whyard said, before I could think of something else to add. 'How do you know about that? I suppose if you write detective novels you become a bit of a detective yourself, don't you?'

'I'm sorry,' I said. 'I...'

'No,' she said. 'If you know, you know. I was wondering if I should tell that policeman or not.'

'Look, I – '

'No, listen for a moment. Then you can advise me what to do. Julie said you might be the best person to talk to. You know about police procedures and all that stuff don't you? Frankly, it's a relief to be able to talk about it, particularly now he's dead. It can't have been too long after he and Miriam got together, although I didn't know that at the time. We were a school group who had won a creative theatre competition and got through to the national finals. Every group were given fifteen minutes to do what they wanted. On the night of our performance we were told there was somebody famous in the audience. And there he was – Kenneth Preston. I suppose I was seventeen and dazzled, but I wouldn't have done it if I'd known he was married. I'd just about forgotten about it until he turned up here a couple of days ago. He was looking straight at me as he had done all those years before. You could see him giving me the sexual onceover. Some men do that. You get used to it. The thing was, he didn't recognise me but I could see him running through the possibilities. It didn't take him too long to make up his mind. This time I was too old for him to bother.'

'But didn't he recognise your name?'

'He never knew what my surname was.'

'So you didn't tell him about the suspicions you and Julie had about there being a secret room?'

'He's the last person on earth we'd speak to.'

Molly Whyard was shifting uneasily in her chair. 'I'm sorry about her, really I am, but I can't say I'm sorry about him. So Julie said I should ask you what was the best thing to do.'

'I'd have a word with Superintendent Addinson,' I said. 'Better he finds it out from you than someone else.'

'You're right. That's the best thing to do. Thank you Mr Knight. You've made up my mind for me. I'll tell him straightaway.'

I wondered how Addinson would take the news that one of those who had been at Langham on the fateful night had a motive for murder that was entirely straightforward. I had wondered why Molly had been so dismissive of Kenneth's films, despite apparently seeing them all. Now I knew why. Not that I thought it was possible that she had murdered Kenneth.

The murder method, the locked room, wasn't a direction she would have embraced, although she and her sister had had their own suspicions of the existence of the room. Her sister? Julie Whyard read crime fiction and Molly would surely have confided in her sister about what had happened with Kenneth, if she had confided in anyone. Perhaps they were acting as accomplices to each other.

A figure was passing. It was Emma Hale, dressed in a fetching ski jacket and leggings, and with a bobble cap on her head, was making her way to the outside door.

'Emma,' I said.

'Oh it's you,' she said. 'I didn't see you hidden away there.'

For a sex symbol she was looking both tired and angry, but then the last time I had seen her on her midnight ramble she hadn't looked entirely cheerful.

'There's something I meant to ask you. Maybe now isn't the time but...'

'You might as well,' she said. 'None of us can leave here so we might as well talk. What is it you want?'

I had hoped that if we got into a conversation I could find a way of teasing out the person she had been intending to see on Monday night and whether that was the same person she had been expecting when I had blundered into her room but, now I thought about it, there was no easy way into the subject.

'It's probably not a good time to ask but my son is a great fan of yours. He's always reporting back on your appearances in the tabloids.'

'Tell him not to believe everything he reads.'

'It wasn't that. He wants you to kick off a charity football match.'

'What's the charity?'

'Preserving wildlife. Twenty things you can do to make your garden more of a nature reserve.'

'I'll see what I can do. Ask him to phone my PA. Here's her card.'

'That's extraordinarily kind of you.'

'It's a good photo opportunity. If we ever get out of here.'

She made Langham sound like a prison camp.

'It shouldn't be too long,' I said soothingly. 'What has happened to Kenneth and Miriam is terrible.'

'Miriam is a real tragedy.'

'She certainly is,' I said.

Just for a second I thought I saw a look of venomous hatred cross Emma's features. The next moment it had entirely disappeared, so I was left wondering whether I could have imagined it. She had been looking at the reception table where Molly Whyard was talking to a woman I didn't know, presumably Jenny from the village. Behind them Florence Hammond was also waiting for a word and I remembered that a similar look had also graced Florence's features when I had first arrived at Langham. Emma had been present then now I thought about it. As I watched, Emma walked out.

Before I had time to put my thoughts fully into order I saw that Jerry was striding towards me.

'There you are,' he said. 'I was wondering what had happened to you.'

'Sit down,' I said. 'I've got lots to tell you.'

'That will have to wait. Addinson wants to see you again.'

'Does he?' I said. 'Now?'

'Now,' Jerry said.

It was an unwelcome distraction. I needed to get my thoughts in order and work out what I had just seen.

26

FOURTH WALL

ADDINSON WAS SITTING BEHIND the old wooden desk with the red leather top in the incident room. He had added an antique lamp with a green glass shade that cast a comforting pool of light over the papers in front of him. The chair in front of the desk was now padded, more comfortable than the one that had been there before. I wondered where he found the time to improve his surroundings and where the additional furniture had come from. He waved me to the seat in front of the desk and indicated a bottle of water and a glass off to one side.

'Mr Knight,' he pronounced with the ingratiating smile he had adopted since my wrongful arrest, 'I'm afraid I need to ask you some more questions.'

'Fire away,' I said, nodding myself into the conspiracy of friendly co-operation that he seemed eager to encourage.

'Locked-room mysteries,' he continued. 'You're something of an authority on them, aren't you? Your author page for instance.'

'I've done some blogs. They were a distraction to convince myself I was doing something worthwhile when I should have been finishing the next Tom Travis book. There's always a temptation to rush off into criticism if one finds oneself short of inspiration, particularly if you have an English Literature degree.'

'I'm sure you're being much too hard on yourself,' Addinson said benevolently, 'personally I find everything you write on crime fascinating. But to get to the point you were talking to Kenneth Preston about the possibilities presented by locked rooms weren't you? He kept copious records of his discussions on the project with everyone he spoke to. In fact, Miriam Preston also recorded a lot of the advice she received from Mr Davis about the general availability of poisons in the countryside. But let's get back to Kenneth. From the notes he left it seems you'd given him a number of ingenious scenarios that he could have used in a film version of *Murder Unseen.*'

'I was just responding to questions he'd asked. That's what I'm here to do.'

'So if I could quote from one of your essays – "*a locked-room mystery is one in which a murder is committed under circumstances in which it seems impossible for any perpetrator to commit the crime.*"' He put the paper down. 'Although, as you go on to say, all locked rooms in crime fiction aren't locked rooms at all. They just appear to be locked rooms but there is always a way in for a monkey with a razor, or a glazier who can mend a window-pane, or a carpenter who knows about sashes. It appears to be impossible, that's the great attraction, but it isn't, it's just improbable and, in the best crime stories, ingenious.'

'That's about it,' I said. It didn't seem safe to say anything more.

'So I was wondering whether your discussions with Kenneth Preston had caused you to reflect on what might have happened to him in real life? He died in a version of a locked room. It could be bolted from both the inside and the out. There was no other way into the room other than through the door. There were no chimneys, windows, trapdoors, nothing. And once the room was locked, it was locked. It was a real locked room, not like the ones in the crime fiction you've alluded to where you're just waiting for it to be explained to you why it isn't. Although, of course, in this instance, there was a way of opening the room from the outside.'

'Which wasn't used,' I said firmly. 'Nobody could have drawn the bolt across from the inside except Kenneth Preston.'

'Indeed sir, but let's see what happened after that. He sat down and poured himself a glass of the Glengowrie. The whisky was laced with cyanide. The bottle has a screw top covered in foil. The Prestons had a reputation for living on the edge but they would hardly carry a poisoned bottle of whisky around with them. Maybe Miriam's death was an accident as they tried out something for the film, but it's difficult to see this as a heartbroken Kenneth committing suicide.'

'I'm not sure it was more unusual than his wife's death. Miriam Preston would have needed to be in a precise position for the bird to have killed her like that. I mean I'm no expert on people being bludgeoned to death but...'

'There's the pulley murder in the train station in *Terminal Man*, isn't there? I would have thought that was quite similar.'

'I'm not good on mechanics and terminal velocity and that sort of thing. Jerry Davis is the man for that. In fact, he advised me on whether that whole scene was viable. He's good at that sort of thing, anything mechanical, anything you can fix with your hands...'

Or, on recent evidence, anything at all. Jerry had put in an impeccable performance on crime fiction; poisons; the backgrounds of the main players; the etymology of Suffolk names; anything and everything criminal that had been raised. It had been impressive.

'But, whatever Mr Davis' role, it was you who was advising Kenneth Preston on possibilities for scenes in *Murder Unseen?*'

'Absolutely, but those were just ideas. When it comes to whether they could be carried out in practice, my first port of call is always Jerry. If he says something can be done, that's good enough for me. In fact, pretty much any unusual method of murder featured in a Tom Travis novel will have been run past him and modified if he raises objections. I've only run into trouble when I haven't consulted him. I came in for a lot of criticism about the exploding handbag in *Killing Spree.* I'm sure some people who read crime fiction do it just to see if they can spot some discontinuity or other. They had a field day with the bag. I've learnt my lesson. I consult him on anything unusual now.'

'So you think up the initial ideas and check with Mr Davis whether they can be put into practice?'

'That's pretty much it.'

'And if you were to put them into practice in real life you would look to him to assure you they were practical? I know crime writers like to try their methods out.'

'We don't tend to do experiments.'

'Don't you?' Addinson sounded surprised.

'No.'

'I seem to remember in one of your blog pieces you said you did. What was it now?' Addinson looked up at the ceiling trying to recall the memory from his overstocked mental library of my complete crime writings. 'Ah yes, I remember what it was. Not that it was very complicated, I grant you. It was the verger wasn't it who used the garden dibber as a dagger. It was icy if you remember, rather a neat touch as it couldn't have been done otherwise, and...'

'I'd forgotten that,' I said. 'It was a one-off and, as you say, it wasn't very complicated. I had been getting criticism about Tom's deductions. I needed to get the dibber right. The exploding handbag hadn't gone down well, as I said, and there was even a furore about the light from the prism. So I wrote the piece to rescue Tom's credibility.'

'Tom's?'

'And mine of course. I am the author.'

'As you say. But if you were arranging something, shall we say, *unusual*, in the way people died, what I understand you to be saying is that you would be turning to Mr Davis for advice on how the procedure might be carried out. He showed what he could do with the wiring of the secret room. I'm sure he's also an expert on unleashing a mechanical bird.'

'Any engineer would be, I imagine.'

'And Mr Davis has more than one degree in engineering according to his *LinkedIn* page. But let me ask you another question. If you were writing a crime novel and you had a series of unusual deaths, possibly involving a high degree of mechanical competence, would your chief suspect be an acknowledged expert in the field, or somebody who claimed to have no knowledge at all about how anything was done?'

'Probably the man who claimed to know nothing,' I said. 'But that would be in fiction.'

'Hasn't it occurred to you,' Addinson continued, 'that the deaths of Kenneth and Miriam Preston, have something of the *fictional* about them? They could easily have been lifted out of a crime novel. That's curious, or perhaps it isn't, given that Langham is, or was, populated by a host of creative people – a crime writer, his adviser who is an expert on the mechanics of more unusual murders, a film director, his rich wife, a producer, a magnate of Asian extraction, two leading men, one of whom seems to believe he is Tom Travis, a femme fatale, an intern, an ex-army man with a conviction for GBH, and a glamorous receptionist. Hardly a normal cross-section of the population.'

'GBH?' I said.

'Jack Catesby. A drunken brawl in a pub. The only reason he didn't end up inside was his war record and the fact that Nick Wallace vouched for his character and said he would lose his job if he was given a prison sentence. It was in the papers.'

'I didn't see it,' I said. 'But you're missing one of the characters – a Police Superintendent with a taste for literary crime.'

27

AVAILABLE LIGHT

'ADDINSON IS CONVINCED I did it. That's why he keeps interviewing me. He won't rest until he finds enough evidence against me – or, to put it more accurately, us.'

I waited for Jerry to contradict me, either by saying that my supposition was wrong or by denying his own involvement. Instead he nodded his head.

'To be fair,' he said, after five seconds of what, to judge from the slightly idiotic look on his face, he regarded as mature reflection, 'you can hardly blame him. Everything that has happened does feel a bit like being in a Tom Travis novel.'

'And the police expert on Tom Travis just happens to be here by chance, does he?'

'Unfortunately, yes,' Jerry said. 'But it is chance. I checked with Molly Whyard. They were expecting a police superintendent called Gleason to turn up. But there was a car accident involving his daughter and he had to pull out. There's no doubt about it. Addinson didn't know he was coming. It can't be some convoluted plot to enmesh you. We need to put that notion aside. What you need to work out is why everything here seems to implicate you. Addinson pretty much offered me immunity from prosecution if I would testify against you. He seems to think you dream up mad ideas and then get me to help you put them into practice. He was virtually suggesting I was an accessory to murder.'

'It was you who assured me that that the pulley incident in *Terminal Man* could have worked in practice. Are you sure Addinson really thinks it's the model for Miriam Preston's death?'

'The similarities are pretty much there for anyone to see.'

Jerry was right. They were. I remembered I had been through a host of different scenarios before deciding on the one that I had used in *Terminal Man*. So maybe I wasn't the best person to see it? But if I just read what I had finally settled for in the book, it would have been as obvious as Jerry was indicating. There wasn't too much doubt about it. It was obvious. Any competent policeman would see that.

'He was also eager to talk about the secret room,' Jerry continued. 'He's checked it out with his expert. She's confirmed everything I said. We need to get our stories straight for Kate and Faith on what has been happening here by the way. What have you been telling them?'

'I was able to get away with a few generalities about accidents and things taking a day or two to work out but that I hoped to be home in a few days. I need to phone her again. She has already left a couple of texts. But what have you told Faith? They're bound to be speaking even if she is in Edinburgh.'

'As of yesterday the twins have both got colds,' Jerry said, 'so luckily Faith is concentrating on them, not me, or you, but that may change once they get better. Luckily it's icy up there and she's worried about taking them outside for fear that would make their condition worse.'

'That's helpful, but we need to be able to tell them something definite pretty soon.'

'If you're not arrested,' Jerry said gloomily. 'Addinson just needs the weight of the evidence against you to reach a tipping point. In fact, as far as I can see, he could have arrested you already.'

'He did arrest me if you remember. And you. Or rather, he went through the motions.'

'Maybe he's just biding his time. Not that I would count on it. It could happen at any moment. An arrest would give him breathing space with the press.'

'Anything he has against me is circumstantial. Surely somebody up his chain of command must see that?'

'Senior Investigating Officers are very much in charge of events once they're appointed,' Jerry said. The ACPO guidance in their *Murder Investigation Manual* is very clear on that. But they do need to act responsibly. There's a section on *The Use of Hypotheses* that's helpful on bias. As far as I remember it went something along the lines of – "*Hypotheses must not be based on 'flights of fancy'. They should be developed objectively. SIOs should be aware of the dangers of making assumptions or believing that assumptions made by others are fact.*"'

'That's a remarkable feat of memory.'

Jerry looked sheepish for some reason. Perhaps it was the imminence of possible arrest and incarceration that focused my thoughts. I might not have any effective knowledge of mass and velocity but Tom Travis was a follower of the classical method until he had veered off course in *Murder Unseen*. He was professional and impartial and his cases had been solved by reason and logic. Like Sherlock Holmes, I had instilled him with detailed knowledge of particular subjects. I had been partly inspired by Jerry. His encyclopaedic knowledge had once extended to any gadget known to man. Except that Jerry now had a second string to his bow in his knowledge of *anything at all*. Or, rather, it might be more accurate to say that he *seemed* to have a second string.

'In fact, I've underestimated you.' I continued. 'I've always thought of you primarily as a sort of super-handyman, with engineering qualifications thrown in. I've seen you as the ultimate practical person with a gadget to hand for any job that might crop up. But I've never thought of you as a master of fact and memory. That's been terribly impressive over the last few days.'

'One does one's best,' Jerry said modestly. 'To be frank, much of it is down to this memory system Faith has been advocating, although I do have a pretty good memory.'

'An almost miraculous one.'

'Hardly.'

'I mentioned it to Kate. She said that Faith had told her about it. It's an organisational thing isn't it? As I understand it, you imagine that you're in your house and you arrange the memories room by room. That means they're tethered together and can be retrieved easily. I must say over the last few days I can't really imagine you living in a normal size house any longer but a mansion, and a large one at that.'

'That's pretty much it,' Jerry said, 'but we're getting a bit away from the point, aren't we? If Addinson is just following his own hunches, he's bound to trip himself up. I could go through what I remember of the manual and see what else might help us?'

'That's generous,' I said, 'but perhaps I should do it myself.'

'You could certainly print it off,' Jerry said. 'But that's pretty laborious. It's more than two hundred pages.'

'I wasn't thinking of doing that, just borrowing your glasses.'

'Sorry?'

'I want to borrow your glasses.'

'This is hardly the time for foolery is it? I mean, Addinson could arrest you at any minute. And me as well, come to that. We should stay focused on him.'

'If you could just give them to me.'

Jerry reluctantly removed the glasses from his head, took a last look at them, and handed them over to me. I put them on.

'ACPO Murder Investigation Manual,' I said. 'What year was it Jerry?'

'2006.'

'ACPO Murder Investigation Manual 2006,' I pronounced.

'What's this all about David?'

'There's probably some sort of on/off switch. You wouldn't have handed them over so promptly otherwise. Ah yes, here it is.'

'What are you doing David?

'ACPO Murder Investigation Manual 2006,' I said. The index to the guidance was set out in front of me on a giant screen. I took the glasses off. 'And what are these?' I said.

'What are those?'

'Yes.'

'You mean the glasses, do you?'

'Yes.'

'They're smart glasses,' Jerry said. 'Synched to my devices. The latest you can get, or they will be when they're marketed.

It's an optical head mounted display. It's just like a computer really. These ones are experimental. Korean. I've got friends in the business.'

'Voice activated?'

'Yes.'

'Right,' I said. 'That's why you've been declaiming questions to the ether. So, were you going to tell me?'

'Tell you what? You wanted a knowledgeable assistant. You got one. If you'd known what I was doing you might have given the game away. Besides, the means are neither here nor there are they?'

'You could have told me.'

'I didn't want to spoil the impression. I thought it was better if just one of us knew. I mean, it's what you always say – better to keep something back. You wouldn't have had so much confidence in me if you had known how I was getting the material. And that would have meant that people would have been more likely to twig what was happening and we would have both lost credibility.'

'Would we?'

'You're not good at dissembling,' Jerry said.

'Have you told that to Addinson? He seems to think I'm world class.'

'Addinson thinks you've prepared the ground so well that you don't have to lie. Although the evidence against you is overwhelming, there's no way that it can be used because you can always provide a good reason why things are as they are. He thinks you're mocking the justice system, and the police.'

'Does he?'

'Of course he does.'

'Are you sure?'

'Yes, and if I could have the glasses back...'

I took the glasses off.

'We need to get a plan in place for Addinson,' Jerry said, putting them back on. 'We need to find out about what you told me about stylometry and the Metropolitan Police. And new techniques in UK policing. Something is coming up now. You could see for yourself if you were wearing these. There was something in *The Times* in the summer. It's an article on the frontiers of crime.'

He made to hand the glasses to me but I waved them away.

'I need to think things through. See if you can find out what sort of weight a court would give to these sorts of techniques. I'm going to my room to think.'

'Sound plan,' Jerry said. 'I'll do what I can.'

Back in my room I consoled myself with the thought that Molly Whyard was probably telling Addinson about her liaison with Kenneth Preston at that very moment and that I had, at least, solved the problem of Jerry's omnipotence. But that was where the good news ended. There were other matters that made no sense at all, like how the traces of Miriam's fingerprints and DNA had ended up in my bedroom.

28

INTERMISSION

Tom Travis always maintains, just after the midpoint of the story he's involved in, that until you understand everything, you understand nothing. It's a conceit of detective stories that the truth is somewhere out there and, when revealed, the world will be a more ordered place than it was before. This sort of fantasy makes crime fiction popular and had annoyed Friedrich Dürrenmatt. In the real world, chance takes more of a hand. Put more bluntly, the bad guys tend to get away with it.

In the unstable world I was now living in we had been summoned to the library so that Addinson could brief us on what had been going on.

'I appreciate this must be an ordeal for all of you and I thank you for your co-operation over the last thirty-six hours...'

Addinson's voice had a slightly ponderous note that I supposed he felt was appropriate for the circumstances we found ourselves in. There was probably a whole section in the ACPO Murder Manual on the tone you needed to adopt if you wanted to detain a group of celebrities in an isolated country house, but you weren't yet ready to unmask the murderer, or even tell the assembled company how many murders there had been.

Them and us, I thought, them and us. And you could cut that a number of ways – them, the dead, us, the living. And the whole process was open to endless further elaboration.

'There will be further statements as matters progress. At the moment we are treating events here as... unresolved...'

Them – there was another version of them. Them could be the staff at Langham – Molly Whyard, and Jack Catesby. And when it came to Molly Whyard, a small insidious voice inside me was saying, you had the beginnings of a motive for killing Kenneth, not to mention that Jack Catesby had a conviction for GBH. Yes, those were positives I needed to concentrate on.

'The press and media are bound to try to establish what contact they can with you...' Addinson had reached another point in his checklist. 'I would urge you to be circumspect. Indeed, you may wish to say that the police have asked you not to comment on events here while the investigation into what has happened is ongoing...'

I looked round. Rufus Stone had the air of a man who was poised to win the first set of a tennis match. His eyes were flitting from person to person as though he were arranging events at Langham into a coherent narrative – Kenneth's cut lip; the sudden blackout that had preceded it; the falling bird of prey that had severed Kenneth's jacket and been instrumental in Miriam's bizarre death; Kenneth's poisoning in a room secured on the inside; the destruction of the moth man's light; and anything and everything else that came to mind. At the moment he was gazing fixedly in my direction.

'I hope to be able to make a further announcement tomorrow on how long we need to hold you here...' Addinson said blandly.

'I'm sorry,' a voice said. 'Do you mean you can't yet give us a date when we can leave?' It was Emma Hale. She didn't look pleased.

'I would ask you all to be patient. That doesn't mean of course that you can't visit one of the surrounding villages in daylight hours...'

'So, I can't leave, that's definite is it?'

'I'm afraid I need to ask you to stay...'

Addinson substituted a shrug of his shoulders for more definite words. Perhaps he couldn't face up to telling the assembled company that they would have to remain at Langham until he found enough evidence to be certain my arrest would hold up in court.

Emma Hale was looking at Harry Leung, who was favouring her with a supporting grimace. Catesby and Molly Whyard looked bored, Florence Hammond looked greyish and worried, the tall police sergeant supportive, and Matthew Tabard as blank as ever. Nick Wallace was looking at his phone, Jerry at the floor, and Rufus at last looking at everyone else.

I thought about the list I had made early on Monday evening before all the fuss had started -

1. *Who had Emma Hale been waiting for when I had blundered into Newton?* **Not known.**

2. *What is the best way of influencing Kenneth Preston?* **Irrelevant now he is dead.**

3. *Why had Leung been convinced we had met before?* **Explained.**

4. *Was the steak and kidney pie incident an accident?* **Not according to Rufus, at least I think that is what he was indicating.**

5. *Why was Miriam Preston so interested in poison?* **Irrelevant now.**

6. *Could I get Tom Travis's career back on the straight and narrow?* **Not so pressing a question as it had been.**

7. *Did I have a chance of signing Emma Hale for a charity football match.* **Yes.**

8. *Why is Matthew Tabard in a downbeat mood?* **If one believes the tabloid press...**

9. *Is Rufus Stone certifiably insane?* **Possibly. But vital to everything that is happening in some way.**

10. *Why did I have a sense that events were about to get out of control?* **I have a good sense of intuition.**

But there were at least as many new questions as the ones that had been answered -

Who had been there when Miriam had been killed?

Who had poisoned the Glengowrie?

Why had Kenneth bolted himself into the secret room?

Why were Miriam's DNA and fingerprints in my room?

What the hell was happening?

'It's getting cold out there,' Jerry grumbled. 'This place could be cut off.'

'I've been thinking,' I whispered, as we moved to the other side of the room. 'What if everything that has happened here revolves around sexual jealousy?'

'You should keep that thought to yourself. Kate might not be too impressed. Miriam Preston was giving you the eye. She was an attractive woman and she did have a hundred million pounds. You didn't do anything did you? You were eyeing up Molly Whyard as well.'

'Don't be ridiculous. The only person I could have been said to have been flirting with was Emma Hale. And that was a simple case of mistaken identity.'

'She was pouring you Krug wasn't she? And she offered to let you shower in her room?'

'Be serious Jerry.'

'Just saying how it was.'

'Rubbish,' I said, moving away, 'let's talk later.'

I hadn't thought for a moment of seducing Molly Whyard, or Emma Hale, but I could still smell the smoke in the cold air when Miriam had passed me the cigarette and that look in her eyes as though she was undressing me. What had that been about? I was still trying to work out the answer when I bumped into someone.

'David, I'm so sorry,' Nick Wallace said, 'that was clumsy of me.'

'No, no, my fault,' I said.

'Actually this is opportune. I've been talking to Harry. I know now really isn't the time, but *Murder Unseen* isn't going to get made for the time being. They were thinking of another director but he's not interested and Emma is definitely not keen to continue. So this stage of the project is pretty much done. But that's the norm for the film business. It happens all the time and sometimes a project takes years to put together. Without Kenneth, well...'

Nick's voice trailed off and he gave one of those shrugs that suggested that Fortune, with or without a capital F, had deserted us.

'Of course that doesn't mean you won't get paid for the full two weeks that you were contracted to be here...'

I wasn't really listening. I was thinking about Addinson's obsession with crime fiction and, in particular, Tom Travis and his creator, David Knight. Kenneth Preston had been found dead in a locked room (of which genre he considered I was a noted theorist and commentator) and Miriam Preston had met her death in an impossible crime, or at the very least in circumstances echoing the plot of *Terminal Man*. Add in any number of other factors such as stylometry; Miriam Preston's fingerprints in my room; my fingerprints on the bottle of whisky that had poisoned Kenneth; and everything – at least from my point of view – made very little sense.

29

FAST CUT

IN THE DINING ROOM Rufus Stone was alternately drinking from a glass of wine and a coffee cup.

'You can almost see his brain working,' Jerry said. 'He's sorting things out. Now is the time to talk to him.'

'So what if he thinks he's the murderer because of *Murder Unseen*?'

'That gets us off the hook. But it's not likely that he has a convenient blank in his memory when it comes to remembering how he did it, is it? That doesn't make any sense. He's not putting all that intellectual effort into unmasking himself is he? Some people say he's a borderline genius. That's why we need to find out what he's thinking, particularly if Addinson is convinced that anything that happens here is down to us. I need to get out of here. Faith is pretty frantic about the twins and their colds. She needs support. So now would be a good time to go over and talk to him. If there is anybody here he trusts it's got to be you.'

'Fine,' I said.

Fine wasn't exactly the word that summed up my mood. Jerry was right. I couldn't really believe that Rufus had anything to do with what had happened to Kenneth and Miriam Preston. The problem was I couldn't believe that anyone else at Langham had anything to do with what had happened either. My normal Tom Travis crime novel is stuffed with individuals who have a motive for killing. Here, except for Molly Whyard, Jerry, and myself, nobody seemed to have such a motive. There was the mystery of Emma's behaviour – but that was a broken love tryst rather than anything else. And did I really believe Molly Whyard would murder Kenneth in revenge for what had happened so many years before? Come to that, Jerry and I were mostly in the frame because of Addinson's assumptions from the past. It wasn't satisfactory, but then it wasn't a crime novel. In a crime novel the necessary clues would have been planted by now.

'So are you going to talk to him or not?' Jerry said.

I got up and sat myself down next to Rufus.

'We need to talk about Kenneth Preston,' I said decisively. It's a technique that works well in Tom Travis novels but only when I think I need to insert an element of plot to push the story along.

'Do we?'

'Yes. Particularly the steak and kidney pie incident and the fused lights.'

'Which should be considered together.'

'Although…' I said doubtfully.

'No, no,' Rufus said impatiently, 'it's clear. There were a number of salient features, but three are crucial. It's easy enough to enumerate them – 1) Kenneth was the only person eating the steak and kidney pie that night. Miriam Preston told us it was the same dish he had eaten the night they became engaged and he had personally requested it. She told me that he was so concerned that it should be identical to the one he had eaten in Paris that he went into the kitchens to ensure they were using the best cuts of steak. I should have asked her where in Paris one finds a restaurant serving steak and kidney pie but I didn't. The key point is that Kenneth was the only person eating the dish that night. Anyone tampering with it could be certain that it would be delivered to him. Then 2) the fusing of the lights the moment he cut into the dish was too convenient to be coincidental. It's clear therefore that the whole thing was planned in advance. Kenneth would have noticed the shard of glass if the room hadn't gone dark. When the lights came back on everyone would have had their own version of what happened and he would have had nine witnesses. There might be nine different accounts as to precisely what had occurred but it was clear something had happened – that's another point to hang on to. And 3) there was your involvement. He did ask you to sit next to him didn't he?'

'It was on the seating plan, I didn't have any choice.'

'No, I don't suppose you did. Who would have put the plan together?'

'Nick Wallace and Florence Hammond I suppose. But they would have been acting on Kenneth's instructions.'

'That must be right,' Rufus said decisively, 'and your fingerprints were found on the glass, weren't they?'

'I picked it up. Kenneth was bleeding. I wanted to know why.'

I spoke in as measured a way as I could but something that Rufus had said had alarmed me. How did he know that my fingerprints had been on the shard of glass?

'Understandable enough,' Rufus said curtly. 'But that's by the by. We need to concentrate on more significant events –

Kenneth's second accident in particular – the one involving the pterodactyl. I say *accident* but it wasn't one.'

'And you know that for certain?'

'There was no way it could have happened simply with a rope coming loose, certainly not with that degree of precision. Besides, there are marks on the mezzanine floor in the studio that indicate that there was somebody there lowering the rope that was attached to the bird. It wasn't dropped, at least not until the last few feet. It would have suffered more damage if it had been.'

I thought back to Kenneth's scream. The first people to join me had been Nick Wallace and Harry Leung. They had been talking together beforehand so, unless they were working together, neither of them could have been Kenneth's accomplice. Other than that I couldn't rule anyone else out apart from Jerry and myself.

'Kenneth had an accomplice. That's another fact we must hold on to. One of Kenneth's key characteristics was his reputation for digging deep into the souls of his actors and actresses. If he's making a murder mystery, he wants his cast to be tense and under threat, not knowing who might be murdered next and who the murderer might be. So he stages the incident with the steak and kidney pie. The cry of pain he utters is real, as is his blood. For once it seems that it is the director who is on the line as well as his actors. It ratchets up the tension they all feel. That's the logical explanation.'

Stories of Kenneth's ruses to reduce his actors to raw emotion were scattered over the web. No Arab epic could be made without a month with the Tuareg in the desert. No gritty slice of British life without lodging for weeks in a bedsit above a fish and chip shop in Neasden.

'The bird gashing his jacket is more problematic,' Rufus continued. 'It's clear that it wasn't an accident either, but pre-planned. Just as Kenneth must have had an accomplice to turn out the lights, he needed an accomplice to fake the accident with the bird. There are the marks on the mezzanine floor where you would expect them to be. There's no doubt about it. And there's no doubt that the two actions are linked. But it's too elaborate simply to be another way of Kenneth keeping his cast on edge. There's another reason for it.'

'I think it's clear...' I remembered Tom Travis doesn't like to be interrupted when he is in full flow.

'No, no,' Rufus said. 'You need to think about what happened to Miriam Preston. That is the key to all this. Consider how they dress for example...'

There was another sound in the dining room. Rufus' mobile was ringing. He looked down at it in that dismissive way Tom Travis has in dealing with modern communications. I waited for him to say he wouldn't be bothered by the call.

'I'm sorry,' he said, 'but I need to take this.'

He got out of his chair and moved to the end of the room. The chair beside Harry Leung was vacant. Emma Hale, who had been earnestly talking to him, had left.

It was five minutes before Rufus returned to the table. He looked preoccupied.

'You were saying,' I prompted, 'the incidents that happened with Kenneth, the bird and the gashed jacket and what had happened to Miriam. You were about to tell me what you thought had happened.'

'Oh that,' he said dismissively. 'It's just a hypothesis. It might be wrong. We need to discuss it some other time. I need to go.'

'I could tell you my theory,' I said desperately.

'I said I need to go.'

'The phone call,' I said. 'Who was it from?'

A smile danced briefly over his features.

'I don't suppose there is any harm in you knowing,' he said. 'It was Claire Moriarty.'

30

BACKDROP

'CLAIRE MORIARTY?' JERRY SAID. 'Are you sure he said *Claire Moriarty?*'

'Of course I'm sure.'

'But she's a fictional character.'

'She was until ten minutes ago.'

'I thought you were thinking of killing her off?'

'I was.'

I had been. I was fond of Claire but somehow I couldn't envisage Tom Travis as half of a detecting couple. The trouble was, I had built Claire up too much to simply detach her from Tom. I had also installed a frisson of sexual excitement between them. She wasn't a character who could be allowed to fade away completely. But, if she rejected him, he would be diminished in the eyes of my female readers and, if he rejected her, he would seem ungallant at the very least. So I had sent her deep undercover on active service for her country at the end of *A Grave Mistake* as a compromise solution. It gave me a couple of years to sort the problem out before the next book was due. But clearly, wherever she had gone, it hadn't been far enough.

'But you didn't kill her off, did you?' Jerry said in accusing tones.

'You know I didn't.'

'You should have got rid of her once and for all.'

'Some characters aren't that easy to get rid of. Look at Sherlock Holmes.'

'You could have done something more definitive than having her topple into the Reichenbach Falls. Shot in the head for example. But never mind about that. What was Rufus saying before he got the call? He seemed to be getting quite animated. What was he telling you?'

I ran through what Rufus had said about Kenneth's accidents.

'And then?' Jerry said.

'And then he got the call from Claire.'

'So we're no further forward than we were?'

'We know that Rufus thinks neither of the events involving Kenneth was accidental. He's suggesting that in both incidents Kenneth acted with an accomplice.'

'But we don't know why he thinks Kenneth was acting like that?'

'No,' I said. 'I think he was just about to tell me when the call came.'

'But that may be helpful in itself.'

'How?'

'Think about it. Somebody sees you in deep conversation. What do they conclude? They must think Rufus is telling you about the case. I did. What's the explanation? It's obvious isn't it? Somebody knew he was about to pass on significant information to you and staged the phone call before he had time to tell you the full story.'

'How could anyone have known that?'

'They didn't,' Jerry said. 'They could see he was talking to you and not being his usual taciturn self. What could you be talking about other than Kenneth and Miriam Preston? And the people seeing you talk know they're the murderers. They know they've got to stop the conversation before he gives you the information.'

'So who are they?'

'It could have been Emma Hale. She was in the room with us. She could see what was going on. She left the room a couple of minutes before the call was made. She could play an upper-class Home Counties young woman without any difficulty.'

'How would she know his number?'

'Mobile numbers were included in that info sheet in our rooms. Everyone here knows Rufus' number.'

'I suppose you're right,' I said reluctantly. 'That's not helpful.'

'There's one thing that might be helpful,' Jerry said. 'From where I was sitting, he looked pretty eager to take the call. That tells us something doesn't it?'

'I don't get it.'

'Tom Travis regards all modern devices like mobile phones as an intrusion into a civilised life, doesn't he? He wouldn't normally take the call, would he? That's what's in the books isn't it?'

'Yes, but...'

'So why does he take this call? The answer must be that he was expecting it. That's why he took it. That must mean she's been in contact before. He knew who it was.'

'She's not real, even if she does phone him. I should know. I made her up.'

241

'Maybe he knows she isn't real but he's decided to go along with it.'

'Why should he do that?'

'Maybe he knows she's an imposter.'

'That's fantastic.'

'No, it isn't. I don't know how far he's sunk into this Tom Travis dream world but, whether he believes she exists or not, he's going to know all about her from the descriptions in the books. She'll need to be true to your descriptions if she is going to convince him. Otherwise he's going to see her for what she is – false. In fact, that's the most likely explanation, isn't it? He's still the same logical thinking machine you created but he knows the person impersonating Claire Moriarty isn't the real Claire Moriarty. That's why he has taken the call – to further the investigation. Didn't you tell me once that Kate used to do amateur dramatics? It isn't you behind all this is it David? It needs somebody who is deeply immersed in Tom Travis to come up with a plan like this. Someone like you David.'

'What about Bob Addinson? He's as immersed in the Tom Travis books as I am. And anyway, why on earth would I want to get Kate to impersonate Claire Moriarty and get her to talk to Tom, I mean, Rufus?' I said.

'Addinson is convinced that you find it difficult to patrol the boundary between fact and fiction with any certainty. We haven't been at Langham Hall a week yet but the whole place is reeling under the pressure of impossible crimes and locked rooms. Addinson thinks it's all coming from you. You're directing everything. He'll take the view that Claire Moriarty is just another addition to the world you've been creating here.'

'I didn't have the locked room installed. That was here when I arrived. You can't blame me for that.'

'You're the one who pushed the Whyard sisters into speculating on its existence and giving us an indication where it was. If it hadn't been for you we would never have found it.' Jerry sounded as though he was finding his case more and more convincing.

'Without you we would never have been able to get that door open.'

'I just assessed the situation I found. Anybody would have done the same.'

'Except the number of people walking around who just happen to have a knowledge of super magnets must be limited. That was why Addinson was suspicious. He thinks I'm – or rather we – are obsessed with committing the perfect crime. He'll be certain we've worked everything out in advance.'

'You should have a detective with an engineering background in that case. Then that sort of thing wouldn't seem so unusual,' Jerry retorted. 'In fact, I think I'll write a novel myself. There are not many engineering detectives at large, are there? Your agent Debbie needs to take on someone with real depth when it comes to deduction. Well? What do you think of that?'

Normally I'm drawn to arguments with Jerry. At this moment I needed to think.

'That could be a good idea.'

'That's good,' Jerry said in a tone that was halfway between mollified and baffled. 'Thanks. And look, I'm not really suggesting that you got Kate to impersonate Claire Moriarty. I'm sure she could carry off the role to perfection if you had asked her but I'm not suggesting you have, unless of course you have, which would be sensible in one way.'

'In what way?'

'Rufus is happy in the skin of Tom Travis and everything that has happened here has played into that. But if you want to get real information out of him before he's ready to give it, you have to disarm him. I'm not sure he was going to tell you anything concrete before he got that phone call, except perhaps a cryptic epigram. So I don't think we've lost anything much. Get someone to play his girlfriend and you might get a different result.'

'So you think that is what the phone call was all about?'

'If you haven't got a better idea.'

I hadn't.

'I've been thinking about Miriam Preston and the bird that killed her,' I said a couple of minutes later. 'I mean, you remember how it was hanging in the studio. I just can't see why she would stand there and let it kill her.'

'Run me through what you found in the studio again,' Jerry said. 'As much detail as you can provide.'

As I spoke, Jerry got a notebook from his pocket and started to ask me questions, the answers to some of which he turned into mathematical equations. Then he asked about the look of serenity on her face and whether she might have had her eyes closed when the bird struck the back of her head and killed her.

'I don't understand how it happened,' he said eventually, 'or rather, I understand how it happened but I don't understand why she would have let it happen. What would have made her just stand there, probably with her eyes closed, waiting for something to bludgeon her in the back of the head? It doesn't make any sort of sense at all.'

It didn't, but then neither did the fact that Kenneth had locked himself in the secret room and drunk a glass of

Glengowrie laced with cyanide. But there was something to be optimistic about in what Jerry had said. Rufus certainly seemed to have views about what had actually happened at Langham. More than that, somebody was impersonating Claire Moriarty and trying to find out what those views were. Who, but a murderer, would do that?

31

BALANCE

THE NEXT MORNING THERE was a new figure standing bedside Molly Whyard that I didn't recognise, a man in his mid thirties dressed in a sharply cut suit. As I moved closer his face broke into a cheery grin as though he might be preparing to sell me a used car that also happened to be the bargain of the century. Then he was standing directly in front of me. He was wearing designer glasses and his eyes were a piercing blue.

'Mr Knight?'

'Yes.'

'Let me introduce myself. Detective Chief Inspector Marriott,' he said flourishing a police identity card. 'I'm here to help with resolving whatever has happened. My understanding is that you're the scriptwriter for *Murder Unseen*. Is that right?'

'That's it. I'm here, or I was here, to help Kenneth Preston on the film. It's from a Tom Travis treatment I wrote.'

Which wasn't exactly true I thought. Was that a record? Telling a lie to a policeman within the first few seconds of talking to him? But he was nodding in a friendly way as though the answer I had given had been the one he had been expecting.

'And you discovered the bodies of both Miriam and Kenneth Preston?' He made it sound as though I had been put to some inconvenience.

I found myself saying it wasn't just me and, when it came to Kenneth Preston, there had been four of us, including Addinson.

'Of course there were,' he said soothingly, 'and Superintendent Addinson tells me that you and your associate…'

'Jerry Davis.'

'…were extremely helpful in locating Kenneth Preston's body which was in a locked room. How was that?'

'Mr Davis and I had found the room previously. It was something that Molly Whyard, she's one of the receptionists here, and her sister Julie, who looks after the library, had alerted us to. Or rather, they had suspicions that William and Helen Graves, the owners of Langham, might have done building work along those lines.'

'And you're interested in locked rooms?'

'Professionally. As a crime writer I'm always interested in what a building might contain, priest's holes, secret rooms and the like. If you can find something like that, you're halfway to a story.'

'How interesting. And the Superintendent told me that Mr Davis managed to find a way into the room?'

'He's an engineer by training. He spotted some wires that he thought must be a failsafe device.'

'Fascinating. And Mr Davis, what is his precise role?'

'I suppose you'd call him the assistant screenwriter more than anything else but he helps me develop plots.'

Marriott nodded again.

'He's also an expert on poisons, isn't he?'

'I'm not sure I'd call him an expert.'

'I believe Miriam Preston was asking him a lot of questions about them.'

'Jerry has been mugging up on poisons and the like before we came here. They're still the stock in trade of many crime writers, particularly those, like myself, who are more interested in classical crime stories. Jerry helps me find exotic ways of killing people. In the average detective book these days there is normally more than one murder. I rarely go with any ingenious methods of murder without running it past Jerry. In fact he helps me make most of them up.'

I was bracing myself for his follow-up question about the similarities between Miriam's death and the method I had employed in *Terminal Man* or locked-room mysteries, but instead Marriott seemed distracted by a speck of dust on his suit that he finally flicked off with a cultivated fingernail.

'It must be difficult for everyone here,' he said. 'I'm sure everyone is eager to get out of Langham.'

'I'm sure they are,' I said. Particularly the murderers, I thought.

'But where is the Superintendent this morning?' I said instead.

'He's been summoned to London to see the Commissioner. I'm not sure why. I think he was due to report on some study he was leading on office communication systems. He'll be back sometime later today. I'm here to provide additional resource. It's a high profile case.'

'Murder is always high profile isn't it?'

'Do you think it's a murder case?'

'Surely there's no question about that?'

'We need to keep all possibilities open. The Superintendent told me that Kenneth Preston was intent on using the bird in the studio here as a murder weapon in this film you were helping him with.'

'He was.'

'And I believe his wife was helping him out in devising a method and that's why you went to the studio after you couldn't find them in their suite. You presumably thought they had gone there to refine murder methods?'

'That's right. They had gone there before, or rather Miriam had joined me and Kenneth in the studio on a previous occasion.'

'What do you mean by *joined*?'

'She played the part of the corpse. Then some other people came in.'

'Who were they?'

'Harry Leung and Nick Wallace. They gave Miriam a round of applause. She was good in the part. She used to be an actress.'

'And?'

'Kenneth asked me for some sort of scenario to explain the situation and I made one up. I can't remember quite what I said but I came up with some version of stabbing. Of course, in reality, Miriam Preston wasn't stabbed to death but bludgeoned by the bird. It hit her in the back of the head. To be frank, in some way it was a copy of a murder method in *Terminal Man*.'

I wasn't sure why I was quite so forthcoming except that I suspected that Addinson would have briefed him already on the similarities between Miriam Preston's death and the passage in *Terminal Man*. I waited for the follow-up questions that were bound to come but Marriott seemed preoccupied by something else.

'Don't you see the direction in this?' he said.

'I'm sorry,' I said.

'The direction, don't you see it?'

'I'm not sure I understand what you mean.'

'Kenneth Preston was a famous director. He was trying to direct a murder, or rather, he was trying to direct a murder in which a mechanical bird was involved. Do you see now?'

'I'm sorry...'

'The whole occurrence could have been a tragic accident.'

'What?'

'Kenneth and Miriam go to the studio to explore what options they have for the bird killing somebody. But the whole thing is fated. Miriam is standing where you found her body. She must have been concentrating on something and not seen the bird coming. Kenneth is fiddling with the ropes to repeat the stabbing experiment. The rope comes loose for some reason and before he realises what is happening, the bird has struck Miriam in the back of the head. Perhaps he is standing on the mezzanine and can't even see where his wife is. So he doesn't feel the need to shout a warning, or perhaps he does but it is too late to register in Miriam's brain. Either reason would explain why she looks so untroubled. So the bird flies through the air and kills her. Kenneth is heart-broken. The classic crime universe has betrayed him. Miriam is dead. He takes the whisky bottle, goes to the secret room, closes the door from the inside, and commits suicide.'

'So he knows the Glengowrie is poisoned?'

'Of course he does. It is he and Miriam who have put the poison in the bottle.'

'But why would they do that? They can't know that Miriam is about to have an accident.'

'Of course they don't. The Glengowrie is a prop.'

'A prop?'

'I was talking to Nick Wallace in the grounds. He told me that was the sort of thing they used to do. They both liked living close to the edge. It's a continuation of what Kenneth does with his actors, positioning them so they think they are going to fall into the abyss. What better way of concentrating the mind if you are planning a murder melodrama than to have poisoned your own bottle of vintage whisky? Nick seemed pretty certain that was the sort of thing they would do.'

32

PUSH IN

'SO, WHAT DO YOU think of our new policeman?' Nick Wallace said. 'Harry Leung tells me he's one of the brightest and the best the Met have got. Harry thinks he's here to take the case over from Addinson.'

'Addinson outranks him doesn't he?'

'He could be recalled. He seems to have the most eccentric theories about what happened.'

'He's not alone. Marriott seems to think we might be dealing with two tragic accidents. Miriam was killed in an accident and Kenneth committed suicide in a moment of remorse.'

'Is that such a bad outcome?' Nick Wallace asked wearily. 'Everyone here needs a rest. We've all been shaken up by what has happened. If we could all go home, we could all escape. Emma Hale, for one, is desperate to leave. She's hardly speaking to me. Harry Leung wants to get her, and everyone else, out of Langham as soon as he can. If Marriott can get that done, I'd be happy to go along with it. Addinson may be convinced he's got a couple of murders on his hands but the only person who is keener than he is on sorting everything into neat parcels is Rufus Stone. You were right to be worried about his immersion in the Tom Travis role. Identifying with a pizza chef is one thing, identifying with a detective when a murder has actually been committed is quite another, particularly if that detective has murderous tendencies of his own. Frankly, for Rufus' sake, I hope Marriott's view prevails.'

'And you really think they could have poisoned an expensive bottle of whisky? It doesn't make any sort of sense to me.'

'For normal people, no. But Kenneth and Miriam Preston weren't exactly your man and woman in the street. And they had a number of friends who didn't think the normal rules of society applied.'

'Meaning what?'

'Meaning that you and I might think it completely mad to poison a bottle of whisky costing several hundred pounds but that might be the attraction for them. Getting hold of poison wouldn't be difficult either. They knew all sorts of shady people, particularly since Kenneth decided he would be directing a crime film. Besides, he always had a soft spot for villains of various kinds; from his accountant to a hit man he met in a nightclub. He said they were more authentic than most people. They could have brought the poisoned whisky with them.'

'Hardly,' I said. 'The whisky was a present for Kenneth. Miriam picked it up from the office. I was with her. They couldn't have brought a bottle of poisoned whisky with them. It was delivered to Miriam here.'

'But if the bottle was delivered here, how did she get the poison into it? And where did she get the poison from?'

'You've already answered the last question. They have shady friends. If Miriam wanted poison she just had to ask one of them to supply her before they came to Langham. Let's suppose she has the poison with her. It's not difficult to get it into the bottle. There's nothing more than a cork stopper covered with a foil wrapper. All she has to do is remove the stopper, put the poison in, re-cork the bottle and replace the foil.'

'As easy as that?'

'Yes.'

'I suppose you should know,' Nick Wallace said. 'I imagine it's a problem you come across all the time – in your fiction.'

He was staring at me. I found myself staring back.

'Although there is another problem,' I said.

'Which is?'

'I don't see Kenneth as the suicidal type, whatever may have happened with Miriam and however bad he might have been feeling.'

'So what does Marriott think happened? That Kenneth committed suicide?'

'That's what he said.'

'Tell me in detail.'

I repeated what Marriott had said to me. Occasionally Nick Wallace nodded his head.

'But,' I said as I finished, 'I can't believe Kenneth committed suicide whatever the circumstances.'

'He might not have known the whisky was poisoned.'

'So are you saying that she deliberately set out to poison him? I suppose she does seem to have been obsessed with poison as a murder method. She talked about it a lot.'

'With you?'

'More with Jerry.'

'Your poisons expert.'

I didn't like the direction the conversation was proceeding in.

'He may be,' I said. 'But the reason why we're here is to answer questions we're asked about killing people.'

'Don't get me wrong,' Nick Wallace said, damping down an imaginary fire that had flared up around him, 'I don't think any of this has to do with you and Mr Davis. I don't think she was trying to kill Kenneth. Why were they in the studio in the first place? They wanted to work out how the bird could be used to kill someone. That was Kenneth's obsession and she was ostensibly trying to help him find an answer. But maybe she was getting tired with the problem? Maybe the whisky wasn't there to let Kenneth celebrate any solution they came up with? Perhaps she was intending to tell him that it was poisoned while he had a glass raised to his lips. She might even dash the glass from his hand with a theatrical gesture. As far as she was concerned, the more dramatic the moment that could be created, the better. I know Kenneth and Miriam. This is her opportunity to ensure he knows that she knows what he has been doing all these years – particularly his endless dalliances with young actresses and to let him know she's not prepared to put up with it any longer. She poisons the whisky in the Chinese Suite before they go to the studio. They've been talking about her providing funding for Kenneth's Graham Greene project so she wants to emphasise the power she now has over him. The money she has come into gives her much more control than before. The poison is symbolic of that. The only problem is that when it comes to her big moment with Kenneth and the whisky, she's already dead; a victim of a tragic accident with the bird.'

'So you think that's what happened?'

'If we think Kenneth wasn't the man to commit suicide whatever the circumstances he finds himself in, and I agree with you that he wasn't, then Marriott is right. It is an accident. We'll probably never know quite what happened. The only thing I'm saying is that the Prestons weren't the loving couple that feature in the press.'

'But why would he go to the secret room to drink the whisky?'

'I can't answer that. But he did and, given the door was locked from the inside, there's nobody who could have poured the whisky and drunk it, apart from himself.'

'So you're saying that Kenneth is appalled by the accident and Miriam's death but, instead of raising the alarm, he decides to go to the secret room, lock himself in, and start drinking the whisky she has given him, unaware that she has poisoned it?'

'Nobody could have locked the door from the inside apart from him. And it's an explanation that gets us out of here!' Nick Wallace looked warily around him as though Emma Hale might be approaching. 'But I need to be out of here.'

No sooner had he gone than Jerry appeared.

'So what's happening?'

I ran through the conversations I had had with DCI Marriott and Nick.

'So we can all leave,' Jerry said when I had finished, 'I could go with that.'

'What?'

'It explains the facts and the danger is that if that isn't the story, they'll pin it on somebody here.'

'And who might that be?'

'You,' Jerry said.

'Rubbish,' I said.

'If you say so,' Jerry said dismissively, 'but remember, if they want to pin something on you they'll probably want to pin something on me as well.'

'The police don't operate like that.'

'Addinson does and he's got a fixation with crime fiction. Anyway, think about it. You might also be interested in what I've been doing.'

'And what have you been doing?'

'Establishing all the facts. That's when everything will become clear. Tom Travis always says…'

'Never mind about Tom. What facts have you been establishing?'

'I've been researching Florence Hammond. You probably don't know about her and Matthew Tabard.'

'What about them?'

'They knew each other as children, or rather their families used to go on holiday together. They were different ages then but that doesn't make any difference now of course.' Jerry tapped his glasses. 'It's all there if you know where to find it. Florence's older sister has an enormously informative *Facebook* page with a comprehensive picture gallery of her life. There's Matthew on the beach with a spade and large sandcastle with a much younger and admiring Florence looking up at him. There's Florence as a young girl and Matthew who looks like he's about to go off to university. And there's plenty more of the two families. I reckon she's been in love with him for more than a decade and now she's finally got him.'

'Is this relevant?'

'It could be,' Jerry said, 'No sooner does he get rid of that tennis player Abbey Frost for Emma Hale than he switches his attentions to Florence. Do you think Emma's the person he fell asleep over? No wonder Nick Wallace is avoiding Emma. Even he couldn't sort that one out.'

'Is this relevant Jerry? It must all be good tabloid fodder but that's about it.'

'Or it could be the key to everything that has happened here. Rufus seemed pretty interested when I spoke to him.'

'His judgement is probably distorted by Claire Moriarty's appearance. If he's talking to her he's not going to be his normal detached logical self. He's not going to be making key deductions and noting them down in his small blue notebook with lined pages, is he?'

'He may be,' Jerry said. 'Tom's method is pretty much tried and tested. He assembles the facts and works through them logically. Then he makes a few notes of the key points he is sure of, drops a few subtle hints, and then gives the full picture when he has all the suspects assembled. From what you were saying about the conversation you had with him last night, he's pretty much sorted out what was going on with Kenneth and the steak and kidney pie and that accident with the bird.'

'If that has got anything to do with anything.'

'It must have something to do with something. What you mean is whether the incidents had anything to do with Kenneth's death, or, for that matter, Miriam's.'

'That's what I mean, is it?'

'Of course it is.'

'So, what's the answer?'

Jerry seemed to be struggling with his reply for a moment. Then he said 'Tom thinks they have.'

'Not Rufus then.'

'Tom, Rufus, it doesn't really matter does it? If anything, you've got a superior version of Tom in Rufus. You may not want to acknowledge it, but it's the truth.'

'So I just sit around waiting for Tom, or Rufus, to solve the case?'

'Cases,' Jerry said.

'While trusting he's not being distracted by Claire Moriarty's presence?'

'I expect it will speed him up,' Jerry said confidently. 'He'll want to impress her.'

'So you don't think we will be sitting round here for weeks.'

'I didn't get that impression at all when I spoke to him. You've got to remember you've got a supercharged Tom Travis in Rufus, like the real thing but better and Tom, if you remember, has a hundred per cent success rate. Rufus will want to emulate that.'

'Even if he finds I'm most likely to have committed any murders that have taken place?'

'That's not going to happen, is it?' Jerry said.

'Any reason why?'

'Because you would need an accomplice to pull off the stunts with the steak and kidney pie, and the bird, and the obvious accomplice for you is me and I know I didn't do anything.'

'So the main reason you're sure that I didn't do anything is because you didn't do anything.'

'It's an important factor,' Jerry said. 'You've also been unlucky in being the first person to find both of the bodies.'

'There was a group of us that found Kenneth's body.'

'That's fair,' Jerry said, after he had weighed up my statement for a few seconds. 'But even with all the weight of the evidence that can be assembled against you, you've still got two or three things in your favour. The first is I'm sure Rufus is convinced you haven't done anything wrong.'

'So my own detective will clear me?'

'If you like. That's rather well put actually.'

'And that will happen soon, I imagine, given that he's supercharged?'

'I'd expect so. There's something else in your favour. You're the obvious suspect and the obvious suspect never does it.'

'That wouldn't convince anyone outside a book. I thought you said there were other things in my favour?'

'There are. Think about Claire Moriarty's appearance. That indicates there is somebody else interested in finding out what progress Rufus is making, other than you. I'm sure the police could track whoever it is through telephone records. And who is that likely to be? There's one obvious answer – the murderer. And given it was a woman's voice there's two more deductions we can make. A woman could be the murderer or the murderer has an accomplice. Besides which, from what you've said, DCI Marriott is looking to wrap the case up. I can't see him believing all this has happened because of some concern you have about the boundaries between fiction and reality when it comes to crime. So you're, we're, off the hook, one way or another. Marriott, according to Rufus, is the best the Yard have got. Perhaps we should go with him if we want to get out of this?'

Jerry seemed certain enough and perhaps he was right. He might even be right about whoever was impersonating Claire Moriarty being the murderer. Perhaps I should leave everything well alone and let Marriott's influence prevail. *Murder Unseen* might still be a Nick Wallace production but it would never be at Kenneth Preston's direction. It might never go into production at all. Either way, my chances of making Tom less murderous would be enhanced. That was what I had always wanted, wasn't it?

33

ASPECT RATIO

IT WASN'T UNTIL LATE afternoon that I came across Addinson striding into the entrance hall and simultaneously divesting himself of his black overcoat.

'You must be pleased,' he said in a sour tone.

'I don't know what you're talking about,' I said.

'Don't give me that.'

'If this is about Kenneth and Miriam Preston...'

'Of course it's about Kenneth and Miriam Preston.'

'Then I haven't done anything,' I said. 'You've got the wrong man. It's somebody else. It isn't me. It could be a woman.'

'Of course it's a woman. It wouldn't be done without her approval – one way or another.'

'I don't understand. Really I don't.'

'Tell that to Leung.'

'What has Sir Harry got to do with this?'

There must have been some genuine note of doubt in my voice because when Addinson spoke again the brittle edge to his voice had softened.

'You don't know, do you?

'No,' I said firmly.

Addinson looked round the entrance hall. Apart from the two of us, and a new woman from the village behind the table, the place was deserted. The woman was eyeing her nails intently as though on the brink of some life-changing decision. Addinson nodded and then turned back to me.

'I'm off the case,' he said, 'or I will be by the end of the week.'

'Off the case?' I found myself saying in a puzzled tone. 'What do you mean?'

'I'm no longer the Senior Investigating Officer on this case, or I won't be by close of play on Saturday. DCI Marriott will be taking over.'

'That's not usual is it?'

'No. Normally the SIO is only replaced in an emergency. That means that the officer in charge can investigate without interference from the powers that be. I've just seen the Commissioner. I suspect she will have spoken to her directly on the *not wanting to intrude into operational matters but feeling that she needs to be aware of concerns that have been expressed* line.'

Her? She? Then it fell into place.

'She being the Home Secretary?'

'She being the Home Secretary. Her husband went to the same college as you and Leung.'

'It's nothing to do with me,' I said firmly. Leung might have hinted he was in a position to do me a favour but I hadn't asked him to. Maybe he was doing a favour for someone else at Langham – someone like Emma Hale. What had she been doing the night the Prestons had been killed? I was convinced she had been seeing her lover. Perhaps I needed to discuss possibilities with Jerry. I shook my head. I was convinced the cause was a man. Emma wanted out of Langham to be away from him and she had influence with Harry Leung. Having Addinson removed from the case and substituting the more media conscious Marriott would improve her chances.

'Perhaps I believe you,' Addinson said. He seemed alarmed at the possibility.

'There's something I need to tell you,' I said before he had time to examine his beliefs more deeply.

'Now?'

'Yes. It's a telephone call that Rufus got.'

'A telephone call?'

'Yes,' I said.

'Let's go into the library then. There are a couple of things I need to clear up with you, come to think of it.'

'I hear you've already met DCI Marriott,' Addinson said as he sank into an armchair opposite. 'I get texts on my phone. From colleagues.'

'So when is Marriott taking the case over?'

'Saturday, midnight.' Addinson's expression suggested we were discussing the end of civilisation. 'He's one of the Commissioner's blue-eyed boys. The press like him because he feeds them information on the cases he's working on so they don't have to put in too many hours to get a story. That goes down well with them. Marriott is the rising star in their eyes. He's probably here to wind things up.'

'Why?'

'We don't want to look ridiculous or incompetent. That's always a possibility in a high profile case like this. The Commissioner will want to avoid that at all costs.

The line in London is still that Kenneth and Miriam suffered tragic accidents. If Marriott can't find a culprit that can be delivered with cast iron evidence, that may be the way it stays. Two more unsolved murders wouldn't be good for the Met's reputation. The Home Secretary and the Commissioner aren't keen on rising crime figures. Besides, the Prestons were well connected. It doesn't do for matters to shamble on.' Addinson gave a short, unconvincing, laugh.

'So you think there's a possibility that the case might simply be closed down?'

'Exactly. Although, hopefully, there may be developments over the next couple of days. Mr Stone seems to have an appetite for pursuing matters. But you had something you wanted to talk to me about?'

'Claire Moriarty,' I said.

'One of your best characters in my opinion. I'm hoping she will appear in the next book. Will she?'

'I haven't quite decided,' I said. 'But that's not the point.'

'So what is?'

'She's appeared in real life. She phoned Rufus.'

'Really, sir? How do you know?'

'I was there when he got the call.'

'Did you hear her voice?'

'No.'

'So, how did you know it was her?'

'He told me. At the end of the call.'

'And he was convinced it was her?'

'He seemed to be. But that's not the point either. The point is why would anyone impersonate Claire Moriarty?'

'Do you know when this call was made?' Addinson said. 'Would around ten yesterday evening be the right sort of timing?'

'How do you know that? Have you got his phone tapped?'

'Oh no,' Addinson said breezily, 'the Commissioner wouldn't like that at all. But there's no need in this case. PC Alison Tyler has excellent powers of recall.'

There was a sudden buzzing in my head. It was the moment when you find the ground under your feet isn't the ground at all. 'I'm sorry,' I said. 'I'm not sure...'

'It's straightforward, sir. PC Tyler was acting under my instructions. She's a talented amateur actress. I'm sure Mr Stone found her convincing.'

'So it wasn't Claire?' I said.

'No, sir. Claire Moriarty is a fictional character.'

'I don't mean that. What I meant to say was whether Rufus Stone believed that it was Claire he was speaking to.'

'That's something of a moot point. He could have believed it was her, or he could have believed that it was somebody who had taken a great deal of trouble to ensure that it was more than a passable impersonation. I did take a couple of hours making sure she was properly briefed. In any event, he was prepared to tell her what he was planning to do when she phoned. Incidentally I did emphasise to PC Tyler that she shouldn't give any hint as to the nature of the mission that she was undertaking or when it might be completed. You have no cause to worry about that.'

Addinson had the manner of a man bestowing a favour.

'So what is he planning?'

'He wants to get everyone together on Saturday so that he can, what shall we say, solve the case, or he might have said cases, Alison wasn't sure. Perhaps he wasn't either. He's thinking of approaching me and asking for my assistance in setting the whole thing up.'

'So…'

'I might have tried to dissuade him before I had my meeting with the Commissioner but now I think it's rather a good idea.'

'And DCI Marriott? What would he think?'

'He might take the view that helping an unhinged actor retreat into his own special version of madness was not advisable. But then he's not in charge for another,' Addinson looked at his watch, 'fifty-four and a half hours. Of course he has a future career to think of. I've just got a couple more days.'

'And you think Rufus knows something?'

'He may do. Giving him a platform to expound his views may be a career-ending decision but then my career has come to an end. There is one other matter that gives me hope.'

'Which is?'

'It wasn't just Claire Moriarty who has been in touch with him. DI Fosbury has apparently surfaced as well.'

'Dick Fosbury?'

'Yes sir. Not entirely a rounded character to my mind. No inner life to speak of but convincing enough if his primary function is simply to pass information on that Tom Travis wouldn't normally have access to. And of course you have sketched in elements of the physical man that were enough for Mr Stone to be absolutely certain that it wasn't Dick Fosbury who had called him, but an imposter. He had no doubt about it. Fosbury had lost any trace of that Black Country accent that you gave him.'

I had a momentary surge of elation. Claire Moriarty might have turned out to be a policewoman but the appearance of Dick Fosbury suggested the murderer was impersonating the Police Inspector to find out how close Rufus was to the truth. More than that, it suggested that the murderer was male. It was the beginnings of an alibi. Why would anyone impersonate Fosbury unless he had been up to no good and was anxious to find out if Rufus was really on to the truth? I felt a surge of elation. Addinson clearly didn't think the impersonator was me. I might have had one *get out of jail* card removed with the revelations that Claire Moriarty was a policewoman, but the impersonation of Dick Fosbury had given me another.

'But there was something else I wanted to discuss with you,' Addinson added affably. 'If you could follow me to the incident room.'

34

AXIS OF ACTION

'NEW EVIDENCE,' ADDINSON SAID as he sat down behind the desk. He produced a couple of A5 notebooks from a drawer. They both had black covers. They looked familiar.

'Have you seen these before?'

'Kenneth Preston was writing in one of them when we had a workshop earlier in the week.'

'A workshop?'

'We were exploring who we were and how we related to the roles in the film version of *Murder Unseen*. It was something Kenneth wanted to do. It was a technique he was fond of – particularly for his theatrical productions.'

'We?'

'Jerry Davis and myself, Kenneth Preston, and the main actors in the film – Emma Hale, Matthew Tabard, and Rufus Stone.'

'And when was this?'

'It must have been Monday afternoon. It seems a long time ago now but it was only three days.'

'So this was after Kenneth's accident with the bird?'

'Yes, that happened around lunchtime. I thought Kenneth was a bit shaken up at the time but an hour or two later he had recovered. You wouldn't know anything untoward had happened at all. We did some breathing exercises and then Kenneth encouraged us to think of the sad things in our lives that had affected us.'

Addinson nodded approvingly as though I had passed a test.

'And he asked you where the inspiration for making Tom Travis a murderer had come from. Let me get this right.' He opened one of the notebooks and started flicking through it. 'Ah yes, here it is. He asked you how you discovered the flaw in Tom's character.'

'He certainly asked me something like that.'

Addinson looked at the notebook as though he might have been examining a tablet of stone.

'He must have made this note contemporaneously so I imagine it is an accurate account. Others who were there remember the question being asked.'

'Then I'm sure that was what he did ask,' I said. 'I just couldn't remember the precise words.'

'Perfectly understandable,' Addinson said, in a tone that suggested the reverse was more likely to be true. 'And what was your answer?'

'I think I said it was just something that came to me.'

'A sudden flash of inspiration?'

'That about sums it up,' I said.

'So, can you tell me anything more?'

'Not really. The problem of inspiration and its origins has baffled critics over the generations.'

'I wasn't thinking so much of looking at it as a general proposition,' Addinson said, 'but asking you whether it might have been something more personal, more localised, something that might have happened to you? Or a story you had seen in the press? A tale of justified revenge, something like that? I just wondered what had given you the idea. Otherwise making one's detective a murderer seems like a dead end. I wondered how you were intending to carry on the series?'

Somewhere inside me, close to my stomach, a ball of unease was beginning to expand into a faint, but slowly intensifying, sense of nausea that began to grip every part of my body.

'You may be right about Tom,' I said. 'In fact, I rather agree with you. His actions in *Murder Unseen* could be regarded as something of an aberration.'

'And you have no idea if there was something specific that triggered this *aberration*? Could it have been something that happened to you personally?'

'Nothing I remember, but then I suspect inspiration is like that. Essentially inexplicable. At least to me, and I suspect to any number of writers. I'm sorry but I can't help you. It's a mystery I'm afraid. I'm so sorry. Perhaps we should concentrate on something more definite?'

'Then let me try a hard fact on you.'

'This isn't stylometry again, is it?'

'No, not at all. It's something that Kenneth has written in his notebook. You can see for yourself -

DK very keen to use the bird
as a murder weapon.

And further down the page I saw that Kenneth had added –

Very Keen!
He'll find a way!

Addinson was subjecting me to an enquiring look. 'You're not contesting that DK is anyone but you?'

'No, of course not.'

'And that you were advising Kenneth Preston that the bird could be used as a murder weapon and that you would find a way to make sure that happened?'

'I think Kenneth was keener on using the bird in his film than I was. That was the first thing we talked about when I met him after I arrived on Saturday. He was in the studio. Miriam joined us. They were keen, or at least Kenneth was keen, that the bird should stab its victim to death. Kenneth drew a chalk line round Miriam while she was lying there. It's probably still there if you look for it.'

'It is.'

'Kenneth had scarcely finished the chalk line round Miriam's body when Harry Leung and Nick Wallace arrived. I think Nick was pleased that progress was being made. He'd only hired me because Kenneth had insisted. I really have no experience in screenwriting so the fact that things seemed to be going well was good news. There was a lot riding on *Murder Unseen*. Nick told me that, if the film went well, they were thinking of helping with the funding package that Kenneth was hoping to put together for his film about Graham Greene.'

'Clear enough,' Addinson said. 'But Miriam Preston wasn't stabbed to death by the bird. It bludgeoned her to death, a blow to the back of the head. In fact, it's strongly reminiscent of an event in *Terminal Man*, isn't it? You're not contesting that, are you?'

'No.'

'And you and Mr Davis knew about the secret room where Kenneth Preston was found?'

'Yes.'

Addinson picked up the second notebook.

'Miriam Preston's notebook,' he said, 'is identical to her husband's. Easy to mix up I imagine. You'd have difficulty distinguishing one from the other. Perhaps they didn't have secrets from one another.' Addinson's tone was ambiguous. 'But you can judge for yourself. Let me see now...'

He was flicking through the pages.

'Ah yes, here it is...'

> "It's curious he should affect me so much. I just get the sense that he is the person I have been waiting for all these years. He's married and has two sons but that needn't necessarily be a problem. Divorce wouldn't be near my first option and maybe he feels the same..."

'Did you?'

'I'm sorry. What do you mean?'

'Feel the same? About some sort of liaison with Miriam Preston?' Addinson gestured towards the other notebook. 'Kenneth is full of suspicion that that is the case. His notes are a little coded but it's clear what he's thinking. He doesn't know for certain who it might be but he suspects it is someone at Langham. Miriam's mood has changed. She's skittish, more like the girl he married and, that tell-tale sign, she's started buying him expensive presents. From what's been written,' Marriott tapped both notebooks with his index finger, 'I'd say that there's one obvious person to put in the frame – you, Mr Knight.'

'Me?' I said.

'You. "*He's married and has two sons…*"'

'That's ridiculous. There might have been some harmless flirting, or people might have assumed there was, but nothing of any substance, I'm a married man…'

'With two sons,' Addinson said drily. 'So you wouldn't deny that you felt something for Miriam Preston?'

I thought of her eyes illuminated by the flame of the lighter.

'Mr Knight?'

'There was a certain, what shall I say, *camaraderie*, between us. But sharing a cigarette is hardly a crime is it?'

'I understand you don't normally smoke.'

'I don't.'

'And the fact that Miriam Preston was a newly very rich woman didn't come into your thinking?'

'No.'

'So she's a very wealthy and attractive woman who appears, from the view of observers, to be flirting with you. But you don't really notice. Would that be a reasonable summary?'

'There may have been an element of flirting. But it was nothing more than a harmless diversion.'

'If you say so.'

'What else could it have been?'

'Perhaps you felt you were people inhabiting different worlds from the ones you had thought yourselves confined to. She was suddenly rich and you were a writer commanding million dollar fees. Perhaps you both felt your luck had changed and that you needed to reward yourselves. Money buys a lot of room to experiment with a new life.'

I had a fleeting sense of regret that Addinson seemed to have abandoned his sense that any motives I might have were related to the boundaries between fact and fiction. That was something that had a noble ring; this was altogether more tawdry: a mixture of money and sex.

'This call you mentioned,' I said. 'The one that Rufus Stone had with someone who was imitating Dick Fosbury. What do you make of that?'

Addinson shrugged in a paternal manner that suggested he was not so much interested in who had called Rufus as to what Kenneth and Miriam had written in their infernal notebooks. It didn't improve my mood, but then any surge of elation that the news that someone had been imitating Fosbury might have brought, suddenly collapsed. The appearance of Dick Fosbury wasn't so much a lifeline as something else entirely.

'Are you quite well, sir?' Addinson said. 'You look rather pale.'

35

DISSOLVE

'I CAN'T SEE WHY you're blaming me,' Jerry said indignantly. 'It was a sound plan. Addinson had the same idea and he's someone whose judgement I respect. There are two people Tom is going to confide in – his girlfriend and his closest police colleague. I'm surprised that Addinson didn't try that as well. Perhaps he did. Perhaps that's why Rufus didn't believe I was Fosbury. Having two Fosburys phone one after the other would be a distinct giveaway.'

'He didn't believe you because you couldn't do a Black Country accent.'

'I dispute that. It wasn't the accent so much as Fosbury's children.'

'What?'

'I mean, he's got a boy and a girl hasn't he? I was talking to him when I realised that I couldn't remember which one of them was the oldest. I think it's Sarah but then I thought it could be James. It threw me so much that my accent slipped.'

'So he didn't tell you anything?'

'Nothing at all.'

'He told the policewoman he was planning a denouement for Saturday and intending to ask Addinson to help stage it.'

'Did he tell her anything else?'

'Apparently not.'

'Not entirely a surprise. We could have deduced that ourselves. You've described it enough times. It's pretty much the same at the end of every book. Tom drops a few hints that he knows what has happened and then asks everyone to assemble. He runs through the main facts of the case, seems to implicate a particular person, and then reveals it was someone else. The guilty party makes a bolt for it but is apprehended or dies while trying to escape. The key clue is revealed and the book ends. It's a tried and tested way of wrapping things up. Rufus is bound to be following it. If anything, knowing there is somebody trying to get information out of him by pretending to be Dick Fosbury, will make him re-double his efforts to get every last detail nailed down before he names the murderer.'

'I wish I had your certainty,' I said. 'Frankly I'm not sure I understand where Rufus is coming from. He seems perfectly able to reject Fosbury as a fake, but seems to accept Claire as real. But some part of him must know that she can't be real either.'

'He's playing a part,' Jerry said authoritatively. 'He's happy to believe in the good fakes but ready to dismiss the bad ones. It's perfectly logical.'

'Is it? How?'

'Look at it this way. If the people were real it would be possible for someone to be impersonated, but if that impersonation is not up to par, it will be rejected out of hand. If it's more realistic it means that somebody has taken a lot of trouble to enter the world he wants to live in. Why shouldn't he go along with it?'

'So you really think he is going to stage this denouement, or whatever Addinson called it, do you?'

'Who's going to stop him?'

'Marriott doesn't seem the type to play along with this sort of thing. Besides, he's got an obvious suspect – me.'

'That may be the case,' Jerry said. 'But I thought you said he only takes charge at midnight on Saturday. Rufus has a couple of days to get his case together. He just needs Addinson to go along with what he is planning. And I thought you said he seemed inclined to do that.'

'He wasn't happy with the way he was treated by the Commissioner.'

'There you are then,' Jerry said. 'He's coming round. In fact, it's probably the perfect ending to his career – a blending of fact and fiction. I can see why he is warming to you. I can't see why you're looking so gloomy.'

'I have every reason to look gloomy. Addinson kept referring to incriminating notebook entries from Miriam and Kenneth Preston. I saw Kenneth making some of the notes so there's not much doubt they're genuine, even if both of them have misread the situation.'

'Misread?' Jerry said. 'What do you mean by that?'

'According to entries in her notebook Miriam Preston rather fancied me as the new love of her life, the person she had been waiting to meet for all the years that she had wasted with Kenneth.'

'She wrote that?'

'Words to that effect.'

'In her notebooks?'

'There's no need to sound so incredulous Jerry. I may not have got the words exactly right but that was what Marriott read out.'

'Did he?'

I thought of the flick of flame from the petrol lighter and the sudden illumination of her cheekbones.

'Yes. Addinson seems to think it gives me a motive for murder.'

'Which is what?' Jerry asked.

'I wanted to kill Kenneth so that I could be with a rich and attractive woman...'

'Plausible...'

'And I killed Miriam so that Kate wouldn't find out I was having an affair...'

'Or Kenneth kills Miriam in a fit of jealous rage and you kill him in revenge,' Jerry said with an undue amount of conviction.

'That's what the suicide note Kenneth left said.'

'Remind me.'

'He regrets killing Miriam in a fit of jealousy. According to Addinson, his police experts would be prepared to swear it was Kenneth's handwriting but there were two anomalous facts. Whoever had written the note had done so wearing gloves, probably those latex gloves doctors wear. There were no fingerprints on the document or any traces of who might have written it.'

'So if it was Kenneth who was writing the suicide note, he was wearing gloves for some reason. And the second anomalous fact?'

'It wasn't written in Kenneth's style. In fact it was written in a style he never uses but one that I use in my blogs. You can deduce all this apparently from stylometric analysis.

It's a new technique the Met are introducing.'

'So from the handwriting it's definitely Kenneth, but from the stylometric analysis it definitely isn't, and to confuse matters further, according to you, he appears to be wearing latex gloves or some such to make sure he leaves no fingerprints on a document that he is both certain to have written but clearly didn't. Tricky. Sounds like one of your plots.'

'I didn't do it,' I said. I was trying to remember something.

'And I didn't help you,' Jerry said absently. 'But you need to bear in mind that juries might think that as you're a crime writer used to making up complicated plots, you might be in an ideal position to make this one up. Ridiculous, but you'd only need a couple of crime readers on the jury for the idea to take hold. That's the sort of thing Addinson would think. Are you sure he's come round? David?'

'Sorry. I was miles away. What did you just say?'

'If you have a couple of crime readers on the jury...'

Jerry started talking again and by the time he was finished I was nearly convinced that I should turn myself in. And he hadn't even mentioned Miriam's DNA and fingerprints in Heisenberg.

'So,' I said, when he had finished, 'we need to sort this out before I'm in front of a jury being cross-questioned about how I make up my plots and the role played by others in helping me make sure that everything I put down on paper is watertight.'

'Others?' Jerry said. 'Do you mean Kate?'

'No, I mean you.'

'That's not completely fair. You're the main mover in this. I just help out on the details, if you ask for help that is. I'm just a sort of facilitator.'

'An accomplice.'

'More an assistant.'

'It's the same thing.'

'Is it?'

'Yes.'

'If you say so,' Jerry said with reluctance.

'It's what Addinson thinks anyway. As far as he is concerned, if anything untoward has happened here everyone who was staying overnight at Langham on Monday evening is in the frame.'

'I was just thinking,' Jerry said. 'Who was Matthew Tabard with the night that Kenneth and Miriam got murdered? My money was on Emma.'

'It's definitely not her.'

'Then it's Florence, except that doesn't make too much sense given how pale she has been looking. Mind you, that story in the tabloids isn't going to cheer anyone up. Not that the fact they were together all night makes them innocent in the first place. They could have been acting together.'

I sighed slightly. Given Jerry's analysis, it didn't seem important to know whether Florence and Matthew had been together or not.

'But you're tired,' Jerry said. 'We should concentrate on essentials. One thing we need to do is put out the word that Rufus has solved the case.'

'Why?'

'It will help smoke out the murderer or murderers.'

'Will it?'

'Yes.'

'You don't think we're putting too much emphasis on Rufus do you?'

'What other choice do we have?' Jerry said after a moment's reflection.

36

PREQUEL

'NOTEBOOKS?' NICK WALLACE SAID. They're not relying on those notebooks that Kenneth and Miriam kept are they? Kenneth could be irritating that way. Anything he wrote down was very much his own version of events. If there was ever any sort of dispute about what had been agreed, he used to read his entries back to me as though they were the absolute truth. He told me that you had promised to give him all sorts of options about how that bird might be used as a murder weapon. In reality, that might mean he had simply mentioned the subject to you in passing. That's just how he was. If you need someone to say that he was prone to exaggeration and tended to write down his own version of events rather than what actually happened, you only have to turn to me.'

'That's helpful,' I said.

I was about to ask him about Miriam Preston's diaries and whether she was prone to the same sort of exaggerations as her husband when I saw Addinson behind us.

'I'm sorry to interrupt gentlemen, but I've just remembered something else that I need to discuss with Mr Knight.

If you could give us a few minutes Mr Wallace...'

'Of course,' Nick Wallace said, 'I'll catch you later David.'

And, with a supportive touch of the arm, he was gone.

'Let's go over by the fire,' Addinson said. He settled himself in an armchair and looked behind him to check that Nick Wallace had left.

'I want to make sure we understand each other,' he continued.

'You might think,' I said, 'that my whole purpose in life is to put two fingers up to authority, but you would be wrong.'

'I confess that the possibility had crossed my mind, sir. Your propensity for becoming the chief suspect for any suspicious death that you encounter is marked. I can just about accept that discovering the bodies of Miriam and Kenneth Preston was chance but I confess I half suspected you might be trying out some new option for your novels. The utterly blameless character seemingly trapped by the weight of the evidence but where none of the evidence is actually... conclusive.'

'A number of us found Kenneth Preston's body.'

'That's true enough.'

'And I didn't have anything to do with the deaths of the Prestons.'

'I wouldn't expect you to say anything different, sir,' Addinson said in a cheerful tone. 'But let me get back to specifics. There are the traces of Miriam Preston's fingerprints and DNA in your room. I wondered if you had anything further to say about that?'

'I can't explain how they came to be there. I can only tell you that I was never in the room with her.'

'If you fear it might be embarrassing for, say, your wife to hear about it, you can rest assured that if you tell me now it will simply be between the two of us. You have my word.'

Addinson was subjecting me to an irritating man-to-man look as though he was about to tell me a dirty joke. I suddenly felt exhausted.

'I was never in the room with her,' I said.

'So, whatever else might have happened, you're absolutely clear that Miriam Preston has never been in Heisenberg?'

'Not while I've been there.'

'Thank you, sir,' Addinson said. 'That's very clear. So let me summarise – although you have all sorts of explanations as to why your fingerprints or traces of fibre from your clothes might be scattered around Langham, you have no explanation as to how traces of Miriam Preston come to be left in your room?'

'No,' I said.

'And these similarities,' Addinson continued, 'between what has happened at Langham and events that occur in your books. I am sure you must have been thinking about them. Do you have any further thoughts about that?'

'No,' I said.

'Or the fact that you seem to have an unerring ability to always find yourself at the centre of events. I wondered if you had any idea why that might be?'

'None,' I said. 'No, that's not right. I suppose it must be chance.'

'Chance, sir? Nothing other than that?'

'What else could it be?'

'The thing is,' Addinson said, after a moment, 'this case needs solving. I think we both agree on that. And I've got just over two days to do it.'

'Two days?'

'Oh yes,' Addinson emitted a chuckle that didn't sound at all avuncular, 'the reason that I shall no longer be the

Senior Investigating Officer in a couple of days is that I shall be retiring.'

'But you've just been promoted.'

'And that will be reflected in my pension. That's the best deal the Commissioner was prepared to offer. Getting one of my colleagues to impersonate Claire Moriarty certainly wasn't her idea of following the normal procedures. It won't be Marriott's either.'

'That stratagem with Claire will be a masterstroke,' I said, 'if it produces results. Did your police colleague get anything out of Rufus?'

'He told her he was in the last stages of fitting his ideas together, but hesitant to divulge them before he had the final piece of the jigsaw in place.'

'That's a traditional...'

'Tom Travis method,' Addinson finished. 'Let me ask you something else. The poison in the Glengowrie. Have you any idea how it might have been put into the bottle?'

'That wouldn't be difficult. Jerry Davis researched it. It's a cork stopper under a foil top. All you would need to do is to remove the foil, remove the stopper, pour the poison in and replace the stopper and then the foil. Anyone could do it.'

'Indeed they could,' Addinson said. 'In fact, in their production videos they make a virtue of the fact that they put the foil on by hand and the process isn't automated. They seem to think it help justifies the price they charge. Their website has a video outlining the process. They even point out the irregularities because they do everything by hand.'

'And anybody at Langham could have seen that video?'

'It's not difficult to find, so yes. Curiously enough, Miriam Preston recorded the method in her notebook.'

'Did she?'

'Not that she says she has seen the video. Rather she says she has been talking to an expert on poisons. One here at Langham.'

'That was probably Jerry.'

'She doesn't mention a specific name. It could be you, Mr Knight.'

'It wasn't. I've never had such a conversation with her. It must have been Jerry if it was one of us. But you'll need to ask him that question yourself.'

'Not you then, but let me raise something. My colleague impersonating Claire Moriarty may not have got a great deal out of Rufus but she was certain he had embraced Tom's desire to bring every case to a conclusion. He seemed certain he could do that. In fact, he's asked me to get everyone who was in Langham Hall the night that Kenneth and Miriam Preston died together on Saturday evening. Of course in one of your novels there wouldn't be any doubt this was the right course of action and he wouldn't need my help. I've never quite understood why all the suspects agree to being rounded up in that way given the inevitable outcome, but that's not the problem here. The problem is whether I agree or not. I know that you have been talking to him. You didn't hint that was what he should do, did you?'

'No. But if Rufus wants a meeting, he'll have something to say. Did you tell him that it can't be any later than Saturday night?'

'I've made that clear.'

'Then I imagine he's got a solution. Tom Travis would.'

'So you think I should agree?'

'Yes,' I said. 'I would welcome the truth. I've got nothing to hide. From what he says, Rufus has worked out what has happened with Kenneth and Miriam.'

'He seems to think, from what he was saying to Alison, that events here are connected. They may be nothing of the kind, but I think he should have the opportunity to deliver his verdict. Marriott won't like it but he's not in a position to stop me. They haven't got time to fire me before Saturday night, even if they wanted to. Besides, I have a great deal of faith in our detective.'

I wondered how much of Addinson's faith in Tom Travis extended to the creator of the character.

'So,' the Superintendent continued, 'do we have a plan?'

'Before I answer that,' I said, 'I'd like to know where you are on the case?'

'Where the police are do you mean? Until the close of Saturday we're treating the deaths of Kenneth Preston and his wife as suspicious. From Sunday morning I think DCI Marriott may conclude that what we have on our hands are a pair of tragic accidents.'

'Meaning what?'

'That you can all go home.'

'And leaving whatever Tom may say to one side, what do you think about me?'

Addinson got to his feet and warmed his hands in front of the fire.

'I'm inclined to believe you're innocent of any wrongdoing at Langham despite the weight of the evidence against you. Let me put that more positively. I've come to the conclusion you are innocent *because* of the weight of the evidence against you. Take Miriam Preston's fingerprints and DNA traces in your room. You could have said that she visited. That would have been simple enough. But you chose not to.'

'I'm not sure I understand.'

'It's straightforward. Imagine Tom Travis is investigating. In the early stages of your books suspicion builds up against one innocent character after another until the moment the real murderer is unmasked. That's not what is happening at Langham. All the evidence is building up against one person – you, Mr Knight.'

'And?'

'I think it's improbable. I think the facts as we know them indicate something else.'

'Which is?'

'I think you're being framed. But I did ask you a question, Mr Knight. Mr Stone is asking for everyone to gather on Saturday evening? Is that a plan you would support?'

'Yes,' I said.

37

TRACKING SHOT

'FRAMED?' JERRY SAID. 'ADDINSON said you're being framed?'

'Us – he thinks we're being framed.'

'You don't think he's just humouring you? Because he wanted your support for this plan he has with Rufus?'

I thought about it for a moment. 'No.'

'He could be right I suppose,' Jerry said in a dubious tone. He looked round the room. 'Then who can it be?' he added.

We were in the library drinking coffee, and eating expensive ginger creations that were enrobed, according to the box, in plain chocolate. The only person missing from those who had been at Langham the night that Kenneth and Miriam Preston had died was Molly Whyard. She was probably manning the front desk until the drawbridge was raised. I wondered whether the fact that we were all in the same room observing each other was designed to be some sort of mutual insurance policy against any further nefarious act. It had been Nick Wallace who had suddenly seemed seized of the need for some sort of group activity to raise the general spirits of the company. It had momentarily seemed a good idea although now the lethargy produced by free alcohol had taken over.

'We should check who is drinking what,' Jerry said. 'Any murderer here will want to keep a clear head and stay alert.'

'So are we looking for people who are drinking a lot and discounting them, or are we assuming that any murderer or murderers will want to appear to be drinking a lot to disguise the fact that they aren't drinking very much at all, because they want to keep as clear a head as possible although they'll also want people to assume they're plastered?'

'I don't think it's that complicated,' Jerry said, 'it's mostly looking out for people who are behaving out of the ordinary.'

'So what is ordinary? The only inveterate drinker I'm aware of is, or rather was, Kenneth Preston. So if he was suddenly refusing drinks that might be suspicious but that's a pointless speculation because he's dead.'

'Leung seems to like a drink.'

'Not as much as Kenneth. Put a bottle in front of Kenneth and he'd go for it.'

'A habit which killed him,' Jerry said.

Drinking, as far as Kenneth had been concerned, had been something of a reflex action. Not that he had been obviously drunk, or even in the first stages of intoxication, when I had seen him at Langham. Perhaps he had been a functioning alcoholic.

'Although,' Jerry continued, 'that doesn't help very much with the question of who is framing us now, does it? Except that it can't be Kenneth or Miriam.'

'They're still very much players from the grave. A lot of what Addinson and Marriott think depends on what Kenneth and Miriam have written down in these wretched notebooks. Although Nick Wallace told me that Kenneth tended to exaggerate anything that had been agreed. He would say that in court if he had to.'

'That's helpful,' Jerry said. 'And anyway,' he added more brightly, 'maybe Rufus is writing it all down.'

'Why would he be doing that?'

'There's that scene in *Death of a Socialite* where Fosbury is trying to emphasise the fact that however brilliant Tom is, he needs to ensure that he doesn't get ahead of himself. We discussed it at the time. You made Fosbury a completer/finisher. He might have been there to pass on police information that Tom would find useful, but he was also there to make sure the case was watertight.'

'It was a good way to give plot summaries to my readers. I made Fosbury a completer/finisher to fit into that.'

'You also made him obtuse.'

'I wanted a plot summary, not people flagging up clues. And anyway, I don't bother with obvious clues like how far the parsley has sunk in the butter. Mine are more about stressing the key questions and challenging the reader to come up with plausible explanations of what events fit the facts, to match against what Tom comes up with at the end.'

'And Rufus is coming up with something?'

'Addinson seems to think he is.'

'And what do you think?'

'I think he knows more about the case than anyone else here. Getting to the truth gets us out of here.'

'I thought Marriott was getting us out of here in any case?'

'The truth is safer. I think Rufus will get to that. Come to think of it, we could help the process.'

'How?'

'We could tell people that we've been told that Rufus has solved both cases and the solution is something he's going to announce on Saturday evening.'

'Or we keep mum and wait for Marriott to let us go.'

'There's no guarantee that's what is going to happen.'

'So we tell people that Rufus has a solution. That's the plan, is it?'

'If you've got a better solution, tell me now. If you haven't, Rufus will move things along. Up till now Tom has always come up with a solution. Look at the analysis Rufus has done on Kenneth's accidents. I'm sure he'll do the same.'

'Tell me,' Jerry said, changing the subject, 'are you still interested in where Emma Hale went the night Kenneth and Miriam Preston died?'

'All information is valuable,' I said. 'I've been thinking about it. Perhaps she went to see Matthew Tabard after all. He told her that, despite the fact that he had left Abbey Frost, and despite what the tabloids were saying, he was in love with Florence Hammond. She got the hump and has been looking to leave ever since.'

'Perhaps,' Jerry said, 'but there may be a way to check that. It all depends how serious William and Helen Graves are and what detailed records they have.'

'Serious about what?'

'Energy conservation,' Jerry said. 'In fact, I think I'll check if Molly Whyard is about. She, or her sister, will know the answer. And remind me, what time did Emma Hale leave her room on Tuesday night? If you can give me the precise time that would be good.'

'What are you talking about?'

'I'll tell you if it works out,' Jerry said. 'You can use it in one of your books if I'm right. So what was the time she left? As accurately as you can.'

'That's not difficult. I'm sure it was the sound of Emma's door in Newton opening and closing that woke me up. There were clocks striking midnight in various parts of Langham and anyway, I remember looking at my watch. It was just after midnight.'

'How much after midnight?'

'Two or three minutes past, no more.'

'Good,' Jerry said. 'That's clear. And can you tell me what time you left your room and when you returned and where you went precisely? Whatever you can remember and as precise as possible.'

I spelt out the details as far as I could. As I recounted what I had done I found that my account sounded implausible. Jerry, however, didn't question it and instead irritatingly insisted on reading time and location back to me to ensure he had recorded both properly.

When he had made a further and final check on my account, he cheerfully enquired 'Aren't you going to ask me what it's all about?'

'I thought you said you couldn't tell me until you'd reached a successful conclusion, so the answer is no. I need to concentrate on whatever is happening here.'

'Please yourself,' Jerry said. 'But if something happens to me overnight, you'll never know.'

'That's hardly likely to happen is it?' I said.

'It could do. Knowledge is a dangerous commodity when there are murderers about.'

'So you think somebody might get rid of you just because you know, or think you know, or think you can work out where Emma Hale went the night that Kenneth and Miriam Preston were killed?'

'It was you who thought that it was important to establish who Emma Hale was visiting, wasn't it?'

'Was it?'

'So you said.'

'Then it is.'

'Right, I'll sort it out for you.'

'Great.'

'No sooner said than done. I think I'll have a word with Molly Whyard now if she's still about.'

'Good idea.'

'And it you're thinking of going to bed, be careful. You never know what might happen.'

With an expansive flourish of his arms and hands that suggested that whatever he was engaged in was key to everything that had happened at Langham, Jerry got to his feet and left the library. Once he had gone I gave a sigh of relief. As far as I could see his exit had hardly been noticed. Rufus was talking to Emma Hale, Addinson to Marriott, and there was a small group as usual around Harry Leung – Jack Catesby, Nick Wallace, Matthew Tabard and Florence Hammond. It appeared innocent but at least one of the people I was looking at knew what had happened to Kenneth and Miriam Preston.

Jerry didn't return. After ten minutes I got to my feet and went into the corridor to ring Kate. As far as I could see my exit caused as little interest as Jerry's had done. For a moment I told myself that Marriott was right and both Kenneth and Miriam Preston had been the victims of tragic accidents.

Iain was still awake, and using the upstairs extension, when Kate answered. I reassured him that Emma Hale was still prepared to kick off his charity football match and his presence ensured that Kate's questions about what was happening at Langham were less direct than they otherwise would have been.

When I went back to the library Jerry was non-committal about the information he might have extracted from Molly Whyard and instead joined the group that was still clustered around Leung.

I hung on for a few more minutes but then decided to go to my room. I had a half-awake dream. Real detectives, not Jerry, but Tom Travis and Dick Fosbury were having a heart to heart talk. I was the waiter at their table but, whenever I got near enough to hear what they were saying, they were talking about what sort of pen would work on the starched hotel napkins that had been provided. I was, anyway, distracted by the view through the windows behind them – an infinitely long beach stretching away to a horizon where the land and the sea merged. I had no idea where we were and what time of day it was. To judge from the light it must have been lunch. But there was no sign of any other diners or food come to that. It didn't make a great deal of sense but then neither did anything else at Langham.

PART FOUR

FRIDAY — SATURDAY

38

SPECIAL EFFECTS

I AWOKE WITH THE world ringing in my ears. I remembered waking before and being in a dream in a restaurant with a long beach. There had been people at a table but who they had been escaped me. Now I had a different vision in my head. Emma Hale was in muddy shorts and looked as though she had been the victim of a sliding tackle. Surely her intended role had been a simple ceremonial kick-off? Something had gone wrong. I opened my eyes.

The bedside phone, an antique looking object made of heavy black Bakelite, was ringing. It didn't have a volume control and was more suited to being a weapon than a means of communication. Its tone was somewhere between shrill and alarming. I stretched out a newly wakened arm and picked up the receiver.

'David Knight,' my voice sounded more certain than I did.

'Mr Knight, I hope I haven't woken you sir, but we need to talk.' Addinson seemed to think that antiquated technology was improved by shouting.

'Now?'

'As soon as you can, sir.'

'Fifteen minutes? The incident room?'

'Perfect.'

I put the receiver down. It seemed that my daily routine was not complete without at least two interviews with the police. My arm was shaking. On one of the windows of the room I hadn't managed to close the curtains and something that passed for daylight was creeping into the room.

Fifteen minutes later I was in the incident room. Addinson was behind the leather-topped desk. He was looking benevolent. On a tray in front of him was a triangular steel cake stand laden with pastries.

'Jazz Age design,' Addinson said, following my eyes. 'Can I pour you a coffee? I thought you might not have had time for breakfast.'

'You'd be right.'

'The sleep of innocence no doubt.' As far as I could discern there was no trace of irony in his tone. He was subjecting me to one of his appraising looks. I held his gaze. The look was a second or two shorter than normal. He produced something from a drawer in the desk.

'Have you seen these before?'

These were a pair of white latex gloves in a plastic evidence folder. Addinson tossed them onto the desk in front of me.

'No,' I said after a few seconds scrutiny.

'Are you sure, sir?'

'Yes.'

Addinson reached for a notebook in front of him on the desk, opened it, and scribbled something inside. He looked at me.

'As you are aware,' he said. 'I was beginning to believe you were innocent because of the weight of the evidence against you. It was probably nothing more than a policeman's hunch but one that I couldn't shake off. There was simply too much evidence against you. I thought for a moment that might be the point, that you were engaged in some strange game that despite that weight of evidence, you would still be able to walk free. But that didn't seem right. And now there is evidence in your favour.'

Addinson indicated the gloves in the evidence folder.

'But,' he added, handing me a coffee, 'do help yourself.'

I helped myself to croissants, strawberry jam and butter while Addinson looked on. Finally, when he had handed me my coffee and I had started eating a croissant, he indicated the gloves again.

'You didn't see these in the Chinese Suite, sir?'

'No.'

'So you know nothing about them?'

'No.'

Addinson reached forward across the desk, retrieved the evidence folder and placed it on the table behind him.

'And?' I said.

'Nick Wallace found them. They were in Kenneth Preston's desk in the Chinese suite. They come complete with at least one of Kenneth's fingerprints.'

'I thought latex gloves were designed to prevent fingerprints being deposited on surfaces?'

'That's normally right, sir. But, in this instance, we were able to recover a fingerprint left inside the glove. We tested it yesterday evening. As I said, it belonged to Kenneth Preston. There were other fingerprints belonging to Nick Wallace on the gloves but that was to be expected, given he found them.'

'And?' I said again.

'You'll remember that the evidence we had pointed in a number of different directions. The handwriting on the suicide note seemed to be Kenneth Preston's. On the other hand, stylometric analysis suggested that the word usage was not Kenneth Preston's but one that you habitually use on you blogging activities. Additionally, the suicide note that Kenneth Preston left had no fingerprints on it, which is odd, if it was a suicide note. So a reasonable man or woman might conclude that you, or X, had found a way to forge Kenneth's handwriting, and had used gloves to avoid their own fingerprints being on the note. The lack of fingerprints on the note would indicate that it was likely to be a forgery. So the only problem was that the note seems to have been written by Kenneth himself.'

'If you can detect that stylometric analysis indicates that I had written the note, I imagine stylometric techniques could have been used to generate a note in the first place.'

'That's a fair point, sir, and a question I've asked. I'm expecting the answer will be that it would be complex but not impossible. But it is not going to be an answer that is going to be available before the middle of next week, hence this little chat. The fact that we've found white latex gloves traceable to Kenneth shifts the odds back in favour of him writing the suicide note. And, if you're not involved, we don't have to account for why you were able to forge Kenneth's handwriting style so convincingly. This new evidence is decidedly in your favour. Do have another croissant if you want one.'

In the corridor outside the incident room I met Jerry.

'I wondered where you were,' he said. 'Not that you missed much at breakfast. I had to have the kippers in the end. You would think that pastry was going out of fashion.

Couldn't be had for love or money. I complained to Nick Wallace but he said events were out of his control. You've been seeing Addinson, haven't you? What was it about?'

When I had finished Jerry subjected me to a long, appraising, stare.

'Latex gloves? It's all rather *convenient,* isn't it? One moment all the evidence is stacked up against you and then some white latex gloves appear that convince Addinson you're innocent. More than that, he was beginning to be convinced that you're innocent anyway because there is too much evidence against you. The tide comes in and the tide goes out but Addinson seems to think you never get wet.'

'What's that meant to mean?'

'It's just an observation.'

'I'm not guilty of anything.'

'Addinson agrees with you, so you don't have anything to worry about.'

'Not until Sunday morning when Marriott takes over. I'm not sure he's going to take the same line on this as Addinson has.'

'I can't see why he shouldn't,' Jerry said. 'Anyway,' he continued in a more positive tone, 'Rufus could have solved everything by then. You know how Tom likes to give hints of the way he is thinking to get people to react. Well Rufus was doing that to Matthew Tabard and Florence Hammond. They were breakfasting together and I could hear part of what Rufus was saying. He was going on about the significance of Kenneth and Miriam being the same height and both dressing in black leather.'

'Are you sure he didn't say anything else? That might be a fair point in itself but it doesn't explain how Miriam could stand in the path of the bird and not notice it was about to bludgeon her to death, does it? That doesn't add up at all. Perhaps she was drugged?'

'Apparently not.'

'How do you know that?'

'I did hear a bit more. Florence asked about her. There was some alcohol in her stomach, but not much, and nothing that would have particularly dimmed her senses. She must have been distracted by something else.'

'How did Rufus know that?'

'Addinson must have told him.'

'Addinson?'

'What other explanation could there be?'

'So did he have an explanation of anything? Like why Kenneth drank the whisky and locked himself in the room, or why Miriam didn't notice the bird?'

'Not that I heard,' Jerry said.

'Maybe we know more than that,' I said. 'Rufus thinks it is significant that Kenneth and Miriam could be mistaken for each other. That means that when Miriam was killed, somebody who unleashed the bird could have mistaken her for Kenneth. That rules out Kenneth. He couldn't have mistaken his wife for himself. But if Kenneth was the intended victim he didn't make the most of his reprieve. No sooner had Miriam died from a blow to the head than he was drinking poisoned whisky. Come to think of it, do we know who died first? I've been assuming that it was Miriam and that Kenneth drank the poison knowingly or unknowingly in a grief-stricken response to her death.'

'That may not be the point,' Jerry said. 'Think about it.'

'About what?'

'Who he was talking to.'

'What difference does that make? Tom is always striking up conversations. It enables me to push the plot on by indicating matters that even the most discerning reader may have missed. However, in this case it simply means that Rufus, or Tom, or whoever Rufus thinks he is, is just following that habit.'

'It may well do,' Jerry said, 'but that's not what I had in mind.'

'Which is what?'

'Who he is choosing to confide in. Florence and Matthew. That's significant in itself.'

'How?'

'Don't be dense, David.'

'I'm not. It's a genuine question.'

'It seems that it is,' Jerry said rather grandly. 'The point is this. If you're a detective investigating a crime, you're not going to confide snippets of what you know to the people who may have done it, are you? That makes no sense at all. Therefore, we can deduce that Rufus thinks that both Matthew and Florence are innocent of involvement in anything.'

'You could be right,' I said.

Jerry beamed, being a stranger to irony.

He was still in a good mood a couple of minutes later when Harry Leung appeared.

'I wonder if now is a convenient moment...'

'If you'll excuse me,' Jerry said. 'I have to phone my wife.'

'I wanted a word about Addinson,' Leung said, when Jerry had left.

'I'm not sure he's going to be a problem.'

'That comes from a clear conscience, no doubt, but I wanted to assure you that I have every confidence that DCI Marriott will close matters down satisfactorily.'

'I'm not sure I quite understand.'

'The last close relatives Miriam Preston had were her father and brother. They perished in the plane crash. Kenneth was an only child. Neither of them have any close family to worry about what happened to them. Marriott tells me that the police are minded to go for the obvious explanation. Miriam was involved in a tragic accident trying to help Kenneth put together a scenario for the film. You saw them playing around with the bird, working out how it might kill somebody. So the accident happens and Kenneth, grief stricken, retreats to the secret room and commits suicide.'

'With a poisoned bottle of whisky that just happened to be handy?'

'They both believed in living on the edge. It's the sort of prop they would invest in. You probably know the story about Kenneth, the restaurant, and the venomous snake, don't you? And Miriam was obsessed by poison if you remember.'

'I suppose so.' I said. 'I understand it would be fairly easy to get poison in to that type of bottle...'

'Precisely. The Prestons are both dead. Neither of them have any family to speak of. The circumstances are undeniably tragic but we should all be focusing on going home for Christmas and putting an end to all this. That's what we should all be aiming for. But I need to make some calls, I'll see you later.'

Jerry came back into the room a few seconds later. 'He was looking pretty determined when he left. What did he want?'

'I thought you said you were phoning Faith.'

'There are such things as mobile phones. They can be used anywhere. Faith's number is engaged. But you haven't answered my question. What did he want?'

'He wants everything closed down so that we can all go home for Christmas. He thinks Marriott wants the same thing.'

'Things could be worse,' Jerry said. 'Marriott might have a motive for throwing the book at you. It would look good in the *Mail*. You're already pretty much the *detective of death* in their minds. Even if you were acquitted, they could have a new folk hero – "Marriott of the Yard", the policeman who refuses to bend to the establishment's will.'

'So much for Justice then.'

'I should quit while you're ahead,' Jerry said with a sudden burst of cheeriness. 'If Marriott wants to close the case down, and Addinson is convinced you're not guilty of anything, why object? Besides, it would be good to be back in London. Faith is bringing the twins down at the end of the week. She thinks it's too cold for them in Edinburgh. Plus, I might be able to arrange the odd exclusive interview for you. Rufus thinking he's Tom Travis is a news story in itself, or you could do something on your tryst with Emma Hale.'

'I'm not keen,' I said. 'Besides, what happened with Emma could hardly be called a tryst.'

'That's a good line,' Jerry said approvingly. 'The more you deny that anything has happened, the more people will think it has. It would do wonders for your sales.'

'You're beginning to sound like Debbie.'

'And Nick Wallace told me that any profile you could maintain would be good for any film package they wanted to put back together.'

'I'll think about it.'

'Great,' Jerry said, as though I had committed myself wholeheartedly to any contact he could pull in. 'Great.

You won't regret this. In fact, I think it might be a good idea if I made a couple of calls. No commitment of course, just some sounding out. You'll get a final veto. You should think of getting a publicist full time.'

'I...' I said, but Jerry was gone.

I sighed. Maybe I should just go with the flow if Marriott was eager to close the whole operation down. Only Rufus Stone, with Addinson's tacit support, seemed intent on finding the full, unvarnished, version of the truth.

But maybe I was too steeped in the world of Tom Travis to properly assess the situation. In any novel I wrote about him one suspect would have followed another in being the focus of attention. Here all the evidence seemed to be accumulating against Jerry or myself. Where were the other suspects?

39

STOCK FOOTAGE

IT WAS AS THE clocks at Langham were striking noon that it struck me that the writing wasn't on the wall but in the notebook. One particular notebook.

'The notebook,' I said.

'Which one are you talking about?' Jerry said. 'Kenneth's? Miriam's? Addinson's? Marriott's?'

'None of those. Do you remember that problem in *Death of a Socialite* when I needed Tom to be able to give some exposition of what had happened but he had nobody to confide in?'

'He wrote it down in a notebook that Fosbury had given him.'

'Precisely.'

'And?'

'If Tom keeps notebooks then there's every chance Rufus does.'

'You're stretching it a bit aren't you?'

'I don't see why. What car was Rufus driving?'

'A green Jowett Jupiter.'

'And?'

'OK,' Jerry said, 'you may have a point but I haven't seen Rufus making notes.'

'That's because Tom keeps the existence of the notebook secret. He only makes cryptic notes at the conclusion of the day's activities, just before he goes to sleep.'

'Does he?'

'He does in *Death of a Socialite*.'

'Are you sure?'

'Of course I'm sure. He does much the same in *Terminal Man*. Rufus is bound to have taken the hint.'

'I'm not sure where that gets us.'

'Find the notebook and we'll find out what has been going on.'

'You said he made cryptic notes. Why does he do that?'

'I don't want to tell the reader too much.'

'So even if we do find them, we may not understand what he is talking about?'

'We may not but it will provide us with clues to what he is thinking.'

'Really?' Jerry said, unconvinced. 'Besides, where does he keep this notebook – if he's bothered to have kept one in the first place?'

'That's straightforward. He hides it.'

'That's not good.'

'Yes it is. He hides it under his clothes, normally his socks.'

'So we just have to break into his room and there it will be under his socks?'

'Precisely. Let's do it.'

'No, it's a crazy idea. If Leung is right, Marriott wants to close this case down, whatever Rufus may say tomorrow.

310

He's not going to be able to do that if Langham is rocked by a spate of break-ins, is he?'

'We can't be sure he's going to do that can we? Besides, Addinson is going to give Rufus the stage, or so he says.'

'You should bear one thing in mind before you get arrested for theft.'

'Which is what?'

'In most people's eyes, you qualify as the chief suspect. You found the bodies, and it's statistically the case that people who find the bodies of murder victims are much more likely...'

'I thought you were going to get rid of those glasses. I'm not interested in statistics. Besides, it's only a Yale lock.'

'What?'

'His room is only protected by a Yale lock. You can check with Molly Whyard if you like. They had a security review and that was one of the main areas that needed to be fixed.'

'Molly Whyard told you?'

'That's what I said. Don't look like that. I eased the question into a conversation with her.'

'And you're banking on the fact that when this break-in is discovered she'll forget she ever mentioned to you that the rooms were susceptible to burglary.'

'They'll never know.'

'What?'

'Nobody need ever know. I've done a reconnaissance. As far as I can see the room is wide open.'

'Don't tell me,' Jerry said, 'you're going to remove the side jamb and slide a credit card down to the lock and open it that way and just pray that nobody notices, particularly that a police forensics team doesn't notice, that the door has been hacked about. Isn't Tom a bit of a forensics expert anyway?'

'I don't think we need to disturb the side jamb,' I said, 'and I'm not intending to use a credit card, but this.'

'And what's that?'

'It's a piece of Meccano. It's from that antique set in the library. There's a gap and this is a flanged plate. I've had a look at the door and I reckon if we slide this down we can open the door without having to remove the side jamb at all.'

'We?' Jerry said.

'I regard you as my technical expert. But if you're not keen I reckon in this case I can do it myself.'

Jerry held the plate in his hand.

'I'm not sure you could. It takes a professional touch. But there is another objection.'

'Which is?'

'When are we going to do this? We don't want to be seen entering another person's room. You, in particular, don't want to be seen entering another person's room.'

'So we need a moment when everybody's mind is on something else.'

'Precisely.'

'So how about now?'

'What?'

'Everybody will be at an early lunch. Most of them out of boredom and Rufus to observe what's going on.'

'You're serious about this?'

I nodded.

'This needs to be done properly,' Jerry said.

'That's why I need your help. You're the expert.'

'Then we'd better go,' Jerry said.

Rufus' room turned out to be about the same size as Emma Hale's, if marginally less exotic in its furnishings. It took Jerry about thirty seconds to get in.

'If you're right, it should be in here,' Jerry said, advancing toward a wardrobe.

'And?' I said.

'It's here, under his socks. And let me see, yes, he's written in it.'

'Anything much?'

'Later. Let me photograph the pages. That's the best way. It shouldn't take long.'

It took a little less than a minute.

'Done,' Jerry said behind me. 'We should go.'

'Make sure the socks go back in the right place. Tom has a photographic memory.'

'I took a picture when I opened the drawer,' Jerry said with the complacent air of the accomplished burglar.

I looked at my watch. We would be in and out of Rufus' room within three minutes. If this had been a book there would have been a footfall outside but there wasn't. I looked round the room. *The Practical Poisoner* and the book on sleep disorders, that I had seen Molly Whyard unpacking on Sunday, were stacked neatly on top of each other on a side table next to a leather armchair. The book on sleep disorders had a piece of paper protruding from it, as though Rufus had marked a particular page.

'We need to get a move on,' Jerry said. 'We've got what we came for.'

I opened the door and looked out. The corridor was empty.

'That went well,' Jerry said, when we got back to the entrance hall. 'Let's go into the library. There's not likely to be anyone there,

'So what have we got?'

'See for yourself,' Jerry said.

The first page was headed *S & K.*

'The steak and kidney pie incident?' Jerry said.

'That seems a reasonable assumption.'

There were four options listed -

accident x

scare ?

wake-up ?

plot ?

'That's clear enough but he hasn't seemed to make up his mind about the rest. What do the rest of them mean? Why would someone be trying to scare him?'

'Never mind that for a moment. What's on the next page?'

Jerry looked at his mobile and then held it up so I could see. There were a couple of words and a large cross -

accomplice X ?

accomplices ?

'That could be for the steak and kidney pie incident or Kenneth's accident with the bird, or both, or either, or for something completely different. But consider the X. I don't think that means he has ruled an accomplice out but that it is somebody he doesn't know – X. Rufus was certain that Kenneth Preston had some sort of accomplice when the bird fell on him. Or accomplices, I suppose. What else is there?'

'See for yourself.'

I looked over Jerry's shoulder. There were a couple of words and a question mark -

separate plot?

'That could mean he's doubtful about whether the incident with the steak and kidney pie and the falling bird are linked at all or whether there is any link between what happened to Kenneth and his and Miriam's subsequent deaths.'

'Is there anything else?'

'Just this,' Jerry said. 'See for yourself -'

Kenneth Preston – murdered ?

Miriam Preston – murdered ?

Kenneth Preston – murderer ?

Miriam Preston – murderer ?

'He seems to have covered all the bases,' Jerry said. 'Are you any the wiser?'

I thought for a moment and then shook my head. The book on sleep disorders that Rufus had ordered had been beside his bed. There had been a piece of paper stuck into it, possibly as a bookmark. It wouldn't have taken more than a few seconds to have opened. Even if it had only been a bookmark it might have given some insight into his thinking. As it was there was only one answer to Jerry's question.

'No,' I said.

40

FOCUS

'THEY SAY STORMS ARE forecast,' Leung said, without specifying who *they* were. I gathered from his manner, however, that it could only have been a forecast that had been given on the highest authority. Leung didn't deal with anything but the highest authority. What he could offer in exchange were connections to the Asian markets, an endless stream of gossip, and the persona of the hopeless amateur beset by good humour. When he appeared I was still puzzling over Rufus' notebook entries. I had retreated to the alcove in the library and was looking out over the darkening grounds while the odd snowflake drifted lazily across the mullioned windows.

'My dear fellow, there's something I need to discuss with you.'

His manner was more suited to Lords on a warm June day with the odd ball being caressed to the boundary on the first morning of the Second Test. Here the odd snowflake was being replaced by hundreds of its fellows.

'I've had a number of discussions with DI Marriott. He will be in charge of any further investigations into what happened to Kenneth and Miriam from next week. We've agreed it's the moment to draw all this to a conclusion.'

Rufus would be giving his own version of drawing matters to a conclusion the following morning at ten, according to Jerry. All those who had been at Langham on the night that Kenneth and Miriam Preston had died would be asked to assemble in the library by Addinson.

'But I thought I should give you some advance warning of what is likely to happen given your own close involvement in... *events*. It would also be helpful if we could treat this conversation as confidential. Of course I'm sure that would be the case with a fellow member of the College, but for the sake of clarity...'

I nodded reassuringly. Leung beamed.

'What's the problem?'

'It's the consequences of Kenneth's and Miriam's deaths. There may be some difficulties.'

'Difficulties?' I echoed.

Leung nodded his head.

'In what way?' I said.

Leung moved closer to me. He lowered his voice.

'It's their wills. In the event that she should pre-decease her husband, Miriam Preston left everything she had to him. That might have been sensible enough when their estates were roughly the same size but, because of the inheritance, she died an extremely rich woman.'

'And Kenneth?'

'Should he pre-decease her, Kenneth left everything to his wife. The wills were made shortly after they got married,' Leung added, as if the only way this could have happened had been in a moment of misguided romance.

'But is there anything wrong with them? The way that they were worded?'

'No. Her family solicitor drew them up. It's where the money goes after that. In the event of her husband's death Miriam left her money to a charitable trust associated with her family.'

'Which presumably isn't a problem?'

'No, it's the organisation Kenneth left his money to, should his wife not be alive at the time of his death, that is a little more... *problematic*.'

'So who is it?'

'Cell 52.'

'Cell 52? The anarchist theatre group?'

Leung nodded quickly and with a marked reluctance. I cast my mind back. The group had been involved in a series of anarchist protests that had involved an invasion of the Houses of Parliament, superglue, and the disruption of the Royal Variety Performance.

'Kenneth was associated with them when he was young.' Leung said disapprovingly. 'There was always a bit of the maverick about him. I'm sure he never intended them to get a large amount of funds and, of course, he was much older than his wife.'

'£100 million would certainly fund a lot of disruption.'

Leung nodded. 'Of course,' he added, 'if the tax authorities were to take a strict view, the sum could be considerably less. But any funds falling to a group like that would be a disaster. Besides, we need to consider the greater good. If Kenneth died before his wife then the money goes to a variety of local charities, including one supporting physically disabled children. If Kenneth died after his wife then the money goes to a bunch of anarchists.'

'I can see that could be a problem. But I don't quite see where I come into all this.'

'You were present when both bodies were discovered.'

'So was Bob Addinson, or near enough.'

'I'm sure he won't rock the boat. Marriott tells me he has an enhanced pension to look forward to. It's the police pathologist I'm more worried about. She's a stickler for precision and not necessarily to be relied on to do the right thing.'

Harry Leung shuddered in contemplation of this intransigence.

'And needing Kenneth to die first rules out the theory that Miriam was killed accidentally and Kenneth, in a fit of remorse and grief, retreated to the secret room and committed suicide.'

'Exactly,' Leung said. 'But there are other possibilities we can consider. Kenneth could have locked himself in the secret room as some sort of practical joke, drank the whisky accidentally, and died. Miriam meanwhile, goes to the studio, unaware of Kenneth's death, and tries out one of the murder methods with the bird they have been discussing, and you and Jerry Davis have been advocating. But it all goes wrong and there is a tragic accident. You, yourself, can attest to the look of complete surprise on Miriam's face.'

'Indeed I can,' I said.

Leung beamed encouragingly.

'And of course there is one other thing. I'm not sure if you've heard but Superintendent Addinson seems determined to let Rufus Stone address us all tomorrow.'

'Tom Travis tends to do that towards the end of a book,' I said.

'And quite rightly so,' Harry Leung said quickly. 'And I know that the Superintendent shares your love of crime procedure. That must be the explanation. The point is that whatever happens tomorrow I wanted to assure you that the case will be closed down. It's in nobody's interest that it should continue. The only thing that might stop that is any controversy over the wills and I can't see that happening. Frankly, my dear fellow, we all need to get home for Christmas and re-group in the New Year.'

Leung gave me a reassuring, collegiate, friendly, one of us, tap on the shoulder.

'I understand,' he added, 'that the Superintendent also considers that you're blameless in all this. Personally I never doubted that for a moment. But let's just keep it like that.'

Then he was gone. I wondered if I had understood everything he had said. It had been, at base, a simple exhortation. *Don't rock the boat.*

'So?' Jerry said a minute later. 'Do you know what's going on? Leung is talking to Marriott. They positively clammed up when I got close.'

'Leung thinks I'm in the clear, which means you're in the clear as well. In fact, he's pretty much guaranteed it, although I expect that's conditional on me seeing Kenneth's and Miriam's deaths in much the same was as he does.' I explained what Leung had told me about the Prestons' wills.

'So, we're out of this,' Jerry said, when I had finished. 'That's good. Besides, there's not much of a contest between disabled children and anarchists, is there? We need to take what we have and quit while we're ahead. That's the obvious thing to do, isn't it?'

'I've been thinking about what Rufus wrote in the notebook. What's that thing that Tom says? *Flip it over*? Just suppose it wasn't a plot *against* Kenneth Preston but a plot *by* him. What were the other options? *Scare* was one of them, wasn't it? They're not individual options. You have to combine them. Kenneth wants to convince everyone that he is under some sort of threat and somebody is out to get him. What better way of doing that than by staging an event himself? He's used to staging events. So he lines up a situation when everyone is present at the dinner and then pretends that somebody has laced his steak and kidney pie with a shard of glass. That's easy enough. There's only one steak and kidney pie being served that night. Kenneth doesn't have to do anything but wait for his moment. He doesn't even have to get the shard of glass into the pie. He can have it about his person. When the lights go out he has every opportunity to cry out, extract the glass from his pocket, and cut his own lip.'

'If you think anyone could do that...'

'Of course they could. Think of all those self-inflicted wounds in the Second World War. It's a minor hurdle compared to the prize to be gained.'

I might have sounded certain but I wasn't entirely convinced. A self-inflicted wound in the Second World War offered a passage out of fighting in which you could end up dead.

'And turning out the lights wasn't a problem,' Jerry added. 'He might have had an accomplice but he could easily have done it alone. All he would need...'

'I believe you Jerry. But we need to move on. So tell me what you think the process achieves.'

'He's got a whole table of witnesses to attest to the fact that he's under threat. It's difficult to see how you might cut your lip in normal light but if everything is pitch black, that's explained.'

'And?'

'So what happens at the dinner seems to be an accident, but then there is the incident with the bird where Kenneth gets his jacket serrated. Suddenly the steak and kidney pie incident isn't an accident but intentional. Somebody it trying to scare Kenneth.'

'That makes sense. And remember Kenneth and Miriam dress the same. They are about the same height. From a distance they look the same. Don't you see what that means? It isn't Miriam who is meant to have been killed, but Kenneth.'

'And Kenneth's death?' Jerry said. 'What do you make of that?'

I hardly heard him. I was suddenly transfixed by the white latex gloves. They were the key element tipping the balance back in my favour. One moment everything had been moving against me, leading to the inevitable conviction of one, David Knight, for murder. Then everything had gone into reverse. I tried to remember precisely what Addinson had said. The white latex gloves had been found in the desk in the Chinese Suite. The police had managed to find a trace of Kenneth's DNA in them, proving he had been wearing them. All well and good. Except it didn't add up. I had looked in the drawer in the desk in the Chinese Suite when I had been trying to find Kenneth on the fateful morning. The gloves hadn't been there and Kenneth must have died before that moment. He hadn't discarded the gloves. Somebody else had put them there before Nick Wallace found them and gave them to the police. Somebody who was still alive and at large in Langham.

'And Kenneth's death?' Jerry said.

'What?'

'Kenneth's death. What do you make of that?'

'I'm not sure I know.'

'You should do,' Jerry said.

'Why?'

'You're the one who writes the crime mysteries. You must be able to string some account together. So Miriam gets killed in mistake for Kenneth. What does that mean?'

'Beats me,' I said. In truth I wasn't so much concerned with constructing hypotheses about why and how Kenneth had died as to what he had been doing wearing a pair of white latex gloves.

'You're thinking about something,' Jerry said accusingly.

'No, I'm not.'

'Yes, you are. You've always been secretive. At least you have been over the last six months.'

'Never mind about that. We've got work to do.'

'Which is?'

'Convincing everyone that Rufus will come up with the goods tomorrow.'

41

CHIAROSCURO

The rest of Friday passed inconsequentially. Jerry and I did our best to steer any conversation in Rufus' direction and his genius for solving puzzles and speculation as to what he would come up with in the meeting that Addinson had arranged. We were met with a large degree of indifference although, between us, we did manage to speak to everyone who had been at Langham the fateful night Kenneth and Miriam had been killed, including Molly Whyard and Jack Catesby. Late in the evening Jerry asked how we were doing. I thought for a moment and then shrugged my shoulders.

When I awoke the next morning it hardly seemed that I had slept at all. I looked at my watch. In less than three hours Rufus Stone was due to reveal his version of what had happened at Langham.

Tom Travis always maintains, or at least he does in *A Grave Mistake*, that the truth sets you free. It was not something I believed in, at least not entirely.

My mobile rang.

'David Knight.'

'You are awake then?' Jerry said. 'And your phone is charged.'

'Is there a point to this call?'

'I didn't sleep very well. That's because I've been tossing and turning wondering what Rufus is going to come up with. Have you had any thoughts about that? Perhaps Addinson has been lulling you into a false sense of security.'

'Us.'

'What?'

'Us. Lulling us into a false sense of security.'

'As you like,' Jerry said reluctantly. 'But what do you think?'

'We've got this far. We need to go to the end.'

'Do we?'

'Yes. Look, I need to get my bearings. I'll see you for breakfast in an hour.'

Only the dimmest indications of dawn were showing through the mullioned windows. I made myself an espresso, which I sipped half-heartedly. I wondered if there was any sense in simply asking Rufus what he was going to say. In the books I had given Tom Travis an air of infallibility. Here, his representative on Earth might be experiencing more difficulty. He had, I remembered, put great store in the marks found on the mezzanine floor in the studio. They might be worth checking before the meeting. It wasn't the greatest plan in the world but it was the only one I had, and it gave me something to do.

The police tape on the entrance to the studio proclaiming DO NOT CROSS had been removed and I wondered whether the bird inside had also left. There was no police constable on duty. I hesitated. Did murderers feel a compulsion to return to the scene of the crime? Would anyone encountering me draw that conclusion? Perhaps I should use a more discreet entrance. I decided to get into the studio from the mezzanine floor.

Doubling back I reflected there was a chance that what was to happen in two hours time would be an anti-climax. Perhaps the view that Leung had been advancing that the whole matter was simply two accidents (and that it was clear that Kenneth had died before his wife) was an explanation that meant we could all go home. I went through the door.

The bird had been hoisted up again to the ceiling and was in eye level contact with me. It favoured me with a baleful glance. I dropped down to my haunches and searched the floor for the signs that Rufus had detected. I remembered I had once toyed with the idea of giving Tom an ancestor who had been an expert tracker in the Wild West. I had eventually given up on the idea but it had cost me a frustrating day amending a whole draft of *Killing Spree* to remove the references, including a series of oblique jokes that Dick Fosbury had indulged in. Somewhere somebody sighed. It took me a moment or two to work out it was me.

I searched the area inch by inch without forming any great conclusions. A sense of foreboding started to seep into me. It wasn't the slight twinge in my knee or the thought of what I would say to Addinson if he were to appear that alarmed me. It was something in the atmosphere of the studio itself. When I got to my feet I found I had moved away from the edge of the balcony so that I could see the bird but nothing of what was happening below. I walked to the edge of the balcony and looked down.

A figure was lying on the floor of the studio with its arms splayed out. I ran down the stairs. The body crumpled on the ground before me was that of a man. He was dressed in a blue pullover and elegant slacks of the sort favoured by Tom Travis. With a growing sense of dread I reached forward and turned the body over.

For a moment Tom Travis stared at me, a reproachful look in his eyes. On the right side of his neck the skin was mottled, the result of a blow or an injury he had sustained while falling. It was a situation that Tom would have been able to take control of in a matter of seconds. It was going to take me considerably longer. It wasn't Tom Travis of course. It was Rufus Stone. He was dead.

There was a sound of footsteps from the mezzanine floor. Addinson was looking down.

'Please stand away from the body Mr Knight. I'll come down.'

My limbs felt like lead but they still worked. I got slowly to my feet.

'Is he dead?' Addinson gestured towards the body.

'As far as I can see.'

Addinson walked down the stairs talking into his mobile. After a minute two police constables appeared. Addinson issued instructions. One of the policeman left, the other stood alert a few paces away. Addinson turned back to me.

'How long have you been here, sir?'

'A few minutes. No more than five.'

'You didn't think to summon help immediately?'

'No, you don't understand. I was looking at the marks on the mezzanine floor. I only just noticed the body a few seconds before you arrived. You can only see the studio floor if you get to the edge of the mezzanine.'

Addinson bent down over the body.

'You're right, sir, he's dead.'

He got to his feet.

'Could you tell me how precisely you came to be in the studio?'

I explained while Addinson nodded encouragingly. When I had finished Addinson asked me to run through events again. I wasn't sure I found my story so convincing the second time.

'That bruise on the side of his neck,' I said, 'could have been caused by a karate chop. It could be the work of a professional killer.'

'But not inconsistent with Mr Stone simply trying to check some markings on the balcony edge, overbalancing, and then falling to his death hitting the side of his neck on the way down,' a new voice added. DI Marriott had somehow slid, unnoticed, into the room. 'But we need to get our experts working on it.'

'I agree,' Addinson said. 'I'll send for them.'

'Good.'

'But don't you think it's suspicious?' I said.

'In what way?' Marriott's tone suggested surprise.

'This circumstances surrounding Rufus Stone's death must be relevant mustn't they? I mean, he was due to give his exposition of what had really happened to Kenneth and Miriam Preston later this morning, or that's what I thought he was going to do, but he can't now because he's been killed.'

'Or met his death by accident,' Marriott said firmly.

'It's not likely that he would have died in an accident just before unmasking a murderer, or maybe two murderers, is it?'

'It's perfectly possible,' Marriott said authoritatively. 'It must happen all the time that what we assume to be the logical pattern of events is interrupted by chance.'

I wondered if I had heard Molly Whyard correctly. She had said that the Dürrenmatt novels were intended for Addinson and not Marriott, hadn't she?

I was sure she had. Perhaps Addinson had lent Marriott one.

'But Rufus was intending to unmask the murderer or murderers.'

'If any murders have been committed,' Marriott added.

'Do you know what Rufus Stone was going to say?' I asked Addinson, as Marriott started to give instructions to the police constables.

'Not in any detail,' Addinson said. 'Mr Stone tended to play his cards close to his chest.'

'And do you think he was on to something?'

'Something certainly, but quite what that was is more difficult to know.'

'So you think Rufus Stone met his death by accident?'

'DCI Marriott does, sir. Perhaps that's all that matters.'

42

FILM NOIR

'WHY DON'T YOU HAVE a glass of wine with lunch?' Jerry asked. 'It would help settle your nerves.'

'There's nothing wrong with my nerves,' I said, executing a complex drumbeat with my fingers on the edge of the table.

'If you say so.'

'Rufus was murdered. There's no other credible explanation. He was on to something and somebody silenced him. It's obvious.'

'You're bound to say that.'

'Why?'

Jerry opened his arms expansively.

'That's what you think about all the time. That's what you do. Crime fiction is your way of earning a living. Always thinking where the next murder is going to occur must get into your subconscious. Anything that happens is going to be seen through the lens of a classical murder mystery. And you've had every encouragement from the events here to look at it in that way. One of the deaths was in a locked room, and one an impossible crime, and you have discovered the body each time.

That must fray the nerves. It was bad enough I was there when we found Kenneth Preston. But perhaps the police have every reason to see Rufus' death as an accident? Addinson agreeing a scheme that led to Rufus' death is not exactly standard police procedure. In fact, it breaks any number of police guidelines...'

Jerry was wearing his glasses again. I thought for a moment he might give me chapter and verse on the guidelines that had been transgressed but luckily he seemed to think better of it.

'Maybe it's fine if you get a result but in this case they didn't,' he continued, with a dismissive wave of his hand. 'They've just got another body to explain. Unless it's another accident, the story in the press is going to be *unorthodox police procedures lead to the death of one of the UK's greatest method actors.* It's questions for the Home Secretary and the Commissioner, a blow to Marriott's reputation, and Addinson's lucky if he gets a full pension because of his misconduct. Not good. Not even Leung could handle it. Everything is a lot worse if it turns out to be murder. But a tragic accident in an ill-fated Langham can be managed better There's already a story doing the rounds that *Murder Unseen* is the new *Scottish play.*'

'What?'

'You know the play that no actor names.'

'You're not an actor.'

'That's beside the point.'

'No, it's not.'

'*Macbeth* then,' Jerry said reluctantly.

'There, that wasn't difficult was it? Besides, we've got more important things to worry about than theatrical superstition. If Rufus was murdered, we're partly responsible. We've been hinting to everybody here that he'd worked out what had happened to Kenneth and Miriam. We've made him into a target. If the murderer or murderess think he's worked everything out, they are going to have to act before he reveals who they are.'

'He mostly did that himself,' Jerry said. 'Addinson might not have said as much, but everybody, or at least anyone who has read a Tom Travis novel, must have guessed that was what was intended to happen. But perhaps it wasn't.'

I must have looked baffled.

'Think about it,' Jerry said. 'Why set yourself up as a target if you don't need to? There's an obvious answer. He didn't know for certain who had murdered Kenneth or Miriam, or if they had been murdered at all. If he had done, he would simply have told the police like any normal person. He seemed to be getting on with Addinson. There was no reason not to.'

Except there was a reason I thought. Tom Travis wouldn't.

'Anyway,' Jerry concluded. 'We don't know for certain there were any murders, and we don't know if Rufus simply died in an accident.'

'Yes we do,' I said. 'We know there is a murderer at work.'

'That's news to me,' Jerry said. 'Why?'

'These white latex gloves. Addinson told me that Nick Wallace found them in a drawer in the Chinese Suite. He couldn't have done.'

'Why not?'

'Because they weren't there. I went to the Chinese Suite on Tuesday morning to find Kenneth to say that Molly Whyard was holding calls for him. I knocked but I didn't get any response. I tried the door and it was unlocked. So I went in. The suite was empty. I wondered what had become of them both and decided to check the studio to see if they were there. That's when I found Miriam Preston. But that's not the main point. The point is that when I was in the Chinese Suite I opened the drawer where Nick Wallace had found the gloves. There was nothing there. Nick Wallace couldn't have found the latex gloves when he told Addinson he did. Or somebody must have put them there later. And it can't have been Kenneth Preston. He was dead.'

'So why did you search the drawer?' Jerry said.

'A writer is always searching for material for their next book. I couldn't stop myself.'

'I've always thought crime writing had its darker side,' Jerry said. 'You probably do a bit of shoplifting on the side as well I imagine. But let me get this straight. You're saying someone must have planted the gloves that Nick Wallace found because they weren't there when you checked the drawer. You're also saying that Kenneth Preston used them to avoid leaving fingerprints on the confession he had signed admitting to his wife's murder. Because there were no fingerprints on the confession the police would be suspicious and, as the confession used sentence structures you use in your blogging material and that Kenneth never uses in his own writings, the natural assumption would be that you had somehow found a way to imitate Kenneth's writing but had betrayed yourself by using the wrong writing style?'

'Precisely,' I said.

'But what had actually happened was that Kenneth wrote the confession himself but in a style that was completely alien to him to give the impression that somebody else must have written it.'

'Exactly.'

'So finding the gloves helps Addinson believe what you have been saying?'

'Precisely.'

'So you've got a guardian angel, have you? No, let me phrase that in the way you would. We've got a guardian angel, have we? Precisely what motivation would this angel have? And what chance was there that Nick Wallace would actually find the gloves anyway, and, even if he did, whether he would think to hand them to the police? Why would anyone act like that? Are you sure you haven't misunderstood where they were found?'

'I know what Addinson said.'

'He might have misunderstood what Nick Wallace said.'

'He was clear. All this may all seem unlikely but it's true. But don't you see? Somebody is still directing events. That must mean something untoward is going on.'

'If you say so,' Jerry said reluctantly. 'So what are we going to do now?'

There were a number of answers, although none that I suspected Jerry would find convincing. Something told me I needed to look back over the lists I had made to see whether the questions I had raised were still the key ones.

'So,' Jerry repeated, 'what next? I get the feeling that when Marriott takes charge we can just walk out of here. That's tomorrow, unless you've forgotten. Maybe that's the best course of action.'

Maybe it was. Addinson had believed there was too much evidence against me even before the white latex gloves had come to light. Marriott might not have shared his view but he would accept the evidence of the latex gloves. Maybe I was still trapped in a conventional murder mystery in my thinking as Jerry had been hinting. But there were still those nagging unanswered questions. *Who had Emma mistaken me for? Who had she been visiting the night Kenneth and Miriam Preston died?*

'Although I can think of a plan,' I said.

'Which is?'

'We spread rumours that Addinson is planning to unmask the murderer before midnight. If we do that there's a good chance we'll smoke whoever it is out.'

'Unless...' Jerry said.

'Unless what?'

'Unless he or she kills us first.'

43

JUMP CUT

AFTER SEVERAL HOURS OF spreading rumours about police revelations scheduled for later in the day I almost didn't hear the discreet tap on the door to my room. The enthusiasm with which Jerry and I had started the process had slipped away like sand seeping from a cracked hour-glass. Somehow I had half-expected Addinson to ask for us to be gathered together. That, after all, had been the plan when Rufus was alive. But no call had come and the light had faded and afternoon had become evening and still nothing happened. Dinner passed and Jerry retired to his room to shower, suggesting that we re-group in half an hour. He hadn't said why. I looked at my watch. Addinson would be in charge for a further three hours.

There was a tap on the door.

Nick Wallace was outside in the corridor.

'We need to talk.'

He seemed to be certain about the fact.

'Then you'd better come in.'

The mini bar helpfully had miniature bottles of brandy. A display cabinet at the end of the room had a selection of antique glasses. Soon we were facing each other at either end of a long, slightly austere, Victorian sofa, made of a dark mahogany with, according to the helpful room notes on the furniture contained in Heisenberg, unusually fine brass roundels and castors. The sofa was upholstered in a green silk fabric decorated with a discreet heraldic pattern. I positioned the bolster behind me and warmed the brandy glass in my hand. At the other end of the sofa, some distance away, Nick Wallace was doing the same.

'I was talking to Harry Leung,' he said, 'about where to go with *Murder Unseen*. If we can get things here wrapped up satisfactorily, he seems very enthusiastic.'

Nick Wallace swirled the brandy slowly round his glass. I waited. The future of *Murder Unseen* wasn't the primary purpose of his visit.

'We'd like to keep you on the payroll as a consultant to the project for the next six months, Mr Davis as well, if he's free.'

'That's generous,' I said. It was. Debbie would be pleased. Kate would be pleased. My sons would warm themselves in the glow of my confirmed status as the chief financial support of the family. But I had a feeling that my financial future wasn't the main reason why he was here.

'But before we get on to that, there are few things that are troubling me,' I said. 'These gloves that you found for instance…'

'I was talking to our police colleagues earlier about them,' he said. 'I gather they were a key factor in convincing them you had nothing to do with Kenneth's or Miriam's death.'

'The thing is,' I said, 'that I was rummaging in the Chinese Suite the same morning that Kenneth's and Miriam's bodies were discovered. I checked the draw where the gloves were found. I can't explain why but that's what happened. When I opened it, it was empty. Somebody must have put them there for you to find. It can't have been Kenneth or Miriam. They were both dead. It must have been somebody else.'

'I'm not sure I'd tell Marriott that when he takes over the case. He seems to be of a mind to close things down. I wouldn't give him any excuse to re-open matters. Frankly, I think we all want to get out of this place and forget everything that has happened. I want to make *Murder Unseen* a success. I also share your doubts about making Tom Travis a murderer. It would be fine for a one-off film but not for a series. This could be an important franchise. That's what we should be focusing on.'

'That's great,' I said, 'but about the gloves...'

'That's easily explained. There's no mysterious third party. I put the gloves in the draw myself. I came across them hidden among Kenneth's belongings after his death. I didn't know what they were but I knew Kenneth well enough to know he had been up to something. So I thought it best to leave them somewhere the police were bound to find them.'

Once there had been a great mass of evidence hovering above my head, like the great wave in the Hokusai print. The discovery of the white latex gloves had been key to stop the wave breaking. Otherwise I would have been engulfed by one bit of damning evidence after another. Without the gloves it would only have been Addinson's hunch that there was too much evidence accumulating against me to be believable, that I could have relied on. The gloves had been a game-changer.

'Look,' Nick Wallace continued, 'I'm very happy to say that it was me who put them in the drawer if the police ask the question, but why open the whole thing up? The police are happy. They would have found the gloves anyway if they had done a thorough search.'

'So what's your explanation of events? Why were you suspicious of Kenneth?'

'I'm not sure I can tell you exactly. He had been reading your books and become fascinated by the exotic plots that classic crime novels use – particularly innovative ways of murdering people. You saw them in the studio with the pterodactyl. Miriam was as enthusiastic as Kenneth. The two of them were definitely working on something. Then on Monday night Miriam comes up with a solution and goes to the studio to see if it works. Something goes wrong. Miriam is in the bird's path and gets bludgeoned to death by it.'

'It's what happens in *Terminal Man*.'

'It is, but that's not a great surprise. I know both Kenneth and Miriam had read all your Tom Travis novels. In fact, that's probably where they got the inspiration from unless you made the suggestion to them?'

'No.'

'Although you made all sorts of other suggestions.'

'Yes.'

'There we are then. It all makes sense. They would be thinking about both what you said and what had been in the books.'

'And the poisoned whisky?'

'There's poison in your books, isn't there? The Prestons liked living on the edge. It wasn't just Kenneth, it was Miriam as well. I think that's what attracted them to each other in the first place. This crime project rekindled something. It's only a few days since they reaffirmed their marriage vows. And Miriam came here to be part of it.'

'And the gloves?'

'Kenneth must have wanted to see if it would work in practice. So he used the gloves and composed the fake suicide note in a language he wouldn't normally use.'

'That's an awful lot of trouble to take.'

'Think Kubrick. Stanley was the director that Kenneth most admired, and he was someone who could take more than a year on set until he got the right take. That was the trouble he was having in raising the finance for the Graham Greene film. He would run over budget and be reluctant to bring it to a close.'

'Without the discovery of the latex gloves,' I said, 'I might have been in real difficulty. Convicted of a crime I didn't commit.'

'But you haven't been. And if you leave it now, that's the way it will stay.'

'So what did happen to Kenneth?'

'I'm not sure I know. He knew about the secret room. He told me about it, although not where it was located. I think he didn't tell Miriam about his suicide note experiment and she didn't tell him about the poisoned whisky or what she was planning with the bird. She would have told him about that when she worked it out. She dies and he's in the secret room for some reason with the bottle of whisky she's given him and she's not there to warn him not to drink it.'

'And Rufus?'

'I don't know for sure. He's investigating in the studio but overbalances. It's a freak accident. Of course it looks as though it's part of a wider pattern, but it isn't. It's a coincidence. Coincidences do occur in real life.'

Did that square with what Rufus had written in his notebook? Why on earth had I thought it a good idea for

Tom Travis to express himself cryptically, or keep the solution to a case to himself until the last possible moment?

'I'm not sure that we're ever going to find out what happened to Kenneth and Miriam for certain,' Nick Wallace said, 'unless Rufus did manage to find something more out and told Addinson. Do you know anything more about that?'

I shook my head.

'So hopefully we can all go home tomorrow and concentrate on the future rather than what's happened here. In fact it might be a good idea to sign you up to that new contract I was outlining. Shall we say £20,000 a month as the base figure? I can get something final run up tomorrow.'

I thought of the objectives I had come to Langham with on the Tom Travis series and the fact that they could all be ticked off. I thought of Kate and the admiring looks of the boys. I thought about Tom Travis and the fact he was dead. Then I thought about the beatific look on Miriam Preston's face after her death, and Emma's irritated features in life. There was something there, if only I could find it.

'Is it a deal?' Nick Wallace said.

'I'm not sure,' I said. 'There's something I need to check out with Addinson before he's taken off the case. That might change everything.'

Bluff isn't really a technique I've ever used with Tom Travis. Somehow it doesn't make sense if you have a forensic mind at work to go in for such random procedures.

'You see,' I added, getting to my feet, 'I'm convinced Rufus' death wasn't an accident.'

'Are you?' Nick Wallace said.

'Yes.'

'Then perhaps we need to talk further.'

'I'm not sure that gets us anywhere.'

'I think it's essential,' he said.

'Yes,' I said, 'of course it is.'

In his hand there was a grey object that, even given the dim lighting of the room, could only be an automatic pistol. The inelegant bulge on the end was a silencer. I moved back to the sofa and sat down.

44

EXPOSITION

'FIFTEEN YEARS AGO,' NICK WALLACE said, 'I joined the British Army on a short service commission. I'd done a degree in law but being a barrister or a solicitor didn't appeal as much as I thought it would. Joining the army offered more exciting prospects. And so I ended up in Afghanistan. When I first got there it was a normal war. Suicide bombings were rare. You didn't think that everything that moved might suddenly explode. Everybody's nerve was pretty much in place. The orderly life the army provided suited me, or so I thought, and I increased my short service commission from three to eight years.'

I felt my stomach muscles tighten. Afghanistan? What had anything that had happened in Afghanistan got to do with what had happened here? And why was Nick Wallace telling me this? And why was there a gun in his hand?

'Then things got difficult. We were back in Afghanistan sooner than we should have been. The army was suffering from manpower shortages and our tour of duty in Northern Ireland was cut short. And when we got back it was a different place. Suicide bombings weren't the exception but the rule. You may have felt safe in Camp Bastion but you certainly didn't feel safe anywhere else. Everything was less in control than it had been. Then there was a crisis at home. My father died of a heart attack. I was in Helmand watching the nerves of my men twisting and fraying and he was outside a hardware shop in Tooting clutching his chest. The last thing he said was "I'll be alright in a moment." But he wasn't. He was dead.

'I managed to get back home for the funeral. My mother looked older than I remembered. Her brother came over from Ireland and there were relatives I hadn't seen for years and a funeral to arrange. I thought, when the mourning was over, she would get back to her old self, but that didn't happen. Every time I got home after that she was more listless and ground down than before. But then one time I got back and her spirits had revived. She had decided to use one of the spare bedrooms to foster children. Older children, she told me, "ones that were difficult to place".

'Jane was seventeen, willowy, very beautiful, lovely golden skin, troubled, but in a proper home for the first time. I think my mother had a secret plan that we should link up. Or perhaps it was that Jane was the daughter she hadn't had. She'd told Jane that she could stay as long as she liked. Jane wanted to be an actress. I always meant to ask her why but I never remembered to. Then we were back in Afghanistan and there were other concerns.

'A Taliban column had been disrupted by American jets and splintered into small units. We'd surrounded one of them, no more than twenty men, in buildings in a village. My superiors were keen we should take them out. They wanted to impress the Americans with our effectiveness – but I knew they would surrender if we gave them a chance, and they did the next day. But my superiors didn't see it so much as a triumph of diplomacy as a lack of moral resolve. I hadn't quite disobeyed a direct order but I'd come pretty close and I got the sense that it might be best if the army and I parted company. Not that that was a feeling shared by my men. The average soldier has a strong aversion to a glorious death. They were perfectly happy to wait for the tribesmen to surrender. They would have been happy if it had taken a week.'

'Jack Catesby. Was he with you in Helmond?' I asked.

'Yes. A lot of the guys here were. We don't have to teach them anything.'

'And when he was back in the UK you helped him to avoid gaol on a GBH charge?'

Even as I uttered the words I regretted saying them. Nick had been in an almost dreamlike state. But now he looked at me for a moment with eyes that wondered why I knew what I knew. For a moment I thought he was going to ask me, but then he nodded.

'He was in a pub in Aldershot. There had been an anti-war demonstration when the coffins flown back from Afghanistan were taken through the streets. Some of the demonstrators were still about in the evening and were in the same pub as Jack. They said some things about killing the innocent for the sake of capitalism and he reacted. There was a fight. He's a fit man and a soldier. He knocked one of them out cold. He shouldn't have done, but he did. It wasn't great timing as I'd got a job lined up for him. He would have lost it if he had gone to gaol.'

'And he didn't?'

'No, he didn't. The magistrate had also been in the army. He was sympathetic when the full story emerged. It helped that the person he knocked unconscious had a conviction for domestic violence. Jack had to do some work in the community and pay a fine.'

'And your mother?'

'I got out of the army and went home. Everything was different although I really hadn't been away that long. Jane was no longer there and my mother was in the first stages of dementia. I thought of going back to the law but it was no more appealing than it had been. Then I got a break. I met an old school friend who had connections in the film business and said they were looking for people like me. If I could fix things in Afghanistan, I could fix things in UK film. More than that, he knew of a job that had come up, if I could start the following week. I had an interview that afternoon and they offered me a temporary contract there and then. One film led to another. So that's what I do now. I fix catering for over-mighty stars; I get resources together for perfectionist directors; I know locations where the brick is not such an astringent and mood-destroying red. I found I could work whenever I wanted to. My mother went into a home, slipped into a decline, and then died. I was the dutiful son, visiting every weekend. She liked me to hold her hand. She died one day I was visiting. She was asleep but there was pressure in her hand until it happened. It was like saying goodbye. I don't think she wanted me to go away again.

'On one of the films Kenneth Preston was the director. He would have been at home in Afghanistan – he was interested in what it felt like to kill, or that's what he told me. And we got on. I was able to help him bring his films in on budget.'

'I see,' I said. In normal circumstances I might have been interested in working practices in the film industry. But I was increasingly wondering where this was going. And where it would have got to when Jerry arrived. 'And you were saying your mother died?'

'She did. I'd been letting her house while she was in the home but when she died it seemed a good moment to sell. There were boxes of papers that needed sorting. That was where I found the picture of Jane and a letter. It had been cut out of a local newspaper. Under the picture was an account of the local coroner's verdict of suicide. It said that he had concluded that she had committed the act "while the balance of her mind was disturbed". From his other reported remarks it was clear that he had little sympathy with young women who got themselves into such positions. There was also a letter my mother had written to me but never sent. The letter said that Jane had been trying to get into acting. She had become entangled with a famous director and they had an affair. She had become pregnant but the director insisted she got rid of the baby. She refused. He cut off contact. She approached his wife but was given a similar cold shoulder. In despair, and too ashamed to confide in my mother, she took her own life. Committing suicide meant that the baby died as well. The last thing she did was write a letter. Some part of her needed to explain and she had no family to explain to, just my mother. I found the letter as well.'

I tried to look sympathetic but ended up with my gaze fixed on the pistol he was holding in his hand. It remained unmoving and pointing directly at me.

'The thing was there was another photograph in the folder with the papers about Jane's death. It was of the famous director. A photograph of himself which he had dedicated to Jane with stuff about how great a talent he thought she would become.'

'So who was it?' I said. I didn't need to ask. I knew the answer.

'Kenneth Preston.'

45

WALK-THROUGH

'ARE YOU SURE?' I said. 'I mean, just because Kenneth had sent Jane a photograph, it doesn't necessarily mean he was the father of her child and the cause of her death.'

'There's no doubt about it,' Nick Wallace said. 'He told me himself. We were in a panelled bar in St James', the sort of place where you wonder if you've really made the grade, or whether the barmen are more used to their next customer being the Sultan of Oman or a passing American tech billionaire. It was a couple of weeks after I found the cutting about Jane. Kenneth was a bit out of sorts. He was drinking faster than usual, not that that seemed to be having any effect on him. He was talking about young women. According to Kenneth it wasn't so much their youthful bodies that excited him as the hero worship he experienced as they surrendered themselves to a genius. Seduction, as far as he was concerned, was the conveying of status to the woman whom he seduced. He was certain there should be a more positive noun for the female concerned, *seducee* or something like that. Whatever else happened, the women could always refer back to the magic moment when, for an hour or two, they had had the privilege of engaging with male genius. He said he preferred not to use a condom and I suggested that there must be difficult consequences at times. I was thinking about Jane. Kenneth took the question as not referring to individuals but the class of beings that were young women. Unwanted children were a problem any woman could easily solve for herself if she wanted to. Some of them, impertinently enough, had asked for his help. Some of them had so misread the rules of the game that they had inferred that love had been a factor. He had shaken his head. In the end all young women had disappointed him.'

'And Miriam?' I asked. 'Wasn't she very young when they married?'

'Miriam was different in two important respects. She liked living on the edge and had every bit as much sense of individual worth as Kenneth did. More importantly, she had family wealth. I don't think Kenneth really believed that her father wouldn't support her financially after she married, but that's what happened. She did get a small allowance while her mother was alive, but that ended when her mother died of cancer. At the time Kenneth was doing well in Hollywood and it wasn't an immediate source of difficulty. But he was also losing interest in being the ideal husband, even with his much younger wife. It was still useful for him to keep up the appearance of a happy marriage but he had reverted to trying to seduce any and every pretty young woman he came across. He was discreet but Miriam wasn't a fool. She didn't have any doubts as to what he was up to. She told me she had gone back to her father and brother to seek help but all she got was her father insisting that she had made her bed and needed to lie in it. Her brother wasn't sympathetic either. He didn't want the business he was due to inherit split up. Then, years later, there was the accident with the plane that killed them both. Miriam's position as the sole surviving member of the family coupled with her brother's failure to form a long-standing relationship, or have children, meant that the tax-avoiding family trusts swung into action and she was suddenly a very rich woman. It coincided with a time when Kenneth was looking for capital for his Graham Greene *magnum opus*. It wouldn't need to be more than five or ten million pounds, just a core commitment that he could assemble the rest of the funding around. But Miriam wasn't playing. She claimed her hands were tied by the terms of the family trust and the conservative nature of the trustee that her father had appointed, an elderly solicitor called Hawken, who, according to Miriam, had no artistic appreciation at all. Miriam, according to Kenneth, could easily have found a way of loosening Hawken's grip on the purse strings if she had wanted to, but his acknowledged affair with Jane irritatingly provided an additional reason for Miriam's reluctance. She couldn't forget that Jane had also confronted her. I think there were other reasons as well. Kenneth had lost interest in her acting career. There had been a moment when he would have cast her as Desdemona if a more nubile and compliant candidate hadn't appeared. She hadn't forgiven him for that either.'

'So why did she stay married to him? Why was she here at Langham?'

'There were a couple of reasons. When her father and her brother were alive it would have meant a loss of face. She would have had to admit that she had been wrong. When they were dead she had become an extremely rich woman, much richer than Kenneth, and she was afraid that she would lose some of her new found wealth in any divorce settlement. And then she wanted revenge for his neglect. She wanted to punish him. So she took a lover.'

'A lover?' I said. 'How do you know that?'

'It was me. I had been in bed with her the week before he told me his suspicions. That was in the bar in St James'. I feigned surprise and ordered two more dry martinis. We had several more. That was when he told me he was planning to get rid of Miriam. He didn't put it quite as baldly as that. It was all hedged round by ifs and buts and alcohol, and any action he was thinking of undertaking was very much her fault. I told him that his genius needed to be supported whatever the cost. For a moment I thought I might have gone over the top but Kenneth seemed to believe me. Ten minutes later I told him I would do everything I could to help him get the Graham Greene film made, whatever the obstacles might be.

'The next morning, Kenneth said he might have gone too far. If I had agreed, even in the slightest, I was sure he would have insisted the previous night's discussion was no more than a drunken proposition that wasn't to be taken seriously and one that would dissolve in the clear light of day. I told him I had a condition for my unwavering support – that I should be the principal producer on the film. The possession of an ulterior motive seemed to convince him of my sincerity. He grasped my hand and gave it a long shake. Of course, deciding to rid the world of Miriam and actually carrying out the crime were two different things. But he already had ideas. He was being lined up to direct a crime film. He asked me to organise a workshop to develop the project and cast the primary roles.

Under the guise of preparing to direct a film he could direct a murder instead.'

'But how did I get mixed up in this?'

'You're the fall guy. Kenneth needed an insurance policy. You were it. The *Daily Mail* seemed to think you were a dodgy character. That seemed to Kenneth to be a sign. He didn't have any qualms about framing an innocent man. The opportunity to direct *Murder Unseen* had been offered to him. He had already been to Langham and had a fancy to use the pterodactyl as a murder weapon. Throw in some locked rooms and impossible murder weapons and it all seemed to be effortlessly falling into place. It was one of his more redeeming qualities that he believed in luck and chance. In his notebooks he stresses it's you who is obsessed with Golden Age crime. It is you who asks to sit next to him at the dinner on Sunday. It's you he wants to implicate when the lights go out and he cuts his lip. You helpfully pick up the glass shard that has caused the accident and that means that your fingerprints are on it. I tell Kenneth it's a good omen. It's something we couldn't plan but we can use.'

'You're his accomplice then?'

Nick Wallace nodded.

'But what would Kenneth have done if it had all gone wrong? How would he explain cutting his own lip?'

'That was hardly a problem. If it became clear that it was a self-inflicted wound Kenneth would say that he had been trying to create tension for the cast to play off. Everyone would have a vivid memory of the accident. Then, when they got to the incident with the pterodactyl and Kenneth's gashed jacket, they would conclude that it was not a series of accidents but a series of warnings. When Miriam is killed, the obvious conclusion is that the murderer has mistaken Miriam for Kenneth. The scenario is that Kenneth was the intended victim all along. The only factor we hadn't counted on was Rufus Stone. He was certain that for the second incident Kenneth had an accomplice, somebody to let the bird drop from a few feet. He was also convinced that it wasn't a warning but something that had been contrived to look like one. He was right. It was a plot and Kenneth did have an accomplice.'

'But it can't have been you,' I said. 'You had been speaking to Leung before it happened. There was no way you could be in two places at once.'

'I wasn't. I should have said accomplices. Or rather, someone who would follow orders and not ask questions.'

'Jack Catesby?' I said.

'Exactly. It was Jack who let the bird fall when Kenneth had his jacket pierced. As it happened, the bird was heavier than Catesby was expecting so the first part of the descent was faster than either he or Kenneth were anticipating and he had to use his feet as a break. I'm sure that was what Rufus worked out from the marks on the floor that Catesby had left. But that was helpful in another way. If there was any question of Kenneth having an accomplice, the obvious candidate would be me. I had worked with him closely on half a dozen films. So having a situation where it couldn't be me was more than helpful.'

'And Miriam? What was the guarantee that she was going to show up at Langham?'

'She told me she would and I was able to convince Kenneth she was certain to show if he was nice to her. She had, anyway, agreed they would renew their marriage vows.'

'But they seemed so fond of each other in the studio that evening.'

'They were both on their best behaviour. Both not wanting to give the other anything to object to.'

'But I still don't understand. How was it all meant to work?'

'You need to remember how events would look. Kenneth would have survived a couple of warning attacks – the steak and kidney pie and the falling bird. It might not be clear what was happening at the time, but in retrospect, it would be obvious that Kenneth was being targeted. Then he gets killed, or rather Miriam gets killed because the murderer mistakes her for him. It's not an enormous leap – they are about the same height, they dress the same. It is obvious what has occurred – the murderer has killed Miriam by mistake.'

'But why would Kenneth forge his own suicide note?'

'Remember, Kenneth isn't going to be dead in the third, and most deadly, attack on him, Miriam is. As far as the murderer is concerned – you – Kenneth has been murdered as planned. That's where the forged suicide note admitting to Miriam's death fits in. Kenneth can write his own suicide note but wear gloves to make sure it looks faked and so that your fingerprints, even if there are everywhere else at Langham, are not on that particular bit of paper. The police won't know how you did it, but the words that Kenneth transcribes are identical, in stylometric terms, to the grammatical constructions used on your website. If you have a computer programme it's not difficult to do. Besides, a plagiarism case I was involved in meant I could access material without anyone really asking why. Kenneth didn't like the fact that he wasn't in complete control but I told him that it bound me in. I was also guilty.

He could see the logic of that. There would be no trail at all back to Kenneth, and scarcely one back to me. In his version of the future he will explain to the police that the forged suicide note is evidence that you had been planning to get rid of him. The only thing that has thwarted your plan has been the fact that he has been locked in the secret room by Miriam. You killed Miriam, believing her to be Kenneth, and that prevented her from releasing him.'

'Neat,' I found myself saying. It was. It would almost do for the plot of a Tom Travis novel if it hadn't been so complicated. 'So what was Kenneth expecting to happen?'

'I would lock Kenneth inside the secret room from the outside. There would be evidence that only Miriam and he knew the location of the secret room. So Kenneth's key alibi is that he's been locked in the secret room. When he's released he will tell the police that the he and Miriam had been exploring scenarios of how they might use the bird in the film. Miriam plays a joke on him by locking him in the secret room. She doesn't intend to leave him there for very long. She goes back to the studio as she has an inspiration for something she wants to try out. At the studio you kill her in mistake for him. Kenneth would have an alibi because he was locked in the secret room.'

'But there's still something that I don't understand,' I said. 'How on earth anyone persuaded Miriam to stand in the path of that onrushing bird? She wasn't drugged, the police told us that. I just don't understand how it could have happened.'

'It's not that difficult. She was preoccupied with her own plan to murder Kenneth.'

46

SYMMETRY

I WOULD HAVE ASKED Nick how he knew Miriam was intent on murdering Kenneth if I hadn't been struck by a more pressing concern. What was Nick Wallace doing telling me all this? He already seemed to have implicated himself as an accessory to murder. Why? Murderers don't confess to their crimes unless they have a reason for doing so. But perhaps there was a different explanation to judge by the gun in his hand. Murderers confess if there are no consequences to their actions. They confess if they're sure that the people they confess to aren't going to be around to hold them to account. Nick had a gun fitted with a silencer. The gun was pointed at me. If he were to pull the trigger there would be no David Knight; my sons would have no father; Kate wouldn't have a husband and there would be no more Tom Travis adventures for my readers.

'Kenneth and I,' Nick Wallace continued, 'murdered her. The three of us went to the studio. Kenneth had the bird lined up as a bludgeon. Miriam had to be in a precise position otherwise it wouldn't have worked but she was concentrating on her own plans so she wasn't suspicious at all. Besides,

I was there, someone she could trust because she knew I was betraying her husband. I was in front of her, lining everything up. She stood perfectly still.'

'But...' I found myself saying. But there weren't any words to follow the first one and I tried to distance myself from what I was hearing and concentrate on how I could get out of my current situation. Surely Jerry would be here at any moment? That was the situation I had to handle.

'We were lovers, which helped,' Nick Wallace continued. 'But that wasn't the real reason she trusted me. She trusted me because we planned to poison her husband. That was what she was focused on. The prospect of his death had disabled her normal antennae for danger. She thought trying out the pterodactyl as a murder weapon was an ironic last favour before she got rid of him altogether. She was smiling when the bird hit her. Kenneth had the same sort of grin on his face the moment after it had happened. Then, when he was beside me checking his wife was dead, I noticed the grin had become glacial. I was reminded that I was the only witness to what had happened and that if he wanted to be totally safe he might need to get rid of me.'

'But...' I said again. But there were too many things I didn't understand. I looked up. Nick Wallace had retreated back into his trance-like state but the gun in his hand was as steady as ever.

'For a moment I was shocked by what had happened. I suppose that right up to the instant he let the bird go, some part of me thought he wouldn't do it. The bird seemed to swoop down and smash into the back of Miriam's head in slow motion.'

'But...?' I said, for the third time.

'How did I get in so deep with the Prestons?' Nick Wallace finished off my sentence. 'Is that what you want to know? It's a question I've been asking myself. I think up until the moment the bird hit Miriam I could tell myself that it was revenge for what happened to Jane and the grief that my mother had felt. Then, with the impact, it was something else. There was suddenly no way out, no way back. Up until that moment I was the successful producer who could cope with a difficult genius and bring his films in on time and to budget.'

There was something in his voice. What was it? Pride? And why was he telling me all this?

'I got to know Miriam waiting for Kenneth. One evening she insisted on opening a bottle of champagne for the two of us when Kenneth was mysteriously absent. He had his eye on a young actress hoping for a part in his next film. When he did finally appear we had drunk the bottle and she made a point of saying how long he had kept me waiting. The next morning he apologised for Miriam's manner and the next afternoon she apologised for involving me in a domestic dispute. I became a referee between them, a mixture of friend and employee who was there to hear their appeals.'

'And Jane?'

'That was before I knew about Jane. Finding out about her hardened my heart. The first line I crossed was starting an affair with Miriam. It was easy enough. We spent hours together waiting for Kenneth. One night he sent a message that he wouldn't be back until the next day. It was obvious what he was doing and she was intent on exacting revenge. I just had to go along with it.'

'But I'm not sure I get this,' I said. 'You seem to have more sympathy for Kenneth than his wife. She may be guilty of standing idly by, and I can see that you might think that was callous, but it was Kenneth who seduced Jane. She should have helped when Jane found herself pregnant but surely she is nowhere near as blameworthy as Kenneth, is she? Why would you be so keen on murdering her?'

'I wasn't keen on murdering either of them. All along, up until the moment that Kenneth unleashed that bird, I thought they would stop. But they didn't, and we all know the consequences. I found that Miriam wanted to murder her husband as much as he wanted to murder her. She had no qualms about that, just as Kenneth hadn't. They both needed an accomplice – me.'

'Even so...'

'There's something you need to remember. She was as focused as he was on finding someone to take the rap. And the person they chose was you, David. Her plan was more straightforward than Kenneth's. Only your fingerprints would be on the bottle of poisoned whisky. Her notebooks would reveal her feelings for you. Her fingerprints would be in your bedroom.'

'I still don't understand how that happened.'

'We went there when you and Jerry Davis were engaged in the workshop with Kenneth. I knew where Molly Whyard kept the spare keys to the rooms. We knew you would be occupied for more than an hour. All we had to ensure was that nobody saw us, and Emma Hale, Matthew Tabard, and Rufus Stone were with you, so that wasn't difficult. As it happened there were Kenneth's notebooks as well confirming that he suspected his wife was having an affair, although Miriam didn't know anything about that. Add in Jerry Davis' knowledge of poison and the fact that Miriam would have her own, verifiable, account of what had happened and it was an open and shut case. You murdered Kenneth because you wanted to start a new life with Miriam and her newly acquired millions.'

I thought of the moment that I had returned to Heisenberg and imagined I had detected the faint aroma of Miriam's perfume in the air. But it hadn't been my imagination, it had been reality.

'You need to remember that they both assumed they would be alive at the end of the evening and the other would be dead.'

'But I'm not sure I understand what they thought would happen and what the police would deduce.'

'The police would be told that Kenneth had been locked in the secret room by his wife. Actually it would be me. Having played her prank she had gone back to the studio to test out a method for using the bird and you had killed her in mistake for Kenneth. Kenneth's alibi was that he was in a room that was locked from the outside at the time.'

'But the room was locked from the inside.'

'That's what I found after we had murdered Miriam. It wasn't in the plan that I had agreed with him. I don't know why he did it, but he did. I had a moment of panic. But it was inconceivable he wouldn't have a drink immediately and that would mean he would be dead in minutes. In normal circumstances he might have been more suspicious about Miriam. But if you're intent on murdering your spouse on a particular day, the thought that she might also be intent on murdering you on that same day isn't at the top of your mind. If I know Kenneth, he would have convinced himself that Miriam was remorseful about her affair and the whisky was a peace offering. He wouldn't have hesitated to pour himself a drink. It would have been a reward. But it was a genuine shock to find the door had been secured from the inside. I had been intending to release the bolt anyway to give every opportunity for Kenneth to be named as the murderer of his wife. That plan still stood. After five minutes I released the exterior bolt. He would have come out if he had still been alive. But he didn't and so there he was dead inside a locked room fastened on the inside. It had become a classic crime puzzle, but an accidental one.'

'And Miriam?' I said.

'Her plan was more straightforward. The bird would have descended but she would have been out of the way. But the concept for the film sequence would have been proved. She would have poured Kenneth a glass of the Glengowrie to celebrate the solution he had been looking for. She wasn't a whisky drinker so she wouldn't have joined him, and she would have insisted that the present was intended for Kenneth alone and that he must have the first drink. Kenneth wouldn't have had any difficulty with that. The best way through his natural suspicions was always to appeal to his ego. In his mind it was the natural order of events that he would be drinking the only glass.'

'But her fingerprints would have been on the bottle.'

'She was wearing gloves.'

'But there were no gloves on the corpse when I found her.'

'I removed them.'

'But didn't Kenneth think that his wife wearing gloves was unusual?'

'She said her hands were cold. Besides, he was concentrating on his own plan. He wanted, above all, to ensure that there was no reason why she might back out of the experiment with the bird that was going to kill her. That was what he was focused on.'

'And Miriam?'

'Like Kenneth, she was expecting to be alive. There might be entries in her notebook about you and eyewitness accounts that you seemed more than compatible but that was just one side of the ledger. There was also the renewal of her marriage vows and the testimony of people here that she and Kenneth were getting on again. And they were. If Kenneth had been murdered by anyone, it would be by David Knight.'

'But there would just be you left, not either of them.'

'And I would ensure that David Knight, despite his reputation in some of the tabloids, escapes without censure. It's potentially tricky. There's an awful lot of weight given to the evidence of the dead in a courtroom. Why should the dead lie? It's powerful enough but I could release evidence to prove that it wasn't you. The white latex gloves were only a start. Whatever the weight of the evidence that could be assembled against you, there was always a counterweight that could be summoned. You were safe.'

Nick sounded certain. For a moment I thought of Emma Hale's expedition and my own conviction that it was an integral part of the tragic events of the night. In truth, like my own nocturnal ramblings, it had had nothing to do with what had happened. Events weren't connected in the way that Tom Travis would suppose.

I thought of Miriam Preston's twinkling eyes and the flare of her lighter as she lit my cigarette. I still didn't understand why Nick Wallace seemed to feel she was worse than Kenneth in some way, although combining lovemaking and plans for murder was probably a richer mix than he could stomach.

'Miriam Preston,' I said, 'I still don't see...'

'What you need to remember,' Nick Wallace said firmly, 'is that Miriam Preston wasn't starting from the same position as Kenneth at all. She was much more experienced in matters of murder than he was. After all, she had already murdered her father and brother.'

47

ARRET

'SHE KILLED HER FATHER and her brother?'

'That's what she told me. I'd been summoned to their house in the country. Kenneth was booked on the five o'clock plane to Cannes to accept a prize for his lifetime contribution to European *film noir* and he wanted to use the occasion to drum up finance for the Graham Greene film. We talked about what he might say for a couple of hours until his taxi arrived. When he had gone Miriam suggested we went out for supper and we talked about *noir* and *femmes fatales*. When we got back we went to bed.

'Miriam was angry with Kenneth, but angrier with her father and brother. Vernon Stanhope had become the apple of his father's eye. Marrying Kenneth Preston was meant to make her family notice her more but it didn't work. Her younger brother might not be good at exams, might not have gone to university, might not have her abilities, but he is the child who is going to take over the family business. When her mother dies of cancer there is no restraining influence left. She needs to do something. And conveniently there is a family trust of which she is the sole beneficiary if her father and brother die. It's not difficult to work out what must happen.

'The Stanhope males die in a plane crash over the Channel. The body of Vernon Stanhope is recovered but not that of his father or the pilot. The mechanic employed to sabotage the plane at the private airfield near Deauville is killed in a car accident a week later. It's all very neat and the thing is that it is Kenneth who has made it possible. Everything has been arranged through a Parisian mobster he hangs out with. The relationship with the French underworld gives him, he says, credibility and allows him to come into contact with people from the street. It was probably one of his monologues on the subject that convinced Miriam that there was help at hand, particularly as Kenneth stresses their code of silence in carrying through a job to which they have agreed and the fact that they will take on any job if the price is right. It's just a question of money. And Miriam, as undisputed heiress to the Stanhope fortune, was easily able to pay what they wanted. Kenneth becomes more attentive after the deaths but that's because their relative financial fortunes have changed. For her he's become more of a problem. He may divorce her, or she him, and, if that happens, she is now much the richer of the two of them, and he will be in a position to claim a large settlement. Not that that is going to be a problem. Besides, she finds out he is contemplating killing her.'

'How on earth did she do that?'

Kenneth looked me full in the face.

'I let her wheedle it out of me. I told her I wasn't entirely sure but things that Kenneth had said had alarmed me. I should have spoken earlier but I couldn't entirely believe what Kenneth was saying. The obvious solution was to get rid of him. I told her I would do everything I could to help. We used to lie in bed discussing her plans. Once I could see her watching me. It was only a split second but I could see the intensity in her eyes, which were working out how far she could trust me. That's when I realised she would have no qualms in getting rid of me if she thought it necessary.'

'But why would anyone think I had murdered Kenneth?'

'She was good at imagining an erotic charge between you. There were all sorts of details that would come to light in her notebook. Besides, you tweet about the times you are away speaking at literary festivals. Helpful if you wanted to make sure there was evidence that she was also in the same hotel in which you were staying. Nothing too elaborate would be needed. A receipt for drinks at the hotel bar on the same day you were there would be convincing enough.'

'But...'

'But once Kenneth and Miriam were dead it could all be fixed. The white latex gloves could conveniently appear. I could swear that I had let Miriam into your room. Not difficult because I did. The only thing that might be difficult was the unexpected.'

'Like Kenneth barricading himself in the secret room?'

'Like that.'

'How did Kenneth know about it in the first place?'

'William Graves told him. He was pitching Langham as the ideal place for Kenneth's workshop. It fits perfectly with Kenneth's newfound interest in classical crime. I told Kenneth and Miriam separately and swore them both to secrecy.'

There was a knock at the door.

'You'd better get that,' Nick Wallace said in a whisper. 'Just let me move out of sight.'

I opened the door. It was Jerry looking surprisingly cheerful.

'Bingo,' he said. 'Or to put it more clearly – jackpot time!'

'What is?' I said, giving a sideways glance that I hoped would indicate that we were not alone. But Jerry bustled into the room turning away from where Nick Wallace was lurking.

'I've found out who Emma Hale was going to see the night Kenneth and Miriam Preston were both found dead. Not that it takes us much further forward but at least now we know. You just have to look at the pattern of the lights dimming in the corridors here. All the data is there second by second if you want to interrogate it. I'm certain I know who it is – Nick Wallace. Mind you, I'm not sure how we are going to confirm that.'

'Easy enough,' I said, 'you can ask him yourself.'

'What?' Jerry said. 'What do you mean?'

'You can ask him yourself,' I said. 'If you turn round.'

Ah,' Jerry said following my pointing hand. 'Nick. I didn't see you there. And that's a Glock 17, isn't it?' He paused. 'British Army issue?' he added, after a moment. He was still wearing his glasses.

'Indeed it is,' Nick Wallace said. 'You seem very well informed. But then I suppose you need to be if you advise Mr Knight on criminal matters.'

Jerry looked in my direction for a confirmatory nod. It was a perfectly reasonable gesture. If knowledge is power I suppose it was helpful to know the make of automatic pistol that was likely to be used to kill us both. I wondered if Jerry also knew the make of silencer. If he didn't he could always ask the man in front of us who the British Army had spent years training to kill in a dispassionate and efficient manner. I managed to incline my head in an approximate gesture of assent.

'And you were right about Emma Hale,' Nick Wallace added. 'I didn't know you knew she was on her way to see me the night Kenneth and Miriam Preston were killed.'

'Fine,' Jerry said. 'Good, interesting, but none of our business.'

He didn't sound totally convinced but then he didn't seem to have adjusted to the fact that both of us were being held at gunpoint.

'Perhaps I should explain,' Nick Wallace said.

'That would be good,' I said, 'that would get us all onto the same page.'

Not that I wanted to be on the same page. The likely conclusion at the bottom of the page was that Nick's best option, by a large margin, was to kill both of us. Why come armed with a pistol if you are not intending to use it? Why put a silencer on the pistol if you don't want to be able to kill and then sneak away unseen? Which raised another question. Why on earth was he here? What was he trying to achieve? For a moment I was mystified but then with a growing sense of impending doom I realised that I knew very well. He was here because Jerry and I had spent the last few hours indicating to anyone in Langham who would listen that Rufus had shared some of his conclusions with Jerry and myself. He probably planned a trajectory of killing through the night. Jerry's sudden arrival had simplified his plans. Instead of having to find his victim, his victim had come to him. Addinson must also be in the frame. Perhaps he had already disposed of him.

'Didn't we, David?'

Jerry was suddenly speaking and I hadn't really been listening too closely. Nick seemed to be running over the circumstances of Kenneth and Miriam's deaths. Luckily, the tone of the question was clear that the only possible answer was yes.

'Yes,' I said, with as much authority as I could muster. It seemed to be enough because they both went back to their conversation. It struck me that I wasn't facing a noble end. *Crime Author Dies in Mysterious Circumstances* was probably the best I could muster. Actually there might be too much death and disaster haunting Langham for a headline simply about me. Perhaps it would be more like *Another Death in Doomed Mansion*. And of course it wouldn't be just my death but Jerry's as well. *More Deaths in Doomed Mansion.* They might even give Jerry his own angle. *Eminent Engineer Dies in Doomed Mansion.* Not that Jerry was that eminent but papers always exaggerate the status of anyone who meets a sticky end.

'I'm sorry to hear that,' Jerry was saying. He sounded sincere. What could he have felt sorry about? Had they been talking about Emma?

'I hadn't realised how she felt,' Nick Wallace was saying with more emotion than he had expressed in recounting the deaths of the Prestons. 'I threw away the pearl.' I felt a growing sense of pain in my brain. What game was Nick Wallace engaged in? Why had he told me in such detail about what had happened to Kenneth and Miriam? Why would he tell anyone that? Pulling a gun would have been enough to convince me that he was the villain of the piece, not going into the minutiae of everything that had happened.

'Anyway,' he said, 'time to be leaving. I'd be grateful if you could stay inside this room for the next ten minutes. I'm afraid I can't be held accountable for the consequences if you don't.'

He eased himself to his feet, the gun steady in his hand, as he backed towards the door.

'There's one other thing,' he said, 'it's about Rufus Stone. I killed him. You've probably worked that out for yourself. He was getting too near the truth of what had happened with Kenneth and Miriam. But, gentlemen, I need to leave you. If you don't want to risk getting shot I suggest you give me ten minutes.'

48

ASYNCHRONOUS

A MOMENT LATER, HE was gone.

'Wow,' Jerry said.

'Quite,' I said.

'So what do you make of that? What were you talking about before I came in?'

'It's complicated.'

'Just a second,' Jerry said raising a restraining hand. 'Before you start. We're just going to let him go, are we?'

'Do you have a better plan? That was a gun in his hand, wasn't it? If he wants ten minutes, I'd give him ten minutes.'

'Fair enough,' Jerry said, looking at his watch, 'ten minutes from now then. So, what was he saying?'

'You heard him. He killed Rufus.'

'Before that. What happened before I got into the room? You must have been talking about something important. You don't just find somebody being held at gunpoint every day. Well you don't unless it's in one of your novels. Frankly, it was a shock. So what was happening before I arrived?'

I explained how Nick had been drawn into the orbit of both of the Prestons and been instrumental in their deaths.

For most of my breathless narrative a new thought crashed across my brain. It wasn't so much *what* Nick Wallace had said that I didn't understand, it seemed to fit the facts as I knew them. No, that wasn't the problem. *Why* was the problem. *Why* had he confessed?

'That's what he said?'

'Pretty much. But I meant to ask you. Why were you late? I was expecting you half an hour ago.'

'I was talking to a couple of the security team at the bar. I told them I'd won some money and needed somebody to help me celebrate even if things were pretty black here. There's nothing like a free drink to loosen tongues and we started talking about how things work out, or how they don't. I said I'd often wondered about joining the army and I'd heard Nick was a good boss to work for. They said he was the best. They reckon he's lucky as well.'

'Why?'

'A bomb exploded next to him in Helmond. The blast blew him off his feet and he was concussed, and for a couple of minutes he was out of it. That was when the Taliban attacked. Jack Catesby took control. It was touch and go for a few minutes but they all held together and they all got out. Funnily enough, Nick Wallace didn't seem to be affected by it at all. Catesby got a gallantry medal but his nerves were shot and he's a bit hair-trigger now.'

I had a picture of a dusty place far away from home and a group of men trusting their instincts to save themselves and each other.

Accomplices, Rufus Stone had written. Nick had been an accomplice of both Kenneth and Miriam Preston. And Jack Catesby had been an accomplice of Nick, and their men were trained accomplices of both of them.

'It's coming up for ten minutes,' Jerry said. 'We need to go.'

'Just a second. Tell me what you were saying when you came into the room before you realised Nick was there. About who Emma had been going to see.'

'Nick Wallace,' Jerry said. 'Just follow the record of the lights...'

He launched into an explanation of the method he had used and I left him to his moment of self-congratulation. I needed to get events straight in my mind. On the night that Kenneth and Miriam Preston had died, the most desirable woman of her generation, Emma Hale, had gone off to see her lover and then, half an hour later, she had returned showing every sign of being an emotional wreck. Why would that have happened if it was Nick Wallace she had been going to see? The tabloids might be running the story that she was upset by the loss of Matthew Tabard's affections but they had made up the romance in the first place, although that might explain the look of hatred that Florence had favoured her with when I had first arrived at Langham. Emma might have been upset that Matthew had turned his attentions to Florence Hammond, but somehow that didn't seem right. She wasn't upset about Matthew at all. It was Nick Wallace she had mistaken me for when I had first arrived at Langham. It was Nick she had been going to see that night. It had always been Nick. Something had happened. What could have upset her so much?

'It's time to go,' Jerry said.

I got to my feet, turned the handle, and looked out into the corridor.

'And?' Jerry said.

'No one.'

'Time to move then.'

When we got to the entrance hall we found the lights were lit but the room itself was deserted.

'He can't have left,' Jerry said looking round, 'the drawbridge is up. He must be somewhere in Langham still. We could try the library.'

But the library was deserted. Embers of a fire were glowing red but that was all.

'We should try the studio.' I said.

'Which entrance?'

'The mezzanine.'

Somewhere there was the sound of something happening, distant but distinct.

'That came from the studio. What was it?'

'There's only one way to find out,' I said.

But I had an inkling of what it was. I had once spent an afternoon idling through a number of videos that had been posted on YouTube by members of the National Rifle Association. Most of them consisted of men in baseball hats going off into the American countryside to fire their weapons and use as much ammunition as possible. One of them had been a man who had been trying out a silencer on his pistol. Not that that was the main component of the sound that I had heard, but that had been the start of it.

I could hear our footsteps as we ran up the stairs. We brushed through the police tape and ignored the baleful stare of the pterodactyl. Everything was suddenly quiet.

'He's not here,' Jerry said.

'He's not here,' I said, 'but he could be down there.'

The head of the bird was in a pool of light that shone down from a cluster of spotlights on a gantry suspended from the ceiling. A current of air from somewhere in the building, perhaps from the door we had thrown open, caused the bird to sway slightly. Suddenly, illuminated on the far wall, was the shadow of a razor sharp beak poised to descend on its prey.

'Kenneth Preston probably had a point in wanting to use that bird in the film,' Jerry said nervously.

But I hardly heard him. With an increasing feeling of dread I walked to the edge of the balcony and looked over. Below us a figure lay face up on the flagstones, curiously orderly in manner, as though he was somehow at attention, despite being flat on the ground.

'That's not... is it?' Jerry said.

'It's Nick,' I said. 'It must be.'

For a moment the body was out of sight as we walked down the stairs and I thought that everything might be a dream and that, any moment, I might wake up. But I knew I wouldn't. The new studio at Langham was getting used to death.

Nick Wallace was lying face up on the ground, the Glock automatic in his hand, the silencer attached to the end of the barrel, his face composed and peaceful, the trance-like state he had appeared in a few minutes before, ended for ever.

There was blood oozing from the side of his head and spreading out over the flagstones. Despite the terrible wound, there was a look of something approaching contentment across his features. It was the same look that had played across Miriam's face.

'Do you...?' Jerry said.

But what it was that he was poised to ask I would never know. The remaining lights of the studio were switched on and what had been a cone of brightness surrounded by a world of shadows gave way to something far more orderly.

'Mr Knight, Mr Davis,' a voice said. 'Why aren't I surprised to see you?'

The voice was Addinson's. Behind him was a shadowy figure that was also coming in to the light. It was DCI Marriott.

49

STOP MOTION

'WE WERE LOOKING FOR Nick Wallace.' I said.

'You don't think we had anything to do with this, do you?' Jerry said.

It wasn't an auspicious start. He sounded defensive. Mind you, I hadn't sounded very convincing either.

'Did you, sir? Or you, Mr Knight?' Addinson said.

I didn't know. None of this would have happened, or happened like this, if I hadn't created Tom Travis in the first place. But it wouldn't have happened either if Rufus Stone hadn't been convinced he was Tom Travis, or Addinson hadn't been prepared to give him a platform, or Jerry and I hadn't done everything possible to spread rumours that the case was about to be solved, or Kenneth and Miriam Preston hadn't decided to murder each other. Causation was fundamentally like that – one thing after another.

'Nick Wallace was in Heisenberg,' I said. 'He was with Mr Davis and myself. He left the room about a quarter of an hour ago. He told us to give him ten minutes or he wouldn't be responsible for the consequences. We were obviously concerned about his mental state and were trying to find him. We heard what I thought was a muffled gunshot that I thought might have been a silencer and then something louder, I suppose Mr Wallace falling to the ground.'

'And you're familiar with the sound a gun fitted with a silencer makes?' Marriott asked, in a surprisingly reasonable tone.

'Research,' I said.

'Understandable,' Marriott said.

'Tell me,' Addinson said, 'do you have any reason for supposing Mr Wallace might do this?'

'He told us he'd killed Rufus Stone.' Jerry said.

'Really?' Marriott said. 'When did he say that?'

'A few minutes ago. In Heisenberg. I'd come in to see David and Nick Wallace was there with a gun in his hand.'

'And do you know where the gun came from?'

'I don't think there can be much doubt about that,' Jerry said. 'It's a Glock 17. British Army issue. Actually they call it an L13A1. Arms like this regularly go missing. People take them for souvenirs. One of the security team here must have had one, or more likely, it's something Nick took himself, when he left.'

'So you're saying he *stole* it?' Marriott said with a slight grimace.

'Probably more like taking a souvenir,' Jerry said, unconvincingly.

'Mmmh,' Marriott said, as though he had suddenly found that something he was eating was indigestible.

'More to the point,' Addinson interrupted, 'why was he in Heisenberg?'

'I wish I knew,' I said before Jerry could say anything.

'So he came to your room; you let him in; and he produced a gun; but he didn't tell you why he was there. Is that what you are saying?'

'It's not easy to insist on reasons why somebody might have come to your room if they have a gun in their hand,' Marriott said.

'I certainly didn't find it easy to establish why he was there. But, as Mr Davis has said, he did admit to killing Rufus Stone.'

'Did he say why he killed Mr Stone. Or how?' Addinson said.

'He didn't say anything about how it had happened.'

'Even that it could have been an accident,' Marriott said. 'Imagine two men struggling. He was in the army where men get trained to kill. It might have been some sort of reflex, an automatic reaction, nothing premeditated, no more than manslaughter. And of course Mr Stone would have been trying to emulate Mr Travis who, as I recall, is somewhat handy with his fists.'

'That could very well have been it,' I said

'So how long was Mr Wallace with you in Heisenberg?' Addinson asked.

'It was only a few minutes while I was there,' Jerry said.

'And that was when he told you both that he had killed Mr Stone?' Marriott said, 'and he hadn't mentioned that before to you, Mr Knight?'

'No.'

'And this is suicide, isn't it?' Jerry asked.

'Yes,' Marriot said. 'It's straightforward,' he continued. 'Superintendent Addinson and I were reviewing what had happened at Langham. We were planning to look again at the secret room. We were outside in the corridor when we heard a shot from a gun fitted with a silencer. It was muffled but quite distinctive. We heard Mr Wallace fall and were in the studio a few seconds later. There were just the spotlights overhead but they provided sufficient illumination to show what had happened. There was no possibility that Mr Wallace was alive and no doubt he had shot himself. There wasn't time for anything else to have happened. Then we heard footsteps, which were you Mr Knight, and you, Mr Davis. Of course we didn't know that at the time so we backed into the shadows to see who it was.'

Marriott was looking at his watch.

Addinson was looking at Jerry. 'And why had you gone to Mr Knight's room?' he said.

'We were intending to check up on where we were. I wondered if Harry Leung had said anything to David about *Murder Unseen's* prospects given everything that has happened here.'

'Something, presumably, you assumed Mr Wallace might have wished to discuss when he turned up,' Marriott said.

'I'm sure that was at the back of my mind,' I said. 'I also thought Nick might have more information on when we might be able to leave. And there was one other thing that he seemed upset about. Emma Hale.'

'Emma Hale?'

'Yes, he seemed to think he had wrecked his chances with her in some way.'

'I thought she was dating Matthew Tabard,' Marriott said.

'Affairs of the heart do get complicated,' I said. 'Anyway, he was quite upset wasn't he Jerry?'

'He certainly seemed very cut up about her,' Jerry said. He supported his words with a judicious nod that at least disguised the faint look of surprise that had crossed his features at the way the conversation was developing.

'He must have said something more than that, surely?' Addinson asked. I wondered what Rufus had actually told him.

'Nothing very much,' I said.

'Nothing?' Addinson said.

'He was obviously upset about something and felt he had let the Prestons down in some way, but there was nothing too specific.'

'General grief,' Marriott said. 'Understandable.'

'You'll both need to make detailed statements.' Addinson said. 'In fact, we could make a start on that now.'

'Surely that can wait until the morning, Bob? No need to get into something open-ended on your last day. You can rely on me to finish things off.'

Marriott emitted a short, controlling laugh that seemed intended to reassure but which suddenly seemed sinister.

'So what happens next?' Jerry asked.

'I'm sure everyone can leave tomorrow, if they wish,' Marriott said. 'Of course, as Superintendent Addinson has indicated, we shall need some more statements. But those are best left to tomorrow morning when we are all feeling fresher.'

'So that's it?' I said.

'I think I'm beginning to be clear about what happened,' Marriott said. 'I'm sure that Miriam Preston's death was accidental, a tragic accident that occurred while she was trying to see if some of the methods that Mr Knight had advanced in his books were practical, or, at least, would look practical on camera. Of course, in saying this, I'm clear that no blame for what had happened can be attached to Mr Knight.'

Jerry was nodding, for once, appropriately.

'As for Kenneth Preston,' Marriott continued, 'I'm inclined to the view that we may never know what happened, or what the precise sequence of events was, but we know that Kenneth met his death by his own hand, knowingly or unknowingly. What Rufus Stone was about to tell us all I don't know but I'm disposed to think that his death was as a result of a scuffle with Mr Wallace that got out of hand. Mr Wallace might very well have lashed out as a reflex action. He was, after all, a man who had, contrary to regulations, a British Army pistol in his possession...'

To judge from his tone Marriott set great store by rules. In a few minutes the conduct of the case would formally be in his hands. Despite his admiration for the regulatory life, I suspected he and the Commissioner would want the case shut down with a minimum of fuss. What Nick Wallace had said to Jerry and myself opened up that possibility. Who, after all, was there to bring to justice? Nick Wallace had confessed that Rufus Stone's death had been his responsibility, whether it had been accidental or not. Perhaps Marriott was right and Rufus Stone's view that Langham was alight with murder and mayhem was erroneous.

'Does anyone have any reason to disagree?' Marriott was saying.

Addinson was silent. Jerry was nodding again.

'No, none at all,' I said.

50

CODA

'SO YOU'RE NOT GOING to tell them what Nick Wallace told you?' Jerry whispered ten minutes later. I shook my head.

We were in the corner of the studio. A dark blue sheet now lay over Nick Wallace's body. Beyond the body, Addinson and Marriott were in deep conversation at the bottom of the steps from the mezzanine floor. Addinson, who had started their discussion with expressive movements of his arms, was now as still as Marriott.

'I wonder what they're talking about?' Jerry said. 'I'm not sure Addinson believes a word of what Marriott has been saying. You weren't exactly forthcoming either.'

'We told them that Nick Wallace had confessed to killing Rufus.'

'I still don't understand that,' Jerry said. 'As soon as he admitted he'd done it he was desperate to leave. Guilt, I suppose. But you could have told them what you said Nick told you. That colours everything and gives Nick a clearer motive for murdering him.'

'And it creates a lot of loose ends. Marriott is in charge of the case now, or he will be in a few minutes. I'm not sure he wants to hear anything more, particularly if it's all hearsay.'

'So we just go home tomorrow?'

'I thought that was what you wanted.'

'I certainly want to see the twins, they're 20% older than when I last saw them and Faith would welcome some help.'

'There you are then.'

'But…'

'But… nothing. It's time everyone left Langham.'

Jerry looked as though he might argue further but Addinson was moving towards us. Marriott was issuing instructions to the tall policeman stationed at the main door of the studio. Then he was gone. For a moment Addinson seemed to hover over the body of Nick Wallace and I thought he might pull back the cover but he didn't.

'Bad business,' he said, gesturing at the body.

'Yes,' I said. 'Tragic.'

'Difficult to know precisely why he killed Rufus Stone,' Jerry said.

'Indeed,' Addinson said. 'That's why I wondered if you could shed any more light on what might have happened, sir?'

Addinson subjected me to one of his interrogatory gazes. Unhelpfully, Jerry adopted his own enquiring expression.

'I was curious,' Addinson added, 'if there was even the slightest hint in what Mr Wallace said when he was with you – before Mr Davis arrived? It's not for the record. My official interest in all this ends in a few minutes. I'd just like to know.'

For a moment I was tempted to tell Addinson everything. But it wasn't an impulse that lasted more than a second. I suspected that one revelation would lead to another. It would get back to what had happened on the night that both Kenneth and Miriam Preston had met their deaths. The fact that I had been out of my room observing Emma Hale on that night Kenneth and Miriam had died could lead to endless questions that even Marriott would have felt compelled to pursue.

'I'm as mystified as you are.'

'Really, sir?'

'Absolutely. But let me ask you something in turn. Did Rufus Stone tell you anything that indicated that he might have worked out what had happened?'

'Nothing significant that I can think of.'

'But surely he must had said something for you to agree to summon everyone to a meeting?'

'He told me that neither of the incidents that happened to Kenneth Preston were accidents.'

'Nothing more than that?' I said. 'There have been people here who have been acting suspiciously. I mean it would be invidious to mention individuals but of course there have been Mr Davis and myself, and Mr Tabard has seemed well, out of it, for some reason.'

'Mr Tabard has just been diagnosed with narcolepsy, sir. That was why he was allowed to leave. He had an appointment in Harley Street. I fear some rumours may already have got out to the tabloid press. One of the symptoms is falling asleep in unusual circumstances. But I'm sure you and Mr Davis will treat that as confidential. I know that you, Mr Knight, have a distrust of that section of the press.'

'Certainly,' I said. 'So that's that is it?'

'If Mr Tabard's behaviour has been explained and you and Mr Davis are witnesses that can testify that Mr Wallace admitted to murdering Mr Stone then that, as you say sir, is very probably it. DCI Marriott is keen to close the investigation, and one has to ask who would benefit from keeping it open anyway? Kenneth and Miriam Preston are both dead. They don't have any family living. Rufus Stone never knew his natural parents. I suspect that the explanation that DCI Marriott advanced is as good as any we will get.'

Addinson left the words hanging in the air. The expression on his face was almost benevolent.

'But,' I said, 'this business of whether Miriam or Kenneth died first and therefore who inherits what, that must still be a problem, mustn't it?'

The expression on Addinson's face turned from one of optimism to one of resignation.

'That may not be a difficulty. I understand DCI Marriott has found a new will.'

'Really?' I said.

'Really. It apparently resolves the matter.'

'So all's well that ends well,' Jerry said in a tone of resignation.

'You might put it like that. It will do for me. But then I'm retiring in ten minutes and looking forward to having more time to devote to crime mysteries where everything is explained. But it's getting late. So, unless you gentlemen have something else to say, I wish you both goodnight.'

'Good night Superintendent,' I said, before Jerry had time to say anything.

Addinson inclined his body towards us, like a fictional policeman leaving the stage, and then, like Marriott, he was gone.

'Good news about Matthew Tabard,' I said, 'wasn't it?'

'That he's suffering from narcolepsy?'

'Not that bit. More that his actions are explained and he's not a murderer and that's why he was allowed to go to London. Besides, he and Florence seem to have got together. I imagine that was what he was talking to Emma about in that heart-to-heart you saw them having. It's another loose end tied up.'

'I don't see why you're quite so cheerful,' Jerry said.

'We can leave tomorrow.'

'I suppose there's that,' Jerry said, doubtfully. 'Look, I need to phone Faith before midnight. She'll be wondering what's happening. I'd better do that now.'

'Fine,' I said.

'Are you coming?'

'I think I'll just stay here for a minute.'

'If you must,' Jerry said. He looked round the room. There was the bird above as menacing as ever, and a body with a blue sheet covering it and a policeman by the door. He left.

I looked at my watch and then walked up to the mezzanine floor. The marks that Rufus Stone had found were still there. There was that question that had been in Rufus' notebook. *Accomplices?*

Then it was all suddenly clear, like the moment of enlightenment that strikes Tom Travis towards the end of his adventures. Nick Wallace might have been Kenneth's accomplice, and Miriam's for that matter, but he had needed his own collaborator. He couldn't have been the person who had helped Kenneth fake the accident with the bird and his leather jacket. He had been with Harry Leung at the time the "accident" had happened. It had to be somebody else.

It wasn't difficult to work out who. Nick had needed somebody who would keep silent whatever happened and not be troubled by any events that might subsequently happen – like Kenneth and Miriam's deaths. He needed somebody who would follow orders unquestioningly. Who better than somebody who was used to taking orders and indebted to him? Jack Catesby had been the accomplice.

They had formed a bond in Afghanistan where Jack had saved him. Nick had repaid the favour by getting Jack a job and ensuring he hadn't served a prison term for GBH. It was obvious that Jack was the man. It would certainly have been obvious to Rufus Stone. That was why Rufus had been so certain that what had happened to Kenneth hadn't been accidental.

I took a deep breath. Something about Nick's abrupt confession still didn't make sense. He had no need to confess to murdering Rufus Stone. Marriott, in particular, would have been happy to add it to the long list of accidents that were already bedevilling Langham Hall. So why confess and then shoot yourself? Remorse?

That wasn't the answer. I had no doubt that Nick had felt remorseful and had regretted being dragged down into the abyss by the Prestons, but that wasn't the explanation. If you confess to murdering someone and then commit suicide, nobody else is going to be convicted of the crime. Why would a man determined to commit suicide lie about what he had done? There was an answer of course – he was protecting somebody else – his accomplice, Jack Catesby.

It hadn't been Nick Wallace who had killed Rufus Stone but Jack Catesby. Rufus Stone had been getting near the truth. And Catesby had suspected the truth might do his ex-commanding officer a great deal of harm. He had, after all, been involved in the incident of the falling bird at Nick Wallace's request and perhaps he had been involved in fusing the lights when Kenneth had found the glass shards in his pie. He suspected Nick was moving towards a solution, particularly as Jerry and I had spent hours confirming the outcome. Catesby had decided to act to save his friend and comrade. What had happened? Had Catesby tried to warn Rufus off? Rufus wouldn't have backed down of course, anymore than Tom Travis would. The truth was much too important. So there had been a struggle and Catesby had killed him.

Catesby had been trying to do Nick a favour, and that was what Nick had been doing when he came to Heisenberg. Repaying a favour. When they had been in Afghanistan together he had been the officer commanding. It was he who had implicated Catesby in the insane feuding of the Prestons. It was he who needed to take the rap if anything went wrong. That was what he had been doing by confessing to Jerry and myself.

Besides, he had other reasons for his actions. It wasn't just his involvement with the Prestons but his involvement with Emma Hale. He was the man she was waiting for the evening I had blundered into her room. But why had there been such looks of antipathy between her and Florence? Florence's look made sense if she simply thought that Emma might be trying to ensnare Matthew as part of her general approach to men, but the other way round?

The answer is in front of me. I was back behind the statue of the courtesan in the corridor. I'm waiting for Emma to walk past. And I know what has happened. She has set off on an impulse to see Nick. Her spirits are high. But Nick isn't in his room. He is coming back from the secret room that Kenneth has just locked himself in. He's already been a party to Miriam's murder and Kenneth had suddenly gone rogue and abandoned the plan that had been decided on. He's trying to work out whether Kenneth's actions are a good or a bad thing. He's unnerved by everything that has happened. He's not in control, as he likes to be. That's when he bumps into Emma. He's suddenly, suspiciously, in a part of the building in which two bodies are going to be found in a few hours time. So what plausible story can he make up that gets him out of the situation and is one she won't question? And that she won't repeat. There's only one thing that springs to mind. He's been seeing another woman. Emma's venomous look on Wednesday morning hadn't been directed at Florence Hammond but at Molly Whyard. That is who he has told Emma he has been with. What he only understands at the moment he says it is that Emma loves him and he loves Emma as well. So even as he says it he realises that he is destroying his chances of happiness, but it's not something that he can take back. There's no other explanation that will shield him from suspicion. And, once said, it can't be unsaid.

He has become someone who is not worthy of Emma's love. He has thrown away the pearl. But there are things he can still do. He makes sure he turns back the tide of evidence that Kenneth and Miriam prepared to frame me. But events are getting out of control. Jack Catesby has killed Rufus to stop him talking. He needs to get Catesby out of the situation that he is responsible for. And the easiest way of doing that also offers him an end to the torment he is suffering. That's why he turns up in Heisenberg with a gun. He needs to confess what he has done to someone and have a witness to his confession. As it happens he has two.

I moved towards the body. The tall policeman in the doorway straightened to see what I was doing. For a moment I felt like pulling the cover back and looking at the dead soldier one last time but it was only a momentary hesitation.

The clocks in Langham were striking midnight as I walked out of the studio. I took a last look at the pterodactyl. As I watched it seemed that the mechanical bird transformed itself into a real one. I closed my eyes to stop it diving down towards me.

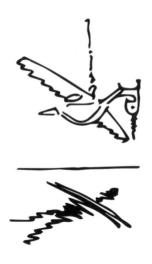

ROGER HARDY

I HAVE LONG ADMIRED Roger's work, which I first came across in Suffolk, but which has since gained a national reputation. I was first attracted to his wonderful paintings of the Suffolk landscape and particularly its woodlands where his vivid colours picked out elements of the trees and the forest that I had not been able to see before.

I have also loved his sculptures and constructions, which sometimes use ancient and discarded materials from the East Suffolk landscape to evoke a poetic and soulful sense of the destinies that life will force us all to face; and sometimes use discarded tools or other objects to create living or invented creatures.

The Sawbird was one of the more playful, if more surreal, of these creations. It was at the Alde Valley Spring Festival that I first saw it suspended menacingly above my head with smoke filtering through it. The evening was dark and it was dangling above a large open fire with logs glowing orange with heat. For a long moment I was taken back to a prehistoric time where it was gliding silently above the primeval swamps of Suffolk.

In addition to wakening the past in my mind, it also struck me that the bird would make an ideal – if fictional – murder weapon. This book reflects that initial inspiration and I am enormously fortunate to be able to add the Sawbird designs to it.

Further details of Roger's work can be found at www.rogerhardy.co.uk.

ACKNOWLEDGEMENTS

I am enormously grateful to those who have helped shape this book. Any book, and particularly this one, benefits from a host of inputs.

Thank you then to my wife, Caroline, for the photograph on the cover and her helpful and wise comments on the emerging text. Thank you to my daughters, Elizabeth and Victoria, for their support, suggestions and design work.

Thank you also to those who have read the book in draft and who have (tactfully) contributed their ideas for improvement, particularly Caroline Aldridge, David Bickel, Mike Hope and Charlotte Wightwick. Thanks also to my proofreader, Gracey Rye, and my book designer, John Chandler.

I am sad that my friend, Bryan Scattergood, who contributed so much to discussions on the overall style of this book in the planning stages and who would have contributed so much to the final version, didn't live to see it published. But thank you Bryan for all those discussions on style. I am certain that this book is the better for them.

And finally, apologies to the muscular Chang, Sir Harry's bodyguard, and secret operative of the Chinese Ministry of State Security, who once featured in these pages. Although he has gone, he remains as real to me as he ever was.

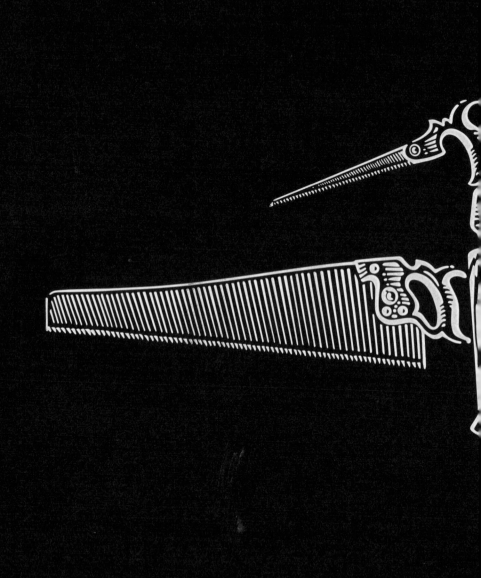